A CROWN IN THE *Stars*

A CROWN IN THE *Stars*

KACY BARNETT-GRAMCKOW

MOODY PUBLISHERS
CHICAGO

© 2005 by
KACY BARNETT-GRAMCKOW

All rights reserved. No part of this book may be reproduced in any form without permission in writing from the publisher, except in the case of brief quotations embodied in critical articles or reviews.

Library of Congress Cataloging-in-Publication Data

Barnett-Gramckow, Kacy, 1960-
A crown in the stars / Kacy Barnett-Gramckow.
p. cm. — (Genesis trilogy ; #3)
ISBN-13: 978-0-8024-1369-7
ISBN-10: 0-8024-1369-2

1. Bible. O.T. Genesis—History of Biblical events—Fiction.
2. Babel, Tower of—Fiction. I. Title.

PS3602.A8343C76 2005

2004025795

ISBN: 0-8024-1369-2
EAN/ISBN-13: 0-8024-1369-7

1 3 5 7 9 10 8 6 4 2

Printed in the United States of America

With love to the Gramckow clan, particularly to
Marietta, Kathi, Al, and Bob.
And to the dear memory of "Pop" Hans, who inspired us all.

Acknowledgments

FIRST AND FOREMOST, to the dear readers who have contacted me: I appreciate your taking time from your busy schedules to send me notes! I've enjoyed hearing from you and pray you've received my replies and my thanks.

To Amy Peterson, Andy McGuire, Amy Schmidt, Lori Wenzinger, Tricia George, Mattie Hill, Malina Pascut, and Vicki Lange of the Moody Publishing team, I really appreciate you all and welcome your input. Also, Mary Busha, my brave agent, our discussions and your steadfast presence are blessings. And LB Norton—did you think you would escape? Thanks for humoring me, and for making me double-check minutiae.

Also, special thanks to Doug Sharp, Vivian Sharp, Richard Geer, and the Revolution Against Evolution crew—it was a pleasure to meet you, and I hope our paths cross in the future!

A belated mention to: The Institute for Creation Research for their terrific study materials and their Web site. I've particularly enjoyed *The Genesis Flood* by John C. Whitcomb and Henry M. Morris.

I have also been remiss, forgetting to mention the Moody Institute of Science video series, *The Wonders of God's Creation,* which was a fascinating part of my research before I ever wrote a word in this trilogy. The observations concerning the "ultimate solvent" nature of water were, obviously, inspiring.

To Auntie Nancy Sutton, your courageous spirit and family stories always inspire me—love and hugs!

Fond regards to: Jeanne Jackson, Jan Whistler, Peggy Shontz, Tammy Harris, Shirley Overholser, Rosanne Fahrenbruch, Vicki Strothman, Pat Janssen-Hall, Jennifer Hills, Natalie Barglowski, Celeste Gilligan—I've appreciated your encouragement, your laughter, and fellowship.

Connie Gourley and the Hazel Dell 4405 crew, I miss you all.

Love always to my parents and family and to my dear Jerry and our sons, Larson and Robert, who bring me back to earth when I'm off in another century.

Above all, Lord, in everything Your will is perfect! Thank You for insisting . . .

Prologue

ON THE SWEEPING fertile plain between the Two Rivers, the Great City sprawled like a collection of tree-garnished mud boxes, encased by protective walls and dominated by the emerging Tower of the Sun—a corrugated brick-stepped mountain that threatened to pierce the skies.

Though still unfinished, the Tower ruled the lives of the Great City's people. Festivals, work, marriages, births, dreams, fears—all were sanctified by the Tower's priests. Nightly they consulted the stars on behalf of the citizens to determine the most auspicious days of Shemesh the Sun.

By their soothsaying, the priests commanded the city. And the citizens welcomed their role as they welcomed the Tower's presence; it bound them together and strengthened them against everything that existed beyond their small lives. In building it, they could boast of challenging the Heavens. They could laugh together in one voice and defy the will of the fearsome, unseen, unnamed, unacknowledged Creator, whose Presence called to their rebellious souls.

Remember the things that happened long ago—
for I am God, and there is no other;
I am God, and there is none like Me.
In the beginning I declare the end,
and from ancient times decree things still to come,
saying, "My plan will hold,
and I will do all that I please to do."
(Adapted from Isaiah 46:9–10)

One

"The earth was not always as you see it today, Shoshannah-child. Before the Great Destruction, the heavens glowed pink as an endless sunrise. The mountains were low and rounded, and the trees were enormous—beautiful and fruitful. And the flowers—they were so sweet that we sometimes ate them! But even more wonderful, little one, were the animals in the world of that time. They didn't fear people as predators or stalk them as prey; they lived around us—often seeking our presence. Yet the earth before was so filled with violence and death that the Most High mourned. To save His cherished creation, He allowed the earth to be swept beneath the waters. But first He warned our Ancient One, Noakh, to build this pen. . . ."

Half dreaming of the earth as it must have been, Shoshannah followed I'ma-Annah through the immense, dusty, dark vessel she called "the pen." Cautiously touching a web-swathed reed cage, Shoshannah murmured,

"You truly lived here for more than a year, surrounded by animals."

"It seems impossible, doesn't it?" I'ma-Annah paused at the base of the pen's central ramp and sighed. Her lovely features saddened as she shook her sleek black hair, bound with gold talismans. "I sometimes despair that the children of my children can't imagine the Great Destruction. But it truly happened."

Grieved by I'ma-Annah's sorrow, Shoshannah leaned forward. "I believe you, I'ma-Annah. I do. How I wish I could have seen the world of that time! It sounds so beautiful. This world must appear *desolate* by comparison."

I'ma-Annah stared at her, surprised. "Yes . . . that's how I felt when I first stepped out onto this mountain. Oh, little one, I cried; it was terrible! But being surrounded by loved ones—like you—eases everything." She hugged Shoshannah, fondly smoothing her wild brown curls. "And I must stop calling you 'little one.' Soon you'll be taller than I am; you're growing up to be just like your mother."

Pleased, Shoshannah asked, "Do I really look so much like my I'ma?"

"Yes, except that your eyes are a bit darker gray, and you have dimples like your father's. But come now. I'll show you the upper level; then we'll join the others before they worry."

They were just nearing the top of the ramp when a large, fur-covered shape bounded out of the shadows above them, bellowing, "Raa-a-aww!"

Shoshannah screamed, clutching the resin-coated railing as I'ma-Annah leapt backward, landing on Shoshannah's toes. But before they could run, the seething shape stood big and tall, dropping its fur cover.

A young man laughed down at them, his clear green-brown eyes sparkling in his tawny, lively face.

"Kal!" Shoshannah swatted at him, furious. "We could have fallen down the ramp!"

"Forgive me," Kaleb said, contrite. But his remorse instantly vanished, replaced by his usual life-loving grin. "I found this shabby old hide and couldn't resist teasing you. I was sure you'd hear me scuffling around up here. I'ma-Annah, I saw where you must have kept the birds—those nets are huge! How long did it take to feed them? I wish I could have been here then—I feel like I missed *everything*."

He held I'ma-Annah's arm protectively, guiding her up the ramp, talking the whole time. "Not that I want to see the earth destroyed again," he assured her earnestly, "but I wish the Most High would grant me such an adventure."

Shoshannah followed them, frustrated, wishing Kal would leave her out of his adventures. Her toes were smarting, and he had stolen her precious time alone with I'ma-Annah. And he was *still* talking and making I'ma-Annah laugh.

When they finally emerged from the vast pen and walked down the huge, dark, summer-warmed ramp, Kaleb helped I'ma-Annah down, then turned to Shoshannah, smiling.

Annoyed, she said quietly, "You have a pimple on your nose."

He touched his nose briefly, bewildered. "I do? Well, you've got one on your chin."

"Oh!" Shoshannah pressed a hand to her chin, glared at him, and marched away.

Kaleb followed her, calling in a need-to-know voice, "But does it really matter?"

Kal, she threatened silently, *I'm going to repay you someday.*

She rejoined I'ma-Annah, who said, "Forgive me, child, for stepping on your foot earlier when I was frightened. Your Kaleb is a rascal—but a wonderful young man."

My Kaleb? Shoshannah stared at I'ma-Annah, dumbfounded, then glanced back at Kal. He raised his eyebrows at her, clearly delighted by I'ma-Annah's verdict.

Still speechless, Shoshannah followed I'ma-Annah down the rocky hillside, toward the tented encampment where their families were preparing the evening meal.

"You *are* going to marry Kal," said Mithqah, round cheeked and full of youthful wisdom, as she helped Shoshannah scrub their dishes outside the women's tent. "He adores you, and your parents love him as if he's their firstborn son. Look how he's working with your father."

Rinsing the last dish in her wooden tub, Shoshannah glanced toward her father and Kaleb, who were covering and tying the horses for the night. Her father, Zekaryah —brown, neatly bearded, and dignified—was nodding as Kaleb talked. He interrupted him now and then with a word or gesture of instruction, which Kaleb swiftly obeyed. They were indeed like father and son.

Years ago, Kaleb's own father, Regem—a shy man who was baffled by his gregarious, daring, third-born son—had asked the strict Zekaryah to train Kaleb to ride horses and use weapons. In turn, Kaleb worked for Zekaryah willingly. And he imitated Zekaryah's rugged leather attire, even wearing his heavy black-brown hair in a thick horseman's plait.

But Kaleb would never match her father's calm, silent demeanor. Shoshannah pretended to be irritated.

"At least he's serious when he's helping my father. Otherwise, I think he lives to torment me."

"You poor thing," Mithqah said, fluttering her black bristly eyelashes exaggeratedly. "Admit it: you love him."

Unwilling to admit anything—even if it might be true—Shoshannah flicked water at her friend's blue wool tunic. Mithqah retaliated, slapping her hand through the tub, splashing Shoshannah's leather tunic and leggings before turning to run. Grabbing the tub, Shoshannah chased her, both of them shrieking and laughing as Shoshannah dashed the entire tub of water over Mithqah's dark head.

"Shoshannah!"

Guiltily, Shoshannah faced her mother, Keren, who had obviously heard the noise and emerged from the women's tent. Tall, incomparable, brown curled and brown skinned with remarkably pale gray eyes, Keren scolded, "If you've ruined Mithqah's tunic, you're going to make her another."

Mithqah wiped her tawny-red face with a quick hand. "Thank you, I'ma-Keren, but I teased her fir—"

"And *you're* going to get more water and finish the dishes." Ritspah—Mithqah's flushed and formidable mother—joined them, her hands on her hips. "I hope you haven't broken anything!"

"We haven't, I'ma-Ritspah," Shoshannah promised, gripping the tub as she stepped closer to Mithqah. If they were going to be punished, they'd suffer together, as always. "We'll go for more water right now."

"You'd better," Ritspah threatened.

Keren nodded stiffly.

Shoshannah peeked at her mother, suspicious. Keren was covering her mouth with her hand; Shoshannah almost laughed with her. But her delight changed to self-consciousness as she walked downhill with Mithqah to the stream. Kal was watching. He flashed her a grin, which Shoshannah reluctantly admired.

After speaking quietly to Zekaryah—evidently asking his approval—Kaleb approached the girls. "Need some help?" he asked.

"No." Shoshannah walked away, resisting Mithqah, who tried to make her stop.

Kaleb followed her. "Shoshannah, listen. I'm sorry I upset you this afternoon. Please accept my apology—your father is watching us."

She paused and looked. Her father was indeed watching them closely—as always. He would expect her to accept Kal's apology.

"I forgive you," she said. *Almost.* She would plan her revenge later. "But, as you say, Father is watching; he might thrash you if we talk too long."

As Kaleb glanced over his shoulder at Zekaryah, Shoshannah hurried Mithqah toward the stream, smiling. Kal wouldn't dare to follow.

"Confess, Ritspah," Keren said as they stepped inside the women's tent. "Their water fight looked like fun; we should have joined them."

"I would have won," Ritspah informed her.

"Perhaps not," I'ma-Annah teased, settling onto a fleece mat, the gold hair talismans fluttering against her neck. "Sometimes even an old woman like me can best a child like you, Ritspah."

They laughed together, then sobered as Ritspah said, "I can't believe how tall our girls have grown. It's frightening. In a few years we'll have to find husbands for them. Do you think you'll ask Shoshannah to consider Kaleb?"

"Perhaps. But I don't want her to marry for quite a while—and Zekaryah talks as if he'd never allow her to marry at all."

"He's too protective." Ritspah leaned down to peer at Keren's toddler-daughter, Rinnah, who was napping, thumb in mouth, on a nearby mat. "*I* think we should send our daughters to visit their cousins in the Tribe of Metiyl. We've refused their invitations twice, but it would be fun for them to have a little freedom before they marry and settle in their own households."

"I suppose you're right," Keren agreed reluctantly. "But I keep thinking of what might happen . . ."

I'ma-Annah eyed Keren severely. "You still haven't told Shoshannah of the past, have you?"

"Only that I lived in the Great City and hated it."

"Let her hear the truth from you before one of your enemies finds her, child."

"What should I say? 'Daughter, you have enemies because I tried to kill the Great King, but our First Father Shem struck him down an instant before.' Forgive me, I'ma-Annah, but I dread it."

"Do you want me to tell her?" I'ma-Annah offered quietly.

The First Father Shem was Annah's own beloved husband. And the Great-King Nimr-Rada's manner of death still saddened her, even after twenty years.

"No, I'ma-Annah, thank you. I'll tell her." *Someday.*

As Keren thought this, baby Rinnah stirred and stretched, her chubby nut-brown face irritable as she whimpered herself awake. Grateful to escape this unwelcome conversation, Keren settled down to nurse her youngest and soothe her into a better mood.

"Well," Ritspah sighed, retrieving a carved wooden spindle and a puffy heap of combed dark wool, "I hope our other children are behaving better than their elder sisters."

"I'm sure they are." Keren absently caressed Rinnah's short wispy black ringlets, thinking of her other cherished daughters, Qetuwrah and Adah, and her sons, Ahyit and Sithriy, who were visiting the Ancient Ones with her brother Eliyshama and his family.

I'll have to tell them everything . . . She hated the thought. They shouldn't have to deal with her enemies. *Time will be enough of an enemy for them.*

She had to stop thinking. She had to fight this bitterness against her enemies. And, sadly, against the Most High.

Two

HIDING HIS IRRITATION, Master Ra-Anan, the bald, smooth-shaven leader of the priests, knelt in his place of honor in a formal, tree-shaded courtyard. The cause of his irritation, the Lady Sharah—his own sister and supposed ruler of the Great City—was emerging from her private residence.

Her golden sandals clicked softly, and her linen robes and pale curls fluttered as Sharah glided into the courtyard and stepped onto a fleece-draped dais. Arranging herself decorously on her fleece-padded bench, Sharah allowed a nervous attendant to check her face paints, then waved her off, nodding to her guardsmen to open the gates. Donning warmth and courtesy like a robe, Sharah now assumed her persona of the City's gracious, tender Mother-Protectoress.

As Sharah received petitions from bowing, worshipful

citizens, Ra-Anan studied her critically, distastefully. In a few years her gorging, tantrums, and drinking into the night would destroy her pale, dazzling, paint-garnished beauty. Then she would be left with nothing but this sham dignity that vanished as soon as her citizens were locked outside her courtyard gates.

I doubt your deluded citizens will call you Queen of the Heavens much longer, Ra-Anan warned Sharah in his thoughts. *Even your son will hate you, if he doesn't already. Where is that boy? Adoniyram, I have too much to do this afternoon without waiting on you!*

The blaring notes of rams' horns echoed outside, making Ra-Anan glance toward the gate. Adoniyram did not appear. Instead Kuwsh, father of the deeply mourned, now legendary Great-King Nimr-Rada, entered Sharah's courtyard. Striking in his habitual gold ornaments and leopard-skin robe, Kuwsh half bowed to Sharah. She nodded, icily proud in the summer heat. Finished with courtesies, and ignoring the citizens bowing around him, Kuwsh sat beside Ra-Anan, an uneasy ally in their political schemes.

His obsidian black eyes glittering in his dusky face, Kuwsh muttered, "Where's our Son of Heaven, Adoniyram?"

Ra-Anan concealed a smile. "Probably planning a grand entrance."

"He should be flailed."

"So should his mother," Ra-Anan whispered in agreement, "when it's safe for us."

"I await the day. Usurpers! I should never have allowed you to convince me that they should live, much less have power."

"They are mere ornaments to please our people; you know that, my lord."

"Hah! By the way, I want to speak to you later."

What now? Ra-Anan wondered, smiling calmly, inwardly seething. "Of course."

Their furtive conversation ceased; Sharah had waved a troublesome petitioner toward them, saying sweetly, "We must be advised, for your sake, by our Priests of Shemesh."

Kuwsh stiffly deferred to Ra-Anan, who studied the rustic petitioner's thin, jutting, bearded features.

"What's your name?" Ra-Anan asked.

"Dayag," the man snapped, glaring.

Ra-Anan chose to ignore his lack of manners—the man was a nobody.

"Present yourself at the tower steps this evening. We will consult then."

"As you say, Master." The man bowed to Ra-Anan, distinctively hostile.

Ra-Anan frowned, watching him move toward the gates. If the man caused trouble, he would be punished.

Now raucous shouts, whistles, and laughter rose just outside the courtyard walls. *Adoniyram.*

Ra-Anan peered through the open gates. The hostile petitioner dropped to his knees and bowed, outwardly humble, but deliberately blocking Adoniyram's progress. Two spear-wielding guardsmen reached for the man but stopped, apparently ordered off by the Young Lord of the Great City.

He's accepting that Dayag's petition! Ra-Anan guessed, furious.

Everyone inside the courtyard paused and watched, futilely straining to hear the petitioner and Adoniyram's response. But Ra-Anan knew without hearing a word; the troublemaker's petition was granted. The man, Dayag, bowed again, then leapt to his feet and backed away, his thin, coarse face triumphant.

Equally triumphant, Adoniyram paused just inside the gate. Though he was simply clothed in an unbleached linen tunic, a leather belt, and roughly laced boots, there was nothing plain about Adoniyram. His height, coppery skin, thick black curls, flagrant, sultry-lashed eyes, and wide, full mouth ensured that everyone in the courtyard, friend or enemy, noticed him.

Smiling, he strode toward his mother and offered her a showy bow. Then he stepped onto the dais, kissed her cheek, and sat easily at her feet. Sharah gave him a smug, prideful look. Ra-Anan watched, nauseated.

Beside Ra-Anan, Kuwsh hissed, "*This* is why I want to speak to you. He's beginning to steal our power by granting favors. We have to rein him in."

"We'll talk, my lord."

"Adoniyram." Ra-Anan detained him just outside the gates.

The Young Lord paused, courteous, but clearly impatient to return to his horse and his hunting.

"Master-Uncle. How may I assist you?"

"How may I assist *you*, Adoniyram? I have failed you in your training."

Adoniyram drew back, narrowing his eyes. "How have you failed me, Uncle?"

Ra-Anan smiled, respecting the young man's surprising instinctive caution; his mother had never been cautious in all her life. And, perhaps, neither had his father. "I have not given you the chance to formally act on behalf of your people. We must encourage your mother to give you a role in her courts instead of sitting idly at her feet.

It would be beneficial if the citizens could observe the two of you working together."

"I've thought the same," Adoniyram agreed genially. "But can she be persuaded to share her glory?"

"For your sake, she must." Ra-Anan watched his nephew's reaction; he seemed interested. "It would be an offense against the heavens, Adoniyram, if your talents were squandered when they could be used to strengthen your kingdom."

"It's not my kingdom, Master-Uncle."

"Because of you, it still exists," Ra-Anan said carefully. "Your birth gave the citizens hope and unity after the death of the Great King, when everything could have crumbled into chaos. Your Lady-Mother has depended upon you, so why should she refuse your assistance now? We must speak with her."

"Without making her angry?" Adoniyram smiled. "Let me know if you or your priests can accomplish such a miracle, Master Ra-Anan; I long to witness it."

Smiling politely in turn, Ra-Anan asked, "What favor did that man, Dayag, ask of you at the gate?"

"Your priests took his river lands, which adjoined the fields near the tower—something about creating another canal. I promised him new lands along the river."

"Do you have such lands to give him?"

Charming and warm, Adoniyram said, "No, my own uncle. But you and your priests do; perhaps we can bargain together and agree on something. We are all reasonable men, and we can't have rebellion among the citizens, can we?"

"There will be no rebellion," Ra-Anan said firmly, displeased. "But I see you are going to hunt. Let's discuss these things tonight or tomorrow over a meal; everything will be settled fairly, I'm sure."

"Thank you, Uncle. You'll hear from me soon."

Ra-Anan watched the proud young man ride off with his entourage of equally proud servants.

Adoniyram, he thought composedly, *I can destroy your life and your mother's life with a few words. But do I wish to destroy you? The citizens almost worship you; therefore, I think I would prefer to control you. The question is* how?

"I saw you talking to Adoniyram," Kuwsh accused Ra-Anan as they rode through the streets of the Great City, ignoring the citizens. "What did you say?"

Determined to placate him, Ra-Anan said, "We agreed to meet later, share a meal, and discuss his role in the kingdom—in your presence of course, my lord."

"He will seek more power as the years pass," Kuwsh said darkly. "There will be a struggle because he is so well liked. I wish my son had lived."

Kuwsh had six sons, but the only one who truly meant anything to him was the one who had died: the Great-King-Mighty-Hunter Nimr-Rada. Very quietly, Kuwsh said, "I should have killed your sister—that *Keren*—when I had the chance."

"It might have been for the best," Ra-Anan agreed, remembering Keren—her idealism, her unshakable loyalty to the Ancient Ones, and her remarkable spirit—amazing in such a tenderhearted woman. "If our Great King were still alive, we wouldn't be facing these troubles now."

"I could still gladly kill her."

"She did not hold the sword that took his life," Ra-Anan goaded him softly.

"But she drew him to it!"

"At the command of those Ancient Ones. What would you do if you had *them* in your power, my lord? I'm curious."

"Those old storytelling fools!" Kuwsh sneered.

But he didn't answer Ra-Anan's question, which pleased Ra-Anan. *You still fear them in your heart,* he thought, satisfied. *Those Ancient Ones and their Most High. They are your weakness.*

Not mine.

"Look at them, my lord," Rab-Mawg muttered. The thin, bald-shaven young Chief Magician-Priest knelt next to Adoniyram on a terrace of the tower beneath the star-scattered night sky.

Feigning indifference, Adoniyram glanced across the dark tree-lined terrace at Father Kuwsh and Master Ra-Anan. They were huddled together like two shadowed vultures, plotting to keep him tethered close where they could watch his every move—and politely counteract all his plans. *Go there. Stay here. Say this, but don't say that. Bow to your mother. Be patient . . .*

Despite all their earlier promises and pretenses of giving him some authority in the Great City, Adoniyram felt as if he were treading water. As if he were living and breathing, nothing more. Beside him, Rab-Mawg obviously felt the same. Ra-Anan usually ignored Rab-Mawg's suggestions or concerns and ordered him to give his full attention to receiving sacrifices and organizing temple ceremonies. As for Father Kuwsh, he shunned Rab-Mawg completely, clearly considering him just an irritating boy who did nothing but play with lamps, screens, smoke, incense, and polished copper mirrors.

Adoniyram, however, considered the young magician to be a potential—though volatile—ally for the future. But for now, he chose to bide his time and pretend disinterest. Watching his would-be enemies, he said blandly, "Let us appreciate them, Rab-Mawg. They are keeping this kingdom intact. Someday, when they're unable to rule, they might have me trained to step into their places."

Me. Not us, Rab-Mawg. Notice how I phrased that. I will rule my own kingdom.

But when? And how could he gracefully topple those two predators from power? Not to mention his mother, whose tantrums and self-indulgences were increasingly difficult to manage. Silently Adoniyram stared up at the late summer constellations: the Serpent, the Lady, and the Child. The High Month of Shemesh, with all its ceremonies, sacrifices, heat, and intricacies, had already passed, leaving him bored.

"When you do step into their places, you will claim your own symbols in the stars," Rab-Mawg said firmly, studying the skies. "But those you should keep." He nodded toward the Lady and the Child. "Those were proclaimed as yours; your people look to you as their Promised One."

Am I the Promised One who will restore the earth to perfection as it was in the beginning? Adoniyram doubted it. The people of this city believed he was their protector. The two manipulative vultures on the other side of the terrace did not. What weren't they telling him?

"I pray to the heavens that I eventually live up to their expectations."

"You will, my lord," Rab-Mawg answered confidently, pondering the stars again.

Adoniyram frowned in the darkness. He needed to pry Master Ra-Anan and Kuwsh off their high perches. What could throw them off balance? How could he make them act so foolishly that the people would rebel and turn to him—Adoniyram—instead?

He could only wait.

Three

"HOLD STILL," Shoshannah urged as she combed her five-year-old sister's dark, springy waist-length curls. "You'll be so pretty when I'm finished."

"I'm already pretty," Rinnah informed her. "Father Ashkenaz called me a pretty bird."

"Father Ashkenaz calls every little girl pretty. But he calls the noisy ones *bird,*" Shoshannah teased. "And you're the prettiest, most noisy bird in the whole . . ." Her voice faded to nothing as their own father's tall, dark form filled the doorway of the lodge. Zekaryah had obviously learned of her latest prank, and he didn't seem amused, as she'd hoped he would be. But surely he couldn't be *too* angry with her—after all, the joke was on Kaleb.

Her stomach tightened into a hard little knot as Zekaryah gave her a stern look. Turning to Keren, who was trimming leather for boots, he said, "Come see what your daughter has done."

"*My* daughter?" Immediately, Keren flashed a worried glance at Shoshannah. "What did you do now?" She hurried outside without waiting for an answer.

"What did you do?" Rinnah begged in an excited whisper.

"Come see." Determined to get her punishment over with quickly, Shoshannah straightened her leather tunic and leggings, shoved her feet into a pair of short boots, and led the capering Rinnah outside. As they hurried through the village toward the stone-and-hewn-timber stables, she almost wished Rinnah weren't so big. To carry a small child was wonderful protection against severe punishment. Instead, she had to content herself with holding Rinnah's hand.

But even before they reached the stables, Shoshannah heard her mother's laughter rising over Kal's indignant protests. And Father usually weakened when I'ma laughed. Heartened, Shoshannah took Rinnah to the woven-fenced herding area where Kaleb was tending his precious new horse, Khiysh.

On seeing the horse, Rinnah shrieked and danced with delight. "You've made him *ugly*!"

The usually tawny Khiysh wore bright face paints—garish, huge red-ochre-dotted "cheeks," flauntingly black-smudged and red-streaked eyes, and Shoshannah's own handprints in red and black along his well-groomed neck.

As Shoshannah hid a smile, Kal beckoned her, frustrated. "Shoshannah! What did you put on him? I saw all this red and thought he was dying!"

Others in the village were gathering around now, laughing with Keren, who was desperately trying to compose herself. Mithqah's parents, I'ma-Ritspah and the sturdy Uzziel, chortled as they stood near Keren. And the tribe's matriarch, I'ma-Laheh'beth, chuckled, while her husband, the bearded, burly, rumbling Father Ashkenaz, laughed and stamped his leather-booted feet.

"Shoshannah-bird!" he bellowed happily. "I recognized your handiwork. Who else would do such a thing?"

Shoshannah flinched, wondering if she'd gone too far. Mithqah sidled up now, her dark eyelashes aflutter with distress. "Kal probably deserved this, Shoshannah, but you've actually upset him. And his brothers . . ."

Alarmed, Shoshannah looked at Kaleb's older brothers, Ozniy and Tiyrac, both serious, almost as tall as Kal, and wonderfully rough hewn. Their big arms were folded forbiddingly across their chests, and their dark eyebrows were raised in her direction. Clearly, in their silent opinion, it was one thing for her to tease their brother, but it was quite another thing for her to make a mockery of a fine horse like Khiysh. And her father obviously agreed with them. Despite I'ma's laughter, he still looked grim.

Zekaryah approached Shoshannah and scooped up the now-quiet Rinnah. "Go help Kaleb. And apologize—I'm watching you!"

"Yes, Father," Shoshannah murmured, lowering her eyes. She hated herself for disappointing him over a mere joke. Not to mention upsetting Kal's brothers, whom she usually counted on as steadfast allies.

"I'll go speak to Ozniy," Mithqah whispered, distracted. She adored Ozniy and was clearly fretting over his sour reaction.

Sighing, Shoshannah clambered over the sturdily woven fence and jumped down into the dusty herding area.

"I'll need some oil," she told Kal. "I used fats and pigments, so water won't work."

He immediately went into the stable and fetched a carved wooden jar and two swatches of soft leather. After dousing one piece of leather with the oil, he handed the remaining swatch and the jar to Shoshannah. She oiled her leather swatch, set the jar away, then quietly approached Khiysh, who was becoming skittish with all the attention. Snorting, Khiysh tossed his head, backing away.

Shoshannah crooned warmly, "Come, come, Khiysh . . ."

As the other villagers drifted off to their daily tasks, the nervous horse settled down and allowed Shoshannah to rub the paints from his face.

Kal grumbled to Khiysh, "If you could see how ridiculous you look, you wouldn't let her near you!" He threw an almost-angry glance at Shoshannah, but his green-brown eyes glinted with reluctant amusement. "Next time you want to make fun of me, Shoshannah, leave poor Khiysh out of it. He doesn't deserve to be humiliated."

"Perhaps there won't be a next time."

Kaleb froze. "What do you mean? Are you giving me up?"

"Do you think I could? No! I only meant that I'm sorry I upset you, and perhaps we should stop teasing each other."

"Where's the joy in that?" Relaxing now, Kal daubed at Khiysh's darkened eyes. "All we need are a few rules."

"*You're* talking about rules?"

He grinned. "Perhaps I've been around your father too long."

"Do you think he's so terrible?" She rubbed a red smudge off Khiysh's neck, ready to argue.

"No. He's a good man. Honorable." Bending to look Shoshannah in the eyes, Kal said, "I could easily endure him as a father-in-law for a lifetime. Not to mention your mother."

Kaleb loved Keren. His voice always softened when he spoke of her, even now, after she had laughed at his cherished horse. And he always insisted that his first childhood memory was of riding a horse with her.

Leaning down again, he whispered, "Listen: I've decided that while you and Mithqah are visiting your cousins, I'll persuade your parents to agree to our betrothal."

"I pray they will." She felt herself blushing now, delighted by his audacity. How could she endure being separated from him for a year? But next month, she would depart with the Tribe of Metiyl after the tribal encampment. "I don't want to leave you; I wish I didn't have to go."

"Have you told your parents?"

"No. They'd listen to me and keep me here—and I'd prefer it—but my cousins have been inviting me for years. I can't disappoint them again."

Kaleb grimaced. "I know. And I suppose, as I'ma-Ritspah says, you should have some time to visit your relatives before we marry." He gave her a teasing-burning look. "After that, I'll keep you too busy."

Embarrassed, Shoshannah started to rub at a black handprint on Khiysh's neck. Kal stopped her. "No, leave the handprints. I like them."

"Really?"

"They're perfect. Others will copy them from pure envy."

She laughed, shaking her head. "I doubt it. They'll just wonder why you don't clean your horse." Her delight faded, and she looked up at him. "What else will you do while I'm gone?"

"I'll go mad," he said, flippant.

"No, be serious. What will you do?"

"Seriously? I'm going to start building *our* lodge."

"Oh, Kal . . ." She almost looked over her shoulder to see if her father was still watching. "Don't; it would look as though we're rushing things. You should wait until my father formally declares our betrothal—and he probably won't do that until I return. He's liable to thrash you for being so bold."

"You're worth the risk. Anyway, I'm so much bigger than he is now; he'd just swipe at me a bit. He knows I respect him." More softly, Kal said, "Beloved, swear you'll never stop tormenting me."

"We'll see," she murmured, pretending to ignore him now.

He smiled, measured his hand against one of her handprints—overwhelming it—and went back to rubbing Khiysh, obviously satisfied.

In the midst of a spring-green field, Keren eyed Shoshannah's stance during bow-and-arrow practice. She could see her daughter's impatience. "Shoulder down. Watch your target."

When Shoshannah heaved a mute but visible sigh and pressed her lips together, Keren said, "Don't even think that. Weaponry lessons are not a waste of your time."

Lowering her bow and arrow, Shoshannah stared at her. "I'ma, *how* did you know what I was thinking?"

Because I have lived behind that same expression, and I remember what I was thinking when I wore it. "Because I am your mother."

Shoshannah straightened. "I'ma, please . . ." She hesitated, then tried again as Keren waited expectantly. "I wouldn't have anyone else as my mother, ever, but none of the other girls in our tribe have to learn weapons unless they *want* to learn them. You don't even make Qetuwrah and Adah and Rinnah practice so much, and they're my own sisters. Why is this so important to you—and to Father?"

You still haven't told Shoshannah of the past, have you?

I'ma-Annah's gentle voice echoed in Keren's memory, chiding her tenderly. Keren glanced across the field at Zekaryah, who was teaching weaponry to their scrawny preadolescent sons, Ahyit and Sithriy. They would be busy for a while; she had time.

She motioned for Shoshannah to sit in the damp grass. Kneeling beside her, Keren summoned her courage. "I have enemies. And because you look so much like me . . . because you *are* so much like me . . . my enemies will hate you."

As Shoshannah frowned, Keren hurriedly continued. "I've already told you that when I was a little older than you, I lived in the Great City. What you don't know is that I was taken there against my will with my sister, Sharah, who is very pale and beautiful. Because she desired comfort and power above all things, Sharah married the Great-Hunter-King Nimr-Rada, though she already had a husband and a son."

"She had *two* husbands at the same time?" Shoshannah gasped, her bright gray eyes becoming huge in her brown face. "Didn't they fight?"

Remembering Sharah's first husband, Bezeq, and their newborn son, Gibbawr, Keren shook her head sadly. "The Great-King Nimr-Rada was unnaturally cruel. He thought nothing of killing anyone . . . men, women, infants. They were less than dust to him. Sharah's first husband, Bezeq, and their little Gibbawr would have been dead instantly if

Bezeq had resisted. And my sister loves only herself. She was happy to leave them for the glories of the Great City. She rules there now, with our eldest brother, Ra-Anan, who controls her every move, I'm sure."

"But . . ." Almost stammering, Shoshannah asked, "Why . . . what happened to make you leave? I mean . . . if your own family rules there now, why can't you return?"

How much should I tell her? Keren wondered. *Do I tell her that the Great King slaughtered my beloved Zekaryah's family? Or that he murdered one of my dear friends, then nearly destroyed another —my sister-in-law, Revakhaw—before smothering his own newborn son and passing the infant's body through the fires of the Temple of Shemesh in that horrible tower . . .*

Haltingly Keren said, "My family members who live in the Great City followed Nimr-Rada. They called him He-Who-Lifts-the-Skies. He pretended to be the Promised One—the 'man born of woman' who will return us to harmony with the Most High, as it was in the Garden of Adan, before that Serpent tempted our Havah. Nimr-Rada craved the worship of everyone on earth. But worship belongs to the Most High alone—which is why I resisted Nimr-Rada. Do you see this scar?"

Lifting her chin, Keren indicated a thin raised weal on her throat. "Nimr-Rada cut me here when he made Sharah and me swear to follow him and the god he created—Shemesh. Not long afterward, Ra-Anan and Sharah conspired against me with Nimr-Rada's father, Kuwsh, because they believed I was a threat to their power. Ra-Anan's followers poisoned me; I almost died."

Shoshannah stared at her, shocked.

Reluctantly Keren continued. "Your father was my guardsman then. He managed to get me out of the Great City and returned me to my family and to the Ancient

Ones. After I recovered from my illness, I sought revenge against Nimr-Rada because he had killed or devastated so many people I loved. I confronted him at a council of all the tribes of the earth. When he scorned the Most High and threatened further evils, our First Father Shem put him to death an instant before I could release my own arrow. Our Shem executed Nimr-Rada for the sake of justice on behalf of the Most High. But I . . . I had merely sought revenge."

There. She had told her daughter almost everything.

Shoshannah watched her beautiful, loving mother and listened to her faltering voice. *How can this be true? It's not possible. My I'ma has enemies? And she tried to kill a king? No.*

And yet, didn't her father still act like a horseman-guardsman? Hadn't he taught all the young men, particularly Kal, to hunt and ride and fight, sometimes ferociously? *And he's so protective of I'ma. And of me. Because I look like I'ma . . .*

Moreover, Shoshannah had often rummaged through her mother's wooden storage chest, fascinated, because Keren had more gold and treasures than anyone else in the Tribe of Ashkenaz. Her mother also had face paints—which she never used now, but which had inspired Shoshannah to paint the unfortunate Khiysh. The paints, gold, fine linens, carved weapons, and gemstones were undeniable evidence of status and power. Her mother possessed all these things. And enemies.

My enemies will hate you.

No, they won't, I'ma. Because I will never go to the Great City. Never.

Shoshannah sat in the Lodge of Noakh, contented, feeling as young as Rinnah, while the dear, ancient I'ma-Naomi combed her hair and talked. I'ma-Naomi's voice was so pleasant and soothing that Shoshannah could have dozed while listening to her. Almost. How many girls could say that the most ancient woman in the world had combed their hair? She nearly laughed at the thought. Truly, these visits with the Ancient Ones were always precious—and too brief.

Unable to restrain herself, Shoshannah said, "I'ma-Naomi, I wish you would come visiting with me."

"Humph!" Naomi sniffed kindly. "You don't need an old woman like me fussing over you, child. You'll have Mithqah for company."

"You don't fuss at all. You know about *everything*. And we'd have such fun—it would be an adventure."

Naomi's combing stopped. "I've had enough adventures for my lifetime, Shoshannah-child. And I don't know about everything—it would frighten me if I did! I'll leave that to the Most High. But you're good to consider me. Even so, all the children of my children know where my dear Noakh and I live. If we leave the highlands, they'd have a terrible time finding us."

Shoshannah laughed, flinging I'ma-Naomi a delighted look over her shoulder. "As if we'd ever misplace you!"

Chuckling, I'ma-Naomi shook her silvery head and resumed combing Shoshannah's curls. "Bah! You go play with your little cousins, child, and enjoy yourself." In a subdued voice she added, "The year will go quickly; you'll see."

"Not quickly enough." Shoshannah sighed, facing forward. Lowering her voice, she added wistfully, "I'ma . . . I love Kaleb. I don't want to leave him."

"You should tell your parents," Naomi said firmly.

"That's what Kaleb said. But then Father would keep me here, and my cousins would think we hate them—or that I'm a coward."

"Let someone try to tell *me* you're a coward," Naomi huffed. "Their ears would burn with the truth!"

Encouraged, Shoshannah said, "I do feel I should go. Anyway, while I'm gone, Kal's going to persuade my parents to approve our betrothal."

"He should speak to his mother first and ask her to speak to your parents—it's only proper. But if anyone could *happily* argue your parents into submission, it's our Kaleb."

Shoshannah peeked back over her shoulder, cautious now. "He's also going to start building our lodge."

Naomi's mouth fell open and she squeaked, "Before your betrothal? Oh! That's too soon—people will talk!" She shook the comb severely. "It's a good thing Kal's so likable. But your father should give him a stern lecture for being so bold!"

Shoshannah leaned over and hugged her tenderly—not fiercely, as she wanted to do. For how could anyone on earth ever forgive her if she crushed I'ma-Naomi with a hug? "I'll miss you!"

"I'll miss you too, Shoshannah-child." Naomi hugged and patted her in turn. She sighed. "Well, let Kaleb make plans to be busy while you're gone—it's good for him. And I am sure the Most High has made wonderful plans of His own for you. Oh, but to build your lodge *beforehand* . . . the scoundrel!"

Shoshannah approached Noakh slowly, reluctant to take leave of the ancient patriarch. He was actually alone, seated on a log, carefully replacing the carved antler blade of a threshing sickle, binding it in place with leather strips and thick, dark resin. His lips puckered in concentration, he glanced up at her, then blinked and looked again.

"Little one." He shook his silver curls reprovingly, while his dark eyes sparkled. "You shouldn't look so much like your mother."

"Then, please, Father of my Fathers, tell me how I should change." She knelt at his feet, smiling, ready to listen.

"I pray you don't change, Shoshannah-child. Your mother has been like another daughter to us; it's a blessing that you are so much like her, never mind how we tease you. Now, *daughter,* please hold this pot for me—I could dump it over too easily."

Shoshannah took the sticky wooden pot tentatively, knowing her fingers would be dark for days afterward. Feeling that she might not have such a chance to speak with him undisturbed for years, she said, "Father of my Fathers, I almost fear being so much like my I'ma. She told me about her enemies."

"Yes, one of her own brothers and her only sister," Noakh agreed, frowning in quiet sorrow. "And our Kuwsh. He was always a little wild, but I never expected such evil of him. It is his pride, Shoshannah-child. When I think of him—and of Nimr-Rada—I believe I have failed."

"I don't believe you have, Ancient One," Shoshannah

said loyally. "You've done the will of the Most High. Kuwsh, father of Nimr-Rada, is the one who failed."

She was afraid she had been too bold, but Noakh grunted mildly, reaching for the small dabbing stick in the resin pot. "Perhaps I should consider the matter in that way. Even so, we must always have things to regret; it keeps us humble, child."

He returned the stick to the pot, wrapped some more leather cordage tight around the base of the sickle to fasten the blade, then sighed, looking at Shoshannah again. "As for your mother's enemies, little one, leave them to the Most High. He knows them. They won't escape Him forever."

Thoughtfully he added, "Rebellious as the children of my children are . . . the Most High will punish them soon. I pray His anger won't overcome us all."

Noakh's quiet words made Shoshannah shiver.

"I've heard something strange," Mithqah said, as she and Shoshannah walked through the busy encampment, seeking the women's tent of the Tribe of Metiyl.

"Tell me," Shoshannah demanded, eyeing her friend's worried, rounded face. Mithqah was becoming more and more serious as the years passed. It was unsettling.

"I heard some of the tribal leaders talking with our First Father Shem. They agreed that the younger generations are aging faster than the previous ones. *We* might die of old age before our own parents do!"

Shoshannah halted, staring, wondering if Mithqah had gone mad. "What?"

"I'm serious, Shoshannah! I was taking food to my father and the others. The instant I walked into the tent, they stopped talking and looked at me as if my hair was green or something. I had to find out what they were talking about, didn't I?"

"So you hid and listened?"

"Wouldn't you have?" Mithqah moistened her lips, glancing around uneasily. "I heard our First Father Shem say, 'We can't continue to deny it.' He did! As if it were choking him."

Father Shem would never joke about something so dreadful. Shoshannah heard her own voice sounding very small and thin. "He meant what he said."

"Should we ask him why he believes such a thing? Perhaps you could ask I'ma-Annah."

I couldn't. How could I even find the words? It would upset everyone.

For the first time in her life, Shoshannah ignored a challenge. "Let us just pray to the Most High that it's not true."

"What do you think?" Mithqah whispered, leaning toward Shoshannah as they ate their evening meal near the hearth in the center of the encampment.

Picking at a bit of venison, Shoshannah studied her parents and then her grandparents—the tall, somberly dark-bearded Meshek and the kind, brown-eyed Chaciydah. Her mother and Chaciydah were quietly sharing their food. And Meshek was talking seriously with Zekaryah. Truly, they seemed right together—she had no sense that the generations were disordered. Until she looked at Shem and I'ma-Annah, who sat with their raucous, fur-clad, wild-haired grandson, Metiyl, and his plump, sociable wife, Tebuwnaw—all of them whispering earnestly, shaking their heads.

"Father Shem and I'ma-Annah seem the same age as their grandchildren," Shoshannah whispered to Mithqah.

"Younger," Mithqah corrected, distressed.

Shoshannah nodded, studying Shem closely. How could Shem possibly be approaching his third kentum—his three hundredth year? Of course he was nowhere near as old as the silver-haired Noakh or I'ma-Naomi, but . . . No. It couldn't be true. And yet . . . *It must be true. Look at them whispering.* Shoshannah felt ill. And scared.

"You are both much too serious," a woman's voice teased lightly.

Shoshannah looked up, instantly forcing a smile. Her mother's dear friend Tsinnah—diminutive, pretty, and rosy brown—knelt beside Shoshannah, smoothing her beautifully fashioned red wool robes. Tsinnah was always well-groomed; Shoshannah felt grubby beside her.

Concerned, tilting her dark, braid-crowned head, Tsinnah asked, "Are you girls worried about leaving with us tomorrow?"

"Oh no, not at all," Shoshannah assured her. "We were just thinking of our parents . . . and grandparents." She knew she sounded awkward and unhappy.

Mithqah simply sat there beside her, mute, her food almost untouched.

Tsinnah clearly suspected Shoshannah wanted to say more, but she quickly changed the subject. "I'm looking forward to our visit. There's so much for us to talk about—a year may not be enough."

Mithqah and I can ask her opinion, Shoshannah thought, relieved. It might be best to talk to someone outside the

Tribe of Ashkenaz. "I think you're right, I'ma-Tsinnah. And perhaps you can teach me how to dress properly—I feel like a wild woman beside you."

Tsinnah laughed, pleased. "Your mother never said such a thing in all the time I was with her in the Great City. She hated to bother with her appearance."

Mithqah scooted closer, interested, as Shoshannah said, "You were in her household there."

Tsinnah's laughter faded, her liquid-dark eyes becoming distant. "Yes. It was a terrible time. Your mother was so brave—I think I might have died in her place."

"But you didn't. You survived."

"Because of her, Shoshannah-child. You should be proud of your mother."

"I am."

A wild disharmony of howls, laughter, and bellowing interrupted their conversation. Kal, eating with the other young men, had wrestled his brother Ozniy to the ground and was busily shoving a fistful of grass into Ozniy's mouth.

"If you steal my food again, I'll make you eat dirt! Are you full? Here, have some more!"

"Nmph!" Ozniy growled through the grass in his lips, trying to squirm away.

Just beyond them, Shoshannah's brothers, Ahyit and Sithriy, whooped with excitement, frisking like two scrawny brown colts as Ozniy finally pushed Kaleb off, then managed to escape.

Shoshannah couldn't help laughing, but Mithqah was horrified.

"Poor Ozniy! I don't believe he was stealing Kal's food at all; I think Kal just wanted to pound on him."

"Enjoy this," Tsinnah said, looking like a child herself.

"After you've married your Ozniy, you might long for someone to give him a good pounding."

Mithqah eyed Tsinnah curiously. "Forgive me, I'ma-Tsinnah, but who told you that Ozniy and I might marry?"

"Your mother. While we were in the women's tent today, she told me that she's seen you watching him. She intends to speak to his mother while you're gone."

"There! You'll marry him when we return, I'm sure," Shoshannah said, pleased for her friend. She was even more pleased to see Ozniy wipe his face furtively, then glance at Mithqah, as if embarrassed that she had seen him beaten. *I should ask Tsinnah if my I'ma has said anything about my marriage to Kal . . .*

"Shoshannah!" Little Rinnah charged toward her now, head down, lip out, followed by the twig-thin, bossy Adah, and the prettier, more reclusive Qetuwrah, who actually looked impatient.

Shoshannah held out her arms, smiling at her sisters. Rinnah dived into her lap and huddled there, glaring at Adah and Qetuwrah. "Tell them I can go with you!"

"Oh, little one." Shoshannah hugged her baby sister, rumpling her curls. "I wish you could. But who will make our I'ma laugh if you're gone too?"

Qetuwrah raised her black eyebrows, seeming almost offended. But Adah tossed her head. "Rinnah, I told you, didn't I? You can't go. Now, stop arguing."

Rinnah's chin quivered. Shoshannah hated to see her cry, and this wasn't how she wanted to part with her sisters.

Tsinnah interposed sweetly, her voice kind but firm. "You each have to take turns visiting your cousins with me. Shoshannah's the oldest, so she's first. Now, don't fight or I won't give you the bracelets I've made for you."

"Bracelets? Where?" Rinnah straightened, her tears forgotten.

As they walked to Tsinnah's tent to retrieve the coveted ornaments, Adah whispered to Shoshannah, "Don't worry about Kaleb. We'll tell you everything he does while you're gone."

"I'm hoping you will." Shoshannah hugged Adah's thin shoulders, enjoying her sister's conspiratorial air—she was a trustworthy tattler. "No doubt he's going to keep the whole tribe in an uproar. If worse comes to worse, beg Father to be merciful to Kal, for my sake."

"You know I will."

Arms linked, the sisters walked onward through the encampment.

"Be sure our Shoshannah stays out of mischief while you're gone!" Uzziel, Mithqah's father, lectured loudly, giving Mithqah a hearty kiss on the cheek.

He turned to wink at Shoshannah, who longed to make an impudent face in return.

His bright eyes crinkling in a smile, Uzziel continued, "And don't run away with any strange young men—I'd whip you both!"

"Don't lose any of your gear," Ritspah added, fastening Mithqah's woolen cloak with a new copper pin, then kissing her good-bye.

While Mithqah uneasily nodded at her parents, Shoshannah kissed her grandparents. Chaciydah wept as Meshek patted her.

Keren looked as if she might cry, but she hugged

Shoshannah tightly, smoothing her curls. "Behave yourself! And return safely. I pray the Most High blesses you."

"I pray He does," Shoshannah agreed, feeling her throat tighten, tears stinging.

She stepped away from them and went to I'ma-Annah and Shem. I'ma-Annah dabbed Shoshannah's tears and said, "Here's a hug from I'ma-Naomi and our Ancient One, Noakh. We'll be praying for your safety."

Shoshannah accepted her hug and looked over at Shem, who widened his big dark eyes at her, fond and serious at the same time. *Is it true?* she wanted to ask him. *Will I die before my parents?* Pushing the fear away yet again, she made herself smile at Shem. "Father of my Fathers, I give you my word I'll try to stay out of trouble."

"But will you succeed?" he asked, giving her nose a light swipe. "That would be a wonder from the Most High."

She pretended to be hurt. He grinned, suddenly looking very boyish, confirming all her fears. *It's true.*

His grin faded. He stared at her as if trying to read her thoughts. Shoshannah couldn't look at him again.

She went to her father, who had been cautiously rechecking her dark little mare, Ma'khole, and retying all her gear. Zekaryah looked so . . . forlorn. Was it possible? She flung her arms around his waist and hugged him with all her might. He returned the hug fiercely, kissing her hair, then patting her silently. Stricken, fighting tears, she said, "I love you."

He could only nod. But he kissed her again as if to reassure her.

Parting with Kaleb was equally difficult. Because they weren't betrothed, they couldn't linger or touch each other. She had to content herself with gazing at Kaleb for as long as she dared, watching him stare after her unhappily as she rode away with Tsinnah and the Tribe of Metiyl.

"She's learned the truth somehow," Shem whispered, watching Shoshannah depart. Annah looked up at her husband, aching at his desolate tone. The truth. She didn't want to discuss it; she would cry. *O Most High, how I wish You could give my children some of my years! Why must this be so? I feel as if the Great Destruction has returned in a different form . . .*

Zekaryah lay staring upward into the nighttime dimness of the leather tent. Keren was curled up beside him, beneath their coverlet and furs, also still awake, he was sure. Again, he wished he could have said good-bye to Shoshannah—warning her to check her gear, to practice with her weapons, to trust no one, and to stay away from the Great City. But his emotions had been too raw—were still too raw—from the men's conversation the previous day. Everything within him wanted to deny the truth he'd been resisting for years. His children could *not* die before him. The thought made him want to rave at the Most High, demanding answers.

Even so, rage would change nothing. And his dear firstborn, Shoshannah, would be gone for a year. Zekaryah prayed she would be sensible and safe. When she returned, he would ensure that she never strayed so far from the Tribe of Ashkenaz again. If their time as a family were to be shortened, then he would be selfish and keep her close.

"She didn't want to leave," Keren whispered suddenly.

Zekaryah could feel her breath, warm against his neck. Turning, he pulled her closer, kissing her cheek, adoring the softness of her skin. "I know." Hardly able to believe he was saying the words, he murmured, "Kaleb loves her. And she loves him."

And if she married him, she would remain with the Tribe of Ashkenaz. She would be happy. Also, Kaleb was of Shoshannah's generation. Their lifespans would be the same—shortened. *Kaleb, too, will die before me.* The thought, finally admitted, was intolerable. Haltingly, fighting tears, he said, "I think Shoshannah has guessed the truth. We should have told her ourselves."

Keren had never seen her husband cry before—not even when their children were born, which had touched him deeply. His grief was unbearable. She wept with him, held him, and lay awake throughout the night, wishing she had found the courage to tell Shoshannah what she had been denying for years—what she still denied. *I will not outlive my children. O Most High, it cannot be true.*

In answer, the wind howled in the darkness outside.

"Do you think it's true?" Shoshannah begged Tsinnah, while they unloaded their gear on the evening of their second day of travel.

"I . . . Wait . . ." Looking claylike, badly shaken, Tsinnah hurried to her husband. Shoshannah regretted bringing up the subject. Particularly when she saw Tsinnah's amiable husband, Khawrawsh, droop like a beaten man as Tsinnah whispered to him. Khawrawsh's father, Metiyl—unloading his sturdy, dusky horse nearby—also hung his head, apparently listening to their unhappy discussion. Soon Metiyl's wife, I'ma-Tebuwnaw, approached Shoshannah and Mithqah, her usually cheerful face puckered, her black-brown eyes brimming.

"I'm sorry. What you heard, Mithqah . . . we're afraid it's true . . ." Tebuwnaw's voice broke. She pulled Mithqah and Shoshannah into an embrace, weeping and rocking them as if she were their own mother, overwhelmed in mourning.

Shoshannah knelt outside Tsinnah's comfortably nondescript circular mud-brick home, pounding almonds with Mithqah, I'ma-Tebuwnaw, and Tsinnah. They had settled into a comfortable routine with the passing months, cleaning, spinning wool, preserving foods, and preparing for visits from the other cousin tribes, who were also demanding return visits from Shoshannah and Mithqah.

The painful revelations from the encampment were no longer spoken of, as if ignoring them would make them untrue. But Shoshannah continued to ponder this dire shuffling of the generations. She had to be brave for her parents' sake. Truly, some potential situations might be ridiculous. Laughable.

Glancing at Tsinnah, who seemed tired this morning, Shoshannah spoke lightly. "I'ma-Tsinnah, if I'll be old and gray before my parents, won't they have to honor me as an elder?"

Tsinnah stared, as if befuddled. "An elder? You?"

While she was evidently trying to imagine such a thing, Mithqah gaped at Shoshannah, incredulous. But

Tebuwnaw burst out laughing and smacked her pounding stone onto its flat base, almost hard enough to break it.

"Trust you, Shoshannah-child, to think of such a thing! I confess, I don't know how to answer you." She turned to Tsinnah. "Daughter, what will we do when our children are older than we are?"

Tsinnah pressed her hands to her forehead, teary-eyed. "I don't know. And I'm sure I'm going to have another."

"You're bearing another child?" Shoshannah gasped, delighted, as Mithqah and Tebuwnaw hugged Tsinnah happily. Like Keren, Tsinnah had not borne a child for years, and—like Keren—she had been baffled by her apparent infertility. "Oh, I'ma-Tsinnah, how wonderful! But don't cry. If our lives are going to be shortened, we shouldn't spend all our time mourning—there's too much to do!"

"I wish your dear mother could hear you," Tsinnah wept. "She would feel so much better—forgive me; I'm going to be sick." Tsinnah hurried away.

Shoshannah tried to not feel abandoned.

"Shoshannah!"

Hearing her name, and seeing an approaching band of travelers, Shoshannah dropped her mending and left Mithqah in the doorway of Tsinnah's house. Yelahlah, a charming and lively daughter of Keren's brother Eliyshama, led a small, plump-bellied mare ahead of her trader-husband's boisterous family.

Laughing, she halted and gave Shoshannah a one-armed hug. "It's so good to see you! Forgive me—I don't dare drop the reins; *he* will drive the horse into a frenzy if I let him."

He was Yelahlah's firstborn son, Rakal. Harnessed into a basket on the mare's back, one-year-old Rakal gave Shoshannah a proud, almost adult look, as if to say, "I rule here."

"You spoiled baby," Shoshannah scolded him warmly, tousling his gleaming black hair. "Why do you give your I'ma such a bad time? Though I'm sure she was like you when she was tiny."

"Oh, how dare you," Yelahlah retorted happily, swiping her black-braided hair off her shoulders. "I was never so spoiled as he is, and it's my beloved's fault, I give you my word!"

Yelahlah was infatuated with her beloved—her brash, attractive, wide-jawed husband, Echuwd. Shoshannah, however, wasn't fond of him. Echuwd needed some kindness to temper his aggressiveness—a balance Kaleb naturally possessed. But it was not Shoshannah's place to criticize; if Yelahlah was happy, then Echuwd—and his equally brash and black-haired family, who were now unloading their packhorses—must be endured. They were close kindred to Metiyl's tribe.

Enthusiastic now, Yelahlah nudged Shoshannah. "I've heard that our I'ma-Tsinnah is finally expecting another child. How is she feeling?"

"Tired and ill." Shoshannah sighed. "I hope I'm not a burden to her; Mithqah and I do all the work we can, but Tsinnah worries that we're bored—though we're not."

"You should visit my husband's family for a while," Yelahlah suggested eagerly. "Let Tsinnah have some quiet time with her Khawrawsh and their family. By the time we're done visiting, she will be feeling better."

Shoshannah longed to refuse, but Yelahlah was already pulling Rakal out of his basket and calling to her husband. After conferring with Yelahlah, Echuwd approached Shoshannah briskly, slinging a water skin over his shoulder, his voice authoritative. "You're welcome to visit, Cousin, but be ready to leave at dawn. My family and I have other things to do and can't be waiting on you women."

"What's this?" Mithqah hissed to Shoshannah, hurrying over to her from the doorway. "What have you gotten us into?"

"Believe me, it wasn't my idea," Shoshannah protested under her breath.

Yelahlah was bounding inside the house to speak to Tsinnah. And Echuwd was going to find Metiyl to tell him that they would take Shoshannah and Mithqah away for a visit with Echuwd's family. Shoshannah hoped she could at least set a time limit on her visit with Yelahlah, without offending everyone.

"Can we hide until they're gone?" Mithqah wondered aloud, grimacing. Like Shoshannah, she didn't care for Echuwd, whom they had met at past tribal encampments.

"Echuwd and Yelahlah would find us," Shoshannah muttered.

Resigned, smiling determinedly, they went inside the house.

Shoshannah studied the rain-swollen western river before them, anxious. Echuwd's family was a short distance away, fiercely bargaining with a group of hard-eyed men who were guarding several donkeys and large, oddly rounded hutlike structures of willow and leather.

As they bargained, Echuwd's family indicated Shoshannah and Mithqah; the strange men looked at them without interest or recognition—to Shoshannah's relief. The farther they traveled from the Tribes of Metiyl and his father, Asshur, the more uncomfortable she became. To find herself at the western river now, instead of the eastern river claimed by her cousin tribes, was distressing.

Gently guiding Ma'khole, Shoshannah edged over to Yelahlah. "Are we already stopping for the night?"

Yelahlah shifted Rakal on her hip, looking as worried as Shoshannah felt. "We're bargaining for those boatmen to take us downriver."

"Boatmen? What do you mean?"

Mithqah joined them, perplexed. "Does your husband's family live south along this river now?"

"No," Yelahlah said, avoiding Shoshannah's eyes. "Echuwd and his family have business downriver. Metiyl and Khawrawsh traded Echuwd's family some newly made tools for some wonderful obsidian and copper and yew . . ."

"I can't go downriver," Shoshannah objected, her hands sweating with a sudden rush of fear. "It's too close to the Great City. I'ma said it would be too dangerous."

"I didn't know we'd be coming this way so soon," Yelahlah explained, distressed. "But Echuwd's father wants to finish their trading before the rainy season begins."

"May I stay here?" Shoshannah pleaded.

Mithqah planted herself beside Shoshannah, silently offering support.

"It wouldn't be safe, and Echuwd won't be happy," Yelahlah began.

Even as she spoke, Echuwd approached them, his

thick eyebrows lifting, his wide jaw set and stern. "What's wrong?"

Yelahlah immediately touched her husband's arm, appealing, "Beloved, Shoshannah's I'ma doesn't want her going to the Great City—Shoshannah might be recognized by her enemies. Could some of us camp here and wait for you to return?"

Echuwd shook his head. "We aren't coming back this way. We'll be turning east and heading home by land."

Shoshannah started to plead with Echuwd, but he snorted. "Don't worry. Just cover your head with something and don't look at anyone. We won't be there for long; no one will notice you." He marched away, pulling Yelahlah and Rakal with him, making Shoshannah feel like a silly child.

Mithqah stared after them, horrified. "I can't believe he's so unconcerned. Do you think we should just leave?"

"The two of us—alone on the steppes? No, that wouldn't be wise. But perhaps we'll be able to wait just outside the Great City; that would be a reasonable request." Deciding this, Shoshannah felt hopeful. Until she realized that those odd huts of willow-ribbed leather were actually the boats.

The boatmen had finished bargaining with Echuwd's family and were filling their now-upright vessels with mounds of straw that had been stashed beneath the overturned boats.

"Mithqah, we're traveling downriver—with all the animals—in those!"

"Well then," Mithqah said pathetically, looking out over the swift-flowing river, "we don't have to worry about going to the Great City. We'll drown along the way."

Four

NEARING THE END of their long river journey, Shoshannah stood beside the patient Ma'khole in the huge round boat, nauseated as much by the looming appearance of the Great City as by the swift-flowing current. The tower, above all, unnerved her. It was like a ridge-patterned mountain of darkened bricks, traversed by countless angled steps, its various levels fringed with trees. I'ma had witnessed this tower's beginning. No doubt the dreadful temple of her mother's memory was somewhere just above that first vast level, hidden by those slime-sealed brick walls.

My enemies will hate you.

Shoshannah pinned her gray cloak securely beneath her chin, using it to hide her quiver of arrows, now looped into the crook of her arm. In addition, her flint knife was in its grass pouch at her waist. But her problem would be her bow; she couldn't hide it. She would have to stay close to Ma'khole to be able to reach it easily.

"We won't be able to wait outside the city," Mithqah whispered, her dark eyes fixed on the tower, scared. "These boatmen will land us in the city itself."

"I know," Shoshannah murmured, feeling trapped. *Kal, I wish you were here. You'd have a plan; you always do. O Most High, help me.*

She pulled her hood over her head, wondering if she would be the only woman in the Great City shielding herself from some nonexistent storm. If so, then others would stare at her, which might be almost as dangerous as wearing no hood at all. In quiet understanding, Mithqah was pulling her hood over her own hair, flashing Shoshannah a brave smile. Shoshannah managed to smile in return. Now if only some of her relatives would also cover their heads, she might have a chance to remain unnoticed among them.

But Echuwd and his relatives, all quibbling and self-absorbed, ignored Shoshannah and Mithqah.

Don't worry. Just cover your head with something and don't look at anyone.

Remembering Echuwd's careless words, Shoshannah cast him a bitter sidelong glance. His disregard for her safety, and Yelahlah's subsequent nervous abandonment of Shoshannah and Mithqah, were like painful wounds. Yelahlah—now silent and holding the squirming, irritable Rakal—seemed so bound to her husband's will that she couldn't insist that they must protect their guests. Hurt and resentful, Shoshannah tried to think beyond her fear.

"If we can hide somewhere until sunset, perhaps we'll be safe," she said to Mithqah, who nodded, wide-eyed, staring up at the tower. "I'll try to persuade Yelahlah to help us."

The boat swayed sickeningly. Her stomach roiling, Shoshannah watched as the boatmen turned their long-poled rudders, guiding their vessel toward a brick-lined inlet near the tower. Ma'khole shifted nervously. Shoshannah rubbed the little mare, equally nervous about disembarking.

The boatmen, however, weren't nervous at all. They maneuvered the boat firmly against an inclined bank, then chased their cargo, humans and animals, sharply outward and upward, the boat tilting with their movements. Then—while Shoshannah stood with Mithqah on the sloped embankment, dazed and afraid—they began to disassemble their craft, calling loudly for bids on their fine, supple willow poles and straw.

As interested bargainers approached, Shoshannah hastily averted her eyes, pulling her hood close about her face and hugging her arrows tight in the crook of her arm. A hand touched her shoulder.

Yelahlah, unnaturally subdued and remorseful, whispered, "Stay close, Shoshannah. We'll find a place to hide."

Grateful that she didn't have to plead for this crucial help, Shoshannah forgave her. No doubt Echuwd was a difficult husband at times, and Yelahlah was probably still learning to cope with his moods.

Kaleb, I thank the Most High that you're not difficult. Only adventuresome. But unlike you, beloved, I don't want an adventure like this . . .

Head down, guiding Ma'khole, Shoshannah followed Echuwd, Yelahlah, Mithqah, Echuwd's family, and their packhorses through the streets of the Great City. She was intimidated by the multitudes of people and terrified of being recognized.

Echuwd and his relatives, however, moved self-assuredly. They visited some enclosed private waste pits—for a bitterly haggled fee paid in obsidian—then headed into the noisy, crowded, brick-paved market street. They had been here often, Shoshannah realized. She heard a man bellow deeply, "Echuwd! Where's that copper you promised me, eh?"

As her husband's relatives scattered throughout the market street, Yelahlah said, "We'll stay over here until my family is finished. Don't worry, Shoshannah; I'm sure we'll leave tomorrow. Meanwhile, let's find some food; Rakal is getting hungry. And we should barter for some grain and water for our animals."

Shoshannah obeyed, quietly helping Mithqah to coax their mares into a gap between two merchants' canopies, positioned against a brick and bitumen wall.

"You can't keep these creatures here!" a sparse-bearded merchant complained from a canopied display to the left, waving his wiry arms at Yelahlah.

Immediately Yelahlah's natural vivacity returned. She smiled at the merchant, delighted as if he had given her a treasure. "Oh, but how could we resist stopping here? You have exactly what we need: food and beautiful ornaments. My husband promised me a ring or a bracelet this journey—wait until he sees these. But first, what foods do you have for us?"

"I'm a jeweler, not a food merchant," the man grumbled. "That's my wife's pastime. Honey-preserved fruits and barley water—the best in the city, I'll admit. But what do you have to trade?"

Yelahlah shifted the wriggling, whimpering Rakal in her arms and untied a leather pouch from her mare. Confident, she pulled out several small, polished, almost-translucent red gemstones. "These are from the north; I polished them myself. And don't tell me they're not fine enough; I know they are."

To Shoshannah's relief, Yelahlah soon gained the merchant's grudging permission for them to stay, as well as a generous helping of the honeyed fruit, barley water, a copper bracelet, and grain and water for their animals.

"No wonder you're the wife of a tradesman, Cousin," Shoshannah told her softly. "You'd persuade the feathers from a bird."

"Oh, I'm not quite that good." Pretending humility, Yelahlah slid her new bracelet onto her wrist.

They fed and watered their mares, then sat down to eat the too-sweet fruit and the sour barley water. Shoshannah turned her face from the street, lowering her head anxiously. If only Echuwd and his family would hurry. But she had a terrible feeling that they would take their time; they were avid negotiators and loved to boast to each other of having bested this tradesman or that merchant in marvelous deals.

If it weren't for their greed, I wouldn't be here, Shoshannah thought, frustrated. Beside her, Mithqah was yawning, drooping and exhausted. Yelahlah was nursing Rakal to sleep. The afternoon stretched before them endlessly. As time passed, Shoshannah relaxed and peeked sidelong from beneath the folds of her hood. Under the merchant's canopy just to her right, a prattling young craftsman, a stout matron, and a thin, stooped man were persuading passersby to inspect the unrivaled beauty of their carvings. Furtively Shoshannah eyed the displays.

Fragile pendants, slender bone hairpins, ivory combs, shallow decorative bone containers, and knives of intricately carved woods, ivories, shells, and gems all glowed in the afternoon light. Shoshannah admired the pendants, but one of the ivory combs drew her attention. It was carved with writhing, gem-flecked hunting scenes like the ones on a small ivory comb, hidden within her mother's storage chest at home. Amazing that it should look so similar . . .

A brown hand slapped down hard over the comb, making everything around it jump, including Shoshannah. Startled, she glanced up into the young craftsman's handsome, mischievous black eyes. He was grinning, until he saw her face. Then he yanked back his hand and cried out, "I'ma-Peletah! Father Tso'bebaw! The Lady is here! She's returned!"

No! Shoshannah scrambled to her feet and started toward Ma'khole, terrified. But the stout matron hurled herself at Shoshannah with surprising speed, wailing a tearful, exultant, head-turning cry of greeting as if she had been longing to see Shoshannah for a thousand years.

"Lady! Have you returned to us? Oh!"

"No, truly, I'm not *her.*" Shoshannah thought she would smother in the woman's embrace. Her hood was tousled now. She tried, and failed, to cover her face again.

Mithqah struggled to pull Shoshannah away from the woman, gasping, "You're mistaken! Please . . ."

Ma'khole was becoming agitated, and the other mares were sidestepping now, threatening to trample Yelahlah, who leapt up, holding Rakal while begging the woman softly, "Hush! Leave her alone!" Rakal wailed, unhappily disturbed from his nap.

Aggravated, the sparse-bearded jeweler beneath the canopy to Shoshannah's left roared, "Grab those animals before they trample things!" Then, seeing Shoshannah fully for the first time, his cry of rage deepened. *"You!"* Turning, he screamed out to the whole marketplace, "Call for the guardsmen! That traitor-woman is here! Tell the men not to touch her—but don't let her escape!"

A few men fled in different directions to summon help, but most people were gathering to stare. Various women, clad in long one-shouldered woolen tunics, gasped at Shoshannah, delighted. Some of the men, however, were unmistakably hostile.

Horrified, the stout matron pushed Shoshannah toward Ma'khole. "Lady, hurry! Oh, forgive me . . ."

Shoshannah grabbed Ma'khole's reins to escape, then halted. *How?* she asked herself. *How can you escape when you're trapped between the wall and that crowd?* This could not be happening. She felt weak.

Mithqah glanced from the crowd to Shoshannah, quavering. "Those men look as if they want to kill us. Oh, Shoshannah!"

Now the matron pushed herself between Shoshannah and the crowd. "Don't you dare hurt her! The Lady never harmed anyone—you know it's true."

"She led our Great King to his death," the merchant argued. "That was harm enough."

Summoning her nonexistent courage, Shoshannah called out, "I'm not the 'Lady.' You're mistaken."

"Liar!" the merchant cried. "Do you think we're fools?"

In tears, Yelahlah answered him above Rakal's wail. "She's not your Lady, and she's done nothing wrong—as I live!"

"She's got the same face and the same eyes and hair—it's too exact to be chance," the merchant pointed out loudly, provoking murmurs of agreement from the crowd.

Now the thin, stooped merchant who occupied the canopy to Shoshannah's left spoke, blinking but firm. "This is not our Lady. Much like her, yes, but not her."

"You sound so sure," the first merchant sneered. "Well, good Tso'bebaw, perhaps we must believe you. The Lady purchased wares from you when she was here—and gave you that land you're so proud of. But how do we know you're not just trying to protect her?"

The stooped merchant bristled, but he spoke clearly. "Everyone knows you have a suspicious mind, Peh-ayr. And, may I say, a jealous spirit. You've never forgiven me for being the preferred one, have you? Let this poor child and her companions go."

Apparently the thin merchant was more trusted by the people of the Great City; the men in the crowd looked less hostile, the women disappointed. But the sparse-bearded merchant fumed aloud, "I say she goes to our Queen of the Heavens."

"Don't be spiteful, Peh-ayr!" the matron snapped, even as she nudged Shoshannah toward Ma'khole. "This young woman has nothing to do with us. What a dreadful welcome you've given her to our city. Go, child, you and your companions, before Peh-ayr thinks of some new trouble."

Yelahlah immediately plopped Rakal into his basket on her mare. And Mithqah scurried toward her own little tawny horse. Swiftly Shoshannah bounded onto Ma'khole, flinging her cloak and quiver over her shoulder and instinctively grabbing her bow.

"Look at her handle that bow—just as the Lady would! I say she should go to be judged," the merchant Peh-ayr repeated, infuriated. "If that Master Ra-Anan finds out about this, do you think we'll escape punishment? And what of Lord Kuwsh?"

Hearing those dangerous names, Shoshannah prodded Ma'khole forward, turning her toward the river once more.

The crowd parted now, but an angry familiar voice lifted above them. "Yelahlah! Where are you going? What's happened?"

Echuwd. Shoshannah hesitated. She had forgotten about Echuwd and his family; they were clustering together staring in amazement—as if they had never expected such a scene. How dare they be so surprised!

"Go, Shoshannah!" Mithqah called from behind her. "Forget them; let's leave!"

In agreement, Shoshannah goaded Ma'khole ahead. But the dark mare slowed skittishly, apparently disliking the brick pavings. Shoshannah was sweat drenched when they reached the end of the market street. And there they were greeted by proud, fleece-cloaked guardsmen, some on horseback, some on foot, all with weapons. Shoshannah snatched an arrow from her quiver, thinking, *One against so many . . .*

A particularly large, muscular horseman—his arms and throat formidably arrayed with clattering teeth and claws from various animals—lifted his own bow, fitted it with an arrow, and aimed it at Mithqah. "You choose," he told Shoshannah coldly. "Give us your weapons or I kill her."

At once Shoshannah offered her bow to the nearest guardsman, pleading, "Don't hurt her; she has nothing to do with this."

"We'll see," he retorted.

Mithqah made a noise of protest, then hushed, clearly terrified of the huge lead guard. But she traded despairing looks with Shoshannah as the remaining guardsmen cautiously surrounded them, returning them to the Great City.

They rode through the market street again, past the

smirking merchant Peh-ayr, past the distressed ivory carver, his sobbing wife, and their ashen young craftsman. And past Echuwd's family, the gaping Echuwd, and the weeping Yelahlah. Shoshannah lowered her head, scared.

As soon as the guardsmen had gone by, Yelahlah turned on her husband and his family as if she would claw them to pieces. "You should have listened to her—and to me! They were our guests! We were responsible for protecting them both; how will you explain this to their parents, and to the Ancient Ones who love them? If they die, you're all to blame!"

Not one of them disagreed. *Amazing,* Yelahlah thought, hating them, hating herself. *I never thought I'd see them speechless.* Wretched, she wiped her face and prayed silently, *Protect those poor girls, O Most High—I am also to blame.*

The thin, stooped merchant approached them now, blinking, hesitant. "If I may, I will offer you my home for the night. Surely you can hear some news of your loved ones tomorrow."

Yelahlah eyed her husband, daring him to refuse. He didn't. Quietly, she said, "I will follow our guests. Perhaps I can plead for them. After all, Master Ra-Anan and the Great Lady are my own close kindred."

She lifted her young son—who was wet—from his basket and swiftly wrapped him in a clean fleece. Then she strode past her husband's family, who silently backed away.

"We say as little as possible," Shoshannah whispered to Mithqah as their mares clopped reluctantly down the bricked streets, past mud-walled, tree-sheltered homes.

"And we give no names," Mithqah agreed softly, her tender face set, though her bristly lashes fluttered, betraying her fear.

"Separate them," the rude, massive lead guardsman commanded. He flashed Shoshannah a look of pure hatred that terrified her.

At once the other guardsmen restrained Mithqah's tawny little mare until she was far enough behind Shoshannah to prevent them from conspiring. But Shoshannah felt they had said enough; they had agreed to protect their families. Now she had to consider her friend's safety. Mithqah didn't deserve to be punished for simply being with her. *At least let me help Mithqah escape . . .*

This southern area of the city seemed quieter. On these streets, the dusky men and women—in fine, long, one-shouldered robes with handsome gold ornaments—were more reserved and proud. Until they saw Shoshannah. They halted, staring at her like astounded children.

Shoshannah squirmed inwardly. She wished she had paid more attention to Tsinnah's gentle advice regarding her hair and clothes. By comparison to these people, she was a coarse creature dragged in from the steppes. *Perhaps I'll behave like such a creature and shock them all,* she thought defiantly.

The guardsmen turned toward a more open street, which led to an enormous residence, protected by high walls and a broad, double-doored wooden gate. Several fleece-cloaked guardsmen stood outside this gate, fending off groups of citizens. Some of the citizens were richly clothed, some poorly. But they all stared at Shoshannah and retreated. The men in particular shied away from her, making her remember that, years ago, if any man even accidentally touched her mother, he was instantly put to death.

Shoshannah cringed inside. *I won't allow that to happen now.*

A gatesman, thickset and rough skinned in his fleece cloak, bellowed to the claw-draped lead guardsman. "Perek, where's Master Ra-Anan? Did he send *her*?"

"Of course he didn't," Perek snapped, tying his bow onto his horse, then dismounting. "And what do you mean, 'Where's Master Ra-Anan?' He left the tower before I did. My men and I were told of *this* as we reached the marketplace." He motioned toward Shoshannah contemptuously, adding, "We brought her here, since Master Ra-Anan said he would meet here with Father Kuwsh and our Lady."

"Well, he's not here yet." The guard tugged uncomfortably at his rough cloak. "Most likely he stopped at his home to eat and rest."

"We'll wait. He's probably on his way." Perek snorted and spat vigorously on the pavings. He sneered at Shoshannah. "Tell us: who are you?"

"I've done nothing wrong," she said, keeping her voice low.

"I didn't ask what you did! Who are you?"

"Shoshannah."

Perek narrowed his eyes. "Who is your father? And your mother?"

Do I tell him? Shoshannah wondered. *It's obvious that I'm like Mother. But what about Father? I think not.*

As she hesitated, Perek marched over to Mithqah and wrenched her off the tawny mare, twisting her arm fiercely behind her back. Mithqah screeched in pain. Scared,

Shoshannah tumbled off Ma'khole and blurted out, "I'm the Lady Keren's daughter. Please, don't hurt my friend!"

"Don't move," Perek commanded sharply. "You stand just where you are, hands at your sides, Daughter of Keren. I don't want to lose any of my men because you've done something stupid."

"Do you think I'd want that?"

"You're undoubtedly a troublemaker, like your mother." The guardsman allowed the teary-eyed Mithqah to stand straight now, but he continued to question Shoshannah. "Why are you here?"

"I was forced to come."

"I don't believe you."

"Believe me; I didn't want to come to this horrible Great City! My cousin's family brought me here unexpectedly —they're traders."

"I'm sure they wish they could have traded you for anything else!"

Shoshannah bit down a harsh response. The guard was still threateningly near to Mithqah. And he was motioning to a lesser guard to hand him a spear. She had to behave.

Voices alerted them all now: servants in pale tunics with white pendants about their necks were hurriedly clearing the street. Just behind them was their master, walking, followed by two beautiful, black-haired women clad in linen and gold. The guardsmen around Shoshannah all bowed, even Perek. Without being told, Shoshannah knew she was about to meet her mother's eldest brother, the dreadful Ra-Anan.

He looked bizarre—bald, white robed, smooth shaven, cold, tall, and proud. Immediately he approached Shoshannah, eyeing her as if she were an odd brick, badly baked. To Perek, he said, "Bring her in when she's called. Don't let any of the guards touch her."

Shoshannah stared after him as he proceeded through the gate, followed by the two women. One of the women —younger, with unbound hair—gazed at Shoshannah searchingly, until the braid-coifed older woman guided her gracefully onward.

Mithqah hurried to stand beside Shoshannah, sniffling moistly and wiping her eyes on her cloak. "That's *him?*" she demanded. "Ugh!"

"My thought exactly."

My enemies will hate you. Her mother had said those words.

I'ma, Shoshannah thought, heartsick, *I hate your enemies. O Most High, help me to behave.*

Someone hurried up to Shoshannah now: Yelahlah, holding little Rakal.

Perek raised a big hand to order her away, but Yelahlah lifted her chin. "I am a daughter of Eliyshama, brother of your Great Lady and of Master Ra-Anan. You *will* let me follow my cousin Shoshannah inside. She's been my guest, and I'm responsible for her. Others might be offended if you refuse."

Perek's hand dropped as if weighted by a stone.

Shoshannah smiled at Yelahlah, proud of her. Mithqah sighed, relieved. They were encouraged by Perek's unexpected submission. A guard spoke to them quietly from the gate, motioning with his spear. "Inside, Lady. Leave your animals; we'll tend them."

Taking a deep breath, Shoshannah obeyed, walking through the gate with her companions.

Five

SHOSHANNAH PRAYED she wouldn't stumble as she entered the huge, crowded courtyard. Yelahlah walked beside her with little Rakal, but Mithqah was clutching Shoshannah's arm, almost holding her back. Hissings and whispers came from the haughty men and women standing on either side of them.

Shoshannah almost forgot her fear. She had never imagined that so much fine wool and linen and so many gold-and-jeweled ornaments existed in the whole earth. Not to mention face paints. Some of the women's garishly painted eyes and lips reminded her of poor Khiysh—though Khiysh might actually surpass them for beauty.

From behind her, Perek growled, "When our Queen of the Heavens appears with her son, you will kneel."

Queen of the Heavens? Shoshannah almost laughed aloud. What did the Most High think of such a title as He looked down upon her? To Mithqah she muttered, "No doubt she can tell the sun, moon, and stars to bow to her as well!"

"Not to mention the wind," Mithqah agreed. "Ozniy and Kal would have a few things to say about *that.*"

If they'd been alone, Shoshannah knew they would have giggled. Their secret joke gave her courage. It also made her forget to kneel.

She stared as a shockingly colorless woman with light curls, richly painted and bejeweled, entered the courtyard, followed by a handsome young man and fawning, tunic-clad servants. Instantly all those gathered, high and low, dropped to their knees. And all, except Yelahlah and Mithqah, touched their foreheads to the pavings. Shoshannah alone stood, incredulous.

A whipping sound cut through the air behind her, and something struck the backs of her legs, felling her. She landed on the bricks, bruising her knees and catching herself with her hands, scraping her palms painfully. Infuriated, she sat up straight and turned, glaring at her attacker, Perek. He brandished his spear at her.

You must truly hate my mother, Shoshannah thought, enraged. Facing forward, she saw that the pale, beautiful woman, now seated on a high, fleece-covered bench, was scowling at her. No doubt she was Sharah; the resemblance to Keren was striking but marred by the woman's exceptional pallor and self-importance.

"Bow, child," Sharah commanded.

"Only because you are the sister of my mother, and we are in your own household," Shoshannah said. And, accompanied by Mithqah and the encumbered Yelahlah, she bowed. When she sat up again, she noticed that the handsome young man seated near Sharah was studying her warily, as if she were a deadly, peculiar thing. She raised an eyebrow at him, bemused. He must be Sharah's son. But the Queen-of-the-Heavens Sharah was talking, her voice low and hard.

"If you speak so rudely again, I will have you beaten. Do you understand, girl?"

Perfectly. Shoshannah nodded stiffly. Mithqah edged closer to Shoshannah's right, clearly reminding her to behave. To Shoshannah's left, little Rakal was squirming and grunting, trying to escape Yelahlah's grasp.

When Rakal yowled in frustration, Sharah said, "You, woman holding the child, who are you?"

Respectful, hushing Rakal by giving him her new bracelet, Yelahlah said, "I am Yelahlah, a daughter of your own brother Eliyshama. Our Shoshannah, here, has been my guest. Please, let us return to our families; we've done nothing wrong."

"Oh, but you *have,*" Sharah said, her sarcasm making Yelahlah stiffen visibly. "You've inflicted yourselves upon us. Now we must decide what to do with you."

A commotion at the gate made everyone turn. A dark man, garbed in a leopard-skin mantle, showy gold ornaments, and a fine linen tunic, swept into the courtyard, his head held high. He was accompanied by a plain, dignified woman, who gazed at Shoshannah, her brown eyes watchful and calm.

But the leopard-skin-draped man seethed. "I've heard the news. This is her daughter?"

"She is, my lord," Master Ra-Anan said politely, inclining his head. "We are discussing what should be done with her."

"Her mother should suffer for her, as I have suffered for my son," the man said. His obsidian-black eyes glittered as he knelt near Sharah, next to Ra-Anan. Everything about this man alarmed Shoshannah; she sensed he had the power to fulfill whatever threats he might make—and he had less self-control than Ra-Anan.

"That must be Father Kuwsh," Yelahlah whispered to Shoshannah nervously, clasping Rakal in her lap.

Shoshannah nodded and focused on the conversation, feeling ill.

Master Ra-Anan was speaking again. "Do we keep her in the Great City then?"

"Yes!" Kuwsh was vehement. The self-possessed woman beside him shook her head, but he paid her no heed. "She stays."

Seated in her high place, Sharah frowned. "Very well, if it pleases you, my lord. But I want her kept out of my sight. And she will have no lands or household of her own—nothing that might give her any power here."

"Of course," Master Ra-Anan said politely. "But what about the death order? Should it apply to her as it did to her mother? I'm not willing to risk my men's lives for her."

"Nor am I," Shoshannah announced, catching a stern look from Ra-Anan. "That death order was a torment to my mother; she still grieves that it was ever—"

"As you wish," Sharah interrupted. "The death order no longer exists for you, or for your mother. No one will die for touching you." She nodded at Perek, who was still kneeling behind Shoshannah. "Slap her."

Perek stood and bowed, then walked around to Shoshannah. She looked up at him, feeling all the blood ebb from her face. He smiled coolly—and then gave her a ferocious slap that sent her reeling against Mithqah. Her left ear stung and hummed with the force of his blow; the whole side of her face burned.

"Shoshannah!" Mithqah's voice trembled, edging toward hysteria, but she helped Shoshannah to sit up again.

As she was trying to steady her spinning head, Shoshannah listened—through her right ear—to Sharah asking, "What about those two women and the child?"

"Send them away," Kuwsh said. "Let them return to their families and tell Keren what has happened to *her.*"

He wants I'ma to come here so he can kill her! Horrified, Shoshannah begged the shocked Yelahlah, "Tell everyone to stay away from here, please! I'll escape eventually, Yelahlah; tell them I will! Mithqah . . ." She looked at her friend, desperate, her voice rising. "Don't let *anyone* come after me; I mean it! I don't want anyone to die—"

"Oh, heavens," Sharah said loudly, cutting through Shoshannah's panic. "She sounds too much like her mother. Perek, shut her mouth."

Shoshannah ducked, trying to ward off Perek. Instead of striking her, however, he tore her quiver of arrows off her shoulder and dropped it, then snatched her arm and twisted it into her back, forcing her to sit up. Streaks of fiery pain shot through her arm and shoulder, passing into numbness. Then Perek grabbed her chin, pulling her head back hard. Shoshannah winced, sweating, struggling to breathe.

"Say one more word and I'll go after your little friend again," Perek muttered. "Perhaps both of them—and the child."

Shoshannah kept still. Even when servants took Yelahlah, Rakal, and the distraught Mithqah away, she didn't utter a sound. But she couldn't prevent her tears.

When they were gone, Ra-Anan said, "Perhaps it would be best if my wife, Zeva'ah, took her into our household."

Sharah agreed with an indifferent wave of her hand.

Now the quiet, dignified woman beside Kuwsh stood. After bowing to Kuwsh, she looked over at the two lovely, graceful women behind Ra-Anan. "I will accompany you."

"Perek, go with them," Ra-Anan commanded. But the order seemed needless to Shoshannah; Perek was gripping her arm as if he would never release her again.

Sharah's son, Adoniyram, stared at the brown-furred quiver of arrows lying abandoned upon the courtyard pavings. The girl was completely uncivilized.

Uncivilized? No, she wouldn't have cared about the lives of others if she were truly uncivilized. Perhaps half tamed was a better description. Or half wild?

But most interesting to observe was the effect this young woman had upon Kuwsh, Master Ra-Anan, and his own mother. Kuwsh longed to destroy her for revenge. Ra-Anan clearly regarded her as a dangerous nuisance. And his mother detested her for trying to protect the lives of others—which was a decent trait in the girl and a loathsome reaction from his mother.

If Shoshannah was exactly the same as her mother, then Adoniyram was forced to conclude that the Lady Keren was honorable. And if she was actually honorable . . .

No. But . . . could my Great-King Father's murder have been justified?

Adoniyram recoiled inwardly. This new thought was contrary to everything he'd been told about the Lady Keren. If she was not a vile, deceitful, seducing traitor, then he had been lied to for his entire life. *Which, knowing my family, is possible.*

He watched as his lovely, spoiled mother and Kuwsh and Ra-Anan discussed the new additions to the tower—which had been the main purpose of their meeting today. But now this half-wild girl had disrupted everything. Particularly Adoniyram's ability to concentrate on ordinary matters such as the building of the tower.

Focusing on the abandoned brown-furred quiver again, Adoniyram thought, *I will learn the truth, Shoshannah. And if you are deceitful, then I will insist that you and your traitor-mother be punished. If not, then I will deal with your enemies for lying to me.*

Perek lowered Shoshannah's arm, allowing her to walk properly and breathe more easily, but he gripped her wrist so cruelly that she couldn't extend her fingers without pain. She longed to promise him that she would behave—for now—if only he would loosen his grip. *He won't believe me,* she thought miserably. *I'ma, what did you do to make this Perek hate you so?*

Humiliated, Shoshannah didn't lift her head or look at the citizens on either side. She trudged through the streets after Ra-Anan's wife, Zeva'ah; her graceful but aloof daughter; and the dignified, big-boned woman who was apparently Kuwsh's wife.

Their destination was a low, sprawling brick residence, enclosed by a high mud-washed wall. At first glance, the residence appeared to be modest. But as Shoshannah followed the other women inside—with Perek still twisting her arm—she was amazed by the beautiful mural-painted walls, the gleaming copper ornaments, fine baskets, exquisitely crafted wooden chests, various types of chairs, and the colorful accents of scattered fleeces, cushions, and gauzy hangings of rare cloth.

"Perek, release her," Zeva'ah said, as if speaking to a child, "but stay near. If she makes any trouble, we'll call you."

Obedient, Perek went outside, giving Shoshannah a last threatening glance.

When he was gone, Shoshannah turned toward the three women, who were all studying her quietly. Zeva'ah's gaze was subtly critical, her daughter's reserved. Kuwsh's wife was stolid, her broad, polished-brown face unmoving.

At last, Zeva'ah exhaled. "You smell like a horse."

"I've been traveling," Shoshannah explained, feeling like a small child receiving a scolding.

"Demamah," Zeva'ah said to her watchful daughter, "tell the servants to bring water to the bathing room, and food and drink for the Lady Achlai. Follow me, child." Zeva'ah said the word *child* crisply, unpleasant behind her courtesy.

While Demamah hurried off to speak to the servants, Shoshannah followed Zeva'ah through a passage to a secluded brick and bitumen-sealed room. The Lady Achlai followed unobtrusively. Zeva'ah eyed the other woman, then gestured toward a short wooden bench, as if resigned to her presence.

Why isn't she more welcoming toward Kuwsh's wife? Shoshannah wondered. Although Achlai didn't seem to require much attention.

To Shoshannah, Zeva'ah said, "If you're going to stay here, you will keep yourself clean and well-groomed, beginning now. Get those clothes off."

Aware of Achlai's impassive scrutiny, Shoshannah looked away, self-consciously unpinning her gray cloak.

Zeva'ah took the cloak as if it were slimy and repulsive. When a flushed, sharp-faced maidservant crept into the bathing room carrying a clay water vessel, Zeva'ah said, "Put that down, Ormah. Then take this and burn it."

Startled, Shoshannah protested, "But that's my cloak!"

"It stinks as you do," Zeva'ah said, unperturbed. "And it's probably crawling with bugs."

"It isn't," Shoshannah argued in distress. "My I'ma combed and spun that wool, and I'ma-Naomi and I'ma-Annah and I'ma-Chaciydah helped her to weave it and to bind the edges—you can't burn it, please!"

Zeva'ah stared at Shoshannah, clearly willing her to submit.

From her place on the small bench, Achlai said, "I will take the cloak, Zeva'ah. If it's infested, I will have it burned. If not, I will be sure it is cleaned."

"Thank you," Shoshannah sighed, grateful.

Achlai nodded and set the cloak nearby but said nothing more. The flushed maidservant scurried away empty-handed.

Other servants were entering and leaving the room now, bringing more water, herbs, garments, oils, coarse fibers, combs, and—to Shoshannah's concern—face paints. Demamah also reappeared and sidled into a corner near Achlai, offering her a drink and some tiny wheat cakes. As soon as everything had been gathered, Zeva'ah pulled the thick curtains across the door. While Shoshannah undressed, Zeva'ah frowned at the soft leather leggings Shoshannah wore beneath her tunic. "I suppose those make sense if you ride horses everywhere. But I wonder at your mother's judgment in apparel."

Don't say anything, Shoshannah scolded herself, while the Lady Achlai silently gathered her clothes, and the hidden knife, as if she were a servant. *Hush and be glad your clothes are safe!*

She was also glad for the scrubbing. Between the dousings of water, the astringent nose-wrinkling herbs, the coarse fibers, and the scented oil, she felt almost renewed. Though she could feel her welts, bruises, and sore muscles, all aching and burning from head to foot—reminders of that terrible Perek.

During her last rinsing, Shoshannah watched, fascinated, as the water bubbled and gurgled down a clay pipe, which apparently drained beneath the brick floor. Then she realized that the women were staring at her. Zeva'ah looked scornful. Clearly she considered Shoshannah ignorant. Shoshannah longed to ask where the water had gone, but she didn't want to confirm Zeva'ah's low opinion of her.

Wordless, Zeva'ah handed Shoshannah some linen undergarments, then a tawny, one-shouldered woolen robe. Shoshannah donned them, still feeling naked when she was fully clothed. Someone coughed outside the curtained doorway, and Zeva'ah called out, "Enter."

The flushed maidservant, Ormah, entered timidly. "The Lady Sharah has sent word that she will take the evening meal with your household tonight. And she will be accompanied by the Young Lord."

Zeva'ah pressed her lips together, then sighed. "Send someone to the market to buy more fruit and meat and bread. Tell the cook to season the meat with good oil, herbs, and salt. Also, be sure the water and drinks are cooling."

As Shoshannah combed her wet hair, Zeva'ah muttered, "I suppose she's changed her mind as usual and wants to speak with *you* about something."

Shoshannah decided it would be wise to remain

silent. She was uncomfortably aware of Achlai and Demamah both still watching her. In the Tribe of Ashkenaz, the women were always laughing, talking, and enjoying themselves when they gathered for bathing or for any sort of work. Here, however, there was no sense of companionship among the women—not even between Demamah and her mother. Shoshannah glanced at Demamah, almost pitying her.

At a sign from Zeva'ah, Demamah held the face paints as Zeva'ah mixed them with an oily concoction. The older woman applied lampblack to Shoshannah's eyes and red ochre to her lips with remarkably thin, delicate wands of wood. When another servant coughed just outside the doorway and announced that the Lord Kuwsh would take his evening meal with Master Ra-Anan's household—in addition to fetching the Lady Achlai— Zeva'ah shut her eyes. Then she stared at Shoshannah, clearly blaming her for disrupting her life.

"Forgive me," Shoshannah murmured, unable to prevent the apology from escaping her lips, but Zeva'ah only frowned.

Kal, Shoshannah thought suddenly, longing for him, dreading the ordeal of meeting that Queen-of-the-Heavens Sharah and Lord Kuwsh again tonight. *How I wish you were here! And how glad I am that you're not! I give you my word that I'm going to escape this place or die trying.*

Achlai watched the girl, Shoshannah, her emotions mixed. The lingering grief she felt for the death of Nimr-Rada, her Great-King son, now mingled with pity for this child with the vivid slap print on her cheek. Surely she must feel as if she had stumbled into a snake pit, with all the snakes agitated and flaring at her. *And my own husband is one of those snakes.*

"Forgive me," the girl had said to Zeva'ah.

But do I forgive you? Achlai wondered silently. *Certainly I must; it's not your fault that my Nimr-Rada was killed. And it wasn't your mother's fault, though she longed for his death. Still, the pain is there if I consider it too much. Forgive me, Most High.*

In the merchant Tso'bebaw's uncomfortably crowded home, Mithqah slumped down before the flickering hearth, refusing to touch her food. Tso'bebaw's wife, Peletah, alternately fretted and wept, trying to console the grieving Mithqah. "I'm sure they won't hurt her; she hasn't committed a crime."

Mithqah lifted her head. "But how can I leave her here? She'd never leave me if I were in trouble."

"She begged us to warn our family not to come—and we must do so," Yelahlah murmured, caressing the now-clean Rakal, asleep beside her. "I'm sure that if Shoshannah can escape, she will. Also, it will be easier for her to escape if she doesn't have to worry that you're here waiting for her."

"But she's already said that she doesn't want to go out onto the steppes alone," Mithqah whispered, thinking aloud. "Perhaps I could bring help to her . . ."

"You *cannot* bring her dear mother here," Peletah said, agitated.

Brisk tapping sounded at the door. Mithqah looked up, praying that it would be Shoshannah, freed and eager to return home.

Instead, a tiny, engaging woman with bright dark eyes

entered the home, led by the now-silent young craftsman who had been with Tso'bebaw and Peletah in the marketplace that morning.

Mithqah slumped unhappily again. But Peletah sighed as if thankful. The newcomer immediately crossed over to the hearth to kneel beside Peletah.

"Tell me everything," she said, mournful.

After hearing Peletah's emotional, hand-fluttering explanation of the day's events, the tiny, bright-eyed woman sighed and said to Yelahlah and Mithqah, "Your Shoshannah has more friends than you realize, my daughters. And if you do bring or send anyone to free her, then send them to me first—I am Meherah, wife of Yabal the potter. My son Lawkham was the Lady Keren's guardsman, with my adoptive son, Zehker. They both loved her, and who could blame them? But tell me, do you have news of my Zehker? I've heard nothing of him since he took our Lady Keren from the Great City."

"Zehker?" Mithqah stared at Meherah, confused. Then she realized aloud, "He's Zekaryah . . . tall and severe and the best in our tribe with horses and weapons."

"That must be my Zehker," Meherah sighed, clasping her hands together, her eyes glistening with unshed tears. "So he is well?"

"He married I'ma-Keren," Yelahlah breathed, delighted. "Shoshannah is his daughter. I was scared of him as a child—but he's a good man. I'ma-Keren loves him."

Meherah beamed at her. "I hoped you could tell me something about him! I knew it wasn't safe for him to come here or to send word after turning against the Great King, but . . . Oh, how my Lawkham would laugh to hear this news!"

"But where is your Lawkham now?" Mithqah asked.

She regretted the words at once; Peletah dabbed at her eyes, while Meherah's smile faded.

"You don't know . . . The Great King killed my dear Lawkham when he accidentally touched our Lady Keren."

"Your son was the young man she still grieves for?" Mithqah asked, horrified. "I'ma-Keren told Shoshannah his story."

"Yes," Meherah said gently. "The Lady Keren hasn't forgotten him; I *am* glad. Others remember his death here, and they've blamed her. But it was that Nimr-Rada; he threw the spear that killed my Lawkham! Our Lady Keren—and my Zehker—retrieved his body from the river for my sake. They risked their lives to honor him; I will always be grateful for that." Her eyes brightened again. "So Shoshannah is the daughter of my Zehker and his Keren? Then she's my granddaughter! We will help her in every way we can, won't we, my Ezriy?"

The young craftsman, seated just behind her, nodded. His eyes were as bright as his mother's. "Of course we will, I'ma."

"But Shoshannah won't want you to put yourselves in danger for her sake," Mithqah objected.

"Oh, we will be careful," Meherah promised.

Grateful, Mithqah murmured, "May the Most High bless you for caring."

"He has, child."

They talked quietly for the remainder of the evening. Mithqah was comforted enough to eat, then to fall asleep. If she had to leave Shoshannah here—at least for a while—then it was good to know that Meherah, Tso'bebaw, and Peletah were here as friends. If only Shoshannah could know it; she might feel better.

Protect her, O Most High.

Six

"THEY ARE WAITING for you," Demamah told Shoshannah, toneless, not looking at her in the flickering lamplight.

She's been sent like a servant, Shoshannah thought, pitying the girl yet again. She rose from the fleece-padded bed in the comfortable little sleeping room where she had been instructed to wait until the others had eaten. Shoshannah was certain they had neglected her during the meal to emphasize that she was not a welcomed guest in their home; she was an enemy.

"Wait," Demamah said, as they were about to leave the room. She looked at Shoshannah now, fearful. "I beg you, Cousin, for the sake of peace . . . when we enter into the presence of the Lady Sharah and her son and the Lord Kuwsh, you must fold your hands before you and bow politely. Like this." She demonstrated an elegant bow, her straight black hair gleaming in the lamplight.

"For the sake of peace? Are they being more quarrelsome now than they were this afternoon?"

Demamah's luminous, long-lashed eyes widened. "No, but wasn't this afternoon horrible enough? I'd think you would want to avoid another slap from Perek."

"I think you're right." Another thought occurred to Shoshannah. "So the Lady Sharah has a son here? My I'ma never mentioned him."

"He is Adoniyram. You saw him today, seated near his mother. Sometimes you will hear people call him Son of Heaven. He was born after the Lady Keren left the Great City. After the death of He-Who-Lifts-the-Skies."

"Why should they call him 'Son of Heaven,' or Lady Sharah 'Queen of the Heavens,' when they are ordinary people?"

"Because the people believe that the Lady Sharah is their Protectoress, and that Adoniyram is the Promised One who will restore us all to the perfection that existed when the earth began." Nervously Demamah changed the subject. "We must go. Please, say as little as possible. Perhaps they'll become tired of questioning you if you're dull."

"Do you think I can be dull?" Shoshannah pretended to be concerned.

Demamah eyed her seriously. "I don't know. But you should try."

"You don't joke much, do you?"

Hesitant, Demamah said, "This is a very formal household. My parents are . . . important."

"For your sake, I wish they weren't," Shoshannah said, making a face.

Demamah gave her a weak smile. "They're waiting."

I think you're not my enemy at all, Shoshannah thought, satisfied. "I give you my word, Cousin, I'll be as dull as possible."

Demamah led Shoshannah from the hushed sleeping room into a narrow, lamplit passage. To their left, a reed doorway stood partly open with a tempting starlit view of a small private courtyard, with its own tree and a garden, which softened the edges of an enclosing mud-brick wall. Shoshannah longed to run outside, but Demamah hastened onward through the dim passage. At the end of the passage was a thickly layered, sound-muffling curtain. Pushing it aside, Demamah led Shoshannah into the huge, mural-painted main room.

Shoshannah fixed her gaze on the braided grass floor mats, but she was aware of Demamah's every move. When her cousin executed a perfect formal bow, Shoshannah copied her. And when Demamah knelt, swiftly smoothing her skirts beneath her knees with a fluid motion, Shoshannah did the same. She could feel all her aching, pulled muscles complaining. She could also feel everyone staring at her. Unwilling to look at them, she studied a collection of copper trays before her, littered with delicate crusts, bones, herb-flecked pools of oil, and fruit pits—the remains of their evening meal. Not tempting enough to make her wish she'd been invited.

"At least she's clean now," the Lady Sharah observed tartly.

I was traveling, Great Lady, Shoshannah thought. *Let me see you travel with no servants and remain clean, sweet smelling, and lovely.* But even as she thought this, Shoshannah chided herself. *Be careful; don't let them make you angry. Perek is eager to slap you again.*

"Look at me," Ra-Anan commanded.

Shoshannah looked warily.

He stared at her hard, suspicious, as if cutting her to pieces in his mind. At last he sat back and said, "Zehker."

Zehker? Shoshannah frowned. What was he talking about?

"He's her father," Ra-Anan said to the others. "She may look like her mother, but her expression just now was *his*. He was my student for years, and he was Keren's guardsman. According to witnesses, he aided Keren in her conspiracy against the Great King. He's the obvious choice."

"That awful wooden-faced Zehker!" Sharah exclaimed, making Shoshannah glance at her. The Queen of the Heavens scowled, her face freakishly pale and malicious. "He hated Keren at one time, I assure you."

"I never trusted him," Kuwsh said decisively, setting his cup on a tray.

Zehker. Zekaryah. Father, did you change your name? Shoshannah felt ill. And angry. Clearly, her parents would be killed if they were ever caught in the Great City. She looked down at her hands, folded tightly in her lap. *I won't talk about I'ma and Father with them. I won't!*

"I've guessed the truth, haven't I?" Ra-Anan asked, so smug that Shoshannah seethed.

"Does my father's name matter? If I'm going to die anyway—"

"Cooperate, and you'll live," Kuwsh said, as if granting a favor. "We want your mother, not you."

"Why do you want to kill her, when you know she was only defending herself and her family against your Great-King son? Your generation might outlive hers anyway! And she will outlive me, no matter what, so I—"

"Stop!" Ra-Anan glared at her forbiddingly as his wife,

Zeva'ah, sucked in a breath and glanced at their daughter. Demamah stared at Shoshannah, clearly bewildered.

The young Adoniyram leaned forward, shaking his head as if he hadn't understood. "What do you mean?"

He doesn't know, Shoshannah realized. But he should. She blurted out, "Our First Father Shem and all the northern tribal leaders have agreed that the younger generations are aging faster than their parents. We'll die before they do."

"Ignore her," Zeva'ah said coldly, recovering. "She doesn't know what she's talking about."

"You're a little tale-bearing traitor, like your mother!" Sharah accused.

Shoshannah stiffened. "My mother *never* betrayed you as you betrayed her, and you know it!"

Outraged, Sharah clawed toward Shoshannah. Her son restrained her, appealing, "Mother, be careful; she's half wild." But Adoniyram scowled at Shoshannah as if he wanted to slap her himself.

The Lady Achlai, who had been silent, kneeling beside her husband, said weakly, "The child is telling the truth."

"She's not!" Sharah cried.

"This is nothing but a rumor spread by our enemies to create chaos for us," Ra-Anan said to Demamah and Adoniyram. "If I had thought it was the truth, I would have told you before." He stared at Shoshannah fearsomely. "You will never speak of this again, or you will be punished as others have been. I will not have turmoil in these lands because of a tale spread by a foolish girl."

Shoshannah complied, bowing her head. *I wish you were right, but I fear you are lying to them, and to yourself.*

"We should have Perek beat you bloody!" Sharah said,

apparently still furious that Shoshannah had dared to reprimand her. But before she could insist that Shoshannah be punished, Adoniyram stood.

"Mother, let's leave this place *now.*"

Brooding, Adoniyram sat on a darkened terrace of the tower. Beside him, Rab-Mawg pretended to analyze the stars, but Adoniyram knew better; the priest's eyes were flickering here and there, agitated in the torchlight.

"Say it!" Adoniyram snapped, losing his much-practiced caution. "Do you think she's right? Will those two outlive me?"

"I've heard this rumor before, and I believe it's false," Rab-Mawg answered stiffly. "But she obviously believes it. Or else she is making trouble."

Adoniyram calmed himself, reasoning aloud. "We should try to learn the truth about this story. She apparently heard it from those Ancient Ones. And I don't believe she's a deliberate troublemaker—she's in enough trouble now without making more for herself. Anyway, what would she gain by spreading such a rumor if it's false? And if it's true . . . her own years will also be shortened; she *is* of our generation." Quietly, he added, "Perhaps that's why I prevented my mother from attacking her."

Sharah had stormed and screamed and thrown dishes as soon as she reached the privacy of her own residence. All her rage had been directed at Shoshannah for being like her mother, Keren, who stupidly trusted those old storytelling Ancient Ones in the mountains. Worse, the girl had dared to voice a truth that the Queen of the Heavens didn't want to accept.

My mother never betrayed you as you betrayed her, and you know it!

Shoshannah's words also implied knowledge of the past that Adoniyram didn't have. What did she know about his mother?

"I say she's dangerous," Rab-Mawg declared. "If she's been in our Great City for less than a day and already created such furor, what else might she do?"

"What else indeed?"

"And," Rab-Mawg's voice rose vehemently, as if coercing Adoniyram to accept his opinion, "you won't be able to prevent someone from killing her eventually. If you decide what should be done with her, my lord, I will assist you in whatever way I can."

"Thank you, Rab-Mawg."

What should happen to this Shoshannah? Adoniyram wondered. She was too straightforward. And evidently honorable. Combined, the traits could be ruinous. That, added to her looks—which were extraordinary now that she was clothed in a civilized manner—made her thoroughly unsettling. Might she be the tool he needed to pry those two vultures from their lofty perches? And to counteract his mother's influence within the kingdom?

Mother, he fumed, *you didn't even consider that, if what this girl says is true, you will live to see my death. Your thoughts were all centered upon how offensive she was toward you. Am I worth so little to you?*

He knew the answer but pushed it away.

As soon as Adoniyram had departed, Rab-Mawg hurried inside the tower's chilly, gold-decked, half-built temple, which was lit by lamps and a hearth and guarded by his own followers—his three fellow priests of Shemesh. They eyed him as they finished their evening meal. All three were thin, black eyed, bald shaven, trustworthy, and devout as he was, clad in pale woolen robes and sandals. And like Rab-Mawg, they despised the arrogant Ra-Anan, the worthless, temperamental Lord Kuwsh, and his equally worthless and temperamental daughter-in-law, the Lady Sharah. They longed for Adoniyram to take hold of the kingdom.

"Listen," Rab-Mawg said darkly, knowing they would hate his news. "Don't repeat this to anyone: We have a potential adversary . . ."

Shoshannah hadn't realized that the comfortable little sleeping room was Demamah's own room. As the servants brought heaps of straw, furs, and coverlets for Shoshannah's bed, she realized that Ra-Anan and his wife intended for her to stay with Demamah, at least for tonight. The thought both consoled and worried her.

While they were combing their hair and preparing for sleep, Demamah was silent. But she cast a wounded look at Shoshannah, which made Shoshannah feel like a traitor.

Clearing her throat meekly, she said, "I'm sorry. You trusted me, but I hurt you the instant I started talking. Forgive me. I should have kept quiet."

Demamah nodded. After a time, she said, "Were you lying?"

Reluctantly Shoshannah shook her head. "No. Our tribal leaders say it's probably true. And I watched our First Father Shem and our I'ma-Annah together with my parents and grandparents. The differences between their generations are obvious."

Demamah settled onto her low, fleece-covered bed, staring upward at the roof beams. Shoshannah adjusted her makeshift bed, smoothing the light woolen coverlet, then flopping back limply to also gaze at the roof.

In a tiny voice, Demamah said, "If it's true, then it's unfair."

"I've thought the same thing countless times. And I've wondered if, perhaps, it's because of this new earth. Our ancient I'ma-Naomi has said that the earth was more welcoming and easier to live in before the Great Destruction."

Now Demamah looked at her, troubled. "Do you believe her? Some say the Great Flood is just a story."

"It's not," Shoshannah said stoutly. She turned on her side to face her cousin. "I've seen the pen, the huge boat they lived in with all the animals. It's wonderful and frightening. I've walked through it. Not only that, but if you could meet our Ancient Ones, Noakh and I'ma-Naomi, and our First Father Shem and his I'ma-Annah, you'd know they were telling the truth." Angrily she added, "How could anyone doubt them?"

"You love them," Demamah observed, sounding wistful.

Something about her voice made Shoshannah stare at her. "Tell me."

"Tell you what?"

"You aren't happy with your life here, are you?"

It was a long time before Demamah answered. "I think I should be more upset by what you've said tonight. But if the remainder of my life is the same as its beginning, then I really don't care how long I live . . . or don't live."

As Shoshannah gaped at her, Demamah whispered, "I haven't been truly happy since your mother left me. When she was here, though I was just a little girl, I knew I was loved."

"What do you intend for her, Master-Uncle?" Adoniyram asked quietly, as he rode out to the tower with Ra-Anan the next morning. Their retinues of servants and guardsmen clattered behind.

"Whatever is most useful for the kingdom—that is what we should intend for her," Ra-Anan murmured, his dark, hooded eyes revealing nothing.

Adoniyram noticed the meaningless polite "we" and the vague explanation. Determined, he said, "Our Lord Kuwsh sees her only as bait for his prey—the Lady Keren."

"It's natural that he does." A brief flicker of distaste passed over Ra-Anan's face at the mention of Kuwsh.

Pleased, Adoniyram said, "I wonder what the Lady Keren's role in this kingdom would have been if she hadn't betrayed my father."

"She gave her oath to be the Protectoress of the Tower: the most revered servant of Shemesh. She would have received sacrifices and offerings from the people."

Adoniyram made his words sound as if he were musing aloud. "I can imagine how my mother and our Lord Kuwsh would resist any suggestion that the Lady Keren's daughter should take her place."

Ra-Anan looked around, as if uninterested. "Our Lord Kuwsh desires only what is best for the Great City. Your Lady-Mother, too, desires the best for her people, I'm sure."

And I'm sure you know she doesn't, Adoniyram thought.

Sighing, he asked, "Do you believe that Shoshannah was intentionally spreading rumors last night?"

Ra-Anan looked at him blandly. "I'm sure she believes she was right." Without a word, Ra-Anan conveyed a sense of triumph, a silent, *I shall outlive you, Adoniyram, so your ambitions to rule this kingdom are useless.*

Adoniyram stifled the urge to smash Ra-Anan in the face; he would probably lose a physical conflict with his tall uncle. Ra-Anan was a devious, unprincipled fighter. Keeping his voice pleasant, he only said, "She might be hiding secrets from us."

"We will learn whatever she knows," Ra-Anan promised.

"If our Lord Kuwsh and my mother allow her to live."

"If they do," Ra-Anan agreed, bland again, staring at the water- and wall-encircled tower, seeming more interested in its emerging form than in the life of the unhappy Shoshannah.

Adoniyram looked over his shoulder briefly and changed the subject. "I see you are training some new guardsmen. I should find some others; mine are becoming complacent and bored with our morning hunts."

"I'll let you know if I acquire any exceptional bowmen during our scoutings."

Bowmen who are also exceptional spies for you, Adoniyram told himself grimly. "I'd welcome your suggestions, Master-Uncle. Will you join me for a hunt tomorrow?"

"Perhaps."

"If not, then don't worry. My Lord Kuwsh might go with me."

Ra-Anan gave him a sidelong look that was surely intended to discourage any hunting or talking with Kuwsh. "Let's see what we can accomplish today; I might have time to ride out with you in the morning."

"Thank you, Uncle." Pretending to think aloud once more, Adoniyram said, "That Shoshannah wore a quiver of arrows yesterday. Do you suppose she hunts?"

"Undoubtedly, if she is Zehker's daughter. We should test her during our hunt tomorrow."

"As you say, Master-Uncle," Adoniyram agreed, smiling inwardly. His mission had been easily accomplished: He would see the girl tomorrow.

After their evening meal, when Zeva'ah had gone to supervise the servants in cleaning and putting away the food, Ra-Anan beckoned his daughter.

Demamah approached and knelt before him quietly, folding her hands in her lap. Her unfailing obedience pleased Ra-Anan. She never argued or behaved sullenly, and her looks and manners were perfect. Her mother had trained her well.

"Did Shoshannah say anything to you last night?"

Demamah looked distressed. "She asked my forgiveness for causing a scene. And she insisted that she had told the truth. She also spoke of the Ancient Ones."

"What of them?" Ra-Anan demanded, scornful. "Another story?"

"She spoke of the Great Flood, but not much more. She loves the Ancient Ones."

"Did she say anything about their worship of the Most High?"

"No, Father."

"The next time you see her, find out if she worships their Most High. I want to know if she is as devoted to such foolishness as her mother was."

"Yes, Father." Demamah hesitated, uncertain. "I haven't seen her all day. She's been barred alone in my room."

"Then she will be eager to talk when she sees you tonight. Be sure you ask her. And tell her that you'll both ride out with me to hunt in the morning."

Demamah bowed her head. "Yes, Father."

Shoshannah curled up in a corner of Demamah's room, homesick and upset at having been left in solitude all day. She'd never been alone for so long in her life. To pass the time, she had created a straw whisk and cleaned the corners of the room. But Zeva'ah was apparently a fervent housekeeper; there hadn't been much dirt to gather, so Shoshannah had given up.

All day, too, I'ma-Naomi's tender voice had haunted her, saying over and over, *I am sure the Most High has made wonderful plans of His own for you.*

Shoshannah closed her eyes hard now, crying to the Most High, "I don't like these plans! Do You hear me? How are they so wonderful? Why did You even bring me here, when I'm obviously so useless?" Then she buried her face in her hands. "Forgive me."

She wept, longing for her parents, for her brothers and sisters, for Mithqah and Ma'khole, and more than anyone else, for Kaleb. He would find humor in this "adventure." He would make her laugh.

A shifting, rasping sound alerted Shoshannah, making her sit up and wipe her face. Someone was lifting the bars that blocked the reed door. A grim, pale-clothed manservant stepped aside, allowing Demamah to enter the room with a small tray.

Demamah set down the tray and gently motioned the servant away. He bowed, glared at Shoshannah, and departed, his footsteps fading in the passage beyond.

"Do they all hate me?" Shoshannah asked, suddenly feeling very tired and forlorn.

"I'm sure they don't." Demamah lifted a fine linen cover from the tray, revealing flat bread, dried fruit, and a bowl of broth. "Look, I've brought you some food. Mother said you haven't eaten."

"Why eat? They want me to die."

"And you've said *I'm* too serious." Demamah's attempt at lightness made Shoshannah stare at her in surprise.

"Do you pray to your Most High before you eat?" Demamah asked softly.

Shoshannah's despair returned, swathing her miserably like wet clothes. "I doubt it would help; He doesn't seem interested in my prayers."

Sighing, Demamah offered her the bowl of fragrant broth, which was garnished with pungent herbs and meat. "I'm sorry, Cousin. But don't be unhappy, please. Listen: Father said that we're to go hunting with him in the morning."

"A hunt? Really?" Shoshannah's spirits lifted—though she was cautious too. "Can I see my poor Ma'khole?" She doubted she would ride Ma'khole; the little mare was never used for hunting and would probably be considered useless by Ra-Anan's men. "If I could just see her . . ."

"Your mare?" Demamah wrinkled her forehead. "I don't know, but I'll ask Father while you eat. Though I won't tell you what he says until you've eaten everything."

"I'll eat!" Shoshannah took the delicate red-glazed clay bowl, inhaling. The food did smell wonderful. Feeling better, she sipped the broth.

Demamah left the room.

"She didn't pray before eating," Demamah reported, hating her role as a spy. "And she said that the Most High wouldn't help her . . . that He doesn't seem interested in her prayers."

Her father raised one dark eyebrow, as if surprised. But he spoke calmly. "Perhaps she will be easier to manage than her mother was. We'll see."

Easier to manage? Demamah didn't like what those words implied. She longed to warn her cousin. And she warned herself too. *Don't become fond of Shoshannah; it will hurt too much when you lose her.*

Seven

"HOW DO I wear this?" Shoshannah wondered aloud, holding up a long, wide piece of linen.

"That will be similar to those leather leggings you wore beneath your tunic when you arrived," Demamah said, busily securing her own garments around her slender waist with a long linen sash.

Shoshannah eyed her cousin's flowing apparel doubtfully. "I think my leather garments covered more. How did you put these on?"

"Like so . . ." Demamah pulled a short-sleeved linen gown over Shoshannah's head and arms, covering her undergarments. Then she tied one end of the long linen cloth around and behind Shoshannah's waist and coaxed her to draw the loose fabric between her knees and wrap the other end around her waist, knotting it in front. Demamah folded, tucked, pinched, and pulled the linen into place deftly, making Shoshannah feel swaddled like an infant. "Demamah," she began hesitantly, as her cousin offered her a long, open-fronted, slash-skirted outer robe, "Don't you have any brothers or sisters? I never hear you speak of any."

"They're all older. And busy. And brothers," Demamah said tersely. "Father sent them to other smaller cities to keep them in order."

"The cities or your brothers?"

"The cities. My brothers are very much like my parents —or they try to be."

"And you never see them?"

"Rarely." Demamah's voice lowered as she wrapped a wide sash around Shoshannah's waist, securing the robe. "My brothers and I don't have much to discuss with each other."

"But you have friends . . ."

"My parents are careful." Demamah tied Shoshannah's sash, tucking in the ends neatly. Finished, she turned away.

No sisters. No friends. No one like Mithqah to laugh and fight and play with, and to whisper secrets to, which couldn't be shared with anyone else. Shoshannah shook her head, unable to imagine such isolation. "You've never been in trouble at all, have you?"

"Not for years, Cousin, but I'm afraid you'll change that. Come now; we have to hurry." She dug into a small wooden box and produced delicate ivory containers of face paints. When Shoshannah began to plead against using the paints, Demamah said, "You'll get me into trouble with my parents if you don't cooperate. Now hold still."

"You're as bossy as my sister Adah," Shoshannah complained. But she submitted to the paints for Demamah's sake.

At last, finished with Shoshannah's lips and eyes, Demamah retrieved a small, heavy obsidian mirror from her box. Tilting her head this way and that, Demamah applied her own face paints.

"You'll have to wear your boots," she informed Shoshannah. "If Mother dislikes them, she will have sandals made for you instead."

"If I live long enough to wear them," Shoshannah muttered wryly, pulling on her boots.

"Don't say such things!"

Shocked by Demamah's fierceness, Shoshannah blinked. "I was joking."

"Please don't joke about death."

Demamah laced on a pair of leather sandals, then went to the doorway, pointedly waiting for Shoshannah to follow.

Feeling disgraced, Shoshannah trotted after her in the gloomy passage. "Are you very angry with me?"

"No." Changing the subject, Demamah said, "I'm sure we're going to be drenched by the rain. But don't let my father hear you grumble."

"I love rain."

"I'll remind you of that later."

As they pushed aside the heavy curtains and hurried through the main room, Shoshannah could feel her "skirt" hugging her waist and hips and dragging at her ankles and calves uncomfortably. "May I grumble about my clothes? They feel too tight."

"Perhaps they'll restrain you a little." Demamah half smiled, softening the effect of her words. "I beg you . . . don't even *breathe* unless you've considered it carefully. Then think several times more."

Shoshannah bit down a teasing response; Perek was

waiting just outside in the courtyard. The misty gray morning hadn't dampened his belligerence. Immediately, he grabbed her arm and led her to a dull tawny-and-black horse, threatening, "Do one thing wrong, Daughter of Keren, and I'll strike you."

Don't worry; I won't even breathe. And it's not because you're smelly.

Perek linked his big hands and leaned down, scowling at her. "Step up."

Squeamishly she obeyed, then gasped as he heaved her gracelessly onto the waiting horse—jarring all the bruises and strains he had inflicted upon her earlier. As she struggled to rearrange her tangled garments, the Son-of-Heaven Adoniyram rode into the courtyard. He grimaced—clearly he must consider her undignified—and Shoshannah made a face at him. Perek swatted her arm and snatched her reins.

Perek, I hate you. She rubbed her arm. Master Ra-Anan was staring at her critically. Demamah, however, turned away. Shoshannah knew she had disappointed her cousin yet again. It had been stupid and childish to make a face at Adoniyram—she *had* to stop being so impulsive.

Adoniyram was riding toward her now. She expected him to scold her. Instead, he gave her a searching look through his long, dark eyelashes, then produced her bow and quiver as elegantly as he might offer a gift.

"Yours, Cousin?"

Sighing, ashamed and grateful, she accepted her weapons—which her father, Zekaryah, had made. "Thank you. Please forgive me for being so rude just now; I deserved that swat on the arm."

Adoniyram smiled suddenly, his copper-brown face disturbingly attractive. "No doubt you keep Perek busy.

Try not to shoot anyone this morning; we don't want any new disasters, Cousin."

She stared after him as he turned his horse to follow Master Ra-Anan's out the mud-brick gate. Adoniyram had been remarkably courteous, despite her telling him that his lifespan would be shortened. *Perhaps he's planning to shoot me instead.* Grimly she slung her quiver across her back and resigned herself to being treated like a child as Perek—now ahead on his own tawny horse—led her spiritless mount outside the courtyard.

Demamah rode up to Shoshannah as they turned from the southernmost street out toward an open field. Very softly, eyeing Perek, she said, "Be careful of Adoniyram; I'm sure he's plotting something."

"As everyone here seems to be doing," Shoshannah agreed beneath her breath. "Except you."

Demamah seemed saddened by her words. Shoshannah watched her curiously, wondering why she seemed so grieved.

She was behaving. She didn't complain about her pathetic creature-horse, Perek's merciless attitude, the sticky mud that might ruin her boots, or her uncomfortable new clothes. And when Ra-Anan spoke to her, she was as mild as Demamah.

Adoniyram seemed disappointed. Waving Perek off, he rode over to her while Ra-Anan was conferring with one of his huntsmen. "I expected some courage from you, Cousin."

"I don't always create scenes," Shoshannah told him,

raising her eyebrows. "Anyway, it's a very quiet morning. I think we're scaring everything away."

"You're bored. I apologize. Next time, I'll have someone bring my leopards." Adoniyram watched her as if he expected her to be nervous or disbelieving.

But her mother had mentioned the leopards so prized by the Great-King Nimr-Rada. "I would like to see them," Shoshannah murmured.

"You've heard about my leopards?"

"I was told your father hunted with them."

"What else have you been told, Cousin?" he asked, leaning closer. "You know more than you've already said, don't you?"

"About our lifespans?"

"About my mother," Adoniyram whispered, his voice beguiling.

Unsettled, Shoshannah asked, "What do you want to know?"

"Everything."

Your mother had two husbands. She abandoned her infant son, your brother . . . It would be so easy to tell him. And so dangerous. Shoshannah looked away. "You must speak to Master Ra-Anan instead. Or talk with your mother."

"I want to hear the truth from you."

"There's nothing I can tell you."

"I understand your fear." An edge suddenly cut beneath his soft words. "But you know I'll persist. Eventually you *will* tell me." He sat up now, looking amiable, as if they had just ended a friendly, unimportant conversation. Ra-Anan was heading toward them, goading his sand-pale horse, clearly displeased.

You don't like it that I was talking with Adoniyram without your permission, Shoshannah realized, anxious. *But Adoniyram is upset that I didn't talk with him as much as he'd hoped. And his mother—that Sharah—would hate me for breathing any of her secrets. Meanwhile, our Lord Father Kuwsh longs for my death—which Perek will gladly take care of, I'm sure.* Silently, closing her eyes, turning her face heavenward, she pleaded, *Most High, how will You save me from them? Or won't You?*

Rain was falling now, like the tears she longed to shed. Somehow, she had to escape.

"Thank you for summoning me," Shoshannah told Ra-Anan and Zeva'ah. She bowed politely, then knelt on the mat in their luxurious main room, now cleared of the evening meal. Zeva'ah raised her eyebrows at Shoshannah, seeming skeptical, but Ra-Anan watched her narrowly.

"Why do you thank us?" he asked, his face and words expressionless.

"Because I *am* thankful. I need your advice, Uncle. Today Adoniyram demanded that I tell him about his mother—and I don't think I should."

"Tell us what you know, child," Zeva'ah urged, smiling, though not pleasantly. She obviously despised Sharah.

Uncertain, Shoshannah faltered, "Perhaps you know . . . It's clear that Adoniyram doesn't. He has a brother. And his mother—I mean, the Lady Sharah—had two husbands at the same time. Her first was—"

"Bezeq," Ra-Anan finished, thoughtful. "They had a son, Gibbawr."

"Yes." Shoshannah sighed, relieved that he knew, and that he was so calm.

Her relief faded as Master Ra-Anan studied her for an unnervingly long time. Then, low and cool, he said, "You are wise to ask our advice. Adoniyram doesn't know about his mother's past. But he should. The next time he asks, tell him the truth."

"I can't," Shoshannah protested, alarmed. "He might be furious. And his mother would certainly be . . ."

"Plead that he say nothing to the Lady Sharah," Zeva'ah interrupted, her dark, lovely eyes gleaming, revealing delight in this conspiracy. "Take Adoniyram into your confidence and gain *his*."

"But . . ." *That's deceitful,* Shoshannah thought. She felt unclean now, staring at her smooth-shaven, authoritative uncle and her exacting aunt. They were unmistakably drawing her into a scheme against Adoniyram, or his mother, or both. Why had she decided to be so open with them—hiding nothing for fear of punishment? She wanted to be left out of whatever they were planning. "Couldn't you tell him?" she pleaded.

Ra-Anan shook his head. "My Zeva'ah is right. He would be more likely to confide in you. But we will confirm your story—for he will certainly complain to us afterward. We'll go hunting again in a few days. You'll have another chance to speak with him then." Smiling politely, he said, "The hunt today was a disappointment; you didn't try your weapons."

Frustrated that he was manipulating her, Shoshannah looked down, pressing her palms hard upon her fabric-clad knees. "Forgive me. I didn't have my wrist guard or any of my gear; I left it with Ma'khole."

"Who is Ma'khole?" Ra-Anan asked, suspicious.

"My little mare." Shoshannah looked at him now, determined to gain at least one favor. "Do you know where she is, Uncle? Or if I might see her and find my gear?"

"If you behave tomorrow," Zeva'ah said, "then in the

evening you might see your Ma'khole." She seemed to emanate a silent warning that Shoshannah must include her when dealing with Ra-Anan.

Shoshannah lowered her head, sickened. She was trapped by these terrible people, who were also her relatives. *Why do You let them thrive, O Most High? They're so sly; they should be crawling in the dust like snakes.*

She feared they would begin to question her again, but Ra-Anan said, "Go. Get some sleep."

Sleep? Did they think she could sleep after *this*? She bowed to them quietly and crept off, aching physically and emotionally. Kal would be ashamed of her for giving in to them, for being so intimidated. *What else can I do?* she wondered. If only she could escape.

As soon as Shoshannah was gone, Zeva'ah looked at her husband, smiling, determined to know his thoughts. "What are you planning? Mischief against our precious Son of Heaven, or his dear Lady-Mother?"

Seizing her hand, pulling her close, Ra-Anan whispered, "Why should we tell Adoniyram such terrible news? Let Shoshannah do it and turn him to us. I give you my word, dear wife; soon he will be so tangled in his own troubles that he won't be able to breathe unless we approve. As for his mother . . . she's destroying herself. But I'll be sure she doesn't destroy us as well."

"And what of the Lord Kuwsh?"

"What of him?" Ra-Anan kissed her hair absently. "Our people hate him more than they hate me. They want Adoniyram to lead them, but we will control him. Kuwsh will be isolated and ignored."

Zeva'ah lifted her face to his, hoping he wouldn't become irritated with her. "Tell me how you will control Adoniyram."

Smiling secretively, Ra-Anan looked into her eyes. "I could destroy Adoniyram with a few words; I know his most devastating weakness. And don't ask me what it is—I won't tell you."

To hide her disappointment, Zeva'ah laughed at him quietly, kissing his cheek, his lips, teasing, "But I want you to tell me *your* weakness, beloved."

Kissing her lightly in turn, he said, "I don't have one."

Zeva'ah sighed. His self-confidence was endless, which was one of the reasons she had been attracted to him; he had provided for her even more splendidly than she had dared to hope. And yet there were problems. The most recent annoyance came to mind—being forced to shelter her bothersome niece. She couldn't help grumbling, "At least that Shoshannah seems a bit easier to control than her mother was."

"She's already been useful. But you, dear wife, are perfect." He kissed her again, becoming ardent now, one hand gliding down her bare arm.

Zeva'ah knew when to stop asking questions.

The next morning, sitting in Demamah's private courtyard, Shoshannah unwound fine woolen yarn off a spindle and wrapped the threads around her upper left arm and hand, making a skein. Usually this was mindless work, from years of experience. Today it provoked memories and longings for her family.

Shoshannah sighed, half dreaming. "When we do this

at home, my sisters usually argue about what color the skeins should be, who received the previous woven garment, and who didn't, and why. Usually, I'm so tired of working the wool that I don't care."

Seated beside her, equally busy, Demamah asked, "Where is 'home'? You always talk about it, and I wish—"

Before Demamah could finish her question—which Shoshannah had no intention of answering precisely—Zeva'ah entered the courtyard, squinting against the sunlight. Her voice displeased, she said, "Shoshannah, you have a visitor."

"A visitor?" Immediately nervous, Shoshannah carefully removed the half-wound skein from her arm and placed it in a basket with the spindle. After a prodding glance from Zeva'ah, Demamah did the same.

"You will say as little as possible," Zeva'ah instructed Shoshannah severely. "Be polite, but don't encourage her to visit again."

Her? Who? Wondering, Shoshannah smoothed her hair off her shoulders—a futile effort, she was sure. She would never look as graceful and lovely as Demamah, who walked ahead of her now through the narrow passage to the main room.

As she stepped past the thick curtains, Shoshannah saw a tiny woman kneeling formally on a mat in the center of the room, her small brown hands clasped upon a folded pile of leather and woolen garments. *My own clothes,* Shoshannah thought, delighted, spying her precious gray cloak. But why had the Lady Achlai sent this woman to her? Any servant could have returned the clothes without a word. And this tiny, pretty woman's dark eyes were filling with tears, though she smiled.

"Shoshannah," Zeva'ah said stiffly, "this is Meherah, your father's adopted mother."

Shoshannah knelt before Meherah, shocked, staring until she remembered her manners and bowed her head. "Forgive me for being rude." Lifting her head, she studied Meherah, who was weeping, exultant.

"Child, you look just like your mother!"

Meherah was so delightfully unexpected that Shoshannah laughed. "I'm glad you're happy about my looks—most people aren't. You're truly my father's I'ma?"

"Oh, you have his dimples!" Meherah cried, touching Shoshannah's face. "Though he smiled so rarely. Is he still very grim?"

"When I misbehave," Shoshannah said, feeling tears start to the corners of her eyes. She longed to fling herself into Meherah's arms and hug her. How wonderful to meet someone who loved her parents.

"Where is he now?" Meherah asked. But then she shook her braid-wrapped head, clearly regretting the question as soon as it emerged from her lips.

Sorely aware of Zeva'ah's prying eyes and listening ears, Shoshannah smiled. "He's in a safe place, I'ma-Meherah. And I pray he stays there."

Meherah sighed, drooping visibly. "I pray so too, child."

Zeva'ah cleared her throat and flung Shoshannah a firm, nudging glance. Unhappily, Shoshannah said, "Thank you for coming, and for bringing my garments from the Lady Achlai. Please, tell her that I thank her with all my might—she didn't need to trouble herself for me."

"Oh, but she did," Meherah protested, leaning forward. "It would shame her before the Most High if she didn't help you when you were so . . ." Her explanation faded beneath a fierce look from Zeva'ah. "Pardon me, Lady." Meherah bowed to Zeva'ah, who lifted her chin indignantly.

Clearly their visit was finished. Zeva'ah and Demamah stood, as did Meherah. Shoshannah followed them out to the main courtyard, hating to see Meherah leave. Swiftly, before Zeva'ah could stop her, Shoshannah hugged the startled Meherah and kissed her cheek. Father would want her to, she was sure. And so would I'ma. Kissing Meherah a second time, Shoshannah said defiantly, "That's from my I'ma, and from Father! I hope I see you again, I'ma-Meherah."

Meherah departed, on foot, and in tears. As Shoshannah faced the tight-lipped Zeva'ah and the wincing Demamah, she realized that she had lost any chance of seeing her precious Ma'khole for many days. But I'ma-Meherah was worth it.

You believe in the Most High, Shoshannah thought to Meherah, amazed, *as does the Lady Achlai. Most High, I beg You, let me see them both again.*

Kneeling alone in Demamah's room, disgraced, Shoshannah thankfully inspected her clothes. As the Lady Achlai had promised, her cloak was clean, and so were her other garments. But most surprisingly, Shoshannah found her knife—in its woven grass sheath—stitched securely inside her cloak. She wondered why Achlai or Meherah had sewn it there. Did they simply want to be sure it wasn't lost? Or were they silently encouraging her to conceal her weapon until she could escape?

Troubled, she folded her cloak and tucked it beneath the coverlets on her bed.

~◈ ◈~

Dressed again for a hunt, which she didn't look forward to, Shoshannah followed Demamah to the main courtyard. But as they stepped outside, Shoshannah saw Ra-Anan threatening two of his men, who knelt before him, obviously terrified. "I don't tolerate drunken fools who wake peaceful citizens, then beat them and steal their belongings! You will never forget this day if you live, I assure you!"

His dark glittering eyes flashed to Demamah and Shoshannah, who bowed. Shoshannah quaked inwardly, trying not to stare.

Furious, Ra-Anan snapped, "You're early! Get out. Go to the stables and find your gear!"

Shoshannah fled with Demamah, who seized her hand and hauled her outside the gate. There they almost collided with Perek, who was approaching, carrying a long, thick, menacing whip.

"Are you escaping, Daughter of Keren?" he demanded.

Shoshannah cowered, but Demamah spoke breathlessly. "My father told us to go to the stables and find her gear. We'll wait there until he sends for us."

"Be sure you do," Perek said, brandishing the whip at Shoshannah.

Already Demamah was pulling her away, fleeing again. Shoshannah couldn't believe how fast her cousin could run in those sandals and tight clothes, her long hair and robe fluttering behind her. Demamah rushed Shoshannah into a plain, low, mud-brick building, which was horse scented and set apart from Ra-Anan's residence. Inside, Demamah collapsed onto a pile of straw.

As Shoshannah dropped beside her, Demamah shut her eyes, gasping, "I don't want to hear them scream when they're punished. I can't bear it!"

Shoshannah looked around, wondering if they were being overheard, though the brick-stalled stable seemed deserted by its servants and all but a few horses. Hushed, she asked, "Do these punishments happen often?"

"Often enough."

"Perek wouldn't kill them, would he?"

"No." But Demamah looked uncertain. And wretched. Glancing at Shoshannah, she murmured, "It's horrible . . . knowing Father has such power. I keep telling myself that he *must* be severe. He has to maintain order."

"And you wish he could be like anyone else."

"Yes." Seeming determined to change the subject, Demamah stood. "Father said we should find your gear. Where is your Ma'khole?"

Taking a halter from a peg near the door, they found the little mare in a pen in the far corner of the stable. Also, in the corner of the pen, Shoshannah found her battered leather pack. She scooped it up and led Ma'khole to the open area near the doorway. There she inspected the mare's dark coat, her eyes, her sides, and her legs. She was well-groomed, placid, and fed, wearing protective leather "boots" strapped to her hooves. Shoshannah eyed her approvingly.

"She's beautiful," Demamah sighed.

"You should ride her sometime," Shoshannah said, stroking the mare's neck, delighted. "She'd love you. Wouldn't you, Ma'khole? I'm so glad to see you!"

A low voice interrupted, "I was told you were here."

Startled, Shoshannah looked up.

Adoniyram sauntered into the stable, his handsome face smiling, yet subtly truculent, daring her to argue. "While our Master Ra-Anan is disciplining his men, Cousin, we can finish our conversation."

Shoshannah's courage wavered. She didn't want to quarrel with Adoniyram, particularly while they were unsupervised in this half-empty stable.

Demamah begged, "Adoniyram, don't create trouble, please!"

"Would I be so rude?" He caressed Ma'khole's dark back. "I merely want to know what our Shoshannah has to say about my mother. And, whatever you say, of course, it will be the truth, won't it, Cousin?"

Was he mocking her? Did he believe she would lie? Revived by her indignation, Shoshannah said, "Of course it'll be the truth, but you won't like it."

"The truth about what?" Demamah whispered, her eyes wide, bewildered. "Does Father know?"

"Yes, he knows. And I have his permission to tell Adoniyram."

Though Shoshannah spoke softly, Adoniyram heard. He inclined his head, polite.

"Of course my Master-Uncle knows everything. And, Demamah, I know you have to tell him whatever we say here, so we'll be sensible; don't worry."

It's true: She's bound to tell Ra-Anan, Shoshannah thought, transfixed. *She's probably had to tell him everything I've said.* She stared at Demamah, her emotions torn.

Demamah looked humiliated and upset with Adoniyram. He seemed not to notice. Smiling at Shoshannah charmingly, he said, "Tell me what you know, Cousin."

Eight

SHOSHANNAH GLANCED around the stalls, praying they wouldn't be overheard. "Give me your word that you won't tell your mother what I'm about to say."

He leaned forward, seeming amused. "If I swear by our Shemesh, who rules us from the heavens, will you believe me then, Cousin?"

Quashing her temper, Shoshannah answered nicely, "Truly, if you have *any* sense of honor, Cousin, your word is enough."

To her satisfaction, his dark eyes widened, confounded, as if his integrity had never been doubted before.

"Shoshannah, don't argue," Demamah pleaded. "Just tell him whatever he wants to know so he will leave."

Adoniyram looked from Demamah to Shoshannah, his expression changing, hardening. "I'm glad you trust me so much, both of you."

"You're the one who doubts I'll tell you the truth," Shoshannah reminded him. "I doubt the truth will be safe with you. Give me your word."

Ma'khole shifted between them, her ears flickering at their voices. Shoshannah rubbed her soothingly, determined to say nothing more unless Adoniyram obeyed. He was too proud. And spoiled.

He sighed, sounding disgusted. "You have my word, though you don't need it, I assure you. And I *do* believe you'll tell me the truth—though, you have to admit most of what you say is upsetting. Now, tell me this secret my own mother has hidden from me."

Shoshannah looked him in the eyes. "You have a brother. Your mother abandoned him and his father—her true husband—for the chance to 'marry' the Great-King Nimr-Rada."

Adoniyram stared at her, silent, clearly struggling within himself, believing her against his will.

Gently Shoshannah continued, "Your brother is named Gibbawr. He's about ten years older than you, and he lives among the northern tribes with his father. He was an infant when your mother left him, forcing my mother to come with her to this Great City. My mother still grieves for his sake."

"Of course she does. She's *honorable*, unlike my mother!" Adoniyram snapped, smoldering, "Don't worry, Cousin. I'll keep our secret." Bowing almost rudely, he turned on his booted heel and strode out of the stable.

Shoshannah realized she had wounded him deeply. Distressed, she looked at Demamah, who looked away.

When Demamah finally spoke, she sounded miserable. "Shoshannah, I give you *my* word . . . I hate telling my father about our conversations, but I have no choice. If he ever catches me lying to him, I'll be like those poor men out there in his courtyard, wondering if I'm going to die."

"I believe you."

"But do you forgive me?"

"Yes." Softly, Shoshannah added, "I hope you have less to tell him from now on."

"I hope so too. Be as dull as you can. *Please.*"

Shoshannah laughed wryly, then sighed. Being dull was far less inviting than an escape. And now that she knew where Ma'khole was sheltered, now that she had her warm, sturdy clothes and her weapons, an escape was possible. She began to make plans.

Adoniyram left the stables, stormed through the hushed courtyard, and entered his uncle's home. In the main room he halted, staring at Ra-Anan, who lounged on a mat drinking from a small gold cup.

Ra-Anan frowned. "Sit down, Adoniyram, please. Since our hunt has been delayed this morning, we might as well talk. Shoshannah told you about your mother?"

"She did." Adoniyram half knelt on a mat, facing his uncle, still staring at him, loathing what he saw. "As you commanded her."

"Did she say that?" Ra-Anan asked, setting the cup on its matching gold tray.

"No, Uncle, she said she had your permission, which was very tactful of her; don't you agree?"

"Yes, amazingly, she's learning some manners. But I must correct one misunderstanding: She *did* ask my permission to tell you, after you frightened her during your previous conversation."

Feeling a reluctant twinge of guilt, Adoniyram said, "I regret frightening her, Master-Uncle, but I wish to discuss her news, not her. It's true then: My mother wasn't rightfully married to my father when I was born?"

Ra-Anan paused, then lifted his cup again. "No. She was not. But don't let it concern you; Shoshannah will remain silent about this, and so will I—as I have been all these years. For the best interests of the Great City."

For the best interests of Ra-Anan, Adoniyram thought defiantly. He managed a polite smile. "May I ask, Uncle, what other secrets are being kept from me?"

"If the need arises," Ra-Anan said, "rest assured, I will tell you whatever you must know to govern this kingdom."

Adoniyram seethed, infuriated by his uncle's secretiveness and arrogance. "Why should you say that I will govern here? If it's true that you'll outlive me, and if it's true that my mother wasn't rightfully married to the Great King, then it's obvious that this kingdom will never be mine."

"It is also obvious that our citizens love you far more than they love me or anyone else, except your Lady-Mother—who will soon squander their affections. Certainly you should govern here." Ra-Anan took another sip from the shining cup.

You are taunting me.

Before Adoniyram could say anything, Ra-Anan put down his cup, severe. "Now, unlike you, I do wish to discuss Shoshannah. She is, for a while at least, a member of my household. For her sake—and for yours—I ask you to treat her respectfully; I want no scandals."

"There will be no scandals, Uncle." *Unless they involve you or Lord Kuwsh or my foolish mother.* But his animosity swiftly faded against his frustrations and concerns. Not long ago, Adoniyram had believed he could gain power and challenge Ra-Anan and Lord Kuwsh. Now, bound by their edicts, wondering if his life might be cut off before theirs, and shaken by this fresh knowledge of his own clouded heritage, he felt almost defeated. Ra-Anan, in particular, would control him.

This is what you wanted, isn't it, Master? he asked Ra-Anan in bitter silence. *You have me in your fist. How can I break free without killing you?*

Another thought occurred to him then: Shoshannah might know whatever else Ra-Anan was hiding from him. *We're going to have another talk,* Adoniyram decided. *As soon as I leave this place.*

Followed by Demamah—and closely watched by Perek—Shoshannah led Ma'khole into the main courtyard. Whatever joy she felt at regaining her cherished mare was dashed by the sight of servants scrubbing sand over the bloodstained bricks in the courtyard.

"Do you think they killed those men?" Shoshannah whispered to Demamah, fearful, as she untied her scuffed leather bag from Ma'khole's back.

"There would have been more blood, I'm sure," Demamah replied beneath her breath, looking upset as she helped with the leather cords. Shoshannah longed to ask what might have happened to the unfortunate men, but Perek was almost beside them now, and she didn't dare risk angering him. No doubt he was the one who had carried out the beating. He had been disgustingly self-satisfied when he had come to fetch Shoshannah and Demamah from the stable.

Guarded by Perek, the two cousins exercised Ma'khole and groomed her until Adoniyram emerged from the house. He glanced up at the clouded sky, as if gauging it for rain. Then he approached Shoshannah and Demamah.

"Since our hunt has been ruined, come ride with me. Our Master Ra-Anan gave his permission, as long as Perek accompanies us." Looking askance at Ma'khole, Adoniyram told Shoshannah, "You'll need a horse—not *that*."

Defensive, Shoshannah said, "Don't insult Ma'khole. My father gave her to me."

"Oh? Why does he—a trained guardsman—allow you to ride this pretty toy?"

"Because she's *safe*, as my father intended. And she's not a toy; I love her."

"You would." Adoniyram beckoned two of his own guardsmen. To Shoshannah's frustration, Adoniyram sent Ma'khole back to the stable, instructing the attendant-guardsmen to return with "proper" creatures. As they waited, Adoniyram said, "Don't sulk; if we race, I'm sure you'd want to beat me. That little mare wouldn't have a chance."

He was right. Worse, Shoshannah realized, if she intended to escape, her chances would be improved if she had a faster animal; she would have to leave Ma'khole here in the Great City. The thought made her ill.

Adoniyram noticed her distress. "Are you still angry with me for insulting you earlier? Don't be. I regret it."

Distracted by his apology, she blinked, amazed. "Really? But you should hate me after everything I've said."

"At least you tell me the truth."

Shoshannah grimaced. "Sometimes I think lying would be easier." Worried, she added, "I hope you'll be well . . . after what I've told you."

Almost inaudibly, he said, "I dread meeting my mother again. I'm rarely surprised by anything she does, but to abandon her husband and infant son . . ."

Listening to his vulnerably soft admission only intensified Shoshannah's uneasiness. He was beguiling. Almost as appealing as her dear Kaleb. She studied her scraped leather boots, at a loss for words. Demamah's slender sandaled feet approached her now, and Shoshannah was grateful for the interruption.

Meekly, eyeing Perek, who lingered nearby, Demamah spoke quietly to Adoniyram. "I asked Shoshannah's forgiveness earlier, and she forgave me. I'm asking yours now. I regret that our parents have made it impossible for us to trust each other."

Adoniyram gave Demamah a careful, thoughtful look, then murmured, "I say we should be more sociable and truthful whenever we can. Also, if certain matters are too dangerous for words, then perhaps we should understand one another in silence."

Demamah relaxed visibly, as if a terrible burden had been lifted from her shoulders. Shoshannah was glad that they were negotiating with each other after separate lifetimes of mistrust.

Giving Demamah a teasing nudge, Shoshannah said, "I'm sure you two were ridiculous, quarreling children. Your wild cousins in the mountains wouldn't have put up with you if we'd grown up together."

"Oh?" Adoniyram grinned suddenly, seeming fascinated. "What would they have done to us?"

"They'd have tossed you into a cold lake or a snow

heap, depending upon the season—and they still might." Shoshannah's mood brightened as she imagined Adoniyram being pitched headlong into a bank of snow; she couldn't help smiling.

"Well," Demamah said lightly, "since there's no snow or lake here, then I'm sure we are perfectly safe, and we can enjoy our morning together."

"Shall we ride to the river?" Adoniyram suggested, as his attendant-guardsmen returned with a sandy horse for Demamah and a tawny-brown horse for Shoshannah.

Studying the lackluster beast fretfully, Shoshannah said, "I think you just want to throw me into the river for revenge."

"I don't. Yet." As he spoke, Adoniyram's expression darkened, slipping into gloom. "Perhaps I should throw myself in."

"Don't say such a thing!" Demamah protested, alarmed.

Knowing she had caused his despair, Shoshannah winced. "You wouldn't try to drown yourself, would you?"

"They'd rescue me," Adoniyram muttered, tilting his head toward his guardsmen.

"Then they'd blame me." Shoshannah raised her voice as Perek drew nearer. "And, no doubt, Perek would beat me."

"I will, Daughter of Keren," Perek growled. He motioned her toward the tawny horse and "helped" her onto it roughly, causing the creature to sidestep skittishly, which agitated Demamah's horse.

Shoshannah quickly guided her horse away from Demamah's, to prevent a small skirmish. Obviously fearing the same thing, Adoniyram and his guardsmen hurried outside the gate to their own horses. Now, unexpectedly, the ruddy, pert little maidservant, Ormah, rushed from the house to Demamah, saying, "I've been sent to accompany you." She flashed a cold look at Shoshannah, as if blaming her.

Another enemy, Shoshannah thought, resigned. She waited as Perek helped Ormah up to ride behind Demamah, then guided Shoshannah's horse after his, outside the gate.

Adoniyram was waiting and nodded as soon as he saw Shoshannah. "Perhaps we should ride to the tower instead. Have you seen it yet?"

"How could I not see such a mountain of brick?" Shoshannah asked, keeping her voice down, knowing Perek would slap her for being rude to Adoniyram.

Adoniyram looked mildly exasperated. "Let me say this more clearly: I'm sure you haven't climbed the tower and visited the new temple yet. We'll go there instead of the river."

To Shoshannah's distress, Adoniyram edged Demamah and Perek away, forcing them to trail behind as they rode along the wide paved market street. Demamah seemed to not mind, but Perek and Ormah would probably report this insult to Ra-Anan and Zeva'ah. Ormah had raised her pretty eyebrows, and Perek scowled, displeased.

Some of the men in the marketplace also looked displeased, but many of the women exhaled squeals and jubilant cries of welcome to Adoniyram—and to Shoshannah. "Son of Heaven . . ."

"He's riding with our Lady—she's been welcomed again."

"She's returned to us!"

They're confusing me with my I'ma, Shoshannah thought, dismayed. She cast a nervous glance at Adoniyram. He was smiling, seeming guileless, but watching the citizens and listening to their reactions. "You *planned* this, O Son of Heaven," Shoshannah muttered, fuming.

He answered with a mock-innocent shrug. She longed for the strength to toss him off his horse. Instead, she suggested sarcastically, "Perhaps we should go to the river later."

"Behave or we will, Cousin."

Now Shoshannah suspected that Adoniyram had merely pretended to consider killing himself earlier to gain her sympathy. He was too smug and proud to want to die. She pointedly ignored him for the remainder of their ride through the Great City.

At the end of the broad market street, they rode across a wide bitumen-coated wooden bridge. Shoshannah was alarmed by the clatter of their horses' hooves over the bridge, and by the silted depths of the canal waters below. Just beyond this unsettling overpass, they entered the gates of the wall-enclosed lands surrounding the tower. Shoshannah stared upward at the structure, amazed. How could mere humans build such a would-be mountain? *O Most High,* she thought, *why do they even want such a thing?*

Rebellion . . . contempt . . . rejection . . . The words came to her like tiny currents in the breeze. Was she imagining *Him* in those dejected words? She shivered, staring at the tower, unable to calculate the sheer numbers of bricks and years it had taken to build to such heights—it seemed to threaten the sky.

Frowning, she asked Adoniyram, "Why do they pour all their strength and time into this tower?"

"You've said the very word: strength. Through this tower, we show our domination of the earth. Also, the citizens will give their devotions to our Shemesh in the temple above." He was unexpectedly quiet, causing her to stare at him. Did he question the wisdom of building such an astounding structure? Meeting her gaze then, he grinned disarmingly, his quick-changing nature again taking her by surprise.

"Let's go up inside; perhaps we can startle some of the priests awake." Turning, he called out, "Perek, guard the horses. Ormah, stay at least ten paces behind us."

Perek glowered ominously, and Ormah eyed the endless stairs with poorly concealed dread. Demamah, however, dismounted willingly, gracefully, with the help of a guardsman. She gave Shoshannah a look that begged her to humor Adoniyram.

Submitting reluctantly, Shoshannah dropped gracelessly to the brick-paved ground, fearing Perek might "help" her. Demamah looked scandalized, but Adoniyram smiled and shook his head. "You behave like a little boy."

"So do you," Shoshannah argued beneath her breath. "Though I'll be completely dignified now."

"Be sure you are. It would be foolish to offend Rab-Mawg and his priests."

Don't worry; I haven't forgotten that men like your "priests" tried to kill my mother. Apprehensive, she smoothed her garments and followed Adoniyram up the high, wide stairs that angled sharply up the sides of the tower.

"Who is Rab-Mawg?" she asked Demamah as they neared the top of the first level.

"Our chief magician," Demamah whispered. Even more softly, she added, "Father says Rab-Mawg is young and impatient, but very . . . acute. Please, weigh everything you tell him—several times."

"What are you whispering?" Adoniyram demanded, pausing, then descending a step to join them. "More secrets?"

Quickly Shoshannah explained, "She was telling me to think carefully before speaking to Rab-Mawg. And I intend to."

"Good," Adoniyram murmured, studying her closely. "And what you don't tell him, you *will* tell me."

"Do you think I'm keeping other secrets from you, Cousin?"

"Are you?"

"None that I know of."

"That's reassuring," he said. But he didn't sound convinced. He started up the stairs again. Shoshannah glared after him, aggravated.

Tugging her arm, Demamah gave Shoshannah a pleading look. Shoshannah nodded reluctantly. In unison, they started up the endless stairs, with Ormah following them at a distance. When Shoshannah looked back down at her, the countless steps seemed to merge together; the effect was dizzying.

Catching her attention, Demamah said, "Father insists we should be reverent when we climb all these stairs . . . to calm our minds before entering the temple above." There was a softness in her voice and in her dark eyes that made Shoshannah stare.

"Just now, you sounded so much like our I'ma-Annah. You even looked like her. But she would detest this place."

Adoniyram heard and turned suddenly, almost wrathfully. "If you say anything like that up there in the temple, Shoshannah, you'll be thrown off the edge of the terrace to your death! Is that what you want?"

She halted on the steps, shocked. "No, of course not. Forgive me. I won't say anything else until we leave. Except . . . why are you so determined to bring me here?"

"I'm asking myself the same question." He resumed climbing.

Is he trying to decide if I should live or die? she wondered, furiously irreverent. *O Son of Heaven, quit tormenting me; make up your human mind!*

With Demamah still clasping her arm, she followed him to the top of the stairs. The uppermost walls protecting the terrace were low and unfinished; Shoshannah resolved to stay away from them. But she lingered, inspecting the numerous small, pampered, mostly dormant trees and plants. The terrace had been coated with bitumen to seal it against the water used to irrigate the mulched, brick-enclosed gardens. Several roughly clothed young men were laboring in a far corner with bricks, slime, and sand, apparently building the foundations of another raised garden.

Gently, as if speaking of normal things could erase Adoniyram's threat, Demamah said, "The trees will be lovely this summer."

I pray I won't be here to see them, Shoshannah thought. But she nodded, determined to remain silent.

Adoniyram beckoned them toward the unfinished temple. As Shoshannah reached him, he said, "Remember, say nothing unless I permit it."

Again she nodded and lowered her eyes, pretending meekness. The pretense vanished as soon as she entered the chilling, lavish temple. Gold, polished stone, and rare gems glimmered at her from every direction, illuminated by deftly placed oil lamps, which heightened the mysterious, humbling aura of this place. And its inhabitants, the priests, added to this daunting impression.

They all looked the same to her, brown, blade thin, with dark, glittering eyes, shaven heads, and smooth faces, all wearing pale single-shouldered woolen robes and sandals. One of them wore a leopard-skin mantle and stared at Shoshannah, unblinking as any predator.

Rab-Mawg, Shoshannah guessed, looking down swiftly as he approached. She understood why Adoniyram and Demamah had warned her against him. Young as he was, Rab-Mawg was fierce. Extreme. And focused on her.

"This is her daughter?" he asked Adoniyram, his voice unexpectedly soft.

Watchful, cautious, Adoniyram agreed. "Yes."

As Shoshannah glanced at her cousin involuntarily, Rab-Mawg suddenly flashed a hand toward her throat. Something thin, cool, and sharp rested just below her jaw. Shoshannah froze. Years of dealing with unexpected teasing shocks from Kaleb and her younger brothers had finally taught her to stand still, hiding her inward turmoil.

As Demamah gasped, Adoniyram stepped closer, warning, "Don't hurt her."

"I won't," Rab-Mawg told him. But to Shoshannah, he murmured, "I've heard that your mother didn't retreat when our He-Who-Lifts-the-Skies put a knife to her throat. I see you are the same."

And I see you are insane.

Rab-Mawg continued, "I was also told that your mother pledged herself—on her own life—to this temple. And she hasn't fulfilled her vows. Perhaps our Shemesh has brought you to us in her place. I believe you should receive the sacrifices and offerings she should have received . . . or be one instead."

Unable to move, Shoshannah prayed she would escape alive. He lowered the knife, smiled politely, and stepped away. Demamah hurried to Shoshannah's side as Rab-Mawg talked to Adoniyram. The rest of Shoshannah's visit to the temple was lost in a haze of terror. She said nothing.

For five days, Shoshannah hid pieces of bread and dried meat and fruits in a bundle within her bedding. For five nights, she arose in the predawn darkness, feigning visits to the privy, allowing Demamah to become used to her early wanderings. She "carelessly" left her belongings and weapons in Demamah's courtyard but otherwise behaved perfectly. And she studied the tree in the courtyard, thinking of her mother. Of I'ma-Annah.

Before the sixth dawn, after the dreadful confrontation with Rab-Mawg, Shoshannah pretended to visit the privy again. But this time, she took her stash of food and went into Demamah's little courtyard.

Stealthily she tied her belongings and weapons together, climbed the tree beside the wall, lowered her belongings down the outside wall with a leather cord, then tied a thicker leather cord to a branch and struggled down the wall, shaking with fear. Halfway down, the cord snapped. Shoshannah landed hard in the dirt, gasping and bruised.

Recovering, praying she hadn't been heard, she snatched up her belongings and sped off in the darkness toward the stables.

Nine

HER HEART THUDDING, Shoshannah set down her weapons and crept into the dark, manure-scented stables. Where were the guards? She waited and listened. Rasping snores sounded from two areas: a stall to her far left, and the opposite corner behind stacks of bundled hay.

Let there only be two guards, she begged the Most High silently. *And let them continue to sleep.*

As her eyes adjusted to the dimness, Shoshannah noiselessly lifted a bridle and reins from one of the pegs by the door, then slipped over to the nearest stall. *Be good,* she thought to the horse, judging its size, offering a dried date. The creature breathed lightly into her hand, nipped up the fruit, then cooperated as she worked the toughened leather bit into its mouth and fastened the bridle. Stroking the horse coaxingly, she opened the reed gate to its stall and led it outside.

I wish you were Ma'khole, she thought, tremulous, wishing she could bid the little mare good-bye. Swiftly, fearing she might awaken the guards, she tied her weapons and few belongings across the horse's sand-pale withers, took a small running start, grasped the mane, and bounded onto its back. She struggled to seat herself, grateful the creature hadn't jolted away beneath her—she was out of practice. But he was well trained. Catching her breath, she guided the horse behind Ra-Anan's residence to avoid the busiest streets and rode south out of the Great City. Shortly afterward, she urged the animal east, away from the boggy, rain-swollen southern marshes. And for the first time in her life, she hated a beautiful sunrise.

Furious, Ra-Anan grabbed the broken leather cord from the ground. Pointing to its match dangling from the tree near the wall, he confronted his shocked guardsmen. "Look at this! You saw nothing? You heard nothing? If you don't find her *now,* you'll see and hear nothing permanently!"

The guardsmen fled, seeking their horses. Perek approached, planted himself in front of Ra-Anan, and bowed. "I beg you, Master Ra-Anan, let me hunt her down."

Ra-Anan waved him on impatiently. Perek snatched his gear, whistled for his horse, and rode out after the other guardsmen, who were scattering in confusion.

Aggravated by their chaotic departure, Ra-Anan headed for the stables. He'd find the girl himself. A stable guard greeted him weakly, saying, "My lord, your horse is gone."

Fool. Disbelieving, Ra-Anan strode into the stable and glanced to the left where his best horse should have been, at an empty stall. He struck the guard to the ground. "In my *sleep*, from behind a brick wall, I heard someone riding a horse past my residence! But you didn't hear someone stealing a horse from beneath your nose! Were you drunk? Get away from me before I kill you!"

While he was fuming, someone rode up outside the stables. Thinking they had caught Shoshannah, Ra-Anan hurried outside. Adoniyram and his three guardsmen looked down at him from their horses, perplexed. For the past week, Adoniyram had visited almost every morning, and Ra-Anan had welcomed him. But now, Ra-Anan stared up at his nephew, disgruntled. "Don't you have a residence of your own?"

Obviously restraining a smile, Adoniyram said, "I do, Master-Uncle, but clearly, it's not as exciting as your own. What's happened?"

Ra-Anan enunciated his words carefully, so he wouldn't stammer in his fury. "Your ungrateful cousin stole my best horse and escaped. Alone."

"So that's why Perek and the others were riding off in such a hurry." Swiftly, Adoniyram inclined his head. "If you don't mind, Uncle, I'll join the chase."

Before Ra-Anan could say another word, Adoniyram goaded his horse away, followed by his guardsmen, all of them eager for this unexpected adventure. Ra-Anan watched them head north onto the main street, then returned to his house. There was no need for him to pursue Shoshannah; there were enough guardsmen after her. Instead, he would question Demamah, who had—reluctantly, he suspected—alerted him that Shoshannah was gone.

Shoshannah rode northeast, intending to find and follow the eastern river—her most trustworthy guide back to the Tribe of Metiyl. She wished she hadn't been forced to travel south from the Great City to avoid people during her escape; the maneuver had cost her precious time. And she half wished she had chosen another horse. This one made her uneasy. He was resisting her commands, testing her, and slowing her down, she realized, according to his own clever nature. If only she knew exactly how he had been trained; then he might behave.

But I don't have time to learn your ways, she thought to the horse. Determined, she urged him onward, praying the creature wouldn't have a tantrum because she wasn't commanding him as he expected. When they reached a long muddied canal, the horse balked at the water's edge.

Twice it swerved from the canal. Twice Shoshannah turned its head toward the water, prodding it forward with her heels and chirruping resolutely. The creature stopped altogether, obstinate, making noises of protest. Soon it would try to throw her off, or bolt away.

What's wrong? she asked him silently. *I'm sure you must cross these canals all the time.* However, the large canal near the tower had a bridge . . .

"You want a bridge," she realized aloud, disheartened. A bridge wasn't possible. And the longer she stayed here, trying to urge this creature across the canal, the more certain she was to be caught. Trying to conceal her desperation from the intuitive horse, she sat quietly and looked around. Where was the end of this canal? Perhaps she could ride along it to the eastern river and follow the river north to the mountains. She could find tribes of cousins to help her along the way. But she would encounter other canals and streams, too, along the way . . . This horse had to learn to obey her quickly.

Don't let a horse rule you. She could almost hear her father saying those words.

"It's only water," she murmured, sliding off the horse, stepping into the mud, determined to win the creature over. Holding the reins, she removed several dates from her battered leather pack, glided one past the animal's nose, and cautiously stepped into the silted water. Clearly tempted, the horse stepped after her.

While she was coaxing it into the canal, a piercing note from a carved whistle echoed distantly through the air, making the animal perk up its sand-pale ears, listening. The note was repeated, followed by the sounds of hoofbeats. The horse huffed and backed away nervously. Alarmed, Shoshannah hurried out of the water to remount the beast, but it bolted toward the call of the whistle and the other horses—like the trained herd creature he was—with her weapons and her gear.

Shoshannah threw down the fruit, longing to scream. Particularly when she realized that Perek was riding toward her like a wild man, well ahead of the other horsemen. In addition to the horse whistle corded around his neck, the guard had a spear. Horrified, praying that the canal would at least slow down his horse, she fled into the water, hindered by the thick silt.

A thunderous splash roiled the water behind her. An instant later, Perek flung himself off his horse, clamped an arm around Shoshannah, dragged her thrashing out of the water, and shoved her face into the embankment. Panicking, breathing sodden earth, Shoshannah tried to see through her disheveled hair. Perek twisted her wrist high into her back until she cried in protest. Then he beat her with his spear, raining brutal, cutting blows on her back, her rump, and her legs, making her scream with pain as she tried to squirm away.

Something heavy crashed over her, knocking her in the ribs. Perek roared as another weight followed the first. Shoshannah gasped as she was dragged by the wrist through the mud. She fought and kicked, unable to wriggle free. Someone was beside her now, clawing at her wrist, hammering at Perek's arm, bellowing, "Let go! Perek, let *go!* Get him away before he kills her!"

Mercifully, Shoshannah felt Perek's grip on her wrist vanish. She was hauled to her feet and saw—through her muddied hair—three guardsmen brawling in the silt, enthusiastically subduing the raging Perek. A man's hand pushed Shoshannah's hair out of her face and forced her to look up.

Adoniyram scowled down at her. "Why would you even think of traveling alone? Are you so eager to die?"

Fighting tears, resentful that she'd been caught, she said, "I'm more likely to survive in the wilderness with true animals."

"Not when Perek is after you. And not when you've stolen our Master Ra-Anan's favorite horse."

"*Ra-Anan's* horse?" Shoshannah's knees wobbled.

"He will probably beat you himself," Adoniyram said, looking around, as if judging their situation. "I think we should return through the least populated area. After thrashing around in the mud, we look like laborers."

I'd rather be a laborer now. Sick with dread, and moving painfully, Shoshannah let him help her onto a horse, while the three guardsmen finished their muddy brawl with Perek.

Ra-Anan was waiting in his courtyard. The instant he saw Shoshannah, he pointed to the paving, commanding her to kneel on the bricks before him. Gritting her teeth against the torments from her wounds, she knelt slowly, cautiously, afraid he would kill her right there.

Ra-Anan raged, "Look at you—you've disgraced us! And *look* at these men." He gestured emphatically.

Shoshannah looked.

Perek and the three guardsmen were crusted with drying mud, wherever their swollen eyes, split lips, and battered noses weren't bloodied. Perek had twisted a supportive band of leather around his right wrist—which was apparently injured—and he glared at Shoshannah through his unscathed left eye; the right one was purpled and swelling shut. Shoshannah winced. He was obviously wishing he had killed her.

Ra-Anan continued to rant at her, his narrow, smooth brown face contorted. "If these men don't heal properly, I won't spare you—do you hear me? You will be severely punished."

Shoshannah looked down, feeling as if she'd been punished already. Her own wrist was sprained, her ribs hurt where she had been kicked, and every place Perek had beaten her burned and pulsed with pain. Her linen garments were also sticking torturously to the bloodied cuts on her back.

"Did you injure my horse?" Ra-Anan demanded.

"No." She barely squeaked out that one word.

"Pray that you're right, *child*," Ra-Anan snapped. "If my horse is harmed, I'll beat you for that too. You are as impulsive and foolish as your mother. What excuse can you possibly give for such stupidity—thinking you could escape? Answer me!"

Stiffening at the insult to her mother, Shoshannah took courage. "I only did what you would have done in my place, Uncle—as my mother did—though I failed."

He lowered his chin at her, staring coldly. Then he called out, "Bring her weapons and belongings here."

A guardsman obeyed swiftly, placing Shoshannah's bow, her quiver of arrows, and her battered leather pack beside Ra-Anan. Scornful, he untied the pack and dumped Shoshannah's gear onto the bricks. All her belongings spilled out: her cloak, tunic, leggings, undergarments, pins, combs, lacings, tiny wooden ointment pots, pilfered food, and her treasured knife, which she had thought would be safer in her pack. Her uncle snatched the knife. "Where did you get this? Did your father make it for you?"

Shoshannah stared at him, mute. Her father had indeed made the knife. Kaleb had carved her combs and ointment pots, her I'ma had taught her to make all the garments, and, of course, her cloak and pins had been created by I'ma-Annah, I'ma-Chaciydah, and I'ma-Naomi. Everything heaped before her was very ordinary, and precious.

"You stole food from my house."

As you would have done, I'm sure, she answered silently.

"You stole my best horse. You've treated my protection of you with contempt. Such contempt should be repaid."

Distraught, she watched her uncle send for a brazier and torches. As she feared, he set her belongings ablaze—but not before Adoniyram stepped forward and claimed her knife, bow, and quiver of arrows, saying, "These are mine; I returned her to you."

Ra-Anan grudgingly allowed Adoniyram to claim the weapons. As the remainder of her possessions smoldered, smoked, and finally caught fire, Ra-Anan asked loudly, scornfully, "Why didn't your Most High save you?"

Watching her cherished possessions burn, Shoshannah swallowed hard, wiping away tears, asking Him the same question. *Why?*

After a merciless scrubbing beneath Zeva'ah's unforgiving hands, Shoshannah limped, under escort, to Demamah's room. When the door was closed and barred—and undoubtedly guarded—Demamah looked up at Shoshannah from a corner where she was huddled like a terrified child.

Her lovely dark eyes red from weeping, Demamah whispered, "You're alive . . . but why didn't you tell me what you were planning?"

"Because you would have had to tell your father."

"Yes, but I would have also begged you to stay; it wasn't worth the risk."

Thinking of her burned possessions—and Ra-Anan's derision—Shoshannah nodded, humiliated. Struggling for composure, she said, "You're being punished because I escaped. I'm sorry."

Demamah trembled. "I hoped I was too old for a beating . . . but I suppose I wasn't." Her voice shook as she continued, "They chopped down my tr-tree."

Shoshannah closed her eyes, picturing the beautiful tree in Demamah's courtyard, hacked to bits merely because she had climbed it this morning. It had been Demamah's favorite place to rest on hot days—destroyed now. *Because of me.* She sank to her knees beside her cousin, feeling wretched inside and out, trying to endure the pain. "I've been nothing but trouble to you."

"You can't help it."

Demamah was serious. Shoshannah stared at her, longing to laugh. Instead, she cried. Demamah touched her arm and whispered tearfully, "I'm so glad you're alive."

"You should have let her die!" Sharah snapped, glaring at Adoniyram in the privacy of her ornate bedchamber. "She's a threat to you—did you think of that? No!"

Adoniyram stared at his painted, gold-ornamented, linen-robed mother, barely able to contain his disgust. "She's no threat to me. And she's your own niece; how can you wish death on her so easily?"

"Because she's like her mother; she will divide this kingdom. I heard how she was admired the other day, riding through the marketplace with *you.* That was stupid of you, Adoniyram! They loved her; she's going to destroy everything if we don't stop her."

"Perhaps I should have let her go."

"You should have killed her!"

"She doesn't deserve to die," Adoniyram argued. "She's done nothing wrong."

"You're protecting her—you're turning against me!"

"*You're* turning everyone against you!" he snapped, his patience worn. "You're so jealous and—"

She lunged, clawing at him like a maddened thing. Adoniyram grabbed her wrists, but not before she managed to rake him with her nails. He held her at arm's length, forcing himself to apologize so she would calm down . . . so they would both calm down. "I am sorry; I was wrong to say that—you're right, she is a danger."

"And you're an ungrateful *fool!*" Sharah kicked at him, still angry. "You never listen to me!"

"I'm listening to you now, Mother." He lowered his voice. "And so are all the servants. They are going to tell Lord Kuwsh and Master Ra-Anan what we've—"

"Those two!" Diverted, her voice laden with scorn, Sharah said fiercely, "They've made such uproars among the people that if it weren't for my settling everything down for them and convincing the people that they're loved, we'd have no kingdom to rule. There would have been a rebellion long ago. And, believe me, Shoshannah could also create a rebellion—she has to be stopped."

"What do you suggest?" Adoniyram asked, quietly prodding her in the direction he wanted her to go. "Ra-Anan will have her under constant guard now. And when Lord Kuwsh hears of her escape, he will also have his say."

"And I will have mine! Kuwsh is nothing."

"He's my father's father," Adoniyram reminded her softly, firmly.

A spiteful expression flickered across her face, as if she'd almost said something to the contrary. It was a fleeting look, but enough to make Adoniyram wonder. He released her and hastily buried his suspicions.

"As I said, Kuwsh is nothing." His mother moved away, defiant as an overindulged child, tossing her pale curls.

Adoniyram hated that gesture. He wished, as always, that she would braid and pin her hair decently like any other matron of the Great City. But he could wish that she would do—or become—countless other things, yet nothing would ever change her. She was utterly self-absorbed.

Preening, she picked up an obsidian mirror and checked her face paints and hair, as if her tantrum had never happened—which was also her way. Sighing irritably, she said, "Have one of the servants take word to Ra-Anan that I will visit his household tonight. I expect to see our dear Shoshannah too. And send word to Kuwsh as well. We should visit together this evening . . . as a family."

Adoniyram wished it could be true. His jaw and throat were stinging; he would have to see if she had left marks on him. If so, then he wouldn't show himself to the citizens in the daylight until he was healed. They could not be allowed to see him as an ordinary man. *Such a Promised One I am . . .*

Holding her sprained wrist protectively, Shoshannah knelt on a cushioned mat beside Demamah, formal and miserable. This unexpected gathering was going to be awful. There was no food to soothe anyone's appetite, but the Queen-of-the-Heavens Sharah was drinking wine, as was Lord Kuwsh, while Adoniyram, the Lady Achlai, Ra-Anan, and Zeva'ah simply stared at Shoshannah. At least the servants had all been sent away. They wouldn't witness the quarrel that was sure to erupt in the tense, silent room.

Sharah started, accusing Shoshannah, "I see you've been injured. It's no more than you deserve. My son shouldn't have saved you—you weren't even thankful." To the others, she said, "Did you see what she did? Look at his face."

Shoshannah looked at Adoniyram's face and was shocked by the livid scratches on his jaw and neck that definitely hadn't been there that morning. He gave her a warning glance. *If anyone gave him those scratches, it was you, Spoiled Lady,* she thought, indignant.

To her surprise, Ra-Anan said, "Adoniyram had no scratches on his face when he returned the girl to us this morning. He must have gotten them somewhere else."

Sharah leaned forward, her gray eyes narrowed. "Are you saying I am mistaken?"

"You have been before," Ra-Anan said, obviously not caring to be polite. "Most of the time, in fact."

Hastily swallowing a sip he had taken from his cup, Lord Kuwsh laughed, his handsome face alight with pleasure at Sharah's disgrace. "Who can argue with the truth? My son—your husband—would have said the same thing, *Lady.*"

"And he would have said many more things about you!" she retorted. "You've always been a troublemaker—and useless to this kingdom except to flaunt your wealth and order others around."

"You've described yourself perfectly," he taunted. As Sharah stiffened, he said, "Don't even think about striking me; I would beat you, and you would deserve it."

"You have no say over me!"

"Someone should."

Adoniyram sighed loudly and moved as if threatening to depart. "Are we here only to exchange insults?"

Kuwsh set down his cup and studied Shoshannah. "No, we are going to discuss this troublemaker. Since she's proven so difficult for you, Master Ra-Anan, I should take her into my household so she won't escape again."

"She stays here," Ra-Anan said flatly. "I am her near kindred."

"And I'm not?" Sharah demanded. "I insist that she come with me."

"You'd kill her on your way home," Ra-Anan snapped. "The Lord Kuwsh and I prefer that she remain alive for now."

"For now," Kuwsh agreed, sounding menacingly tranquil to Shoshannah.

Sharah swirled her cup in her hand, smiling. "Lord Kuwsh wants her alive for revenge—which is understandable. But, Ra-Anan, I don't understand why you want her to live in your household *only*. You must be considering her as a second wife."

Her suggestion was so breathtakingly horrible that Shoshannah couldn't move. Demamah gasped aloud, and Zeva'ah actually looked at Ra-Anan.

Sharah laughed delightedly. "You should see your faces!"

"I don't think they appreciate your joke, Mother," Adoniyram said impatiently. "However, I wish to say that Rab-Mawg and the priests want Shoshannah to live . . . and to fulfill her mother's vow to serve in the Temple of Shemesh."

Shoshannah gaped at him, speechless. Why had he bothered to save her from Perek this morning if he only intended to hand her over to the temple—to Rab-Mawg, who was every bit as dangerous as Perek? *Why are you suggesting this to them?*

"I don't think I was joking about her situation, but you must be," Sharah told Adoniyram tartly.

"How much have you had to drink?" he asked, unperturbed.

"Not enough for you to say anything about it, ever.

Now, listen to me: I don't want this girl to be revered for anything, particularly not in my tower."

"*Your* tower?" Kuwsh demanded, becoming indignant. "You've done nothing toward building this tower, except to say that it must be completed. You haven't parted with any of your lands, or your gold, or your time, or your harvests . . ."

Beside him, the Lady Achlai quietly shifted his cup out of his reach as he scolded Sharah. Ordinarily, Shoshannah would have smiled at such a ploy, but now she was too upset.

As Lord Kuwsh and Sharah quarreled, Shoshannah stared at her traitor-cousin, Adoniyram. He ignored her. Frustrated, she glanced away, unintentionally catching her uncle's attention. Ra-Anan held her glance, smiling unpleasantly, as the suspicious Zeva'ah watched them both.

In a loud, apparently idle tone, he said, "Tell us, Adoniyram . . . what do you think should happen to my guest?"

Adoniyram shrugged. "Truly, Master-Uncle, I don't know. However—now that your horse and my guardsmen are safe—I will say that today was amusing."

I hate you! Shoshannah thought to Adoniyram fiercely. And without looking at her uncle, she thought, *Ra-Anan, you are detestable. You claim to be my protector-kinsman, but you certainly aren't protecting me from Adoniyram and the others as you should. If you had, I wouldn't have tried to escape.*

Her anger gradually faded. And her back and arm and legs were hurting terribly now. She wished this meeting would end. Obviously nothing would be decided for her tonight—Sharah, Ra-Anan, and Kuwsh were too angry with each other to come to any agreement. Trying to ease her bruises and cuts, she shifted, wincing. The Lady

Achlai turned toward her now, her wide brown face gentle with compassion.

I wish I could visit with you, and our I'ma-Meherah, Shoshannah thought sadly. *I hope you pray for me.* Though prayers hadn't helped her so far.

Why didn't your Most High save you? Ra-Anan's voice mocked her from this morning. She felt abandoned. At least in the wilderness, out on the steppes, she would have had some say in her own fate. Here in the Great City, these gold- and linen-clad animals controlled everything. There was nothing she could do.

Adoniyram avoided Shoshannah's gaze. If they were alone, it would have been different. He would have persuaded her that he was not her enemy. But here, surrounded by his relatives, he had no choice but to ignore her as if she didn't matter.

Truly, she was becoming important to him. The realization made him nervous.

Be silent, he ordered her in his thoughts. *Do and say nothing that will create more trouble; next time, I might not be able to save you.*

Ten

"I COULDN'T BELIEVE the Lady Sharah said such a thing about you and my father," Demamah whispered to Shoshannah. They sat on Demamah's bed, stitching Shoshannah's new garments, which would supplement the ones she'd half ruined during her attempted escape.

"She was ridiculous and completely wrong," Shoshannah agreed, shuddering as she worked a sleeve.

After two weeks of punishing isolation, it was easier to discuss Sharah's malicious opinion of Ra-Anan's motives toward Shoshannah. And, after two weeks, Zeva'ah had apparently managed to put her own suspicions aside. She had finally spoken to Shoshannah again this morning—telling her that she couldn't pout forever; she had to help Demamah with daily tasks and prepare for visitors who would arrive later this week.

Curious, Shoshannah wondered aloud, "Who is coming to visit?"

"I was afraid to ask," Demamah confessed, rasping her bone needle against a sharpening stone. "I only know that we have to finish your clothes soon. Mother wants you properly attired for the visit. After this, we help with cleaning, and later cooking."

"So our visitor is a tribal leader?"

"Most likely. Give me your word that you'll be perfect and dull."

Unable to resist, Shoshannah teased, "Of course. I'll copy your every move."

"Don't you dare mimic me while our visitors are here. Father would beat us both." Demamah checked a seam in the pale linen, then said, "I'm glad you haven't lost your spirit; you've been so gloomy these past few days."

"I'm bored," Shoshannah admitted, tying down the last stitch on the sleeve. "I want to go outside, but I don't want to see Adoniyram and his mother. Or that Rab-Mawg."

"I don't think he would have hurt you—he was only trying to frighten you."

"Well, he succeeded."

Softly, Demamah said, "Father knows you tried to escape because of Rab-Mawg."

Easing her wrist, which still ached from the sprain, Shoshannah said, "Thank you for telling him. Is he still angry with you?"

"Not as long as I tell him your every thought. Listen: Tonight I'll tell him that you think our Queen of the Heavens is ridiculous. And that you are gloomy and bored and longing to see your Ma'khole. I'll also tell him that you've threatened to mimic me while our company is here, and I'll complain about it just a little. That ought to satisfy him."

"Good. I'll hush now."

They smiled together, like two schemers, and bent over their sewing again.

"You forgot to tell your father that I don't want to see Rab-Mawg," Shoshannah muttered to Demamah as they slowly followed Ra-Anan up the tower stairs the next day.

"I did tell him," Demamah protested beneath her breath. "But he apparently wants to see how you and Rab-Mawg deal with each other now. Also, I'm sure Father believes he's being generous, allowing you such freedom so soon after your escape. You must try to be grateful."

"This isn't freedom; this is punishment! I think I'll be sick right on Rab-Mawg's feet. That's how I'll deal with him."

Demamah's brown-black eyes became huge. "You wouldn't."

"I should, but I'll control myself."

"See that you do."

"Yes, elder sister," Shoshannah teased. But her smile faded as she continued up the steps. Why was Ra-Anan determined to have her meet Rab-Mawg today? Couldn't he see that the priest was dangerous? Perhaps treacherous—which made him worse than Perek, who was trailing behind them.

Shoshannah exhaled, trying to calm herself. Ra-Anan expected her to climb these stairs and enter the temple with reverence, or at least an appearance of dignity; he would punish her if she misbehaved.

Entering the golden temple, she immediately broke into a chilled sweat. This was truly a place her parents and the Ancient Ones would never want her to visit. It felt . . . godless. Furtively, she wiped her damp palms on her gown as Ra-Anan greeted Rab-Mawg and the three attendant-priests, who bowed, hands folded, properly dignified.

Ra-Anan nodded, saying, "You have a new student. My niece must learn the customs of our Great City, our habits and ceremonies concerning the tower, and the ways of our Shemesh. She must also learn the signs in the stars." Emphasizing each word distinctly, Ra-Anan added, "You will overcome any objections you might have to her character . . . and her parentage."

What about my objections? Shoshannah wanted to scream.

But Rab-Mawg and his fellow priests all bowed courteously. Rab-Mawg smiled. "As you say, Master Ra-Anan."

Like one bestowing a great favor upon them, Ra-Anan said, "She will study here, properly attended, for two mornings a week, while I am meeting with the craftsmen and the builders. I will take great interest in her progress. Also, she will learn of the stars on nights when it is convenient to everyone."

Again Rab-Mawg agreed pleasantly. Shoshannah thought he looked falsely gracious. Perhaps he was planning to kill her after all. To her despair, Ra-Anan said, "I will return by midday. Demamah, stay with her. Perek, make her behave."

Perek bowed deeply as Ra-Anan passed him on the way out of the temple. Then he glowered at Shoshannah, obviously watching for any excuse to punish her. She flinched. Demamah put a cold hand on Shoshannah's arm, seeming as upset as Shoshannah felt. Rab-Mawg, however, behaved serenely.

Inclining his head toward Shoshannah, he said, "Lady, this new responsibility is unexpected, but not unwelcome. You must question us if there is anything you don't understand—that is your duty as our student. However, our sacred temple is *not* the place to conduct lessons. Please, come with us."

Still courteous, Rab-Mawg led them to an unfinished brick-and-bitumen room behind the temple. Shoshannah coughed, almost pinching her nose at the acrid-sharp odor coming from a smoldering stone brazier on a brick stand. The room's murky atmosphere wasn't helped by the full, thickly draped curtains hiding them from the main temple and from another adjoining room. Did these priests hate fresh air?

As Shoshannah wiped her stinging eyes, Rab-Mawg spoke to the three attending priests. "Ghez-ar, Ebed, do we have any food to offer our guests? Awkawn, bring some clay and reeds to record her lessons for today." To Demamah and Shoshannah, he murmured politely, "Please, sit and rest while you wait."

Nauseated, Shoshannah knelt beside the silent Demamah on a fleece-padded mat. Awkawn returned swiftly, bearing a clay trough filled with soft, pliable clay. From his pale woolen belt, he produced several oddly carved reed sticks and offered one to Shoshannah. She accepted the reed and a bit of soft clay, but not the bread or meat or cup of beer provided by Ghez-ar and Ebed. Demamah, too, refused their offer of food—which the priests would rightfully interpret as mistrust.

Rab-Mawg smiled, watching Shoshannah closely. "You are still frightened as a result of your last visit here,

Lady, but you need not be. I was only testing you."

"That knife didn't feel like a test to me," Shoshannah said, trying to keep her voice and her gaze steady.

"Then I apologize for upsetting you."

Seated beside Rab-Mawg, the stick-thin Ebed turned to Shoshannah, sounding wholly rational, almost kind. "We—his fellow priests—understand how formidable Rab-Mawg might appear or behave, Lady. He *was* testing you, but he has no intention of harming you. Nor do we."

I don't believe you, Shoshannah thought. *I am sure you'll turn against me like a pack of predators the instant I anger you.*

Kneeling opposite her, Ghez-ar leaned forward, his eyes gleaming in the muted light. "We are pleased to talk with you, Lady. We've heard that you visit the Ancient Ones. And we remember your mother riding through the streets of the Great City when we were children. At the time, she terrified us."

"But my mother isn't a terrifying person," Shoshannah said, bemused. "The children of our tribe love her—and she adores them. Why did you fear her?"

"We preferred to live," Awkawn answered, his thin mouth twisting scornfully. "We were told, as boys, that her touch meant death."

Cautious, knowing they were probably devoted to the memory of the Great-King Nimr-Rada, Shoshannah said, "That death order was not her idea, or her fault. She cried when she told me about it."

"Yes, I heard that you objected to it your first day in the Great City," Rab-Mawg said, his tone dismissing talk of the Lady Keren and the death order and changing the subject. "Let's resolve one thing immediately: If you are to be our student, you must be convinced you are safe here." He produced his knife from a fold in his sash and cut one of the flat loaves of bread into slender, precise strips. He ate a bit and offered some to Ebed, Ghez-ar, and Awkawn. Then he motioned to Shoshannah and Demamah. "Please, acknowledge peace with us. No one except Adoniyram has eaten here. We would be honored if you would share our food."

And furious if we don't, Shoshannah thought. Demamah took a bit of the bread. Sighing inwardly, Shoshannah copied her gesture and ate the bread. It was dry and throat-cloggingly coarse. Trying to soften it—and recklessly deciding that if they meant to kill her, she would die anyway—she accepted a sip of their beer. It was as strong as anything I'ma-Ritspah had ever brewed for Father Ashkenaz. It was worse than the bread. Her eyes watered again, and she heard Demamah sigh miserably beside her. She would have laughed if she hadn't been so nervous. She coughed instead.

"Will you live, Lady?" Awkawn inquired, his sharp face mocking, as he stood to pass some food to the brooding Perek.

Shoshannah nodded, unable to speak. She was actually sharing food with these temple priests. And she was going to be their student. Even more amazing, they seemed almost normal. Had she been wrong about them?

"Now that we've settled our misunderstanding, we will begin with matters of trade," Rab-Mawg announced, twisting a piece of clay from the trough. He kneaded the clay briefly, flattened it, then briskly wielded his reed marker. "First, the symbol for water—which is most important—is signified by wavy lines, such as these . . ."

He passed his marked clay to Shoshannah. Not knowing what else to do, she copied his symbol for water onto her own bit of clay. Finished, she glanced up and realized that Rab-Mawg's three attendant-priests looked disappointed. Obviously, they had expected to talk with her about her mother. Or about the Ancient Ones and the death of Nimr-Rada.

You will have to wait, Shoshannah told them silently. Perhaps they could discuss these things during future lessons. But why did she need lessons at all, unless Ra-Anan expected her to remain in the Great City indefinitely?

"This represents a stalk of barley," Rab-Mawg said, marking it down as soon as he received his clay from her again. "These—two lines crossing within a protective circle—are sheep. A bowl means food. And six lines, all intersected as the rays of the sun, signify the heavens. We create tokens bearing these symbols for various items that are used by traders when they promise to exchange goods that must be delivered . . ."

He droned on, and Shoshannah struggled to remain attentive.

I'm going to be here forever.

While they descended the tower steps, Demamah whispered, "I am sorry for you—having to endure those lessons two mornings a week."

"You won't come with me?" Shoshannah paused, disappointed, resenting the marked clay "lesson" in her hand. "Mithqah would have accompanied me no matter what."

"In adventures, perhaps. But not for lessons from Rab-Mawg. I'm sure your dear Mithqah would agree with me. Ormah can go with you. And Perek."

"Oh, thank you," Shoshannah grumbled, though she

forgave Demamah instantly. Pattering down the stairs again, she asked, "Are we obligated to those priests now that we've eaten their food?"

"Not if Father forbids it," Demamah said. "Though he will regard them as obligated to protect you while you're in the temple."

I hope they regard themselves as obligated, Shoshannah thought.

"What do you think of her?" Ghez-ar asked Rab-Mawg.

"We will see," Rab-Mawg said, pondering the young woman's reactions during the lesson today. She was—of course—still afraid of him. And he intended to keep her fearful and respectful if she remained in this kingdom—this priestdom. "Let her become used to our presence, and to the temple. Soon we'll learn her true thoughts and judge her from those."

"She looked bored during the lessons," Ebed told them, going toward the smaller room where they slept.

Awkawn snorted contemptuously. "Of course she was bored. She's female. We weren't discussing babies, attire, or the preparation of food. Do we have any herbs left, Ghez-ar?"

"Yes, but we'll need more in a few days." He retrieved a small leather pouch and opened it to display their dwindling cache of "herbs."

Rab-Mawg brooded, considering what they would be forced to trade from their own meager supplies to replenish their beer, incense, and the precious herbs and roots. They used these things routinely to induce the euphoria so critical to understanding the ways of the heavens. The prized euphoria was a benefit that offset their frequent bouts of boredom and frustration.

And Master Ra-Anan was a source of that frustration. The man was enriching himself from goods offered by the people of the Great City and the surrounding tribes—goods that rightfully belonged to the temple and its priests. The Lord Kuwsh and the Lady Sharah were also guilty of this crime, though they had endless resources of their own.

Such guilt must be punished.

"I'll keep watch," Ghez-ar said unnecessarily—it was, after all, his appointed day for temple duty. Rab-Mawg took the pouch from him and went into the small, secluded room where Ebed was kindling fragrant incense within a small clay brazier. When they judged the time to be perfect, Rab-Mawg cast their ration of "herbs" onto the incense. Awkawn closed the curtain securely, and they gathered around the brazier, quieting themselves as they inhaled the precious vapors.

Lulled, Rab-Mawg temporarily abandoned all thoughts of Ra-Anan and the others, giving himself instead to the effects of the sacred smoke and the hope of rest.

Accompanied by Demamah, Shoshannah reluctantly sat in the Lady Sharah's crowded ceremonial courtyard. She hadn't been here since the day of her capture. And nothing—not even twilight, a lavish brazier-lit feast, and a cheerful crowd of revelers—could improve this place for her. Nor did their illustrious visitor, Father Elam of the southeastern tribes of the earth.

Shoshannah studied him, thinking, *Elam—firstborn son of Father Shem and our dear I'ma-Annah—you are not what I would have expected.* He was handsome, of course, with his gleaming black curls, wide dark eyes, and rare smile. But he was also very self-important; he had deliberately waited for a place of honor to be prepared in the feasting area, which must accord him the same level of respect shown to Lord Kuwsh.

However, Lord Kuwsh was hostile. He said nothing to his cousin Elam, though Shoshannah knew from childhood stories that ages ago the two had been raised almost as brothers.

"I'm sure Lord Kuwsh hates Father Elam because of Nimr-Rada's death," Shoshannah whispered to Demamah, who was gathering food in a dish.

"Yes," Demamah replied softly, absorbed in her task. "Listen, we'll share this—there aren't enough dishes for everyone. No doubt Mother will complain about how the food has been served. Look at the gold dishes . . ."

Smiling, Shoshannah looked. Zeva'ah's lips were a tight line in her beautiful face, and she was unmistakably eyeing the Lady Sharah's food—served separately from everyone else's—on gold dishes. Not even Lord Kuwsh, the Lady Achlai, or the celebrated Father Elam were given gold dishes. Adoniyram, too, was drinking from a red clay cup, though he picked at his mother's food as much as his own.

Demamah nudged Shoshannah. "Try this." She took a piece of fish like white meat, dabbed it in oil and herbs, and offered it to Shoshannah, who recoiled, suspicious.

"What is it?"

"Crabmeat. Don't fuss; just take a bite."

Obedient, Shoshannah chewed, swallowed hastily,

then gulped at a cup of diluted wine. "You can have the rest. I'll eat bread and fruit."

"No, you should try other things." Demamah persisted kindly, offering her oddly cooked vinegar-smelling eggs, bird livers, curdled milk, and smoked fish.

"I think you'll poison me before Rab-Mawg does," Shoshannah told her. "I'll eat some fish, if you will leave me alone."

"You're impossible," Demamah sighed. "Anyway, Adoniyram's watching you."

Impatient, Shoshannah took a bite of fish, glanced at Adoniyram, and instantly regretted it; the Lady Sharah saw her and glared.

Lifting one pale jewel- and gold-adorned hand, the Great Lady beckoned her severely.

Shoshannah nearly choked, gulping her fish. "I'm in trouble," she whispered to Demamah. "What should I do?"

"We'll go to Father."

Better him than her. They stood and hurried past the other seated guests to Ra-Anan, who frowned at them for disturbing his meal. Demamah knelt, whispering to him frantically, begging his advice.

Ra-Anan's frown deepened. "Demamah, stay with your mother." Standing, he said to Zeva'ah, "Beloved, I'm going to speak with my sister."

"Please do!" Zeva'ah snapped, looking thoroughly irritated.

"Shoshannah, stay five paces behind me," Ra-Anan told her. He strolled over and looked down at Sharah, who had obviously had too much to drink and was now arguing with Adoniyram. Interrupting, Ra-Anan asked, "Did you wish to speak to us, my sister?"

"I wanted to speak to *her*." Sharah scowled up at Shoshannah. "But now that you're here, Ra-Anan, I told you she's not to be honored in any way. Why is she here?"

"Why shouldn't she be here? She is of our own family."

"Don't argue with me; I didn't invite her!"

Adoniyram said quietly, "Your guests will be upset, Mother. Perhaps we should discuss this later."

"You shut your mouth!" Sharah told him, so loudly that everyone nearby hushed and stared. "If you think I'll endure you lecturing me, you're wrong!"

Adoniyram tensed visibly. "Forgive me. I will remove my offensive self from your presence." He put down his cup, bounded to his feet, and marched off.

Sharah jumped up and screamed after him, "Don't you dare come back until you're ready to apologize!"

Just as he reached the courtyard gate, Adoniyram turned and executed a perfect bow. Sharah threw her gold cup toward him clumsily, splashing her guests instead. Kuwsh straightened, furious, his fine tunic speckled with wine. Beside him, Father Elam stood, clearly offended. Everyone was gasping, whispering, staring.

Shoshannah longed to shrink into nothingness.

Ra-Anan said, "We regret offending you. We will leave at once."

Sharah confronted him, her face vividly flushed with rage. "You wait! I'm not finished talking to you!"

"You are not talking; you are screaming," Ra-Anan told her. "And you have upset your guests."

Sharah waved her hand disdainfully, as if to say, *What do these people matter?* But she lowered her voice to something less than a scream. "Don't you dare bring her into my presence again unless I command it."

"As you say, my sister." Chillingly courteous, Ra-Anan

inclined his head. Turning, he spoke beneath his breath to Shoshannah. "Wait outside with your cousin."

Shoshannah obeyed swiftly, beckoning Demamah as she hurried toward the courtyard gate, passing the curious guards. With Demamah grasping her sleeve, they slipped into a shadowed area to the left beside the outer wall.

"That was horrible," Shoshannah said, leaning against the wall, feeling her heart thud. "I never imagined anyone could be so rude."

"She's usually more restrained in public." Demamah sounded shaken.

Footsteps echoed to their left now, and the girls turned warily.

"I thought I heard your voices," Adoniyram said from the darkness. He drew nearer to Shoshannah, stealthily clasping her wrist. "Forgive me for leaving; did she strike you?"

Shoshannah shook her head. "No, I . . . am well. Thank you." She wished he would let go of her wrist before Demamah noticed. He did, but with a lingering, caressing gesture that seemed too intimate. Shoshannah quickly stepped away, facing him. "Master Ra-Anan told us to wait here."

"I'll wait with you until he appears."

"Thank you," Demamah sighed.

Don't thank him, Shoshannah thought. She felt Adoniyram staring at her. To her relief, Ra-Anan emerged from the gate, guiding the indignant Zeva'ah. And, against all customs and courtesies, Father Elam, the banquet's guest of honor, followed them.

"Since you are my host for the week, Ra-Anan, I'll leave with you," Elam said. He nodded stiffly toward Adoniyram. "I hope you are well."

"Perfectly," Adoniyram agreed courteously. Turning to Ra-Anan, he said, "Master-Uncle, I'd prefer to sleep on your floor tonight. Otherwise, my Lady-Mother will invade my household and ensure that I regret my behavior."

"Of course," Ra-Anan said. They began to walk together through the streets, which were lit here and there by window lamps. "But when it is safe, Adoniyram, we *must* warn your mother that she has just offended all of the most powerful men in the Great City. And from beyond."

Ra-Anan sounded regretful. But, somehow, watching him stride calmly ahead, Shoshannah sensed that her uncle was pleased. As if he had hoped . . . no, *intended* for her unwelcome presence to create a conflict.

He knew this would happen. And Sharah will hate me all the more.

Now Adoniyram was walking beside Shoshannah in the darkness. If he were any closer, he would be touching her again. Shoshannah edged away from him, distressed, praying he would leave her alone. If Kaleb were here, he would dump Adoniyram into the nearest waste pit.

And get himself killed . . . She hastily banished the thought.

Eleven

BLEARY FROM A SLEEPLESS night, Shoshannah stood in Ra-Anan's gloomy courtyard, shivering as she waited for Demamah and the beginning of Father Elam's hunting party. At least the cold air would keep her awake. Puddles of water had collected wherever the paving bricks were uneven, and a drizzling mist lingered, reminding her sadly of the mountains and her family.

Adoniyram emerged from the house alone, studied the gray sky, then sauntered over to Shoshannah, pleased.

"I'm glad we left the banquet when we did; I'm sure the rain ruined whatever my mother didn't. She's probably furious."

"Will you need to avoid her for a few days?" Shoshannah asked, glancing up at him reluctantly.

"Perhaps longer." He leaned toward her with a warm, appealing smile. "Will you be glad if I stay here?"

"You are welcomed, of course," she said crisply. She had dreaded seeing him this morning—so much that the anxiety had cost her sleep. And yet, seeing him now—being alone with him—she could almost hear Mithqah arguing, *Admit it: He's handsome.*

Inwardly, Shoshannah argued in return, *Yes, he is handsome, but he's also a proud, presuming, deluded Son-of-Heaven lord.*

Unconcerned by her aloofness, and clearly expecting her to be grateful, Adoniyram said, "I've sent for your weapons; you should use them this morning."

"Thank you, Cousin, but my hand and wrist protectors were burned with the rest of my hunting gear, so I can't use the weapons."

"We will find something for you. Though your wrists are . . . exceptionally delicate," he murmured.

"Adoniyram, please, I don't want to offend you, but I also don't want you teasing me like this. It's unfair and improper, and you know it."

Immediately, his expression became set, cool. "Very well, I'll leave you alone for now. But listen to me: Whether you use them or not, your weapons will be given to you this morning. You must return them to me at the end of the hunt. Otherwise they might be seized and burned."

"As you say, Son of Heaven."

He had been about to leave, but he paused, frowning. "You say my title so rudely. You don't believe it, do you?"

She fought within herself, fearing she had already caused him enough aggravation, but knowing she couldn't soothe him with a lie. Instead she asked, "Do you believe what your people say—that you're the Promised One?"

Equally somber, he asked, "Do you think it could be true?"

"No. It's not."

"You'll have to explain your reasons to me later. And I expect the truth, as we agreed."

"Of course." Shoshannah was surprised that he had accepted her opinion so calmly. Perhaps he wasn't as deluded as she'd thought.

He leaned toward her again, becoming secretive as more servants entered the courtyard. "By the way, I'm going to be ignoring you in public from now on. I don't want my mother to suspect that I am concerned with you at all, or she will try to kill you. And don't ridicule my titles or role with anyone else—particularly Rab-Mawg."

"Thank you for warning me."

Nodding politely, he turned away, greeting Ra-Anan and Father Elam, who were emerging from the house. Demamah followed them, trailed by the sulky Ormah.

As soon as she saw Shoshannah, Demamah said, "There you are! I couldn't find you anywhere."

"You're the one who disappeared," Shoshannah argued kindly—which was true; Demamah had vanished after their rather skimpy morning meal.

"I went to the kitchen to talk to our cook; she needs our help after the hunt." In a whisper, Demamah explained, "Father Elam brought more attendants than we expected; they've done nothing except eat since yesterday. I noticed the bread portion was unusually small this morning."

"Oh, I thought we were being punished again."

"Thank the heavens, no," Demamah said. She went off to her horse, followed by Ormah.

Thank the heavens. Shoshannah tried to remember if she

had heard Demamah say those words before. She doubted it; she would have noticed. The phrase was like a rejection of the Most High, who surely must feel the words like a cutting betrayal. And yet, Shoshannah felt equally betrayed, certain He had abandoned her.

Why didn't your Most High save you? Ra-Anan's smug question still taunted her, denying the existence of the Most High. And because Ra-Anan had completely rejected the Most High, his daughter, Demamah, hadn't heard all the stories of Him. Only bits and pieces—entangled with mockeries and denials.

I should tell her the Ancient Stories of the Beginning, and the Garden of Adan, and the Adversary—that Serpent. And of the Promised One. I should tell Adoniyram too; they both doubt the Most High.

But how convincing could she be, when she felt so betrayed?

A guardsman entered the courtyard gate now, bearing Shoshannah's weapons. She thanked him and accepted her bow and its quiver, relieved to hold them again. Her parents had fashioned the bow and quiver, her last tangible links with home. Hugging the weapons briefly, she slung the brown-furred quiver of arrows over her back and tested the bow. Her right wrist still ached uncomfortably with the motion of aligning the bowstring to her jaw—another grievous reminder of her failed escape.

Someone rode up beside her now, and she lowered the bow. Father Elam nodded graciously, smiling so much like his Father Shem, but so unlike him that it seemed eerie to Shoshannah.

"I never thought I would see a woman so glad to hold a bow. You're the one who provoked that argument last night."

"Yes, Father Elam." Discomfited, Shoshannah lowered her head.

Somber, he leaned down, asking quietly, "Is it true what I have heard? that my own father said the younger generations will age and die before their elders?"

She nodded, daring to glance up at him. "It's true. Believe me—my generation is one of the youngest, so I have no reason to lie about this."

"I don't doubt you, child. My father would never say such a thing if he didn't believe it. I just wanted to be sure that he had said it. We've wondered . . ." Elam hesitated, as if trying to deal with the thought that his children, and their children, might die before him. At last he shook his head and straightened. "Are my parents and the Ancient Ones well?"

His obvious concern made her relax a little. She answered him warmly, allowing him to see how much she loved his parents. "When I left them, they were well. Please forgive me for being bold, but I'm sure they would have told me to say that they send you their love and greetings. And that they miss you."

"Thank you, child." He appeared troubled. Perhaps a bit guilty.

When he didn't turn his horse away immediately, she felt encouraged enough to ask, "Forgive me, Father Elam, but are your brothers and sisters well?"

He frowned. "Why do you ask?"

Almost faltering, certain she had been too forward, she said, "I only thought that . . . when I see your parents again . . . if I do . . . they'd welcome some news."

"Huh. I rarely see my brothers. Asshur doesn't want to travel this far south, and Lud likes the northern mountain coasts, while Arpakshad stays to the west of my tribes, and Aram has claimed lands on the northwest side of the rivers. As for my sisters—they are all busy with their own tribes."

Too busy to visit the Ancient Ones, who would surely tell them things they didn't want to hear, Shoshannah thought darkly. As for Father Elam, it *had* evidently been worth his time to travel to the Great City to visit much younger distant cousins like Master Ra-Anan and that Queen-of-the-Heavens Sharah, and to receive their hospitality and fawning courtesies. If he truly wished to see his brothers, and the Ancient Ones, then certainly he could also spare time for them.

As she was thinking this, Father Elam said, "Eventually, I will find time to see my parents and brothers and sisters again."

"I'm sure you'll be glad to see each other," Shoshannah murmured politely.

He nodded in silent farewell as Perek swaggered up with Shoshannah's horse—the same dull tawny-and-black creature she had ridden during her first hunt here. As soon as she had settled herself atop the horse, Shoshannah glanced over at Demamah, who lifted her eyebrows wonderingly. No doubt Demamah would have to ask what Father Elam had said—as commanded by Master Ra-Anan, who would insist upon knowing everything.

Shoshannah threw a resentful sidelong look at her uncle as he mounted his favorite spoiled sand-pale horse. He and that horse deserved each other—the scoundrels.

Uncle, I am sure you took me to that feast last night knowing my presence would anger the Lady Sharah. You wanted her to offend everyone there. You're plotting against her. And perhaps against Adoniyram. And me. How can I stop you?

Shoshannah sat with Demamah in the warm bricked kitchen, pitting a small mountain of sticky dried dates. Tedious work, but better than plucking the assortment of fat, lifeless, blood-drained birds, as Ormah and the overwhelmed cook were doing now.

Rain suddenly spattered inside the one small window, making the cook hurry to close the shutters and light oil lamps. Irritated and defensive, she shook her dark-braided head, saying to Demamah, "I have no choice but to light these lamps; you can tell your mother so if she complains about the low oil supply. It'll be too dark to work in here otherwise."

"I know it's true, Tabbakhaw, and I'll tell her so," Demamah promised.

"See that you do!" Tabbakhaw stomped back to pluck the birds, while Ormah smirked, evidently amused that Tabbakhaw had snapped at Demamah.

Graceful as ever, Demamah ignored them. Instead, she began to think aloud, "After this, we'll shape the bread dough. And we should prepare more vegetables . . ."

"If you want more vegetables, you'll have to chop them yourself," Tabbakhaw scolded, whisking a clump of down and feathers into a nearby basket.

"I *am* planning on doing it myself," Demamah answered, giving Tabbakhaw a subtly threatening look—far more restrained than Shoshannah would have been. "And Shoshannah will help me. Though we don't have to."

Mercifully, Tabbakhaw took Demamah's hint and went to work, feathers flying away beneath her fingers as she grumbled to herself.

An amused masculine voice made them all look toward the kitchen doorway. "I've found you. Is work better than my own exalted company?" Adoniyram stepped into the kitchen, smiling.

Demamah shook her head at him. "If you're not going to be useful, Adoniyram, you should leave. We're busy trying to make your food."

"I doubt I'm useful at anything, dear Cousin. However, I've sent for food from my own household. I'm sure your cook won't mind. And I have no intention of leaving. Your mother is sewing—which doesn't interest me—and Ra-Anan and Father Elam are napping, which is also dull, so you'll have to endure me."

As he sat comfortably on the mat with Demamah and Shoshannah, two of his attendant-guardsmen marched in and lowered several heavy baskets onto the floor near the openmouthed Tabbakhaw. Heaps of soft bread, pots of spiced honey, roasted meats, jars of preserved fruits and oils, and bunches of pungent dried herbs scented the air. Also, to Shoshannah's disgust, there was a basket trap full of scuttling, menacing crabs.

Instantly, Tabbakhaw was beaming, praising Adoniyram. "Blessings from our Son of Heaven! How wonderful; these crabs are just what we needed. I'll heat the water at once; thank you, my lord!"

"I'm glad you're pleased. Now, if you don't mind, I'd like to stay here and visit with my cousins."

"Oh yes, let it be as you say, my lord; thank you. We won't disturb you."

Disgusted by the change in the now flattering and fluttering Tabbakhaw, Shoshannah muttered to Adoniyram, "We've been working here for half the afternoon without one smile from her. But you walk in and she's overflowing with compliments—though you didn't lift a finger except to order the food."

"As I said, I'm not very useful." He waved his guardsmen off, taunting them cheerfully. "I noticed you left the wine and beer outside! Don't drink it all, or you'll be punished—you're not in my residence now."

The guardsmen laughed and departed, and Adoniyram settled down, watching Shoshannah and Demamah pit the dates. Carelessly he began to pit a few. To Shoshannah, it was strange to see her privileged cousin doing such an ordinary task; he looked and smelled so clean, so perfect, so wrong for work.

Mithqah, Shoshannah argued silently to her dear absent friend, *it is possible for a man to be too handsome. Adoniyram is proof of that.* Mithqah would have disagreed fiercely, Shoshannah knew. Particularly if Adoniyram had looked at her the way he was watching Shoshannah now, from beneath his long eyelashes.

Softly he commanded, "Tell me why I'm not the Promised One."

Aware of Demamah listening, and knowing that she must report everything to Ra-Anan, Shoshannah said beneath her breath, "You cannot be the Promised One because you aren't born of the sons of our First Father Shem. Actually, of Arpakshad."

"Arpakshad?" Adoniyram looked perplexed. "How can anyone from his tribe restore perfection to us? They have nothing to do with our Great City."

Shoshannah pondered this briefly, then murmured, "Perhaps the Promised One won't be concerned with ruling the Great City. It may be that the Promised One will 'restore perfection to us' with the Most High and then return us to the Garden of Adan. There's so much we don't know."

"Then why are you telling me that I'm not the Promised

One?" he whispered, becoming mildly exasperated. "Since there's so much you don't know . . ."

"Because you wanted to hear what I *do* know." Shoshannah lowered her voice even more, making Adoniyram and Demamah lean toward her. "Listen; if you wish, I'll tell you the stories of the Ancient Ones."

Demamah looked interested, but Adoniyram shrugged, tossed a pitted date into the basket, then reached for another.

Sighing, fearing that he was only humoring her, Shoshannah whispered, "In the beginning, by the Word of the Most High, the heavens and the earth were created . . ."

By the time they finished pitting the dates, Adoniyram seemed genuinely interested, for Shoshannah was telling them of the Adversary, the Serpent. But Demamah interrupted by fetching a large trough of puffy dough. Then they had to show Adoniyram how to select and pat out bits of dough, which amused him. And Zeva'ah entered the kitchen then, disrupting everything with questions, commands, and complaints about the oil lamps—which Demamah quickly defended. Zeva'ah also threw a suspicious parting glance at Shoshannah, who remained silent.

The instant Zeva'ah left, Tabbakhaw announced that she was ready to steam the crabs. Immediately Adoniyram and Demamah went to help her. Evidently, putting an end to a bunch of scuttling crabs was more fun than subduing lumps of dough.

As she watched her mitt-protected cousins laughing and snatching at the doomed crabs, Shoshannah formed another oiled grain-speckled cake of dough. *At this pace,* she thought, *it'll take me all spring and summer to tell them about the Promised One, the histories, and the Great Flood. I don't want to be here that long. But I'm sure I will be.*

Disheartened, she reached for another lump of dough, longing for her home, her family, and Kal.

Twelve

SWEATING BENEATH the late-spring sky, Kaleb wedged a thick mud mixture in between the stones abutting his—and Shoshannah's—new lodge.

"Here's more," Zekaryah told him, slapping another heap of mud-mortar onto the stonework.

Kaleb nodded, still unable to believe that Shoshannah's father was helping him. Or that he had agreed that Kal should marry his daughter. He had expected resistance from Zekaryah, perhaps even some anger. Instead, Kaleb was dealing with Zekaryah's intense determination that Shoshannah's lodge be perfect.

I want the same thing, though, so this is good, Kaleb reminded himself, beating the mud in tight with a padded mallet.

He rested briefly, wiping his mud-spattered face with his equally muddied forearm. Shoshannah would have teased him for looking messy—and he would have loved her teasing. He longed to hear her voice again, ached to see her smile, her dimples . . . He was becoming dull and gloomy without her.

"That will do," Zekaryah said, standing beside him, studying the small, handsomely built lodge.

That will do. A high compliment from Zekaryah.

Kal grinned. "If it weren't so rude, I'd go to the Tribe of Metiyl and bring her home now."

Zekaryah grunted, still staring at the lodge. "Furniture."

Kal almost said that furniture didn't matter to Shoshannah, but that would be a serious mistake. Zekaryah would stare at him instead of the lodge.

"It's wonderful!" Keren called out, approaching them now—her beautiful face bright with pleasure, the edges of her linen head scarf dancing in the breeze.

As they admired the lodge, Rinnah bounded up to them, her curls springing out like dark wood shavings. "Is it finished? Can I go inside?"

"Are *you* finished cleaning out the goat pen?" Keren demanded, eyeing her youngest child.

Rinnah shuffled and dug her leather-clad toes into the dirt. "Well, almost. The goats were playing and—"

"Tie them. And finish cleaning," Zekaryah commanded, silently threatening dire punishments that made Kal want to protect his small soon-to-be sister-in-law.

As Rinnah ducked her head and escaped to the goat pens, Kal said, "I almost let her go inside. I'm going to be a terrible father."

"You'll learn," Zekaryah said.

"But *we* didn't have to learn—we're perfect," Keren added, so demure that Zekaryah flung her a suspicious glance. She laughed, and Zekaryah shook his head, his usual dignity failing as he smiled.

"My children will learn better manners if I pen them with the animals," Kal decided aloud.

"Kaleb!" a voice cried, almost wailing.

He turned, alarmed, to see a bedraggled and weepy Mithqah trudging from the woods into the clearing with her mare, followed by a grim Metiyl and the exhausted Yelahlah and her family. And Father Shem. And I'ma-Annah. The sight of all these travelers terrified Kaleb.

Shoshannah . . .

Followed by Zekaryah and Keren, he ran to Mithqah. He had to hold her up as she cried.

The entire Tribe of Ashkenaz gathered in the central clearing. Kaleb sat between his parents and Zekaryah and Keren, all of them listening to Mithqah's story. Then they stared at Yelahlah and her husband, Echuwd, who knelt with the hushed Rakal on the other side of the central open hearth.

Father Ashkenaz growled to Echuwd, "Our Shoshannah was your guest, under your protection; you should have listened to her fears. You deserve a beating!"

"I am also *your* guest, and under your protection," Echuwd argued, lifting his head to stare at Ashkenaz.

Seething, Kaleb almost answered Echuwd himself, but Ashkenaz stood first. "You are nothing but a man with evil news, Echuwd, which was your fault to begin with! You're not a guest until I've accepted you as one—and I haven't! So don't you dare answer me smartly, you whelp, or we'll pound some sense into that thick head of yours." Quieting slightly, he said, "It's only for your wife's sake that we haven't whipped you already."

Rinnah huddled against Kaleb, quivering like a trapped baby rabbit. As Kaleb hugged her, she cried out, "Is Shoshannah going to die?"

Her thin tremulous voice stopped everyone. Adah and Qetuwrah, kneeling beside Keren, burst into tears, while their brothers, Ahyit and Sithriy, sat and stared in shock, their bony, scraped knees drawn up to their chins.

Seated nearby with I'ma-Ritspah, Mithqah said, "They intend to keep her alive. As bait. Father Kuwsh said, 'Her mother should suffer for her, as I have suffered for my son.'"

"I'll go for her," Keren said.

Immediately Zekaryah shook his head. "No."

Mithqah said, "You can't, I'ma-Keren. Shoshannah doesn't want anyone coming after her. She meant it. She's afraid someone else will die, and that would be worse for her—you know it." Hesitantly she lifted her rounded chin. "But if anyone else *is* willing to go to the Great City to help her, I'll accompany them."

"No." It was Ozniy who spoke, large and foreboding, like an echo of Zekaryah.

Kaleb stared over his shoulder in surprise at his usually calm brother. Ozniy was watching Mithqah steadily, and she looked back at him, seeming both pleased and distressed.

Mithqah's father, Uzziel, cleared his throat. "You'll stay here," he informed Mithqah gruffly. "Your mother and I say you've done enough; Shoshannah would agree. And you have other obligations." As simply as that, Uzziel confirmed that Mithqah would marry Ozniy.

Any other time, Kaleb would have laughed and tormented his brother, but now he was too worried about Shoshannah.

"Forgive me, Father Ashkenaz," he said loudly, "but I must say that I'm going." Certain he had everyone's attention now, Kal turned to Zekaryah and Keren, asking, "Please, do you consider your Shoshannah to be my wife?"

His question was a risk. As head of his household, Zekaryah could declare his daughter married with a single word. He could also set conditions that had to be met before the marriage could take place.

Kaleb watched his prospective father-in-law closely. Would he take offense at being forced to make such a sudden and serious formal commitment? Kal could see the older man thinking. Planning.

Zekaryah looked up. "Yes," he said firmly.

Beside him Keren nodded, smiling, though he saw tears in her eyes. And Kaleb heard his own tenderhearted mother, Pakhdaw, utter a choked, wistful, "Oh . . ."

Profoundly relieved, and married, Kaleb sighed. "Thank you." Tousling Rinnah's curls lightly, Kaleb stood and crossed to the other side of the hearth to face Echuwd.

Now the wild-haired Metiyl called out, "You take whatever he gives you, Echuwd! Remember, I warned you that you deserve this!" But rather than thrashing the unfortunate Echuwd, Kaleb merely spoke to him in a calm voice. "If you stand while I talk to you, Echuwd, I won't touch you. But if I have to drag you to your feet, you'll earn scars."

Echuwd stood, looking up at Kaleb, who subdued his impulse to pound the man to dust. "You'd better pray for my wife's safety, Echuwd, because if she dies, *your* wife will have to find a new husband. I will kill *you*." Pausing for effect, he added, "And if I die while I'm trying to save my wife, then my brothers will find you and kill you. So be sure you pray."

Echuwd flinched and retreated in sullen, humiliated fear. Kaleb didn't pursue him. He turned, intending to go sit with his parents again until the meeting ended, but nearly collided with his brothers, who were standing just behind him.

"We're going with you," Tiyrac said.

Kaleb stared at him, calculating. "No, you're not."

Before they could start an argument, the First Father Shem stood, accompanied by I'ma-Annah. Acknowledging his authority, Kaleb and his brothers quickly returned to sit with their parents and Zekaryah and I'ma-Keren.

Calm and deliberate, Shem said, "There must be no further quarreling. Echuwd, because of your willful disregard for Shoshannah's safety, I assure you that Kaleb and Shoshannah's families have the right to demand your life for theirs. However, for Yelahlah's sake—for everyone's sake—we pray that won't happen."

Echuwd knelt stiff faced beside Yelahlah, who looked ashen, as if she would faint.

Clasping I'ma-Annah's hand protectively, Shem said, "Your Ma'adannah and I agree that we must accompany Kaleb to the Great City. Shoshannah is being held there because Kuwsh is determined to avenge his son's death—despite the fact that I executed Nimr-Rada according to the will of the Most High, for being a murderous rebel. But the Most High will judge between us. Therefore, we'll go with Kaleb."

Metiyl shook his head, his nostrils flaring. Father Ashkenaz started to rumble words of protest, but beneath Shem's unblinking gaze, he actually halted, then shrugged.

"As you say, Father Shem. We'll keep watch over the Ancient Ones while you're gone."

I'ma-Annah spoke to Kaleb's brothers, her gentle voice easing their tension. "You have obligations here, Ozniy, so you should stay. As for Tiyrac, if he wants to go with us to help his rascal brother—with his parents' permission—then we welcome his company."

I'm the rascal brother, Kaleb thought, trying and failing to be indignant. He was grateful to I'ma-Annah—he had meant to take Tiyrac with him all along. His pretense at a quarrel was only to ensure that the stubborn Tiyrac wouldn't change his mind.

Now, Tiyrac lifted his chin at Kaleb menacingly.

Kaleb glared at him, pleased.

With Ozniy's help, Kaleb covered the lodge's stonework with hides, matting, and rocks to ensure that it would dry evenly while he was gone. As they set the last stones in place, Kaleb said, "After you and Mithqah are married, move in and guard this place for us until we return. I'll tell Father and I'ma that you have my permission. That will give you time to build your own lodge."

"Shoshannah won't mind if others live here first?" Ozniy asked, grateful but concerned.

"It can't be helped. I don't know how long we'll be away, and I'd hate to leave it abandoned—or else Shoshannah will meet clans of mice when she walks inside for the first time." Kaleb thumped his brother's shoulder, scolding, "You should have been building *your* lodge while Mithqah was gone. Did you think her parents would refuse you?"

Ozniy shrugged, self-depreciative. "Her parents could have chosen anyone else. I didn't know she was so interested in *me* until a few months before she left."

"You weren't paying attention," Kaleb said, rolling his eyes in mock disgust. "She's been watching you for more than a year. I didn't say anything to you because I knew she'd be embarrassed and because Father Ashkenaz wouldn't have liked it. And Shoshannah would have been angry with me for weeks." Thinking of Shoshannah, Kaleb's joy faded. Quietly he said, "I'm sorry we'll miss your wedding."

Embarrassed as their father when confronted with sentiment, Ozniy turned gruff. "Mithqah and I forgive you. Just be sure you all return safely."

"We will. Though I wish Father Shem weren't going with us; it worries me that he's putting himself in danger. I . . ." Kaleb stopped and stared, confounded, as Zekaryah rode by, guiding three horses: Keren's dark one, Zekaryah's big tawny animal, and a sturdy packhorse, already loaded with gear. "He's going with us. I'ma-Keren too."

"I thought Zekaryah told her she couldn't go."

"She's obviously convinced him that she can." Kaleb longed to argue with Zekaryah and Keren, but he knew it would be useless. Truly, if a child of his own were ever in danger, he would do anything to save her. He muttered to Ozniy, "If Ima-Keren's enemies find her, she will die. Pray for us."

"I will." After a grim pause, Ozniy said, "We should go load your gear."

Kaleb hugged his burly, self-conscious father. Uncomfortable, Regem lectured him. "Obey Father Shem and Zekaryah. And listen to your brother once in a while—don't go rushing off like a wild man doing as you please. Ask for their advice; then keep your mouth shut."

Kaleb grinned. "I'll try, Father. Be safe while I'm gone."

He dreaded telling his mother good-bye; Pakhdaw had been crying all morning, and her usually placid brown face was blotchy, her eyes very red. As he kissed her cheek, she began to sob again.

Kaleb bent, facing her almost nose to nose. "I'ma, think how calm everything's going to be without your rascal son here. You should be glad I'll be gone for a while."

"That's no help," she complained, wiping her eyes with her sleeve. "You just bring our Shoshannah home and settle down. And don't get your brother into trouble."

Hearing this, Tiyrac protested, "I'ma, do you think I'd let him talk me into anything?"

"Kaleb has always convinced you to do as he pleases, Tiyrac, and you know it." She patted Tiyrac's face as if he were tiny again. "Just be careful. I love you both."

Visibly discomfited, Tiyrac kissed her good-bye, nodded to their father, then marched off toward the horses. Kaleb hastily told his parents about his bargain with Ozniy, hugged Pakhdaw in farewell, and fled.

Heartsick, Keren kissed her daughters. Qetuwrah and Adah clung to her and sobbed. They felt so fragile as she held them. Was she wrong to leave her five younger children in order to be near her firstborn? *I should stay . . .*

Ahyit and Sithriy leaned against her, patting her back—too "adult" to hug her like mere babies. Keren hugged her sons fiercely and kissed their faces.

Sithriy pulled away slightly, solemn, looking just like his father. "You'll bring her back safely, I'ma."

Keren wished she felt as confident as he sounded. Rinnah burrowed between her siblings now and hugged Keren's waist. Keren picked her up, swaying, fighting tears. "Little one . . . be good for our I'ma-Ritspah."

Rinnah sniffled. "But I'm going to stay with I'ma-Pakhdaw. She needs me."

"You just hope she won't make you work as hard as I'ma-Ritspah will," Adah said knowingly. She turned to Keren. "I'ma, don't worry; Qetuwrah and I will make them behave. We'll take care of everything."

Beside her, Qetuwrah nodded, saying brokenly, "And we'll clean the lodge."

The girls were already making plans to be without her. The boys expected her to go—though they also expected her to return, which might not be possible.

"Remember us when you pray," Keren said, kissing them all again. *O Most High, please guard them!*

"We'll stay with the Tribe of Metiyl while you go on to the Great City," Zekaryah explained to Kaleb and Tiyrac, as they led their horses down a hillside trail. "Until then, as we journey, you'll practice with your weapons. And we'll make plans. You won't be able to just ride into the Great City and demand Shoshannah's return."

Absorbing this information, Kaleb looked down the trail to Shem, I'ma-Annah, and I'ma-Keren, who were following Metiyl, the disgraced Echuwd, Yelahlah, and Rakal, who rode proudly atop Echuwd's horse. "What about Father Shem and I'ma-Annah? Have you persuaded them to stay with you?"

"For a while," Zekaryah answered, toneless. "But he's a First Father."

Meaning you might not stop him if he decides to ride into the Great City and confront his enemies, who could kill him.

"How can we find Shoshannah?" Kaleb asked.

"You'll become guardsmen—you and Tiyrac."

Kaleb groaned inwardly. "That will take time."

"Yes."

Give me patience, O Most High.

Accompanied by Keren, Annah noticed Yelahlah slowing as they picked their way down the hillside. When Annah and Keren drew nearer to her, Yelahlah faced them, tired, worried. "I haven't told you . . . Sharah apparently has a son who is the same age as Shoshannah—perhaps a little older."

"Nimr-Rada had a son with Sharah?" Annah thought, *How terrible to have such parents.* "Did he seem well mannered?"

"I don't know," Yelahlah said, eyeing her son and her husband. "Sharah was so hateful and sent us away so quickly that I had no time to watch him—though he is a very handsome young man." She glanced at Keren. "Father Kuwsh, too, was hateful. Oh, Keren, so many in the Great City blame you for Nimr-Rada's death."

Keren nodded, as if unsurprised, but her color faded. "I pray Shoshannah hasn't been treated too badly."

Giving Keren a pathetic sidelong look, Yelahlah asked, "Can you forgive me?"

Annah saw Keren struggling to restrain the hurt and rage she felt over her daughter's predicament. She clearly blamed Yelahlah, though she loved her. As Annah hoped, Keren finally nodded, subdued. "Yes. I know you tried to help her . . . afterward."

Yelahlah was obviously disappointed that Keren's forgiveness wasn't wholehearted. But what could she expect? Surely Yelahlah would feel the same way if her own Rakal were endangered by someone else's foolishness.

To divert them, Annah wondered aloud, "Do you suppose your cousin Tsinnah has had her baby yet?"

Counting off months on her fingers, Yelahlah said, "If not, then it's any day now."

"I'm glad for her," Keren murmured.

Annah noticed her wistful tone; Keren was evidently longing for another child.

Keren caught Annah's glance and said, "I'ma-Annah, does Father Shem really intend to go into the Great City and confront Sharah and Ra-Anan and Kuwsh?"

"If need be," Annah replied, dreading the thought. She looked ahead at her husband, who was talking with Metiyl. "All I can say for certain is that my Shem and I feel compelled by the Most High to go with you. Our Noakh and I'ma-Naomi agreed, so surely there's a reason —though I am afraid to know what that reason might be."

"It's not too late to turn back," Keren offered. "I'm not trying to be rid of you, I'ma-Annah, but . . . what if Kuwsh and the others no longer respect your age and your status as our First Father and First Mother?"

"If that is true, then the children of my children have no regard for anything, including the Most High, which means that I've failed completely." Pondering this, Annah said, "I would despise living with such shame."

"We need you to live," Keren told her, widening her pale gray eyes—suddenly looking very young and distressed.

Cherishing Keren's obvious concern, Annah said, "We also need you to live, Keren-child. Don't forget that."

Keren looked away, shrugging as if she had already given up the thought of survival. Watching her, Yelahlah seemed ready to protest. But then she lowered her head despondently. In silence, the three women continued along the rocky, downward-sloping path.

Thirteen

"DO YOU THINK we have enough of the crimson to continue the pattern?" Demamah asked, crouching beside Shoshannah in the small, private courtyard. They both studied the emerging cream-and-crimson woolen pattern in the ground loom, which extended for half the length of Demamah's garden.

"I'm sure we've figured it accurately," Shoshannah mused, resting her chin on her fingertips. "But if we're in doubt, we could make this as a border, reduce the crimson in the main pattern, then finish the other end of this fabric as we've begun it, so the edges will match. And if we have some crimson left, we can make a belt."

"For me?" Adoniyram asked, startling them from the shadowed doorway. "Thank you, dear Cousins." He strolled into the warm afternoon sunlight, bare chested and coppery brown, wearing a simple fleece wrap. His dark curls shone, fresh scrubbed, and he smiled appealingly at Shoshannah.

She made a face at him, exasperated. How brazen of Adoniyram to come into Demamah's private courtyard unsupervised. Why didn't Ra-Anan and Zeva'ah restrain him? Pushing back her hair, Shoshannah said, "The belt's not for you. We're making this fabric for Aunt Zeva'ah."

"I'll ask her for it then," Adoniyram said, crouching beside her. Whispering, he added, "And when I wear this fabric, I'll remember that your hands have touched every part of it."

"Oh, you'll remember; I'll weave some itching burrs into the area covering your backside—and it would serve you right!"

Demamah looked scandalized, but Adoniyram laughed warmly—as attractive as Kaleb in a playful mood.

Disturbed by Adoniyram's nearness, Shoshannah arose and stepped around the low wooden loom. He grinned and moved as if to follow her, but she put up a defensive hand. "If you're going to visit, then you stay *there* and don't interrupt us; we're working."

Sobering a little, he said, "I give you my word . . . I'm here for a reason."

"Then say it," Demamah commanded, winding some of the precious crimson thread onto a slender shuttle. She had begun to adopt Shoshannah's dictatorial air with Adoniyram, which he enjoyed—to a point.

Adoniyram remained silent for such a long time that the young women both sat back and stared at him, forgetting their work. Looking hard at Shoshannah, he said, "I wanted to warn you: Our highest day of Shemesh is approaching. Whatever happens, you should not attend the ceremonies in the tower."

Before she could request an explanation, he said, "Our Great King died on that day, at the hand of Shem, because of your mother. You could be blamed in her place. Some of the celebrants might demand your blood for revenge."

Confounded, Shoshannah said, "The Great-King Nimr-Rada was *your* father, Adoniyram. If anyone should want my blood for revenge, it should be you. Why are you warning me about this?"

"Because I would be bored without you," Adoniyram teased, clearly deflecting her question, forbidding her to pursue the matter further. "Now, since I've said everything I'm allowed to say, it's your turn to talk. Tell me again what the Ancient Ones say of that Serpent in the Garden of Adan."

Shoshannah hesitated, longing to demand a straightforward answer to her question.

But Adoniyram prompted her, "Remember? 'Now the Serpent was more crafty than any animal . . .'"

So he *had* been listening to her recitations for all these weeks. Encouraged, Shoshannah temporarily abandoned her curiosity at his lack of vengefulness, picked up her shuttle, and resumed the story. "He asked the woman, 'Did the Most High really say . . .'"

Adoniyram listened to the restful cadence of Shoshannah's narrative, admiring her slender, always-busy hands working the shuttle through the threads on her loom. *I would be bored without you,* he thought. *You've given me a sense of being part of a family for the first time in my life—quarrelsome as that family can be. But more than that . . . how can I*

demand revenge for the death of a man who probably wasn't my father?

His mother's unguarded expression on the night of Shoshannah's escape had run through his mind again and again: hateful, triumphant, spiteful at the mention of Kuwsh and the Great-King Nimr-Rada. Now, months later, Adoniyram was finally beginning to confront the reality of this new shame, which must remain hidden. His mother had certainly betrayed her "husband" Nimr-Rada. It would be just like her to stupidly, maliciously give herself to another man for her own petty retaliation against slights, imagined or deserved, from the Great King. *I am the result of her revenge.*

In a way, Adoniyram was relieved to think that he wasn't the son of Nimr-Rada—who was by even the most loyal accounts a brutal, blood-loving man. But he still felt a wholehearted resentment toward his mother. Watching Shoshannah, he wondered how his life would have been with honorable, respectable parents he could admire. Parents like Shoshannah's.

"I will put animosity between you and the woman, and between your descendant and her descendant. . . ." Shoshannah recited, her voice intensifying. "He will bruise your head, and you will bruise his heel."

Pondering her words, remembering the histories she had recited earlier, Adoniyram thought, *If the Great King was not my father, then another man was. And perhaps he was a descendant of Father Shem. Perhaps even of the Tribe of Arpakshad. Shoshannah, beloved, what if you are wrong? What if I am the Promised One?*

To Shoshannah's Most High, he thought, *Reveal the truth, if You live.*

In the unfinished room behind the temple, Shoshannah watched as Rab-Mawg sipped from a cup and inscribed sun symbols on a pliable clay tablet. Soon he would expect her to copy the symbols and recite their meanings to him again. But Rab-Mawg's thoughts seemed to shift all of a sudden. He stared at her coldly. What was wrong with him? Was he drunk? Most mornings he was decisive and sharp as flint. Other times he seemed to speak to her from a fog. But now he watched her as if she were evil, an enemy conspiring against him.

Worried, longing to hurry her lesson so she could escape, Shoshannah asked, "Are you well?"

Rab-Mawg's black, unfathomable eyes narrowed fiercely. He thrust the tablet away, mashing its soft contours against the brick floor. "I meant what I said."

What had he said? When? To soothe him and avoid a scene, Shoshannah nodded. "Of course you did."

"Then why are you so rebellious, resisting me?"

"Forgive me," Shoshannah whispered humbly, panicked. How was she resisting him? He wasn't making sense. Beside her, Ormah shifted uncomfortably, edging away.

"You thought I didn't mean it," Rab-Mawg persisted, standing, approaching, making Shoshannah scramble to her feet. His eyes looked odd—glazed, intense—and his color was heightened. "I'm telling you, Daughter of Keren, *she* hasn't fulfilled her vows."

I'ma, he's referring to you. "You're right; she hasn't."

"But *you* will," Rab-Mawg said, belligerent.

"As you say." She looked down at his clenched hands. He held no knife this time, but she was still afraid—he was behaving so oddly. By now, Ormah was scuttling through the doorway. Shoshannah tensed, ready to run after her.

"Enough," Perek growled, coming from behind the linen-draped temple doorway. Ghez-ar and Ebed followed him, their eyes wide, nervous.

"She thinks I'm lying," Rab-Mawg said, smoldering, fixated on Shoshannah, who struggled to remain calm.

"She will do as you say," Ebed assured Rab-Mawg cautiously. "But she's called away now. She has to go."

"She should stay," Rab-Mawg muttered, harsh, glaring.

"She will return," Ghez-ar said. His voice was tranquil, though Shoshannah saw him sweating. "And meanwhile, you can rest and have something to eat and drink."

"He's had enough already," Perek retorted.

Ebed frantically waved a bony hand, signaling Perek to hush.

Rab-Mawg saw the movement and stared at his assistant. "What are you doing?"

"Swatting flies," Ebed lied, sweating as profusely as Ghez-ar.

Irritated, Perek said, "We're going. Rab-Mawg, take a nap and be sober for the lesson tomorrow night. Master Ra-Anan won't be pleased."

Rab-Mawg moved toward Perek, but Ghez-ar and Ebed grabbed his arms; they were wrestling with him as Shoshannah hurried from the temple. Perek followed her, though Shoshannah was sure he would have preferred to beat Rab-Mawg.

Outside, the guard gave her a shove. "What did you say to make him so angry?"

"I didn't say anything," Shoshannah protested.

"You should've noticed he was drunk; I'll wager you said something rude."

"It wasn't simple drunkenness, Perek, I'm sure. He's imagining things. Ask Ormah if I said anything rude—she was beside me during the whole lesson."

"We'll see," Perek snorted as they hurried down the endless bricked stairs. Ormah was rushing ahead of them as if Rab-Mawg was after her. When they finally reached her, she was in the tower yard bowing to Ra-Anan. Irritable, he waved some guardsmen out the gates, instructing them to take several pack-laden horses to his home.

Jabbering like a frightened child, Ormah said, "Master, Rab-Mawg threatened us! Shoshannah must have said something during her last lesson to make him angry."

"You were at my last lesson," Shoshannah reminded the maidservant firmly. "If I'd said anything wrong, you would have tattled on me that same day."

Ormah's pert little face darkened, and she appeared ready to argue, but Ra-Anan lifted a hand to stop her. "Ormah, go to your horse. Now. Perek will help you." Frowning at Shoshannah, he said, "Tell me what happened."

"Uncle, I give you my word; it was more than drunkenness. Rab-Mawg was talking wildly, and his eyes were odd." She pleaded, "Don't make me study with him tomorrow night. If he's in the same mood, he will throw me over the edge of the terrace, I'm sure."

"He won't touch you," Ra-Anan said coldly. "I will be there, and I will speak to him about his behavior today. *You* quit making excuses to avoid your lessons."

He didn't believe her. Sick at the thought of facing Rab-Mawg again, Shoshannah trudged toward the horses. Perek resentfully tossed her onto the lackluster mount now considered her own, then rode ahead, leading her horse and Ormah's away from the tower.

As they passed through the brick gates, a rough, thin, sharp-faced man spat toward Ra-Anan's back after Ra-Anan and Perek passed by. Shoshannah stared at him, amazed by his open hostility. He returned her look, defiant.

The guardsmen near the gate ignored him.

Uneasy, Shoshannah asked Ormah, "Did you see that man?"

"No, I didn't," the young woman answered snippily.

It was useless to talk with her; Ormah would probably pout for the remainder of the day. Concerned, Shoshannah tried to describe the man to Perek.

He gave her a disgruntled look. "Don't make more trouble for yourself, girl."

She would speak to Ra-Anan after the evening meal. Surely he would be in a better mood and listen to her then. Though perhaps her experience with Rab-Mawg had shaken her so much that she was seeing danger where none existed. Her fear lingered.

"What did you give Rab-Mawg?" Ghez-ar demanded as Awkawn blearily wandered out from the sleeping area.

"I've just awakened. I didn't give him anything." Awkawn rubbed a hand over his rough-whiskered face, staring at Rab-Mawg, who was now sitting against a wall, disoriented and clutching his head, guarded by Ebed.

Baffled, Ghez-ar looked around and spied the mashed clay tablet and the clay cup beside it. Inside the cup was a murky liquid with a thick, foul-looking residue at the bottom. Rab-Mawg had evidently been experimenting on himself with some of their latest "herbs" and had underestimated the strength of this mixture. Worse, he had impatiently tested his potion during the girl's lessons—a terrible mistake. Ghez-ar frowned. Their revered chief magician was obviously becoming dependent on the herbs for his "visions," seeking Shemesh.

We must stop you from destroying yourself—and us.

The next night, as she knelt with Demamah on the darkened terrace beneath the star-scattered sky, Shoshannah watched Rab-Mawg and listened to him, shocked. He was soft-spoken, courteous, and baffled by her account of his wild behavior the previous morning. "Surely she misunderstood me."

Impatient, Ra-Anan snapped, "Don't pretend with me! Perek said you were raving. Whatever you drank, don't drink it before her next lesson. Any more scenes like this, and I will beat you both."

"I regret worrying you, Master." Rab-Mawg sounded wholly sincere.

Was he the most convincing liar in the world, or did he truly not remember his terrible behavior? While Shoshannah was deliberating, Ra-Anan beckoned her severely. "Come here. You will behave now and not waste any more of our time with your foolish excuses; sit and pay attention. These lessons are for your benefit."

Lessons, Shoshannah thought bitterly. *Stories created from your own little minds to fit pictures in the stars.*

Gracious, as if forgiving her for accusing him unjustly, Rab-Mawg inclined his head toward Shoshannah. Behind him, Ebed, Ghez-ar, and Awkawn watched her, clearly worried. They were probably hoping she wouldn't persist with her accusation—though it was true. No doubt they feared that Master Ra-Anan would dismiss them from their coveted, honorable positions as servant-priests in the tower of Shemesh.

What would the four of you do then? she wondered, as she and Demamah knelt a little nearer to the priests. They would have to become ordinary farmers and tradesmen, or canal diggers. It would be quite a tumble for them if they were removed from their golden temple on this tower. *I'm sure you would do almost anything to keep your positions here, including killing me.* Scared by the thought, Shoshannah paid careful attention as Rab-Mawg explained the patterns in the stars.

"We are now in the month of Shemesh, with the Serpent, the Lady, and the Lion, represented by these stars here and those stars there. Soon, the Promised Child will be revealed over there." He rested his hands on his knees, his face shadowed. "These signal the times of harvest, which are followed by the days of balance—of weighing and measuring grain. In the coming months, you will see the symbol of our Great King riding the eagle of Asshur, for he conquered those tribes."

Father Metiyl's tribe. And Tsinnah's tribe, Shoshannah thought desolately. *She's had her baby by now. And it seems as if I never visited her at all.* Sternly she scolded herself, *Don't think of them! Finish your lesson so you can leave.*

The detestable Master Rab-Mawg talked for half the evening. She forced herself to listen to him and to repeat what he had told her. She indicated which stars were a part of her lesson tonight, and why. And she recited which stars were to appear in the following weeks. By the time she finished, even Ra-Anan was pleased with her. "Very good, child."

Though his tone was patronizing, it was the first time he had actually complimented her. But having his approval felt more like a betrayal of her parents than an accomplishment.

Demamah had been silent throughout the evening. Now, however, trailed by two guardsmen, she clasped Shoshannah's arm, delighted, as they pattered down the moonlit tower stairs. "You did so well! That went so easily —thank you!"

"Were you afraid I'd create another scene?"

"Of course."

Despite herself, Shoshannah laughed in the humid, bug-rasping summertime darkness. Feeling better, she scampered down the last stairs after her uncle, heading toward a torch-bearing guard who waited with their horses.

Suddenly other footsteps rushed at them from the darkness. A shadow collided with Ra-Anan, jostling him, obscuring him briefly. Ra-Anan cried out sharply, then roared and lashed out at his attacker. Shoshannah heard scuffling, an appalling choked squawk, and a terrible bone-crunching noise, followed by a loud, hollowish thud.

Guards rushed past Shoshannah and Demamah, toward Ra-Anan, and Demamah shrieked, "Father? Father!"

"Demamah, hush!" Ra-Anan snapped. After a brief pause, he disentangled himself from the shadows and from a form lying limp on the brick pavings, and returned to the torchlight.

Shoshannah clung to Demamah, horrified, staring at Ra-Anan. The side of his face was gashed with blood and he was limping, his expression terrible, unearthly in the wavering light.

"Uncle . . ." As Shoshannah was trying to gather her wits, the guardsmen dragged a body into view: a rough, thin, death-staring man with blood oozing from his bashed nose. She shrank back. "That's the man I saw yesterday."

Warily Ra-Anan studied her, then looked around. "To your horses, both of you. There may be others."

They obeyed him in shocked, hurried silence.

Fourteen

IN THE MORNING LIGHT, Adoniyram stood in his uncle's courtyard, staring at the would-be assassin's leather-shrouded body. Ra-Anan eyed Adoniyram accusingly. "This is the same troublemaker you encouraged us to compromise with some time ago."

"I remember. He was Dayag—a fisherman." Adoniyram looked away from the dead man's battered features. Determined to correct his uncle, he pretended ignorance, asking, "Did we fulfill the promises made to him when his lands were claimed by the temple priests?"

"They offered him lands in exchange, which he rejected."

Inferior lands, away from the city and the river—which was his livelihood, Adoniyram reminded his uncle inwardly. *And that was your fault; you know it. You control everything here, including your priests.*

Studying the long ointment-laden slash on Ra-Anan's face, which would leave a scar that could never be hidden, Adoniyram said, "I hope there are no others in the city who think like him."

"*He* is dead," Ra-Anan said crisply, satisfied. "And I will destroy any others just as easily. One blow to the throat and two to his head." Contemptuous, he yanked the leather shroud closed and signaled to his guards. "Tie this thing and dump it in the river south of the city."

While the guards hurried to obey, Ra-Anan limped toward his residence again. Adoniyram followed, suspecting that his uncle's fight for life had been more desperate than he implied. In addition to the facial gash and the limp, Ra-Anan's right hand was bruised and swollen, and he was moving cautiously.

Keeping his voice neutral, Adoniyram asked, "Are my cousins well?"

"Still sleeping." Ra-Anan was terse. "They were unhurt, but badly shocked. I'll acquire more guards to reassure them."

And to reassure yourself, Adoniyram decided, entering the main room. *You were badly shocked too, Master-Uncle. You thought you were unbeatable. But perhaps you were wrong. And so was I.*

"If you find any exceptional bowmen, remember, you've promised them to my household."

"We will see," Ra-Anan muttered, easing himself onto a heap of cushions.

Zeva'ah entered the main room now, perfectly robed, flaunting gold cuffs and a new red-beaded necklace hung with flat, gleaming gold leaves. She carried a copper tray laden with flat bread, dates, seared spiced fish, a fine gold plate, linens, and four gold cups—also new, Adoniyram decided. Obviously Ra-Anan had "accepted tributes" from tradesmen that were meant as offerings for the tower priests. No doubt tradesmen and priests alike were furious with Ra-Anan.

Zeva'ah set her tray on the woven mat beside her husband and cast a searching look at the gash on his face. He ignored her, reaching for a piece of the soft bread and some fish.

Ormah entered the room now, bearing two clay pitchers.

"Go wake the girls," Zeva'ah commanded as the maidservant set the pitchers beside her. "They can't sleep all day."

Ormah obeyed meekly but sneaked a smiling glance at Adoniyram before leaving the room. He averted his gaze.

Ra-Anan ate in silence, but Zeva'ah maintained a trivial, sociable conversation with Adoniyram until Demamah and Shoshannah emerged from the curtained passageway. Both girls were barefoot and clad in simple linen gowns and robes. And both looked wonderfully drowsy and young without their usual face paints. They immediately bowed and knelt, worriedly peering at Ra-Anan. He frowned, causing them to straighten and focus on their morning meal.

"Your father is well," Zeva'ah told Demamah, smiling too brightly as she poured diluted wine into the gold cups and passed them around. "Thank the heavens and go about your work; last night was nothing."

You can't pretend your enemies are nothing, Adoniyram argued silently, undeceived by his aunt's smile. *Poor Dayag was only one of many.*

Demamah accepted her mother's verdict quietly, as

did Shoshannah. They shared Demamah's gold cup and picked at their food, downcast.

Adoniyram forced himself not to stare at Shoshannah —tempting as she was. Let Ra-Anan and Zeva'ah guess at his feelings toward her; he wouldn't confirm them openly. He knew full well that they used Shoshannah to lure him into their household, but he wasn't going to fall into whatever else they might be scheming. *I may use you instead.*

A commotion sounded from the courtyard: horses snorting, men calling to one another, servants running. Zeva'ah put down her gold cup and smoothed her robe. A guardsman rapped lightly at the wooden door frame, coughed apologetically, then bowed and announced, "Lord Kuwsh has arrived."

Ra-Anan quickly swallowed his entire cupful of watered wine, flashed a chilling glance at Adoniyram, and muttered, "No doubt your mother will be here soon also."

She will need to gloat, Adoniyram thought. Nodding politely, he said, "I'm sure you are right, Uncle."

To emphasize his less exalted status, and to put his enemies at ease, Adoniyram set his food aside and stood to greet Lord Kuwsh. Demamah and Shoshannah also stood, folding their hands before themselves and bowing as Kuwsh entered the main room.

Showily garbed in new linen robes, massive gold cuffs, and a gold collar, Kuwsh waved a dismissive hand. "Sit. Eat."

Adoniyram sat down without a word, watching and listening. Demamah and Shoshannah knelt, eyeing Kuwsh anxiously.

He ignored them but sat beside Ra-Anan. "You look remarkably well. My servants told me you were badly wounded."

Pouring himself a cup of undiluted wine—though it was not his custom to drink so much—Ra-Anan said, "Your servants are useless as spies; you should dismiss them."

"Perhaps I should. Obviously they exaggerated." Kuwsh studied Ra-Anan now, critical. "If that cut was the worst of your injuries, then you're fortunate. However, I'd advise you against going out before it's healed. That's a nasty slash."

"Yes, it would be a mistake to seem vulnerable," Ra-Anan replied, his tone acidic. "I've decided to forgo the temple ceremonies. I'll send offerings to the priests instead."

"The more the better." Kuwsh pointedly surveyed the new gold cups.

Ra-Anan gave him a sharp, forbidding look. Adoniyram bit down a smile and finished his drink.

"Will you have something to eat?" Zeva'ah asked Kuwsh gently, offering him the gold plate containing a bit of fish, some bread, and dates. Kuwsh accepted but only toyed with the food.

Another servant rapped humbly at the outer doorpost, stepped in, and bowed to Ra-Anan. "Master, the Lady Sharah is coming with her household."

Adoniyram wished his mother weren't so predictable. He offered his empty gold cup to Zeva'ah. "I'm finished, thank you, Aunt."

Zeva'ah smiled, but her eyes looked stony. She poured a bit of liquid into the cup, wiped it dry with some linen, then refilled it almost to the brim with straight wine for their drink-loving Queen of the Heavens.

"Trust her to arrive and create a scene," Kuwsh muttered.

Adoniyram seethed. How ridiculous of Kuwsh to accuse Sharah of creating a scene when he was enjoying Ra-Anan's misfortune just as much.

Soon enough Sharah swept into the room, haughty, fleshy, pale, and overladen with jewels and gold. To Adoniyram's disgust, her curls were unbound, and her linen robe swept the floor behind her. He greeted her with a dutiful kiss, then offered her his place and sat on a mat nearby.

"I see you're still alive," the Great Lady said to Ra-Anan sarcastically. She nodded to Kuwsh, then glanced at Demamah and Shoshannah, who stood and bowed. Scowling, Sharah waved a petulant hand. "Oh, if you must stay, then sit down!"

The girls sat.

Sharah accepted the wine from Zeva'ah and laughed at Ra-Anan, triumphant. "What a scar you'll have! See what happens when you make the citizens hate you?"

"Remember your own words, my sister," Ra-Anan warned, baring his teeth at her.

Sharah sniffed, pleased. "*That* won't happen to me, ever. The people adore me, and you know it. I'm like their own loving mother."

And unlike mine, Adoniyram retorted in his thoughts. He longed to escape now, to take refuge with Shoshannah and Demamah, to tease them and laugh with them, to listen to stories, and to persuade them to hunt with him as they hadn't done for weeks. Instead, he had to listen as his mother demanded Ra-Anan's account of the murder attempt for her own amusement.

While she listened, Sharah sipped from her cup and repeated self-righteously, "*That* won't happen to me; I haven't made enemies for myself the way you and Lord Kuwsh have done."

Adoniyram noticed Ra-Anan and Lord Kuwsh's offended scowls and wondered, as always, how his mother could be so deluded.

Shoshannah refrained from squirming in the presence of her elders. All the gold manners and pride in the world wouldn't make Lord Kuwsh, Lady Sharah, and the smoldering Master Ra-Anan and his Zeva'ah into wonderful people. She hated being bound to them. And yet, it would have been truly horrible if Ra-Anan had died last night.

She froze at the thought, staring down at the mats, suddenly realizing how close she had been to disaster. If Ra-Anan died, Zeva'ah would toss her out like rubbish. She might escape, but more likely someone else would claim her to fulfill a private scheme: Kuwsh. Sharah. Rab-Mawg. Or Adoniyram.

Sick to her stomach, she reminded herself that of the four, only Adoniyram hadn't expressed a wish to kill her. And although he had openly defended Rab-Mawg's claims toward Shoshannah, she feared that, given the chance, Adoniyram would make her his wife. He had indicated his desire toward her often enough. And marrying him would be another kind of death. She would have no hope of ever returning to her family. Or to Kaleb . . .

As Shoshannah stared at the mats, dazed, the Queen-of-the-Heavens Sharah raised her voice indignantly. "These are new cups! And that is a new necklace, Zeva'ah. Did you think you could hide them from me?"

"This is my home; I have nothing to hide," Zeva'ah said, an edge beneath her courtesy. "My beloved gave these to me the day before yesterday."

"You're jealous because they snatched them before you did," Kuwsh taunted Sharah.

Ra-Anan said, "Sharah, this is not your concern."

"Isn't it? I think you have taken what should be mine."

Shoshannah closed her eyes during the petty quarrel that followed, reminding herself to be grateful that Ra-Anan was alive.

Shoshannah heard Demamah stirring in her sleep, apparently disturbed. The attack on Ra-Anan had affected her badly. She wasn't eating and obviously she was sleeping poorly—as was Shoshannah.

I'll talk with her tomorrow, Shoshannah thought, bolstering her own lagging courage. *Her father is alive and we don't have to attend the ceremonies at the tower, which we've both been dreading.* Truly, there were mercies . . .

Turning her thoughts toward the Most High, as she hadn't for weeks, she wondered, *Are You here and guarding me after all?*

Wearing a leopard-skin robe formally clasped over his left shoulder, Rab-Mawg inspected the sparkling gold-covered altar. Fragrant wood, spices, and resins were all there, perfectly arranged, ready to be lit during the ceremony tonight after he had received the offerings. Satisfied, the young chief magician-priest relaxed, smiling to himself. Today, the highest day of Shemesh, was indeed a day to celebrate. For the first time, he would have the worshipful citizens to himself during the ceremony, unrestrained by the presence of Master Ra-Anan.

Furthermore, Ra-Anan had sent gifts to the temple to atone for his absence. Or, more accurately, he had returned some of the goods he had stolen earlier.

You survived, Rab-Mawg thought, regretful. *But if there was one attempt on your life, there may be another, and the next attack might succeed. Then I'd be free of you. Perhaps next year at this time, you'll be gone.* And then Shoshannah would fulfill her mother's vows.

I'm glad you are afraid of me Shoshannah, he thought. *Even if you don't trust in our Shemesh, or follow him, you will follow me.*

Now, contemplating the girl's near-disastrous lesson, Rab-Mawg frowned, troubled. The new mixture of herbs, seeds, and rhizomes had been more powerful than he had expected. Too powerful. He had gained no vision from the potion. Instead, he had lost his memory of that whole day and the next morning. Ghez-ar and the others had been alarmed and furious that he had endangered their places in this temple.

Next time I will be cautious. And there would be a next time. He was convinced that this new mixture, properly measured and balanced, would provide the euphoric appearances and understanding he sought from the heavens.

Ebed, Ghez-ar, and Awkawn emerged from behind the linen draperies. Rab-Mawg nodded and smiled, letting them see that his eyes were clear, that he was sober and ready for this all-important day. Mockingly, he said, "We should pray for our Master Ra-Anan's full recovery."

They all laughed together.

Fifteen

IN THE TWILIGHT, amid echoing canine yips from the surrounding grass slopes, Kaleb sat with Tiyrac and the others before the small evening fire. But he was uncomfortable, aware of Zekaryah staring at him.

At last Zekaryah spoke. "You're too perfect."

"That doesn't sound good," Kaleb muttered to Tiyrac beneath his breath. His concern heightened as Zekaryah half knelt behind Kaleb, grasped the thick horseman's plait that Kaleb had proudly worn for years, and began to slice it off with a flint blade.

Everyone but Echuwd and little Rakal groaned in loud protest. I'ma-Keren cried out, "Zekaryah, no!"

Don't argue, Kaleb warned himself, shutting his eyes hard. *It'll grow back. This is for Shoshannah . . . though she would laugh.*

Beside him, Tiyrac growled as Zekaryah gave his hair the same treatment.

"Don't bathe," Zekaryah instructed. "Hands and face only."

"What-what do you mean?" Tiyrac sputtered. "We'll get fleas!"

"Even better."

Resigning himself to misery, Kaleb mourned aloud, "We'll look and smell like animals."

"Good," Zekaryah said, brandishing their severed plaits at them.

Keren approached him now, holding out one demanding hand. "Give those plaits to me; their mother will want them."

I want mine, Kal thought. Curious, he glanced sideways at his brother's brutally chopped locks. "You look worse than I do."

Tiyrac snorted, then really stared at him and grinned. "Well, your whole head looks crooked."

"Crooked or not, it's still prettier than yours!"

Hearing this, the brawny Metiyl slapped his knees and bellowed and howled with his irrepressible laughter until they all joined him—relieving their tension with merriment.

When they could breathe again, Kaleb stood and circled around the fire to Father Shem. Kneeling before him, perfectly reverent now, Kaleb begged, "Pray for us, please. And for Shoshannah."

Shem smiled. Kaleb might be a scoundrel and unruly at times, but he trusted in the Most High with all his might—which was considerable. Thoroughly satisfied, Shem gripped Kal's shoulders and prayed for him. For Shoshannah. For them all.

At dawn Keren hugged her son-in-law tight, determined not to distress him with her tears—Kal was almost too tenderhearted. "You be safe!" she ordered, looking up at him severely. "Find Shoshannah and rejoin us as soon as you can."

Hugging her, almost crushing her in response, he said, "I'ma-Keren, please don't worry."

"But I will."

Turning to the big, self-conscious Tiyrac, Keren hugged him too. "You're like my own sons, you and your brother. Thank you for doing this."

"Perhaps the Most High will bless me," he mumbled, abashed yet hopeful, his green-brown eyes shining like Kaleb's. Obviously, despite his growling, Tiyrac was looking forward to this adventure as much as his brother.

"Remember your lessons," Zekaryah commanded them roughly. "Trust no one. And follow the river south."

"We'll remember; you have my word," Kal agreed, giving Zekaryah a solid, hard-fisted parting thump on the shoulder before going to mount the restless Khiysh.

Watching them leave, Keren swallowed her urge to cry. Joining her comfortingly, I'ma-Annah said, "We'll pray for them constantly. But, oh . . . their hair is so badly chopped—those poor boys! Zekaryah," she accused gently, "they look horrible."

"They'll live."

"I'm sure they will," Shem agreed, watching the two

adventurers ride over a small, grassy hill and out of sight. "But if they don't rejoin us within a reasonable time, I *will* go after them."

Recognizing her First Father's quiet, unshakable determination, Keren groaned to herself. Her distress increased when Metiyl agreed threateningly, "If so, then you'll take me with you. We'll see this Great City."

Weeks into their journey, riding a short distance behind Kaleb, Tiyrac complained, "You smell like rotten meat."

"Well, you're riding downwind," Kaleb reminded him.

"Let's not discuss *that!* The stew you made last night could purge the innards from a bear."

"The bears look and smell better right now." Kaleb sighed, exhausted, sweating beneath the warm late-summer sun. To their right, the great western river flowed so temptingly cool and swift that he could hardly resist flinging himself into the water. He craved a thorough scrub, a shave, and a good night's sleep. Not to mention a decent meal. Would this journey never end? "We've got to be nearing the city."

"Even so, let's camp for the night and try some fishing," Tiyrac suggested. "Then we should tend our gear."

As much as he hated to give up any daylight travel time, Kal had to agree with his brother. They needed to restring their bows and replenish their supply of arrows. And the horses were tired. Khiysh was becoming irritable, snapping at shrubs and grass and hinting broadly that he would toss Kaleb if they didn't stop soon. "You catch the fish, and I'll tend the gear," Kaleb offered—fishing was one of Tiyrac's favorite pastimes.

Tiyrac grinned. "Done."

Working swiftly, they dismounted, rubbed and covered their horses, then staked their lead ropes deep into the earth, allowing the weary creatures to graze without escaping. While the brothers were busy clearing an area for a small hearth, Khiysh huffed and issued a challenging, stomping snort. Kaleb straightened and turned to see the target of Khiysh's threats.

Horsemen. Five of them. Tiyrac exhaled deeply, sounding worried. "Too late to escape them."

"We don't want to escape them," Kaleb reminded him.

"*You* don't."

"Do you have your knives?"

"Yes," Tiyrac snapped. "Do you have your brains?"

In better spirits now, Kal gave his brother a complimentary shove. "You're improving."

"Shut up and keep an eye on them."

"Yes, master."

The lead horseman was the biggest of the five, but size didn't matter; they were drawing their bows, aiming for Kaleb and Tiyrac. Kaleb was surprised by his own calm. He had never met any of these men, but thanks to Zekaryah, he understood them. He could almost hear Zekaryah warning, *Don't fight unless you must.* Tucking a thumb loosely into his belt, Kaleb watched them approach.

While the lead horseman and a fellow horseman held their arrows aimed at Kaleb and Tiyrac, the other three swiftly dropped to the ground. One hurriedly rummaged through the brothers' gear while the other two headed for their horses.

Immediately Khiysh reared and lunged, while Tiyrac's horse, Nashak, furiously bit toward the horsemen who had interrupted his grazing.

"I go with my horse," Kaleb told the lead horseman.

"If you fight us, you'll die!" the man snarled.

"I didn't say I would fight you," Kaleb pointed out, reasonable. "I said, 'I go with my horse,' that's all."

One horseman stopped rummaging through Tiyrac's gear and called out, "Ghid'ohn, look at these." He lifted Tiyrac's bow and quiver, his small brown eyes gazing fixedly, meaningfully at the lead horseman.

Suspicious, still wielding his own bow and arrow, Ghid'ohn asked Kaleb, "Who are you? Where did you get weapons and horses like these?"

"We grew up with these things," Tiyrac said in his deepest, most impressive rumbling voice.

"My first memory is of riding a horse," Kaleb agreed. "I've never been without one. Or without my weapons."

"You'll be without them for now," Ghid'ohn told him. "Kneel, both of you. Dibriy, Ye'uwsh, tie them both tight. Double the cords, then search them for weapons—they're coming with us."

"Well," Kal whispered to Tiyrac, elated, "that was easy!"

"Shut up."

Sixteen

"HERE! FROM YOUR MOTHER." Ormah scurried into Demamah's courtyard, dumped several skeins of plain wool onto the mat beside Demamah, and darted away again.

Shoshannah lowered her fringe work and stared after the maidservant, bemused. Ormah was rushing as if Zeva'ah were at her heels. "She's in a hurry."

"She has to finish her work before attending the festival this evening," Demamah explained, picking at the skeins of wool. "The young women of the city place offerings into the river to commemorate the death of . . . a young guardsman. After they've recited his story and mourned his fate, they light lamps, then dance and feast in the market street after dark."

"What young guardsman?" Shoshannah asked, her mother's stories rising uncomfortably in her memory.

Demamah fidgeted with the yarn, not looking up. "One of your mother's guardsmen, Lawkham. They say he loved her and she provoked him to anger the Great King so terribly that . . . he was put to death. His body was thrown into the river."

"And it was my I'ma's fault, of course," Shoshannah muttered, infuriated by this twisted version of her mother's past.

Her words soft, but bitter edged, Demamah agreed. "Of course. It could never have been the fault of our Great King."

Knowing that Demamah had no part in the awful stories told of the "Lady Keren," Shoshannah controlled herself and went on fringing the edge of the crimson-and-cream fabric. But resentment burned at her until she finally said, "It's amazing the people haven't killed me because of my mother."

"I'm sure most of them don't blame you or wish you harm. And we know the truth, you and I."

"Yes, but it's terrible when no one else wants to believe it." Shoshannah yanked fiercely at a knot of woolen fringe, uncomforted.

Finished with her evening meal, Shoshannah stared into nothingness, tracing and retracing the rim of a copper platter with her fingertips, frowning.

By now, surely, the women of the Great City were gathering, drinking and stirring themselves into an emotional state, mourning over a warped recital of Lawkham's death. The truth wouldn't matter to them; they would cling to their own story, further embellishing it beyond recognition. *It wasn't fair.*

Across from Shoshannah, Zeva'ah sighed, sounding exasperated. "Quit sulking, Shoshannah. You've ruined our whole meal with your bad mood."

Shoshannah looked up, startled. "Forgive me, Aunt. I was being thoughtless."

"On the contrary," Ra-Anan said smoothly, "you were thinking too much about something. What is it?"

Shoshannah hesitated. Her aunt and uncle stared. Lowering her head, she confessed, "I was thinking about this festival and . . . regretting its origin."

"Its origin is regrettable, but the whole thing is merely an excuse for crowds of foolish girls to play in the streets after dark," Ra-Anan told her. "Forget them. And forget that old story—as they've forgotten it."

"It's not just the girls who are foolish; Tabbakhaw is going too," Zeva'ah announced, disapproving. "You'd think she has no sense at all."

"You didn't forbid her?" Ra-Anan asked, turning to his wife, revealing the still-vivid, welted scar running down the left side of his face toward his throat.

Zeva'ah sniffed. "I thought of forbidding her, but she would have been in a temper for weeks, and our meals would have been tainted. However, I did tell her not to return with Ormah if they were sick from their drinking."

"You should have forbidden them to attend such absurd, childish revels; they represent our household," Ra-Anan said, his deep-set eyes narrowing, his mouth tight.

Zeva'ah tensed, visibly defensive, and Demamah plaited her fingers tightly together in her lap. Recognizing the signs of an impending quarrel, Shoshannah considered saying or doing something rude so she would be dismissed from the room.

A loud, insistent tapping on the main door interrupted both her thoughts and the looming spat.

Perek called out a rough greeting, then entered and bowed, his dark forehead furrowed with displeasure. "Master, forgive me. There's a crowd of marketplace women at the gate, demanding that *she* join them." The guard's leather-strung collection of animals' teeth and claws clattered alarmingly from his right bicep as he gestured to Shoshannah.

Aghast, Shoshannah squeaked, "Me?"

"Yes, you!" Perek snorted. "They're threatening to create trouble for our household unless you offer tribute to that young man who died for your mother's sake."

No. I can't. She glanced at her uncle, hoping that he would refuse, but Ra-Anan lifted an eyebrow, actually considering the idea.

"Please, Uncle, no," Shoshannah begged, trying to keep calm.

Beside her, Demamah leaned forward, distressed enough to actually speak. "Father, wouldn't they kill her?"

Ra-Anan leaned back, coldly reasoning aloud. "She'd be guarded. And those women from the marketplace command half the city's trade; they can't be ignored."

"They could make our lives miserable if they refuse to serve our household," Zeva'ah told Shoshannah, obviously glad to smooth over her quarrel with her husband by taking his part. "I'm sure you'd live, child."

I'm afraid I won't.

"Be sure they don't harm her, but don't upset their ritual," Ra-Anan told Perek, his decision apparently final.

Shoshannah listened, appalled. *They're handing me over*

so easily. She knew that arguing would only make matters worse.

Even Perek didn't dare resist, though the brawny guardsman looked stupefied, as if he couldn't believe that his master was commanding him to shepherd a flock of women.

"You can go outside as you are." Zeva'ah stood and motioned Shoshannah to her feet. "Just watch what you say and don't insult anyone."

"I wish you'd come with me, Aunt," Shoshannah said, challenging her cautiously. "I don't want to bring any disgrace on your household."

Demamah stood and looked from her mother to her father. "Please, let me go with her; I'll keep her out of trouble."

"Absolutely not!" Ra-Anan snapped. "You two will stay here, where you belong."

But obviously I don't belong here. "Forgive me, Uncle. Aunt." Shoshannah bowed to them formally, coldly. Almost shaking with rage and hurt, she stalked outside to the courtyard, which glowed crimson and violet in the sunset.

Perek followed her. As soon as they were far enough away from the main residence, he began to vent his fury. "You've been nothing but a problem from that first day—I should have killed you when I had the chance! Now this! Guarding a bunch of silly females . . ."

"Most men would be glad to change places with you," Shoshannah interrupted angrily as the guards opened the gate. "It's a good thing you're not married. Your poor wife!"

A wild chorus of feminine laughter greeted them, scaring Shoshannah. Hands gripped her wrists, her elbows, her gown, pulling her into the crowd of triumphant women.

"His poor wife!" one young matron echoed, laughing at Perek.

Shoshannah realized suddenly that she had said just the right thing; as awful and rude as it was, it pleased these riotous women. She also realized that she was now safer with them than with Perek. He looked as if he could spit fire.

"Off we go, Daughter of Keren," someone chanted singsong into Shoshannah's ear. "To the river!"

They're going to throw me in . . . and Perek won't rescue me.

Herdlike, they rushed Shoshannah away from Ra-Anan's household, laughing, exulting, forcing Perek to hurry after them toward the market street, where they were joined by other eager celebrants. Here and there men leaned out from doorways or stood in small groups, watching the "silly females" parade past. Embarrassed, Shoshannah tried to ignore them. But at the end of the market street, a familiar figure on horseback made her almost stop in her tracks. Adoniyram. With two guardsmen.

He acknowledged her with a barely noticeable nod, then gave his attention to the other unmarried girls in the crowd, smiling at them, admiring some of them openly, making them shriek and giggle.

You didn't warn me not to attend this *gathering,* Shoshannah thought to him, infuriated. He was apparently here to amuse himself. But perhaps he would intervene if she were threatened by these unruly women.

Some of the matrons and younger girls carried slender bone flutes, and they began to play these now, the melancholy notes rising in the air, subduing the gaiety of the celebrants. As they approached the dusk-washed river, the women hushed. Sighs, whispers, and a mournful, overwrought narrative threaded through the crowd.

"He loved her, forbidden, this young guardsman . . . but she scorned him . . . a mere guardsman . . . Still he remained devoted! For her he died . . . then she regretted what she had done . . ."

Listening to their recitation, Shoshannah stifled her disgust. These women made her mother sound cold, hard-hearted. *Like Sharah.* The celebrants were nudging her toward the riverbank. A matron, sturdy and determined, thrust an object into her arms: a large, oblong wooden container filled with aromatic spices, dried flowers, and an alarmingly lit taper, which would soon set the dish aflame. It was a boat, Shoshannah realized. An offering. "Set it in the river, Daughter of Keren."

Still seething, but knowing she had to obey, Shoshannah went down to the water and waded in, gasping quietly at its coldness and at the thick silt oozing upward into her sandals. Zeva'ah would be furious if the sandals were ruined. Feeling the current pulling at her garments, Shoshannah lowered the now-kindled offering into the water, praying she wouldn't set her hair afire. The craft flared spectacularly, its glow reflected in the dark current that was drawing it away downstream.

Other women set their offerings adrift behind Shoshannah's, keening in ritualized wails. Shoshannah watched the fiery boats and listened to the wails, suddenly mesmerized, feeling as if her mother's story had come alive before her eyes.

My mother stood in this mire. Somewhere nearby, she and Zekaryah had pulled Lawkham from the river and mourned with her attendants. They had carried Lawkham's body through the streets of the Great City to his grieving family. *I'ma, how awful that must have been for you, and for Father.* She ached to think of them, and of the young Lawkham and his family. Lawkham had been a bit older than Kal . . .

Whispers arose behind Shoshannah now, tiny exclamations of horrified delight. Curious, Shoshannah turned. Three women stood at the river's edge, separate from the crowd, two holding flaring torches, another, tiny and pretty, hugging herself vulnerably. I'ma-Meherah.

Amazed, Shoshannah waded out of the river, rushing toward her adoptive grandmother, who held out her arms.

"Shoshannah-child . . ."

As the women behind them crowded nearer, Shoshannah hugged Meherah and kissed her, gladdened and grieved. "I was just thinking of you . . . of your whole family."

"Here I am, child," Meherah said fondly, as if they had been together from Shoshannah's infancy. "And I won't leave your side until you're safe again."

Surprised, Shoshannah pulled back, studying Meherah's tender, bright-eyed face. "Who told you I was here?"

"The Young Lord's guardsmen. And my own daughters. They heard rumors in the streets today—so I would have come no matter what. Though I usually don't."

For Shoshannah alone, Meherah whispered, "They don't mourn my son; they offer tributes to someone they've imagined." Raising her voice, Meherah said, "These are two of your own aunts, Hadarah and Chayeh."

"You look so much like your mother," Hadarah sighed, holding her torch safely out of range as they embraced in greeting.

From behind them a woman cried, "Meherah, come away from the water!"

"Peletah, you timid thing," Meherah scolded her loudly, warmly. "Come meet my Shoshannah-child!"

Feeling safer now, Shoshannah followed Meherah up the riverbank, where the robust Peletah and the other women crowded around them, chattering, obviously enjoying the scene tremendously. They reentered the Great City together, singing, laughing. The merchant wives offered Shoshannah honey cakes, spiced meats, drinks, and fruits. And they taught her the tiny gliding-skipping steps of their dances, lit by countless lamps, tapers, and torches.

Forcing down her resentment at the lies they had recited about her mother, Shoshannah danced, smiled, and talked with the women and girls of the city. But she deliberately ignored Perek, Adoniyram, and his guardsmen, who watched her from the shadows.

Adoniyram secretly admired Shoshannah as she danced. She was lovely and delightfully unassuming, winning the affections of the city's matrons and daughters as he'd hoped. They would honor her because of this night. *That will infuriate my mother. And antagonize our Lord Kuwsh . . .* It would also provoke the increasingly unstable Rab-Mawg to insist that Shoshannah must fulfill her mother's vows. Unfortunately, it would also help Ra-Anan's popularity, for he was sheltering the girl, and he had presumably allowed her to come here tonight. *But I will find some way to deal with you, Master-Uncle, as I have dealt with the others . . .*

It had been so easy to subtly encourage his own unwitting gossip-loving servants to spread this thought in the market street: that Shoshannah should join these women tonight. The risk to Shoshannah had been worth the result. *Beloved,* he thought, eyeing Shoshannah from beneath his lashes, *we will win.*

"Aw, what a stench! I say we should scrub them first!" the guardsman Ye'uwsh complained, his scraggly, squared brown face contorted, grimacing as he tightened the ropes around Kaleb's and Tiyrac's wrists. "They'll kill half the city."

Kaleb scoffed amiably, though he secretly hoped Ye'uwsh's complaints would persuade the others—a ducking in the river sounded like bliss. "Are you going to scrub me, Ye'uwsh? Hey, maybe you can pick the bugs from my hair!"

"No," Ghid'ohn said, half grinning at Kal's taunt, "we'll lead them into the Great City, stinking to the heavens like the animals they are. As for the rest of you, shave and clean yourselves. We don't want anyone to say that we look like these two."

While Kaleb tried to ignore the torment of clean water so close by, Tiyrac growled beneath his breath, writhing miserably, chafing at the cords that bound them. "I itch! Augh! You owe me for this, Kal."

"I know. But at least we'll have everyone's attention—and that's what we want."

"Anything, if it'll get me a bath!"

"I hope Shoshannah won't see me this way."

"I hope she does."

"What are you going to do with them?" Dibriy asked Ghid'ohn, prying for information as usual.

Not trusting the sinewy, nosy Dibriy for an instant, Ghid'ohn said brusquely, "I'll do exactly what I was commanded to do. Now go scrub and shave."

Whom do you serve? Ghid'ohn wondered. *Master Ra-Anan? Lord Kuwsh? Our Queen of the Heavens, or the Young Lord?* Whoever it was, Dibriy would spill all the information he had gathered. Therefore, Ghid'ohn was determined that there wouldn't be much to spill, except for the knowledge of these two stinking monsters they had dragged in from the steppes. Ghid'ohn wished he could trade these two mountain dwellers to the highest bidder. *I'd be rich.*

Yawning, Shoshannah sat with Demamah just inside the cool, dim house, wearily picking through heaps of dried lentils and peas. "I wish I could have a nap."

"You'll sleep well tonight," Demamah comforted her. "But that's the last time Mother lets you out for a festival. She's upset that you returned without your sandals."

"I had blisters from dancing; my feet hurt so badly that I removed the sandals. My Aunt Hadarah promised to hold them. Or maybe it was Aunt Chayeh; I don't remember. I should have tied them to my sash."

"Mm-hmm, that's true," Demamah agreed. Smiling, she cast a sidelong look into the sunlit courtyard, watching Ra-Anan, who was listening to the architects present their ideas for the final stages of their grand tower. "At least Father was pleased with you."

Yes, but that will encourage him to hand me over to the next rowdy gathering. And then I might not return safely. Reluctantly, Shoshannah considered thanking Adoniyram for his apparent protection last night. But something about his conduct during the festivities had unsettled her—and it wasn't just his blatant flirting with all those young girls. He had been so calm and unsurprised to see her amid the crowd . . .

Zeva'ah entered the main room now, smiling, the fringed crimson-and-cream wool garment in her arms. "I should still be angry about your sandals, Shoshannah, but you and Demamah did such fine work on this fabric that I find myself excusing you."

"Thank you, Aunt," Shoshannah murmured, picking through the lentils. She was going to hear about the sandals for months if they weren't returned, she was sure. *Please, Hadarah, or Chayeh, don't forget to return them!*

"And," Zeva'ah continued, "you impressed the women of the city; they're sending little gifts to you. Food mostly, which I've sent to Tabbakhaw in the kitchen. So, obviously—despite your objections—you enjoyed yourself after all."

"Once I knew I would survive," Shoshannah replied, in what she hoped was a teasing tone. *Once I'ma-Meherah was with me . . . yes, then I had fun. I was with some of my own family again.*

Zeva'ah clearly resented Shoshannah's teasing. Throwing her a sharp look, she smoothed the fabric in her arms and changed the subject. "The next garment you make should match this; I'll arrange for more crimson. But you should make it of even finer thread."

There was a brief commotion at the gate as Perek and some guardsmen streamed inside, bowed, and knelt, waiting for Ra-Anan to finish his meeting. Shoshannah looked away, uninterested. Ra-Anan's dealings with his guardsmen were usually dull and dominated by her uncle's own unchallenged commands.

She continued her sorting, listening to her aunt's preferences in threads and colors, while stifling the impulse to yawn again.

Then Demamah gasped, "Oh! Look at those two coming in now—they're at least as big as Perek!"

"And *filthy*," Zeva'ah said, shocked, moving closer to the door to stare at the two men who had offended her. "Surely they aren't being considered as guardsmen."

Shoshannah glanced at the two men, then gaped, clutching handfuls of dried lentils. The bound, grimy, thick-bearded, skin-crawlingly unkempt man now kneeling before Ra-Anan was Tiyrac—dear, grumbling, mush-hearted Tiyrac! And just beyond him, hands also bound, was . . . *Kal.*

She almost said his name aloud. But the word stopped in her throat, she was so badly shocked. They were here. Kal was here. And scruffy, with an oily, hacked, uncombed mane. How could this be her usually tidy, almost-vain-of-his-hair Kaleb? *What's happened to you?*

Think! She scolded herself, rubbing the lentils from her sweating palms. *Kal and Tiyrac would never willingly go anywhere looking so awful, not even to a waste pit.* She studied her beloved and his brother again, touched and tortured by their captivity. *You've done this on purpose. For me. I wish you hadn't, but I am so glad to see you!*

She was grateful that Zeva'ah and Demamah were so fascinated by the two filthy apparitions in their courtyard that they were ignoring her completely. While they stared, Shoshannah calmed herself, listening hard.

"You are brothers," Ra-Anan said, arrogant, looking as if he smelled something putrid. "Move back, then tell me your names."

Tiyrac scooted backward on his knees, then answered unwillingly, "Tiyrac."

"And I am Kaleb, the younger," Kal said, his sociable voice at odds with his loathsome appearance.

"What tribe are you from?"

"We've been disowned," Kaleb answered, still pleasant. "We have no tribe."

Ra-Anan frowned. "Why?"

"Fighting. Too many complaints about our behavior."

"At least they simply disowned you," Ra-Anan said pointedly. "Here, we are not so merciful if you break the rules. You have no wives?"

"No," Tiyrac said, abrupt.

Kaleb shrugged, wonderfully casual. "My beloved is somewhere; I think her family is hiding her from me."

Hearing this, Shoshannah nearly choked—delighted that he was able to enjoy himself, filth and all. Ra-Anan eyed Kaleb darkly. "You need not concern yourself with her now; you will both be in my service until I dismiss you."

"Your men have my horse," Kaleb said. "I go with him."

"Shut up about your horse," Tiyrac growled. Facing Ra-Anan, he demanded, "What if we want to leave?"

"You won't be leaving."

"Meaning you'll keep us here against our will?"

"You'll prefer to stay. If you don't, we send others to find you. And if we find you, then you'll both suffer," Ra-Anan informed them, looking aggravated. He was also recoiling slightly, his thin nostrils twitching.

A persistent outcry from the street stopped the interrogation. A lean, dignified guardsman opened the gate, spoke to an unseen person outside, accepted something, then shut the gate again. His dignity fading, the guardsman dangled Shoshannah's just-returned sandals from his fingertips, obviously not knowing what to do with them.

"*There* are your sandals," Zeva'ah sniffed to Shoshannah. "Go get them, then come right back."

"Yes, Aunt." Nervously Shoshannah stepped forward, bowed politely to her uncle, and accepted her sandals from the discomfited guardsman, thanking him. She was aware of Kaleb's presence the whole time. When she dared to glance at him, she saw that he and Tiyrac were openmouthed, frankly scandalized by her one-shouldered linen gown. But then Kal's eyes gleamed suddenly, clearly plotting mischief.

"Do you always let your women walk around half naked?" he asked Ra-Anan, sounding completely amazed and naïve.

He was pretending, Shoshannah knew, but he still made her flush self-consciously. She wanted to throw her sandals at him.

Ra-Anan stared at Kaleb for a long instant, then sneered and spoke to the other guardsmen. "Be sure these animals are clean, properly clothed, and *polite* before presenting them to me again. Get them out of here."

The guardsmen all grimaced and turned their faces as they hauled Kal and Tiyrac away, shoving them roughly. Shoshannah knew that if either brother did anything wrong, he'd be punished severely. Perhaps killed. *Behave!* she begged Kal silently. To the Most High, she prayed, *Be with them, please . . .*

She strained as much as she dared to watch them departing through the gate. There was no mistaking Kaleb's jaunty walk; he was enjoying himself and planning more mischief. Trembling, heartsick, Shoshannah went back to sorting the lentils.

Zeva'ah turned away from the door, indignant. "Half naked indeed!"

~~

"Did you *see* her?" Kaleb hissed to Tiyrac, still awestruck by his unexpected glimpse of Shoshannah.

"I saw her," Tiyrac muttered. "And it was enough. Control yourself."

"No wonder your beloved is gone," Ghid'ohn told Kaleb grimly. "You probably insulted her every time you opened your mouth. Now you're going to have a bath."

"A what?" Kaleb asked, pretending ignorance again, making Tiyrac glare at him.

"A bath," Ye'uwsh said, shoving him forward. "Something you've never had before. The nearest mud puddle will improve you, I'm sure."

Vastly relieved, Kaleb sighed. This day had proven better than he'd dared to hope. Despite the shock of her face paints and bare shoulder and arms, Shoshannah looked perfectly beautiful and well cared for. And she had seemed concerned; her heart was unchanged toward him. Elated, he blessed the Most High.

He decided to quarrel—just a little—about having a bath.

Seventeen

"YOU—KALEB—LOOK," the guardsman-turned-stablehand Dibriy complained. "You've missed a pile. Clean it up!"

I haven't reached that stall yet, Kal answered silently, scooping the manure. *If you hadn't been slapping your lips together all morning, you would have noticed that I've been working in a pattern.*

Kaleb worked for Dibriy and the other guardsmen as he had always worked for Zekaryah: willingly, remembering that by proving himself trustworthy with small, unpleasant tasks, he would eventually be granted more agreeable responsibilities. His goal was to guard Shoshannah. Or at least to tend her horse officially. He had already found Ma'khole, who was too fat now but otherwise healthy. The little mare had recognized Kaleb, bumping him in greeting; Shoshannah would be pleased. If only he could tell her.

Perhaps today I'll see her. This hope—and the alluring memory of her in that new gown—made captivity bearable. But he had been watching for days without seeing her, much less speaking to her. And there were other problems. He wasn't allowed to talk with Tiyrac, and he was separated from Khiysh.

Most High, he thought, trying not to complain, *let me see a way to get out of this Great City alive with Shoshannah and Tiyrac and the horses. There must be a way.*

As soon as Kaleb had finished spreading the stalls with fresh straw and grasses and filling the troughs with water, Dibriy commanded, "Weaponry. Now."

Weaponry. Grimacing, Kal retrieved his "weapon"—a blunted pole—from a corner of the stable. This was a toddler's weapon. And his weaponry instructor, that Perek, wasn't much more impressive. He was volatile and blindly devoted to their Master Ra-Anan. *So now we're going to dance around in the mud and I'll pretend to learn what I already know.*

"Do you think you're clever?" Perek sneered at the end of their "lesson," gouging Kal with a pole. "You couldn't defeat a dung heap!"

And I think you see me as a threat, Kaleb decided. *That's why you're harassing me constantly.* He reminded himself to be patient. For Shoshannah. Clenching his jaw, he endured Perek's taunts.

Perek stalked, swatted, prodded, mocked, and smacked at Kal the whole way to the gate of Ra-Anan's courtyard. Kaleb cast sidelong glances at Perek's shadow behind him as they walked, gauging Perek's movements, bracing himself for each blow.

Perek, you're a horse dropping.

He saw the shadow of the next strike coming and gritted his teeth; Perek jabbed his blunted pole into Kal's rump, making him yelp. Around them, all the guardsmen snickered. *Enough.*

Judging Perek's position, Kaleb pivoted, ducked, and slammed an end of his own weapon into Perek's groin. Perek dropped onto the damp street, screeching horribly. The other guardsmen froze. Seeing their shock, Kaleb said, "I didn't intend to hit him quite *that* low. Perhaps he doesn't want children."

As a crowd of citizens gathered to stare and laugh, the other guardsmen hastily grabbed the anguished Perek by his arms, dragging him inside the gate, where they were supposed to present themselves to their Master Ra-Anan. Kaleb followed, trying to guess what sort of punishment the master might inflict upon him.

Ra-Anan emerged from his residence, studied Perek's curled-up form on the courtyard pavings, and frowned. "Who did this?"

Bowing politely as he'd been taught, Kaleb knelt. "I did, Master Ra-Anan—in self-defense."

Perek managed to pull himself upright, shaking his head in denial, rasping thinly, "An . . . unprovoked attack!"

When no one else denied this lie, Kaleb thought, *So, I get blamed.*

Master Ra-Anan's deep-set hooded eyes narrowed, almost closing. "My men *never* strike one another. You are undisciplined and rebellious."

"Perek attacked me first," Kal explained. "The others are afraid to tell the truth. Perhaps you should question them in secret."

Dangerously quiet, Master Ra-Anan asked, "Do I take orders from you?"

"Never, my lord."

"Master."

"Master." Kaleb felt his punishment coming. "Do as you think best." *Wrong,* he realized as soon as he said the words. Again, he had told Ra-Anan what to do.

His thin lips curling, Master Ra-Anan stared at Kaleb ominously, while speaking to the other guardsmen. "Ghid'ohn, Dibriy, Ye'uwsh, escort him to the tower grounds. Hand him over to the commanders there. Tell them that if he causes trouble, they can entomb him inside a wall."

As they went out the courtyard gate, Kal told Ghid'ohn, "Don't worry; I won't fight you. You still have my horse."

Ghid'ohn shook his dark head, disgusted. "As your brother always says, 'Shut up!' If you can behave, I'm sure you'll be out of there in a few weeks."

A few weeks more of no Shoshannah. Kaleb sighed. *Most High, not that I'm complaining—I lost my temper—but did I truly deserve this?*

At nightfall, in the shadows of his own secluded courtyard, Adoniyram listened to his informant, the wiry, usually ineffective Dibriy. "He felled Perek, my lord! Right there in the street, as if he's been felling men Perek's size all his life."

"Is he a good bowman?" Adoniyram asked, pretending disinterest. "If he isn't, then I've no use for him."

"He had bows and arrows when we captured him," Dibriy said. "And he didn't look starved, so I'd say he's a good hunter."

"I suppose that's a start. Tell me about this man."

Under the watch of a weapon-laden guard, Kaleb stepped onto a dipping, swaying reed boat and lifted a coated basket of a dark, resinous substance onto his shoulder. Bracing himself, he climbed the canal bank and hauled the basket over to his fellow laborers, who were waiting with a pair of oxen that bore a load of the resin-filled baskets.

The two leathery, disgruntled workers, Qasheh and Zeh-abe, scowled when they saw him. "We're supposed to hurry, Kal," Zeh-abe complained. "The overseer is waiting, and I don't want to miss my evening ration."

"If we miss the rations, then you can have mine," Kal said mildly. To his amazement, Zeh-abe looked pleased. Kaleb decided not to enlighten him. He tied the basket onto the nearest ox, and Qasheh rapped the oxen forward with a staff as Zeh-abe led them from the canal bank.

"Forget missing the rations," Qasheh warned. "The overseer will have us beaten if we're too slow. Kaleb, now that I think of it, why don't you thrash the overseer? If you knocked Perek over, you could manage *him*."

Reaching up to steady the slime-laden baskets, Kal said, "I don't need any more trouble. I want to be done here as soon as possible."

"Do you think you'll be pardoned before us? We've been here in the mud and slime for almost a year."

Curious, Kaleb asked, "What did you do?"

"What everyone does," Qasheh answered belligerently. "We got drunk and wandered into the wrong house. When the owner confronted us, we realized our mistake and left. He went to Master Ra-Anan and accused us of beating him and stealing a cloak."

"And did you?" Kal doubted the surly man's story.

"*I* didn't steal anything," Zeh-abe said, indignant. "I don't even remember that night."

"That must be maddening," Kaleb soothed, adjusting his hold on the baskets, aware of their guard, who was drawing closer now, within earshot.

"It is maddening," Zeh-abe said. "I'm not guilty, but here I am, suffering for it. And I was beaten half to death by Perek too."

"Who hasn't been?" Qasheh snorted. "I hope you gave him a lifelong injury, Kaleb."

I hope I didn't. Kal resolved to work with someone else tomorrow.

Coerced by the impatient guard, they led the oxen thudding over the timber bridge toward the tower. Kaleb looked upward as they passed through the tower gate, still amazed that humans were building this brick-and-slime mountain. More amazing to Kal was that ordinary citizens apparently came to work on this structure freely, side by side with the less fortunate men who slaved here against their will. The citizens were proud of their tower, openly declaring that it was their way to heaven—as if they could force their way into the presence of the Most High, whom they refused to acknowledge.

This pile of bricks wouldn't help their lofty ambitions,

Kaleb knew. Nor would the Most High. *Aren't You angry with them?* Kal wondered, gazing upward at the clouding heavens. *I fear I'd be less patient than You, O Most High.*

"You!" An irritable, thick-bearded guard to Kaleb's right prodded him fiercely with the butt of a spear. "Get up those steps; you've been ordered there. Move!"

"Atop the tower?" Kaleb asked, startled, trying to bide for time to reason through this new difficulty.

"Yes! *Move!*" the bearded guard snapped, his brown eyes small and glaring. "He's been waiting long enough."

He who? Unwillingly, Kaleb mounted the steps. The bearded guard followed him, exasperated, pushing him along. As he climbed, Kaleb heard Zeh-abe proclaiming loudly, "I get his ration! He gave it to me . . ."

Work would be interesting tomorrow on an empty belly, Kaleb decided. Praying to face this unexpected situation with dignity, he calmed himself and looked around. The higher he climbed, the more Kaleb appreciated the view from the tower. A light breeze skimmed his face. If he closed his eyes, he could almost imagine that he was on a mountainside, free again. But he didn't dare stop and close his eyes—the guard wouldn't put up with it.

At the top of the unending stairs, a voice greeted them, amused but cool and watchful. "No doubt this is the one."

To his left Kaleb saw a dark-curled, polished young man near his own age, clothed in a plain wool tunic, a broad crimson belt, and thickly-laced boots. If this young man had not been giving him such a critical, hard-eyed look, Kaleb would have dismissed him as a vain and spoiled city boy. *He has power here,* Kal decided, and bowed as he'd been taught.

The young man looked surprised, and he mocked Kal genially. "I was told, Kaleb, that you have no manners, and a stench to level the city—perhaps even this tower."

"I've learned about baths here," Kaleb answered, liking him, not bothering to suppress a grin. "But manners are a struggle."

"All the better." Leaning forward, the young man addressed the bearded guard politely. "Thank you for bringing this Kaleb to me. What's your name?"

"Dawkar, my lord," the guard said, bowing, ridiculously pleased.

"Dawkar," the Young Lord repeated, as if memorizing the name. "Thank you again. If he doesn't behave, I'll return him to you."

Bowing a second time at this courteous dismissal, the guard went down the tower steps, almost swaggering. Kaleb would have enjoyed the man's delusion of triumph, except that this young "lord" was watching him, judging him coolly.

Smiling, the polished youth said, "I'm Adoniyram. I hear you toppled the dreaded Perek."

"After Perek struck me too many times to count, my lord. I regret losing my temper." Kaleb was uneasy, realizing that this Adoniyram was Sharah's son. "Perek's going to be after my blood now, I'm sure."

"You might fare better with my men," Adoniyram said. "You're bigger than any of them; just don't pound on them too much."

"If they don't attack me, I won't touch them." Kaleb remained agreeable, but he wanted to argue. He didn't want to join this Adoniyram's household, which was removed from Ra-Anan's and, therefore, from Shoshannah.

But the Young Lord was already walking down the tower steps, talking as if the decision was made.

"I'm told you can hunt; that's good. My uncle, our Master Ra-Anan, has been promising to send me a bowman for some time. Since you've caused him enough trouble that he's tossed you here, I'll take you into my service. You'll find I'm not quite as demanding as my uncle, but I do expect to be obeyed." He paused, glancing back at Kal, hard and serious. "I also believe in punishing my men if they push me too far."

"I'll remember, my lord," Kaleb said, trying to remain hopeful.

"Have you eaten today?" Adoniyram asked. He sounded genuinely concerned.

"I gave my ration to someone else."

"You'll get another. You'll also have to follow me to my residence on foot. And my guards will accompany you so you won't 'lose your way.'"

Reluctantly, temporarily accepting his fate, Kaleb followed the Young Lord down the stairs, wondering at the unknowable will of the Most High.

"I still haven't forgiven Ra-Anan for letting *her* rule the women's festival," Sharah grumbled, settling into the most comfortable fleece-padded seat in Adoniyram's residence and looking around. "Really, Adoniyram, you need better furnishings. And why don't you have anything out here for me to drink?"

"Because I didn't know you were coming today, Mother," Adoniyram said, smiling, looking so much like his father that Sharah smiled in return.

She was so glad he was handsome—she would have detested an ugly son.

Lifting his eyebrows charmingly, Adoniyram added, "By the way, my uncle didn't willingly allow Shoshannah to 'rule' the women's festival; the women demanded that she attend. I'm sure he was furious."

"Don't even say her name in my presence!" Sharah snapped. "We've got to insist that Ra-Anan and Kuwsh get rid of her soon. My worst fear is that she's going to steal the citizens' affections, and yours too. She's untrustworthy—a little liar who wants to divide this Great City. I want you to stay away from her; do you hear me?"

"I hear you, Mother, truly. Now, if you'll forgive me the wait, I'll find something for you to drink." He went through a small doorway toward the kitchen.

Satisfied that drinks were forthcoming, Sharah smoothed her flowing curls and adjusted her linen robe. She toyed with her clever new serpentlike bracelet—pure gold with lovely little red-gemmed eyes, winding around her wrist marvelously. It made her arm look slimmer and finer, like ivory.

"Here," Adoniyram said, bringing in a cup and a small clay pitcher. He poured something into the cup and offered it to her with a gracious half bow.

Sharah wrinkled her nose, offended by the simple clay cup and its contents. "This is plain barley beer. Don't you have any wine?"

"I can't often afford trading for wine, Mother, but this beer isn't too bad. Now, what were you saying about Ra-Anan?"

"I was actually talking about the girl; you need to persuade Kuwsh and Ra-Anan to get rid of her. If her family merely *believes* that she's here, it's enough to draw them into the city. She doesn't have to be alive for Kuwsh to get his revenge."

Her son stared at her, shaking his head as if he were going to argue.

"Don't be stupid!" Sharah cried. "You know what a danger she is—and if it's a choice between letting her live or saving our places in this kingdom, then there's really no choice at all, now is there?"

"Give me a little more time, Mother, please," Adoniyram said, half kneeling beside her, affectingly softspoken. "The more we disagree with them, the more Ra-Anan and Kuwsh will refuse your request."

More time? She had waited long enough already—the girl had to be dealt with. Sharah was almost ready to take matters into her own hands. But before she could say so, Adoniyram changed the subject.

"Have you heard about the guardsman who defeated Perek? I have him here in my residence."

Diverted, Sharah took a sip of the beer, grimaced at its nasty taste, and put it down. "He actually defeated Perek?"

"Ask him for yourself." Once more, Adoniyram left her alone.

Restless, she stood, looking around his main room. It looked like a miserable merchant's home. Revolting. She was going to tell Adoniyram *now* that he must decorate his residence properly. Wasn't he the Son of Heaven? Her only child?

Not your only child, a tiny thought nagged.

The only one worth anything, Sharah argued silently, exasperated, pushing the strange, troublesome thought away.

Adoniyram reentered the room, grinned, and bowed to her teasingly as he extended one hand toward the doorway. An impressively tall, muscular, attractive young man entered the room and bowed. He was slightly paler than her Adoniyram, with gleaming black-brown hair smoothed back into the beginnings of a guardsman's plait. A truly good-looking young man.

She couldn't resist speaking to him. "I see now that you *could* have beaten Perek. Didn't he leave a bruise or scratch on you at all? Turn around, let me see you. Turn, turn!"

The young guardsman raised a surprised eyebrow, but he turned politely and then faced her again, studying her—admiring her, Sharah was certain.

"Well," she said, pleased, "do you speak at all, or do you only stare?"

Wide-eyed, he said, "You look so much like that girl in Master Ra-Anan's household; you could be her mother, though you're pale as a chunk of fat."

Sharah stared, trying to absorb this outlandish, unbelievable statement. *Pale as a chunk of* . . . "What?"

To her horror, he began to repeat blithely, "You look so much like that girl in our Master Ra-Anan's household; you could be her moth—"

"Out!" Adoniyram commanded, charging between them, waving the stupid man from the room. "Go back to the kitchen! You need to learn some manners!"

While Sharah was trying to gather her stunned, scattered thoughts, Adoniyram followed the uncouth guardsman out, staring until he was apparently gone from sight. Then, passing a hand over his face, Adoniyram returned to the main room.

"Mother, I'm sorry—I would never have believed he could be so rude."

"If he were in my household, I'd have him beaten!"

Sharah cried, trying to recover from the shock of his ignorant comparison. *As pale as . . .* She couldn't even finish the thought without cringing. The big fool had made her feel *old* and *ugly!* Unable to speak, she marched out of her son's residence, ignoring his apologies.

"You said that on purpose, didn't you?"

Kneeling before Adoniyram in the main room, Kaleb lowered his head, still horrified. That overpainted Sharah-woman was remarkably similar to I'ma-Keren and Shoshannah in height and features, but terrifyingly proud and . . . *flirtatious.* He had been so frantic to be rid of her attention that he had said the first coherent thought to cross his mind. And the truth had stopped her as he'd hoped. Now, Adoniyram would certainly return him to the mud pits.

Relentless, Adoniyram persisted. "Admit it; you said that on purpose, didn't you?"

"Yes. Please forgive me. I've never been so scared of anyone in my life."

Unexpectedly, the Young Lord dropped into the fleece-draped seat and laughed, shaking his head. "You were scared? I've never seen anyone shock our Queen of the Heavens so badly—not even that girl you referred to. My Lady-Mother hates her enough to kill her. Remember that from now on, won't you? Also . . ." Adoniyram's voice hardened. "The girl you saw in Master Ra-Anan's household is nothing like my mother. Never compare them again."

Adoniyram passed a hand over his face as if trying to wipe away a grin. "I can't *believe* you said such a thing to my mother. Just stay out of her way when she's here, and you might live."

"Thank you, my lord." Kaleb sagged, relieved that he wasn't going to be returned to the slime. Until now, he hadn't realized how much he wanted to stay in Adoniyram's household. He would have a little more freedom here. And from what the servants had said, he would probably accompany Adoniyram everywhere as soon as he was "presentable"—including visits to Master Ra-Anan's household.

A blessing. Thank You, Most High! Just keep that Sharah away from me, I beg You.

While they finished their morning meal, Zeva'ah said, "Ormah is unwell." Zeva'ah sounded as if she blamed the maidservant for being female and needing her monthly days of seclusion. "Demamah, you'll have to go with Shoshannah to her lessons today."

"Yes, Mother," Demamah replied dutifully. But while they were preparing to leave, Shoshannah heard her sigh, apparently dreading a morning in the presence of the unpredictable Rab-Mawg.

As they went out into the sunshine to their horses, Demamah tugged at Shoshannah's arm. "That's one of those awful brothers."

Shoshannah looked, almost smiling when she saw Tiyrac, clean, mannerly, and looming beside Demamah's horse. Before she could say anything, Demamah whispered, "Look at the red in his hair!"

"His coloring *is* different from the others, isn't it?" Studying the fiery tinge in Tiyrac's dark, sunlit hair,

Shoshannah realized for the first time how odd he must appear to Demamah. Shoshannah had never considered his coloring or size to be unusual; all the men in the Tribe of Ashkenaz were tall, red brown, and burly. Unable to resist teasing her cousin, she asked, "Do you suppose he's a brute like Perek?"

"I hope not," Demamah whispered, alarmed. "I think he's going to tend my horse today."

"I'll pray for you . . ."

Obviously scared, Demamah approached her horse and looked up at Tiyrac.

He hesitated, bowed, and linked his hands, offering her a foothold to mount her horse—as neat and careful as any other guardsman. But he seemed distressed when he turned away from Demamah. And he stole a quizzical look at Shoshannah.

She stifled a laugh.

"Daughter of Keren," Perek growled at her, "quit staring at *that* one! Come here."

Shoshannah obeyed meekly, not wanting Perek to become suspicious. And she was worried because Perek seemed to consider Tiyrac to be an enemy. *Please don't let him make trouble for Tiyrac,* she prayed fervently. *And let me see Kal soon.*

No one had mentioned Kaleb since he struck down Perek and was taken to serve in Adoniyram's household. But Ra-Anan was furious. And Shoshannah had been too upset over Kal's punishment to rejoice over his victory against the guardsman. She was desperate to know that he was well. *Tiyrac must also be concerned . . .*

She watched Tiyrac furtively as he bounded onto his own dark horse, prepared to follow Demamah on their excursion to the tower. As they rode north on the market street, another procession of horses rode toward them, heading south: Adoniyram's household, apparently returning from an early hunt.

Shoshannah was worried when Ra-Anan greeted Adoniyram with a rude nod. But Adoniyram spoke to him courteously, seeming pleased with a successful hunt; his guardsmen were hauling a brace of netted, wrung ducks and, wonderfully, a fine lion's corpse. Adoniyram smiled at her secretively as he rode past. And behind Adoniyram, riding a weary brown horse, was Kal.

She gave him a cautious hint of a smile, then tossed her head and sniffed, loudly repeating Zeva'ah's indignant complaint. "Half naked indeed!"

Kaleb's eyes sparkled as he rode past.

Perek, riding his own horse just behind Shoshannah, growled a wordless threat. Shoshannah held her breath fearfully, but Kal said nothing. The danger passed in an instant, departing with Adoniyram's triumphant household.

Relaxing, Shoshannah exulted inwardly, *He's safe! He's well!* She wanted nothing more than to escape with him. And Tiyrac, of course. She tried to think of a plan.

Adoniyram turned to look at his new guardsman as they rode out of the market street. "What did she mean, 'half naked'?"

Grimacing wryly, Kaleb hung his head. "The women of my tribe don't bare their shoulders. So, when I saw first saw her in our Master Ra-Anan's courtyard, I was shocked. I asked the Master if he always lets his women run around half naked."

Agreeably shocked himself, Adoniyram laughed out loud, making all his guardsmen crane their necks and lean forward. Dibriy had left this little bit of gossip out of his story about Kaleb, apparently considering it too dangerous to repeat. "You said that to him? In front of her? I don't believe you!"

Adoniyram could just imagine Shoshannah's face when she'd heard Kaleb's idiotic remark. "I'm amazed you're still alive. You're going to apologize to them." Grinning at Kaleb's confounded expression, Adoniyram said, "We'll both apologize and give my uncle that lion's hide. Though I don't know what sort of gift I could send *her.*"

"I'd think an apology would be enough, my lord," the big man grumbled amiably.

"You're a lout." Adoniyram liked his new guardsman better all the time.

Kaleb wondered why Adoniyram hadn't insisted that he must also apologize to the Lady Sharah. Odd. Had the Young Lord wanted his own mother to be insulted? *You are a strange bird,* he told Adoniyram silently. *But so is your mother.*

Eighteen

"YOU'VE RUINED MORE apparel in one year than I have in five," Demamah chided softly, examining Shoshannah's broken sandal strap as they sat in her courtyard.

Shoshannah winced at the comparison. And at the burning of the caustic salt-ash-fat ointment she was dabbing on her raw big toe. "I couldn't help tripping."

"You shouldn't have been running. Mother's not going to be happy."

"I'll mend the sandal somehow—though I'd prefer new boots. I could make them myself if I just had a swatch of good leather."

Practical as always, Demamah pointed out, "Good leather will cost us a measure of barley."

"Forget the boots then, though they'd cover my injury. I'm going to lose my toenail."

"It will grow back."

"Eventually." While she let the ointment seep into her wound, Shoshannah gazed morbidly at the stump of the once-beautiful tree in the courtyard. *It was my best chance for escape. If I had waited until Kaleb and Tiyrac were here, we would have succeeded. Why couldn't I have controlled my fear? Most High, why am I always so foolish?* Zeva'ah entered the tiny courtyard now, brisk and so flawless that Shoshannah's spirits sank even further. Didn't her aunt ever have an untidy day? Wasn't her hair ever messy?

Zeva'ah frowned. "Why are you two sitting here doing nothing? I came to tell you that Tabbakhaw will need your help; we're expecting company tonight." Suspicious, she stared down at Shoshannah. "What have you done now? *Look* at your sandal."

Humbled, Shoshannah said, "I'm sorry, Aunt—I'll mend it. I tripped."

"You won't be able to make it look right again," her aunt snapped. "But I suppose Adoniyram and our Lord Kuwsh won't be surprised; you always look rumpled."

Adoniyram, Shoshannah thought, her gloom lifting. *Perhaps Kaleb will attend him!*

"Will the Lady Sharah and the Lady Achlai also visit?" Demamah asked, wrinkling her forehead in apparent concern.

"The Lady Sharah, no—thank the heavens. It seems she's pouting for some reason." Zeva'ah sighed. "But the Lady Achlai . . . perhaps. And that filthy guardsman will apologize for offending us, as he should have done weeks ago, before Adoniyram stole him. Adoniyram, too, will apologize for his rudeness." Zeva'ah's lovely features smoothed graciously now, as if she were already practicing the perfect look of forgiveness in her mind.

Secretly thankful for the warning that she would see Kal tonight, Shoshannah wrapped her injured toe in a strip of linen, then stood, bowing politely to Zeva'ah. "I'll go help Tabbakhaw, Aunt."

"Don't cause trouble," Zeva'ah warned. "I don't want any scenes in the kitchen today."

"I'll watch her, Mother," Demamah promised, joining Shoshannah.

Zeva'ah flashed her daughter a skeptical look. "As you always 'watch' her while she creates turmoil?"

"Forgive me." Demamah bowed, seeming to accept this criticism. But as they hurried toward the kitchen, she became indignant, whispering to Shoshannah, "Why does Mother say such things? As if you intend to create trouble—you don't! And she shouldn't insult Adoniyram's new guardsman—if he's like his brother, then she's misjudged him terribly."

"And I say she shouldn't complain about you," Shoshannah agreed softly, hobbling, deciding it was safer to ignore the subject of Kal and Tiyrac. Though she was amazed to hear Demamah say anything for Tiyrac and against her mother. *Will she ever rebel against her parents completely?* Shoshannah couldn't imagine such a thing.

"I regret insulting you and your household; I beg your forgiveness," Kaleb said, bowing to Master Ra-Anan and his beautiful, formidable wife, while he recited his brief speech—as instructed by Adoniyram.

As Adoniyram had predicted, Master Ra-Anan accepted Kal's apology with a nod, as did his proud wife. Then Adoniyram waved Kal—a mere guardsman—quietly out of Master Ra-Anan's impressive main room. Dejected, Kaleb bowed and parted. It was pure torment to leave his Shoshannah inside with those disturbing people. She seemed so isolated and defenseless that Kaleb longed to snatch her and run away.

His misery eased as he stepped into the courtyard and saw a large, familiar shadow waiting for him. "Tiyrac! You're loose?"

"For now." Pounding Kaleb's back in a rough welcome, Tiyrac said, "Let's get to the stable before Perek finds you—he's eating in the kitchen."

After nodding courteously to the guard as they strode through the gate, Tiyrac became grim. "As soon as you were sent to the tower, they brought Khiysh into the stable for Master Ra-Anan."

"So Ra-Anan will use him?"

"If he can."

"I pray they don't kill each other," Kaleb muttered.

"The guardsmen are betting on Khiysh against the Master."

"I doubt that's a good thing."

They hurried through the dusk into the stable. To Kal's surprise, Ghid'ohn was there with Ye'uwsh, and a number of the stable hands. They shouted approvingly when they saw him, and Ye'uwsh yelled, "You're still clean! I thought we'd have to douse you again."

"Good to see you're alive," Ghid'ohn grunted. "Sit. Eat with us."

"We owe you at least a meal." Ye'uwsh's black eyes glittered. "Perek hasn't lifted a hand to anyone since you beat him!"

The others laughed and applauded in agreement. They pushed Kaleb into the seat of honor—a hay bale—

and shoved food and drinks at him. They mockingly reintroduced him to Khiysh and then told him all the gossip from Ra-Anan's household.

Kaleb listened to every scrap of talk about Shoshannah but volunteered no news from Adoniyram's household. They didn't notice his unaccustomed silence—they were simply pleased to see him again.

I'm being honored for misbehaving, Kal thought, smiling. *Well, that's a change.* It was small comfort while being separated from Shoshannah.

"Your parents should have been here by now to rescue you," Lord Kuwsh grumbled to Shoshannah as they waited for their meal to be brought from the kitchen. "Do you think they're glad to be rid of you after all?"

"Perhaps, my lord." Shoshannah acknowledged Lord Kuwsh politely, then lowered her eyes. But not before his wife, the Lady Achlai, gave Shoshannah a sad, apologetic smile.

You hate this situation, Shoshannah thought to the unhappy Achlai. *I thank you for wanting to protect me—though you can't.*

"She continues her lessons?" Kuwsh asked Ra-Anan, looking irritable.

"She is learning of our city. And of manners. You must admit she behaves better than before."

When Kuwsh agreed with a reluctant shrug of approval, Ra-Anan continued, "My priests have formally requested that she be trained for the temple."

"I still say she shouldn't. Those priests are troublemakers as it is. They'll conspire against us to steal our power."

"My Lady-Mother fears the same thing." Adoniyram sounded measured, cautious. "Actually—and I am telling you this in confidence of your silence—she also believes you are managing the situation badly. She intends to have Shoshannah put to death if she gains too much favor among our people."

"Adoniyram!" Demamah gasped, staring at him until her father glared at her.

As Shoshannah listened, not entirely shocked, Lord Kuwsh bristled and spoke through clenched teeth. "Tell your mother, Adoniyram, that she does not rule here."

"Our niece is proving useful," Zeva'ah said defensively, to Shoshannah's surprise. "It's no benefit to anyone if she's put to death."

"Not yet," Ra-Anan corrected.

He made Shoshannah feel insignificant, and more certain than ever that her eventual fate meant nothing to him.

"The girl is innocent," Achlai said heavily, not looking at her husband. "To put her to death would be a crime, worse than what happened to my Nimr-Rada."

She defends me for Your sake, O Most High—protect her.

Lord Kuwsh was frowning at Achlai as if he wanted to strike her. "Don't think that you speak for me," he told his wife.

Gently, almost kindly, Achlai murmured, "I know I don't speak for you, my husband. I regret offending you."

An apology that was not an apology, Shoshannah decided. But Kuwsh would look foolish if he scolded his wife further.

Glowering, Kuwsh addressed Ra-Anan and Adoniyram in the tone of one who expected to be obeyed. "I don't seek the girl's death unless it's necessary; her mother is the traitor who should die. But—again—I do *not* want her in that temple, receiving offerings from the people. Such a visible presence in this kingdom will give her too much power. As for your priests, Ra-Anan, you must control them. They were entirely too pleased and proud of themselves during the ceremonies of Shemesh."

"They were rejoicing," Ra-Anan said, fingering the livid scar on his jaw. "But they will be restrained." He threw Adoniyram a warning look. "You will say nothing to them on your next visit."

Adoniyram's full mouth curved in a self-mocking smile. "I doubt anyone would pay attention to me, Master-Uncle. I have no power here. Indeed, I feel like a mouse, trying to avoid being clawed by lions."

Kuwsh and Zeva'ah laughed at him, while Ra-Anan grimaced. Adoniyram looked sincere, but Shoshannah watched him, trying to decide his intentions. Adoniyram's behavior shifted continually, subtly. He had upset her so often that she couldn't trust him. Perhaps someday she would be able to ask Kaleb's opinion. But that might be hoping for too much. It would be dangerous. What excuse could she possibly make for speaking to an "unfamiliar" guardsman? Even so, it had been good to have a glimpse of him tonight. And he hadn't minded apologizing.

Her parents must certainly cherish her, Achlai thought, touched by Shoshannah's soft, worried expression when Kuwsh had been reprimanding Achlai. *She's a good, loving girl. I wonder why they haven't come to save her. Could they be planning something else?*

Perhaps one of the First Fathers would come to the

Great City and insist that the girl be returned to her parents. Perhaps Father Shem himself would come here. The idea was frightful. *I pray he doesn't!*

That went well, Adoniyram decided, watching everyone from beneath his lashes. Kaleb's apology had been accepted, as his own had been; therefore Kaleb would stay in his household, while Ra-Anan would have to be satisfied with commanding Kaleb's gloomy brother. The others were also warned of their Queen of the Heaven's threats against Shoshannah, and Adoniyram had been able to discern everyone's intentions by their reactions. His mother and Kuwsh did not want Shoshannah to take the infamous Lady Keren's role in the tower. But Ra-Anan, Rab-Mawg, and his priests did. There was going to be a struggle among them all. *Which I must win.*

Tabbakhaw appeared now, bearing a massive copper platter laden with two steaming, dark-skinned roasted ducks, decoratively nested in vegetables. Behind her, the maidservant Ormah proudly flourished the gold serving tray and cups and a large basket of aromatic bread. As everyone gave attention to the food, Adoniyram studied Shoshannah.

You behaved perfectly, Adoniyram thought. *Your manners are improving. And now that I'm welcomed in our Master Ra-Anan's household again, I will visit you often.*

He had missed her. For Shoshannah's sake he would not offend his uncle again. Acquiring Kaleb, however, had been worth the temporary banishment; he would be a perfect commander-guardsman. Eventually.

In the morning sunlight, Shoshannah walked up the tower stairs into the glittering temple, outwardly docile, her hands folded respectfully. Perek and Ormah followed her, already bored. Like Shoshannah, they longed for these lessons to end.

"Here, Lady," a voice beckoned from behind the altar. Ebed stood there, pole thin, freshly shaven, and smiling, wielding an ash-dusted gourd scoop. "Our Master Rab-Mawg is still asleep. You'll have to endure my company until he wakes."

"Why is he still sleeping?" Perek demanded, his voice echoing off the gold-adorned walls.

"I ask your patience." Ebed quietly thrust the scoop into the ashes on the altar, lifting out bits of charred bone and resins. "We offered sacrifices until late into the night for the sake of our Great City, our people, and the crops. Rab-Mawg was the last to sleep. Until he wakes, the Lady Shoshannah can stay here. There's much for her to learn in the temple."

"Don't call her 'the Lady,'" Perek ordered. "She has no title."

"As you say." Ebed nodded but continued to scoop up the remaining ashes.

Exhaling loudly through his flaring nostrils, Perek turned on his heel and stomped to the temple doorway. Ormah shied away from him, scooting toward Shoshannah.

Ebed glanced furtively after Perek, then smiled at Shoshannah, whispering, "There's much you haven't seen here, Lady. Let me wash my hands, and then I'll rejoin you both." He bowed and carried a copper tub of ashes behind the half-drawn linen curtains.

Curious, Shoshannah approached the gold-adorned altar. When the Ancient Noakh or Father Shem offered sacrifices, they offered them upon an altar of uncut rock, gathered from the surrounding land. No gold adorned the altar of the Most High, who had no need for any wealth. *But Shemesh must have his gold.* She studied the symbols embossed into the gold: stylized trees entwined with snakes, flowing waters teeming with fish, and odd *X*'s with their four ends half broken toward the right. As Shoshannah traced the signs, frowning, Ebed reappeared, followed by Awkawn and Ghez-ar.

"Is this also a symbol of your Shemesh?" Shoshannah asked, touching a bent *X*.

"Of course," Awkawn said, irritably. By now Shoshannah knew he rarely liked mornings.

But Ghez-ar's brown eyes lit up, and he came to explain the symbols to Shoshannah and to Ormah, who lurked at her elbow. "The right-bent angles denote the movement of our Shemesh through the skies, Lady. The streaming water signifies life, while the tree, of course, is knowledge, and the Serpent is wisdom."

Wisdom! Shoshannah scoffed inwardly. How could they honor the Adversary, the Serpent?

Oblivious of her scorn, Ghez-ar continued eagerly. "We seek all these things in the name of our Shemesh. And what better place to display these symbols than upon the sacrificial altar?"

"You sacrifice only animals?" she asked, remembering that Nimr-Rada had passed the body of his firstborn son through the fires of his Shemesh.

"Lambs and doves," Ebed answered gently, joining them now. "And in the sight of Shemesh, fire perfects what it consumes, as it perfects gold. What we sacrifice here is never considered lost."

Perhaps to you it's not lost, but my mother and my Aunt Revakhaw grieved horribly for Revakhaw's child, whom they lost to the fire of your Shemesh.

Still enthusiastic, Ghez-ar said, "Lady, I've wanted to ask: Have you ever seen the sun stones, which were possessed by the Ancient Ones? I was told by the elders of my tribe that they are unnatural stones, which glow in the darkness, like cold fire."

Shoshannah shook her head, bemused. "If our Ancient Ones have such things, I never saw them."

"They were probably afraid she'd ruin them," Awkawn observed tartly. "Why don't you show her Rab-Mawg's useless trick with sunlight, Ghez-ar? Since you're so enchanted with it."

"Awkawn, don't be so ready to give up on the idea. It won't be useless if we can correct the image somehow." Ghez-ar disappeared behind a linen curtain and reemerged with a concave metal dish, more brilliantly worked and polished than an obsidian mirror. Nodding to Ormah, he said, "Please, if you could stand just outside the doorway in the sunlight."

"Near Perek?" the maidservant asked, looking uneasy.

"Only for an instant," Ghez-ar encouraged her.

While Ormah obeyed reluctantly, Ghez-ar stood near the doorway, angling his metal dish this way and that until a flash of light shone on a nearby wall. "Look at the image, Lady, carefully."

Obediently Shoshannah approached the light image on the wall, then gasped. It was upside-down, but undeniably . . . "Ormah!"

"What?" Ormah stepped inside the temple again and the image vanished, leaving only a reflection of sunlight.

"Don't show her," an acid voice interrupted, startling them all. Rab-Mawg swept into the temple from the hidden area, sleep rumpled and thoroughly annoyed. To Shoshannah, he muttered, "You hush. Say nothing of what you've seen to anyone."

Shoshannah immediately bowed her head, not wanting to provoke Rab-Mawg. But the wonderful upside-down "image" of the maidservant lingered in her mind. Unimaginable. And apparently secret. Were they planning to use this trick of light in some future ceremony to terrify worshipers of Shemesh?

If your Shemesh were real and worthy of devotion, as the Most High is real and worthy, then you wouldn't need such tricks to show his glory.

"I'll forget what I saw," she promised the testy young Chief Magician.

He leaned toward her, zealously hard-eyed. "No, Lady, don't forget what you've seen; it is a part of your training to remember and keep such secrets."

I would rather forget.

Astride her tawny-and-black horse, Shoshannah rode quietly after Ra-Anan and Adoniyram and Perek through the tall, damp, green and brown grass, alert to every noise. And to Kaleb's presence not far behind her.

Have courage, she pleaded with her spiritless horse silently. *Stay with the hunt.*

She had been trying for several weeks to take down just one animal that would provide leather for decent boots. This morning, the men were planning to drive creatures eastward from these boggy southern grasslands into the open fields nearby, where they could easily slaughter them. Soon these grasslands would be flooded for the season, and hunting would be more difficult. *I must catch something today.* A soft rustling sounded to Shoshannah's right, followed by a squeal. *A sow?*

Her heart thudding, Shoshannah flexed her fingers around her bow stave, set her arrow, and watched. Her horse stirred uneasily.

I don't blame you; boars are dangerous. She was also keenly aware of Kaleb and the guardsmen behind her, stilling themselves, their spears ready. If she didn't get the first shot, the guardsmen would claim whatever they felled. More rustling sounded to her right, and fresh squeals. Shadowed forms, low and wide, slipped through the grass. *I'm going to take a chance.*

Tracing one of the shadows, judging its path from the movements of the grass, she released an arrow into the brush. In less than a heartbeat, the guardsmen behind her charged toward the barely seen herd, roaring, driving the creatures toward the open fields as they'd planned. Shoshannah rode after them, elated. One boar lagged, bearing her arrow behind its left shoulder. Kaleb finished it off neatly with a well-aimed spear.

Shoshannah called to him, thrilled, but pretending irritation. "That one's mine; you know it!"

"Do I?" His look invited her to follow. He dismounted, sauntering toward their prey. Shoshannah flung herself gracelessly off her own horse and hurried to meet Kaleb before anyone else approached.

"Be careful; I love you," she whispered, looking at the boar's ochre-yellow body.

His expression softened for a fleeting instant. "I love *you*. But we'd better change the subject. Should we argue . . . Lady?"

"Let's not. Perek's watching, and I don't want to make him angry; he's the only one who's allowed to beat me."

"Really?" Kal looked her in the eyes, darkly amused, his face hardening. "I want his job then. He's coming now."

Loudly, Perek called out, "That one's not yours, Dung heap!"

Pushing a foot onto the bristly felled boar, Kaleb wrested his spear free, checked its heavy bone blade, and stepped away politely. "I wasn't claiming it—I've already offended the Lady enough."

"Don't call her 'Lady.' She's no one here," Perek snarled, reminding Shoshannah of his confrontation with Ebed in the temple.

"Of course," Kal agreed, dangerously terse.

Shoshannah regretted telling him that Perek had beaten her.

By now Adoniyram was approaching, evidently concerned that Perek and Kaleb might quarrel. Kaleb bowed to Adoniyram. Perek twitched, reluctantly following his example. Adoniyram stepped between the two guardsmen and looked down at Shoshannah's quarry. "Not a bad-sized kill."

"For being shot by a woman?" Shoshannah asked, glad for his presence but disliking his condescending tone.

He smiled. "Don't pick a quarrel with me—you won't win." Turning, he commanded, "Kaleb, haul this thing for her; leave the arrow in its side so we remember it's hers. Perek, please tell my Master-Uncle that he has meat for his household."

"I claim its hide," Shoshannah told Adoniyram. "I'm going to use it for boots; I hate riding in these sandals."

"You'll look ridiculous—like a boy. However, if you must have boots, I'll trade you that hide for some presentable leather. And you should have a skilled craftsman make them; you're not in the wilderness anymore."

Aggravated, recalling her fiercest grievance against him, she muttered, "How could I forget? Anyway, the boots probably don't matter; I won't need them if I'll be living in the temple. The way you've encouraged my uncle and those priests to train me . . ."

"Don't argue about your lessons." In a whisper, he added, "Trust me."

"You make trust difficult!" she retorted beneath her breath. "And since you're so concerned about temple matters, why haven't you persuaded your mother to fulfill her obligations to Shemesh? *I'm* not the one who was first bound by the oaths."

"Nor was she."

"She *is*," Shoshannah insisted, remembering her mother's account of Nimr-Rada extracting her oaths at the edge of a knife. "Your Great-King father said that your mother was also bound by the oaths. But *I* am taking her responsibilities."

Adoniyram smiled at her disarmingly, his voice suddenly warm. "Come now, can you imagine my mother serving in the temple?"

"No," Shoshannah said, refusing to let Adoniyram beguile her, aware of Kaleb nearby, trussing the boar to a stout pole. "I can't imagine her doing anything like work."

Laughing, Adoniyram teased, "At last we've agreed on something."

He's too familiar with her, Kaleb thought, frustrated and envious, lashing the boar's cloven hooves to the pole with needless force. *I've got to get her away from here, soon.*

Nineteen

"I DIDN'T REALIZE that the oath bound our Queen of the Heavens as much as it did her sister," Adoniyram said, grimacing at Rab-Mawg and the others while they shared their evening meal in the living area behind the temple.

"Nor did I." Rab-Mawg faced Adoniyram, unblinking. "Yet she claims to be the loving mother of her people. She ought to be a good example to them and fulfill her vows."

Adoniyram silently accepted a bit of dry, overcooked lamb from Ghez-ar, who bowed, sweating as he asked Rab-Mawg, "Excuse me, Master, but won't the Daughter of Keren be an acceptable substitute?"

"I believe she still follows that Most High."

"Surely, if that's true, she will change," Adoniyram said smoothly, not liking Rab-Mawg's tone. "She does recite the ancient stories now and then, but I've heard that she wavers in her beliefs. If she continues her lessons and eventually fulfills her mother's vows, I'm sure you'll persuade her to turn to our Shemesh."

"No doubt you are right, my lord." Rab-Mawg still sounded displeased. "But whatever the girl does, your Lady-Mother should show her own devotion to our Shemesh."

The Chief Magician had never liked their Lady Sharah, Adoniyram knew, because her only interest in the tower was that it reflected her own glory and added strength to her realm. She had never actually worshiped Shemesh, which frustrated Rab-Mawg.

Warily, Adoniyram avoided the subject and continued their meal. But he thought, *Rab-Mawg, you're becoming arrogant and offensive. If I gain control of this kingdom, you will be replaced.*

Wearing her new soft leather boots, which Adoniyram had insisted upon trading for the boar's hide, Shoshannah scurried up the moonlit tower stairs, distantly followed by the unhappy Ormah and the torch-bearer Perek. She had been praying for rain tonight, to avoid this lesson. But now she was glad the skies were clear, because she'd seen Adoniyram's horse being held by a guardsman at the base of the tower stairs. And if Adoniyram was here, then—perhaps—Kaleb had accompanied him.

Breathless, she turned the corner from the stairs to the terrace, glancing around eagerly. There was no sign of Adoniyram. He was probably inside the temple. But there was a guardsman silhouetted in the moonlight outside on the terrace, unmistakably tall, broad, and armed with a long spear. *Kaleb.*

She ran to him, snatching the chance before her

courage failed her—before anyone else came onto the terrace. He saw her, swiftly looked around, and caught her in his free arm as she hugged him. He felt wonderfully warm and safe as a protective wall. To her surprise, he bent and kissed her lips fiercely, then turned her loose with a gentle, undignified swat that urged her to flee. She caressed his whisker-roughened jaw and ran.

Father would probably swat you, she thought, rejoicing. Their first kiss! Too brief and stolen, but she felt like dancing.

Kaleb watched Shoshannah, adoring the sight of her as she dashed to the edge of the moonlit terrace, her robes and hair fluttering in the breeze. The unexpected sensations of her embrace, her responding kiss, and the gliding touch of her fingertips all lingered, warming him, tormenting him deliciously. He wanted to laugh. *You think we've gotten away with something forbidden, dear wife, but we haven't.*

He sobered, wondering when he would have the chance to tell her that they were actually married. Perhaps Tiyrac could tell her. Kal dismissed the idea as quickly as it came. Tiyrac would be too overwhelmed and self-conscious to get the words out of his mouth. Then he would have to deal with Shoshannah's questions, and her shock. She might even hug Tiyrac, which would undo the poor man altogether.

I'll tell her myself. Most High, give me the chance . . .

Torchlight flared to Kaleb's right. He gripped his spear, alert. Perek and a little maidservant turned from the steps onto the terrace. The maidservant was ignoring

Perek haughtily, and he seemed irritated. Spying Shoshannah, the rude guardsman waved his torch at her, bellowing, "Run ahead of us like that again, Daughter of Keren, and I'll thrash you! Do you hear me? Come here, *now!*"

You thrash her and I'll drop you with the sharp end of this spear, Kaleb threatened him silently, tensing, ready to attack the man.

Apparently summoned by Perek's bellowing, Adoniyram emerged from the temple, followed by those thin, bald, Shemesh-worshiping priests. Swiftly, Adoniyram halted Perek with a single word. "Stop!"

Kaleb followed the Young Lord, keeping a proper distance, watching him and listening.

Adoniyram beckoned Shoshannah. "What's happened?"

Shoshannah sounded happily unrepentant. "Perek didn't like it that I ran up the stairs; he believes I was too far away from him."

Amused, Adoniyram said, "You probably were. When will you learn to behave?"

Never, I hope, Kal thought, resenting the Young Lord's attitude toward Shoshannah. Though he usually treated Shoshannah coolly in public, often ignoring her, Adoniyram was now acting as if he had some claim upon her, almost as if they were betrothed.

What can I do if he takes her for his wife? Kaleb wondered, appalled. He was a lowly guardsman here, with no authority. And all his physical strength wouldn't help him. If he rebelled, Adoniyram could have him killed, and Shoshannah as well.

"Perhaps when I'm old—in a few years—I'll learn some manners," Shoshannah told Adoniyram. But her high spirits faded as the priests approached; she stepped back and bowed.

Kaleb watched, disturbed, realizing she was afraid of these priests.

"Come," the twig-thin leader of the priests motioned to Shoshannah, as disturbingly possessive as Adoniyram, though he bowed to the Young Lord politely. "We will be sure you behave. Perhaps our Son of Heaven will observe your lesson."

"I've nothing better to do," Adoniyram agreed, shrugging.

Kaleb was certain Adoniyram was pretending indifference. *What are you planning, O Son of Heaven,* he wondered, fighting to rein in his temper. *And how can I defend Shoshannah against you all?* He had never felt so useless in his life.

Twenty

ECHUWD SAT at the evening fire and watched his enemies: Zekaryah, Keren, Father Shem, and I'ma-Annah, and Metiyl, who had been guarding him so closely that he couldn't escape. He was a captive in Metiyl's tribe. Worse, he had lost almost a year's worth of profits from trading. All because of that girl, who was too thoughtless to keep her face hidden as he'd instructed.

She and her madman husband will probably get themselves killed somehow. Then I'll be blamed and put to death too. How can I save myself? Echuwd's heart thudded furiously as he considered ways to escape.

An idea, simple and easily accomplished, took hold in his mind. His relatives would be here in a few days, finished with their latest trading expedition in the highlands. They would help him. Mentally he calculated what price must be demanded and rehearsed what he would say. He had to regain what he had lost.

❧

"We ought to depart soon," Keren murmured as her dear friend Tsinnah knelt beside her, holding her infant daughter, Tavah. "News might spread that we're here."

"Another month or so won't matter," Tsinnah whispered. "You'll be safe here for at least that long."

"Yes, but then we'll go north to stay with Neshar and Revakhaw, though I'd hate to put them in danger."

"They won't consider you a danger; they love you. But are you going to take Yelahlah and that Echuwd with you?"

Keren sighed, torn over this still-unmade decision. At last she said, "Father Metiyl believes Echuwd should be kept here until Shoshannah, Kaleb, and Tiyrac return safely."

"I agree with Father Metiyl." Tsinnah stroked Tavah's delicate fingers. The baby, sweet and pretty as her mother, yawned and stretched drowsily.

Keren smiled, distracted her from troubles. "May I hold her?"

Tsinnah fondly passed the baby to her.

Keren relaxed, kissing the infant's soft cheek and wondering at her name. *Tavah. To grieve.* "Why did you give her such a name, Tsinnah? Isn't she a joy to you?"

"Yes, but I fear I'll outlive her and be left with grief instead. And . . . because I have caused sorrow for you, with your Shoshannah."

"That wasn't your fault." Keren rocked Tavah gently, lulling her to sleep.

"I still blame myself." Smiling faintly, Tsinnah said, "By the way, Shoshannah wonders if you will honor her as an elder when she becomes old and gray before you."

Keren laughed, though tears filled her eyes. "How like her. Elder nothing! I'll scold her and send her off for a nap first."

"Always the mother." Tsinnah hesitated. "I pray the Most High saves her for us."

"Yes," Keren agreed, trying to subdue her tears and the feelings of anger against Him. Life would have been desolate without Shoshannah . . . without all her babies . . . She would never regret their existence. Never.

Twenty-One

LESSONS AGAIN. Miserable, followed by Ormah, Perek, and a number of guardsmen, Shoshannah rode behind Ra-Anan, Kuwsh, and Adoniyram through the crowded market street. Strangely clad tribes were visiting the Great City, jostling with the usual merchants, loudly offering peculiar, garishly colored robes, heavy copper and gold earrings, feather hair adornments, furs, and pungent meats and curdled milks that made Shoshannah feel sick.

A rounded, leather-clad young man hurried out and grasped Shoshannah's horse by the mane, halting her. "If you've any wounds, we have cures!" he cried. "Poultices! Herbs! Permanent tracings of protection against all misfortunes!"

Taken aback, Shoshannah stared at him.

He bared his arm, revealing a dark, bluish series of

disfigured lines and dots along his shoulder and forearm. The marks seemed to be etched beneath his skin like permanent bruises. He rubbed them hard, but they didn't smudge. "These can never be scrubbed off! For one measure of grain or half a measure of meat . . ."

"Get away!" Perek snarled, riding forward, jabbing his spear toward the peddler.

"Don't you threaten my son!" A woman garbed in fur and beads stormed at Perek, her anger rousing everyone nearby. "He's only offering remedies—which *you* need for settling yourself!"

"*Stop!* Perek, back away." Apparently provoked by the commotion, Ra-Anan scowled, turning his horse toward them. "Woman, I can have my guards confiscate your belongings and chase you and your family off like rubbish. Don't delay us further. If you want to trade goods here, you cannot lay hands on anyone in these streets." Ominously, he added, "Make a booth and keep to it."

Ra-Anan's cold, scarred, clean-shaven features, his splendid robes, and all his guards apparently convinced the woman. She pulled her son back, but she was fuming. "Make a booth? With what? Nonsense! We've arrived with nothing. Bariyach, come away!"

Drawing rebellious looks after him from other merchants, Ra-Anan rode onward.

Adoniyram slowed his horse to ride with Shoshannah. Eyeing her, he asked softly, "Did that man touch you?"

"No. He touched only the horse's mane." Adoniyram's dangerous tone and cutting stare took Shoshannah's breath away. She had to remind herself not to look back at Kaleb for help. Recovering, she stammered, "I-I'm well. Truly."

"You don't look well."

"I was shocked. He was offering 'protection against all misfortunes.'"

"Why is that so shocking?" Adoniyram relaxed now, shaking his head at her. "There's nothing wrong with protecting yourself against misfortunes."

"He had marks beneath his skin, and scars. They looked horrible."

"Oh, those." Adoniyram was dismissive of her ignorance. "Certain tribes cut patterns into their skin, then rub them with powders to dye them. When the marks heal, the dyes remain."

More at ease now, Shoshannah argued quietly, "But dyes won't protect you against misfortune. Only the Most High can do that—and sometimes we have to struggle through difficulties to learn."

"Then that shows your Most High's cruelty," Adoniyram interrupted, smiling.

Offended by his derision, Shoshannah said, "The Most High isn't cruel; *we* are. I think you're looking for reasons to turn against Him. If He were truly horrible, Cousin, we wouldn't exist. The Great Flood would have destroyed us all. But He loves us—He longs to protect us."

"As He has protected you thus far?"

"Perhaps He has protected me and we don't realize it."

"*I've* protected you," Adoniyram said.

"And you're supposed to ignore me in public. Go away."

"But who will protect you if I go?"

Now he was flirting with her. She had to discourage him. Kal would notice.

"Lady," a woman called from alongside the street ahead.

Shoshannah looked. Several young matrons with dark, tapering braids and lavish shawls were clustered together.

One of them nudged another, who held an infant. "Will you honor her child?"

"I'm no one here," Shoshannah started to say, but the shawl-swathed mother quickly lifted her baby toward Shoshannah. A newborn. Moved with longing, Shoshannah halted her plodding horse and accepted the baby, cuddling it gratefully. She kissed the newborn's forehead, stared into its soft eyes, then returned it safely to the proud mother. "Thank you. What a beautiful child."

Jolted unexpectedly, Shoshannah turned to see Adoniyram riding ahead, leading her horse by the bridle. "Adoniyram . . ."

He looked back at her, raising an eyebrow. "Now I'll have to agree with my mother when she complains that you're stupid and trying to take over her kingdom."

"I can't take her 'kingdom' if I'm truly stupid, can I? Tell her that I just want to go back to my family. Please, Adoniyram, let me guide my own horse, and you can ignore me for the rest of the day."

Bowing his head in taunting silence, Adoniyram released her horse. But he looked pleased.

Attended by Ormah and Perek, Shoshannah wandered onto the rain-dampened terrace. Her lesson was finished and she wanted to leave, but her uncle and Lord Kuwsh were talking with several tradesmen in a far corner of the terrace, gesturing broadly, raising images of the tower's ever-increasing future levels. Adoniyram waited nearby, arms crossed, looking as bored as Shoshannah felt. Kaleb, meanwhile, was near the stairs, long spear in hand, clearly on guard duty. There was no chance of speaking with him.

Sighing, Shoshannah retreated to the moist garden area, studying the raised bricked beds, dormant shrubs, and young trees. To her dismay, Adoniyram followed her, motioning Ormah and Perek back.

"I'm here to protect you again," he teased softly.

Resisting his flirtatious overtones, she argued in a whisper, "That's what you believe. *I* say that the Most High has directed you to guard me."

Adoniyram grimaced, as if her opinion was ridiculous. "He hasn't spoken to me."

"Then you can't be the Promised One. But that wasn't what I meant; I think the Most High has caused you to help me, whether you realize it or not."

"No, I've made all my decisions for myself," the Young Lord argued, unnervingly serious. Leaning toward her, he murmured, "That brings me to another thought: What if I *am* the Promised One?"

"You aren't, O Son of Nimr-Rada."

Hesitant, his words a mere hair thread of sound, Adoniyram breathed, "Tell no one: I'm not the Great King's son."

Shoshannah felt all the blood ebbing from her face. She could hardly speak. Was he serious? "Whose son are you, then?"

"Perhaps a son of Arpakshad."

She stared at him for a long instant and decided he was challenging her. "You don't know that."

"You don't know that I'm not."

Remembering the stories of her childhood, learned

during happy evenings spent with the Ancient Noakh and I'ma-Naomi, Shoshannah said, "I was taught that we will recognize the Promised One by his unfailing love and obedience toward the Most High. You don't love the Most High; you cannot be the Promised One."

"What if I should turn to the Most High?"

Again she stared at him, amazed, doubtful. "Will you?"

He smiled charmingly. "You don't know that either, do you?"

"You're mocking me."

"No, I'm not."

She wished he were.

Perek approached now, beckoning her. Lord Kuwsh and Master Ra-Anan were preparing to depart.

Adoniyram chided himself silently, riding behind Ra-Anan and Kuwsh through the city. Twice today he had broken his own resolution to avoid speaking to Shoshannah in public.

Not wise. And perhaps I said more than I should. Now I will see if she can keep my secrets.

Prodding his horse forward, he joined Lord Kuwsh and Ra-Anan, who were still arguing about how to proceed with building the tower and the temple. But listening to them quarrel over paints, pillars, and stairs, while he tried to suggest his Lady-Mother's preferences as she had instructed, had been dull work today. How could he concentrate after speaking with Shoshannah and, earlier, watching her embrace that baby? He had imagined her holding his own child.

Dangerous.

Willfully Adoniyram subdued those thoughts, which might remain only thoughts if all his plans ended in disaster. He also had to deal with Shoshannah's belief that he wasn't the Promised One. *Is she right?* he wondered, looking up at the clouded skies.

You don't love the Most High; you cannot be the Promised One.

Could he trust or believe in a God who had probably foreshortened his own life, as Shoshannah had said?

A voice seemed to whisper at the back of his mind, *But if Shemesh is your god, you must ask the same question of him.*

Adoniyram considered this, surprised. He felt as if this new thought was whispered by a teacher who was reasoning with him kindly, telling him to be fair.

"You've been talking with *her* quite a bit today," Kuwsh observed, startling Adoniyram into the present.

Composing himself, Adoniyram smiled sardonically to convince Lord Kuwsh that he was annoyed with Shoshannah. "Earlier, on our way to the tower, she was upset by marks that trader had carved in his arm. I persuaded her that they were nothing. Then she had to hold some merchant wife's baby—did you see her? We must convince her to behave more cautiously in public. Otherwise my mother will take offense."

Kuwsh glowered at this, casting a dark look at Ra-Anan.

Coolly, Ra-Anan said, "I will speak with Shoshannah tonight."

Adoniyram maintained a perfect, disinterested mask. But he warned Shoshannah in his thoughts, *If you reveal my secrets to our enemies, beloved, then you won't deserve my protection in the future. Prove to me that you can be cautious.*

Shoshannah tried to remain calm as Ra-Anan scolded her after the evening meal.

"If you insist on resuming your mother's tradition of openly honoring every baby who's offered to you, Shoshannah, then you must understand that you will cause Lord Kuwsh to turn against you."

Softly, severely, Zeva'ah added, "You will also provoke our Queen of the Heavens. She's already threatened to kill you. Do you understand how serious this is?"

"Yes, Aunt." Aware of Demamah's subtle, tense concern, Shoshannah suggested hopefully, "Perhaps Demamah should accompany me whenever I go out into the streets. She can accept the babies and everyone will be satisfied. She would enjoy it, wouldn't you, Demamah?"

"Of course, but not if my parents are against the idea," Demamah agreed, worried.

Zeva'ah shrugged and glanced at Ra-Anan for his opinion.

"I have no objections. Yet." Ra-Anan frowned at Shoshannah. "What were you talking about with Adoniyram today?"

"I'm sorry I delayed you this morning, Uncle; forgive me. We were discussing that peddler's arm; it was covered with dark slashes. Adoniyram said that certain tribes cut themselves deliberately and rub dye into the cuts and—"

"What else?" her uncle demanded, looking dangerous.

Shoshannah squirmed uncomfortably. "Adoniyram was flirting with me. He said that he had to stay to protect me, but I told him I wanted him to just ignore me. Please, Uncle, can you speak to him? I don't want anyone to talk and say things that aren't true."

"If his behavior becomes inappropriate, yes. What else?"

What else could she safely tell? Slowly, painfully, she said, "Adoniyram believes that the Most High is cruel, and that He isn't protecting me, or anyone else."

His voice lowered, hard, Ra-Anan asked, "And do you still trust in the Most High?"

Demamah stiffened beside her. Zeva'ah, too, seemed to be holding her breath.

Looking her uncle in the eyes, Shoshannah answered softly, "Yes."

Ra-Anan stared at her as if she were manure scuffed into his clean house. "If you wish to live, child, you will not repeat this foolishness to anyone—particularly not to Rab-Mawg or our Lord Kuwsh. Now, leave the room."

Shoshannah hurried away, disgraced, but thankful the questions had stopped.

Shoshannah looked up. Demamah entered the sleeping area, shaking her head, upset. "Father said that if he had struck you, he would not have been able to prevent himself from killing you. He asked me if I've been hiding things from him." Demamah's big eyes glimmered with tears. "I gave him my word that I wasn't keeping information from him to protect you. At least not *that* information . . . confessing you still follow the Most High . . ."

She sat beside Shoshannah on the makeshift bed now, staring at her, whispering, "Why did you say anything at all?"

"It was the truth; he would have known if I was lying."

Demamah pushed a hand through her straight, glossy hair. "It would have been better to remain silent. Now he will suspect everything I say."

"I'm sorry." Wondering, Shoshannah asked, "*Is* there anything to suspect of you?"

Clearly unwilling to answer the question, Demamah changed the subject. "Why do you suppose your parents haven't tried to rescue you from here? Surely they love you."

They are trying. But I'm not going to tell you that. Aloud, Shoshannah answered, "They do love me. But I'd rather die than have them risk their lives, and I'm sure they know it."

"You *will* die if you speak so foolishly again, defending your Most High."

Softly, Shoshannah asked, "Isn't your Shemesh worth defending?"

Demamah stared at her, silent.

Alone in her ornate bedchamber, Sharah lifted a small, oval obsidian mirror and stared hard at her reflection in the mirror's dark surface. Her makeup, skin, teeth, and hair were all perfectly groomed. She put the obsidian down and picked up a mirror of highly polished metal and frowned into her gleaming, now goldish-pink image. Still perfect.

Restless, she thrust the mirror away and poured herself some wine. Perhaps she should have ridden out into the city today with Adoniyram. Attention from the citizens usually lifted her sense of gloom. She could have also prevented Adoniyram from speaking to that girl. And she could have taken that infant for herself, forbidding Shoshannah to accept the citizens' adulation.

You are scheming against me, she thought, frustrated. *You're stealing my son, and my citizens. I'm going to insist that Ra-Anan keep you hidden. If he doesn't . . .*

A respectful cough interrupted her. She frowned. "What?"

"Lady?" One of her maidservants approached timidly, her dark head bowed. "A woman has come to the gates with news of your family. She won't talk to me but says that you will want to hear what she says."

Sharah was about to send the woman away unheard, but curiosity and boredom changed her mind. "Bring the woman to me, then leave. And don't let me catch you listening!"

As she waited, Sharah smoothed her expression deliberately and practiced a benevolent smile. If this woman was some fool with news of a cousin or something equally stupid, Sharah would send her away immediately. Hearing footsteps, Sharah flashed her practiced smile toward the entrance of her private rooms.

A nondescript brown-skinned woman bowed toward her, then knelt shakily, obviously scared.

Becoming irritated, Sharah said, "It's late. Not a time I usually receive pleas from citizens."

Moistening her ashen lips, the woman whispered, "This is about Keren, your own sister, Lady. I saw her. Please believe me; there's no mistake. I know where she is."

Sharah took in a breath, then exhaled, delighted. "Does anyone else know? If you've told anyone . . ."

"My husband and children know. And my husband's brother . . . who is married to your niece Yelahlah. But we've remained silent. We will also leave your city at once, if only you could give us the means to support ourselves as we try to return home. There were terrible floods on our lands this year, Lady . . ."

Donning her generous, loving mother expression, Sharah said, "I'll provide for your family this once. But I warn you: If I find out that you've lied, I will have you hunted down and punished. You and your family."

The woman's brown eyes widened, terrified. "I'll tell you the truth, Lady. And others are with her. Please, listen . . ."

As the woman poured out names and descriptions in a muted monotone, Sharah listened, elated. This was news worth paying for, worth hiding. Worth celebrating. Ra-Anan and Kuwsh were going to have fits when she rubbed her victory in their smug faces. Laughing to herself, she hurried away to summon her guardsmen.

Twenty-Two

SHELTERED JUST INSIDE the doorway of Ra-Anan's home, Shoshannah dropped her spindle into her lap and peered outside. As she watched, Adoniyram strode into the crowd of merchants and visitors seated in Ra-Anan's busy courtyard and bowed graciously to Lord Kuwsh and Ra-Anan.

"Look at him," she murmured to Demamah. "Late and not caring a bit."

Kneeling beside her, Demamah stopped combing a puff of wool. "I hope he doesn't upset Father."

Kaleb followed Adoniyram, his usual brisk walk now slow and measured. He positioned himself in a corner, cautiously eyeing everyone. Shoshannah was concerned by his unusual behavior but dared not look at him for too long; Demamah would notice. Reluctantly, she glanced toward the gate just as two trainers entered, guiding two of Adoniyram's leashed leopards in their golden, jeweled collars.

The sleek, showy, almost sacred leopards were reminders of Nimr-Rada, Adoniyram's mighty hunter-"father," and symbols of Adoniyram's status in this kingdom. Everyone in the courtyard watched the leopards, unnerved. Kal, however, studied the pampered beasts as if he were planning how to stop them if they attacked anyone. Adoniyram merely smiled.

If you hoped to disrupt this meeting, Adoniyram, then you've done it, Shoshannah thought. *But what would all these merchants and visitors do if they realized that you're not their revered Nimr-Rada's son?* She often wondered if he had been merely teasing her all those weeks ago. *If it's true, then others must know . . .*

The Lady Sharah would know, of course. Lord Kuwsh, perhaps—he seemed indifferent to Adoniyram, not fond or watchful as a grandparent would be. However, Lord Kuwsh was usually indifferent to others. And if Adoniyram were not Nimr-Rada's son, wouldn't the proud Lord Kuwsh have denounced him at birth? Unless he had some selfish reason to keep Adoniyram alive . . . As for their Master Ra-Anan . . . Frowning, Shoshannah watched her uncle, trying to decide.

Ra-Anan's lips pressed to a thin, impatient line. "Be seated, Adoniyram, please. We are discussing our plans for the festival during the High Month of Shemesh."

"I should leave then, since I have nothing important to say." But he sat near Ra-Anan and relaxed, signaling for the keepers to settle his leopards nearby.

Without another glance, Ra-Anan turned from his nephew to the crowd of merchants again. As if Adoniyram were nobody.

I think you know Adoniyram is not Nimr-Rada's son, Shoshannah told Ra-Anan silently. *But you allow him to stay; you control him, as you control me, for your own purposes.*

"Look," Demamah whispered, combing another puff of wool, "Tiyrac is going to stand with his brother. They seem to guard each other."

She's calling him "Tiyrac" now. Astonished, Shoshannah eyed her cousin. Was Demamah becoming fond of Tiyrac? The thought was both delightful and worrisome. She didn't want Demamah to become unwittingly enmeshed in her own future plans to escape with Kal and Tiyrac; if they were caught, Demamah would suffer terribly. And yet . . .

Unable to squelch her curiosity, Shoshannah asked beneath her breath, "What do you think of him? Is he as bad as Perek?"

"He's much more polite than Perek—and never angry with me. You'd think he was trained to live in the city, while Perek is actually the wild man dragged in from the steppes."

"You've been *watching* Tiyrac."

"No, I haven't, so hush."

Shoshannah hid a smile. Demamah *was* watching Tiyrac. Oh, how she wished she could tease Tiyrac and see him blush and stammer denials that any girl, particularly one so lovely as Demamah, could be interested in him. But that could never happen; if Ra-Anan even suspected that Demamah was fascinated by the young man, Tiyrac would be sent away. And that was the last thing Shoshannah wanted.

To excuse herself for looking at Tiyrac and Kal, she said, "I think they're trying to decide what to do if Adoniyram's leopards attack anyone."

"I'm sure you're right."

By now, Ra-Anan's voice was rising as he spoke to the unwillingly attentive merchants. "This year we will have more visitors than ever before to our Great City. You will have more opportunities for trade, and we will all gain if we are prepared to receive them as honored guests. We expect your assistance in building temporary residences to shelter our visitors . . ."

The High Month of Shemesh. Thinking of it, Shoshannah's stomach tightened. Surely her uncle wouldn't expect her to take part in any of the temple ceremonies, knowing she worshiped the Most High and considered their Shemesh to be a god of their own making.

Their festival is almost four months away, she reassured herself. *I don't have to worry about it yet.* To calm herself, she gazed at Kaleb again, grateful for the sight of him standing there with Tiyrac, safe and well. For now.

Let us escape soon, she begged the Most High. Fearing Demamah had noticed her, Shoshannah glanced at her cousin. Demamah hastily looked down at the combs and wool, away from Tiyrac.

Kneeling on a mat in the temple with Ormah, Shoshannah watched, fascinated, as the priest Ebed rolled a carved stone tube over a soft pat of clay. A fragile picture trail of streams, fish, and rays of sunlight revealed the path of the moving tube. She smiled, delighted. "Ebed, how wonderful! Please, may I see the stone? I'll be careful, I give you my word."

Seeming gratified, Ebed bowed his shaven head and offered the pat of clay and the carved tube to Shoshannah.

"Test the marker for yourself, Lady. This was our Master Rab-Mawg's inspiration. Eventually each merchant in the city, and every priest and official, will have his own special marker, carved in his own particular pattern to seal the tokens of his agreements."

Knowing that Ormah would want to inspect this new type of "marker," as Ebed had called it, Shoshannah gently set it between them. She studied the carved stone, rolled it over the clay, then handed it to Ormah.

As Shoshannah hoped, the maidservant abandoned her usual haughtiness, eagerly applying the stone to the clay. Shoshannah smiled, contented. When Ormah was happy, she was less inclined to exaggerate stories of Shoshannah's misbehavior to Ra-Anan. And the last thing Shoshannah wanted now was to make Ra-Anan more upset with her.

"Are you playing, children?" Awkawn asked, sweeping past the curtain into the temple from behind the hidden room. He threw a belittling glance at Ormah, who frowned.

Reluctant to acknowledge this rude priest, Shoshannah lowered her head and said nothing.

Awkawn planted his bare bony feet directly in front of her. "Rab-Mawg summons you now; you shouldn't linger here unless you're worshiping our Shemesh, O Daughter of Keren."

Shoshannah stood, agitated by his taunt. Had he been talking about her with Rab-Mawg? Slowly she smoothed her garments and walked past the curtains to the hidden room to face Rab-Mawg.

He was waiting, alert but not wild-eyed. And there was no knife in his hand. Grateful for this small mercy, Shoshannah knelt in her accustomed place, with Ormah beside her. The maidservant cleared her throat nervously.

Rab-Mawg gave her a sharp, quelling look, then turned to Shoshannah. His voice stiff, almost clipped, he lectured, "As you are aware, Lady, we will soon celebrate the High Month of our Shemesh."

Shoshannah nodded, not liking his topic.

He returned her look, clearly not liking his student. "You must begin to learn those duties abandoned by your mother."

"My uncle has given you instructions . . ." Shoshannah murmured, allowing her words to trail off, not quite questioning him.

"Yes, he has. But even if he hadn't, I would insist that you fulfill your obligations."

Shoshannah listened, nausea twisting her stomach. She tried to remain expressionless, but the priest stared at her so hard and for such a long time that she began to fidget.

At last he said, "You will have to convince me that you deserve this honor—and the power you will possess. I give you one year." He leaned forward, until she could almost feel his breath in her face. His eyes glittered sharply, as if he dared her to deny what he was about to say. "I know you still believe what those Ancient Ones taught you, and you are contemptuous of our ways—I've been watching you! But I'm telling you now that you *will* abandon those old beliefs. You will faithfully receive offerings and require devotions in this temple. You will become the wife of Shemesh, and you will proclaim his greatness to our people. You have one year."

One year? Then what would happen, if she failed to convince him that she "deserved this honor"? Was he already planning her death? So much for his insistence that she must be convinced she was safe here.

Rab-Mawg continued his lecturing. "Master Ra-Anan and I have decided, too, that our tower is unfinished."

You and Ra-Anan and all the other greedy fools in this rebellious city.

"We intend to continue building until this structure reaches the heavens, until it stands in the clouds. This tower will draw all the other tribes to us and earn such a name for us that, whatever happens, we will be strong and united. We will never be scattered across the earth like straw!" Rab-Mawg's expression was passionately intense, stirred with the kind of devotion that most men reserved for their beloved wives—or their horses.

Ugh! He's in love with this tower, Shoshannah thought, revolted. But a question occurred to her then, one that might calm and distract this bizarre priest. "Please, Master Rab-Mawg, can you tell me anything more about the future of this tower? Has my uncle made any other plans for it, except that it will be a temple?"

The young priest actually looked surprised. He studied Shoshannah, then eyed Ormah, who was now shifting impatiently—no doubt wishing Shoshannah hadn't questioned him. Cool, he inclined his head.

"I have not spoken to your Master-Uncle about this, Lady, but I intend to ask permission to inter our Great King somewhere in this tower. After all, it is being built in his memory, and at his request."

"Inter? You mean to . . . bring his body here and . . ."

"What we can *find* of his body," Rab-Mawg agreed sharply. "Yes. We will protect his remains here. Lord Kuwsh has already interred the head beneath our altar."

"Oh." Shoshannah suppressed a creeping chill of horror, wishing she hadn't pursued the subject. The Great-King Nimr-Rada's body had been cut into pieces after his death. After her mother and father had supposedly rebelled and betrayed him to their Father Shem, who had executed Nimr-Rada. *I'll never learn to think before I speak.*

As she scolded herself for being so foolish, Rab-Mawg said, "In this way, we will honor our fallen king. Despite your mother's treachery, our He-Who-Lifts-the-Skies will never be forgotten." Leaning forward, the priest added, "You could be forgiven and remembered forever, if you fulfill your mother's vows to serve Shemesh. You would be *worshiped,* even if you die before your elders. Just convince us that you deserve such adoration."

I don't want that kind of adoration.

He continued to talk, his face again lit with that awful intensity that made her skin crawl. She wasn't going to be able to fool him for long. He would certainly want to kill her at the end of her allotted year. *One year to escape.* She had to warn Kal.

While they were walking down the stairs, followed by the spying Perek, Ormah criticized Shoshannah indignantly. "You *had* to question him and keep him talking! You can't ever keep quiet, not even when your life depends on it. And"—she shook her head—"I don't understand why you find it so hard to just do what our Master Ra-Anan and the priests ask. It's not the dreadful problem you seem to think it is! Just worship our Shemesh—as you should. It's so simple." Perturbed, the maidservant added, "I wish someone would offer *me* such a glorious place in our Great City in exchange for a few stupid lessons."

I wish they would too! Shoshannah snapped silently,

marching down the stairs, making Perek growl as he hurried after her.

Seated beside his wife in their main room, Ra-Anan scolded Ormah. "Perek was concerned about your behavior at the tower today. Listen to me, girl: You will not speak of Shoshannah or her lessons to anyone. Do you hear me? Don't even discuss her with the cook. If I suspect you of gossiping, I'll have Perek cane you until you can't walk."

Ormah shook, her pointed little face turning claylike with fear. "Yes, my lord."

Ra-Anan waved her out, watching as she bowed and dashed through the doorway to the kitchen. *Can she be trusted?* Ra-Anan frowned until Zeva'ah leaned against him and sighed, clasping his arm.

"Beloved," she murmured, "I hope Shoshannah won't ruin all your plans with her foolishness; she's more like her mother than we first believed."

"If Shoshannah is too much like her mother, then she will destroy herself," Ra-Anan said absently. He wished he could have more time to talk with the girl, to persuade her of her potential role in this kingdom. And to crush her frustrating devotion to the Most High and the Ancient Ones. If only his Zeva'ah weren't such a suspicious, jealous woman, he would personally take control of Shoshannah and her lessons. She must be made to obey.

Eventually, when he declared Shoshannah's new high status, Shoshannah would be popularly acclaimed. Then Sharah and Kuwsh would be provoked enough to behave foolishly, endangering their already eroding hold upon the affections of their people. As for Adoniyram . . . Ra-Anan smiled to himself. *I still control you.*

"Do you still want us to protect this girl, knowing that she worships that Most High?" Rab-Mawg asked. He was watching Adoniyram so closely that the Young Lord wondered how much the head priest suspected.

Swirling the thick beer in the clay cup they had offered him, Adoniyram pretended to think briefly; then he nodded. "She's important to us for now—don't you agree? She's the perfect irritant for our enemies." He paused. "One favor?"

Rab-Mawg smiled agreement thinly—looking so much like Ra-Anan that Adoniyram almost told him of the resemblance. But knowing how thoroughly the young head priest detested his arrogant mentor, Adoniyram pushed the thought away. It was best not to provoke Rab-Mawg. Not yet.

Clearing his throat, Adoniyram asked, "Can we keep this situation hidden from our Lord Kuwsh and my Lady-Mother? I don't care to quarrel with them unless we have to."

"Master Ra-Anan has ordered us to say that the girl's lessons concern nothing more than trade matters, customs, and polite manners. We are forbidden to mention her intended role. But she will fail us as her mother did. You know she will."

"Let me deal with her then." Adoniyram finished his drink, grimacing at the bitter taste it left in his mouth. "Don't kill her; she can't help being who she is."

"She *can* help it," Rab-Mawg contended. "But she won't."

If I succeed, I'm going to pitch you out with the other vultures, Adoniyram thought, loathing his quarrelsome priest-ally. His whole mouth felt dry from their beer. Grimacing again, he said, "I'm going to send you some better stuff to drink, Master-Priest. It won't be wine, but it's certainly better than this—plain water is better. I'm amazed your guts aren't soured from drinking it."

Defensively, Rab-Mawg said, "We've had to brew our own drinks. Your mother, your uncle, and Lord Kuwsh have stolen so much from us that we're going to be begging in the streets soon."

"I'll send you everything I can."

"Thank you, my lord."

"Of course." Adoniyram grinned, provoking a genuine—though pained—smile from the unhappy priest.

You have to trust me for a while longer, Rab-Mawg. Then you'll wish you hadn't. But by then it will be too late.

And Shoshannah, he hoped, would behave long enough to ensure her survival. The thought made Adoniyram nervous. *Am I right?* He wondered. *Is there another way?*

He felt nothing like a Promised One.

Exhausted, peering through the nighttime darkness, Kaleb watched Adoniyram pace back and forth along the edge of the tower's plant-garnished terrace. *Why are we still here? He's finished talking with those priests, and Shoshannah won't be attending any lessons tonight, though I wish she were . . .* Not that it mattered; Kal doubted he'd have a chance to steal another kiss from his unenlightened wife, much less discuss an escape plan.

Most High, he implored, *I am ready to snatch Shoshannah and my brother and leave this accursed place, if only You would show me how! Why must we stay here? And why isn't that Young Lord ready to go back to his residence for some sleep?*

Unable to restrain himself, Kal approached the young man, scuffing his boots just loudly enough that Adoniyram would be aware of his presence. As he expected, Adoniyram turned toward him, a dark outline against the stars.

"Kaleb. What is it?"

"I'm not sure, my lord. But I'm worried by the way you're pacing. Are you going to throw yourself over the edge here?"

Adoniyram gave a short, bitter laugh. "Not tonight. I hope not ever." He leaned against the waist-high terrace wall now, apparently brooding.

Kal stood just far enough away to be polite, but near enough to hear the Young Lord if he decided to talk.

After a brief pause, Adoniyram said, "I am doubting some decisions I've made, though I'm sure they are the right decisions. Do you ever doubt yourself, Kaleb?"

"Sometimes." Kaleb laughed, more at himself than anything. "Usually others do my doubting for me."

More quietly, the Young Lord asked, "Have you ever killed anyone?"

"If I have, they haven't told me." Immediately, Kal regretted being flippant. It would not do to have his new master think that he, Kaleb, would kill anyone. Lowering his voice, firm and serious, Kal said, "Actually, I haven't killed anyone, my lord. And I pray I never do."

"That's what I thought." Adoniyram sounded half disgusted, half amused. "But I am sure that if provoked enough, you could kill someone. Admit it; you would."

"To defend myself, perhaps," Kaleb agreed reluctantly. *Or to defend Shoshannah.*

"Or to defend me?" Adoniyram asked, still amused. "Perhaps you ought to think about that—being my guardsman."

"If you were threatened, of course I'd defend you, my lord. That's my duty." Kaleb grinned, hoping to end the conversation. "However, I prefer to think that everyone loves you so much—and fears my stinking reputation so much—that they won't try anything at all."

"Oh yes, I'm sure you're right. Everyone loves me."

He sounded as if he were jeering at himself. Kal felt a jolt of sympathy for the young man, realizing how very isolated and lonely he was.

Adoniyram turned away from the edge of the terrace and started toward the stairs, motioning for Kaleb to accompany him. "Grab a torch and let's go; I'll clear my head with a hunt tomorrow morning."

Lighting a torch from a nearby smoldering clay brazier, Kaleb frowned. *Who is it you wish to kill?*

As they walked down the stairs, Adoniyram said, "By the way, about a month ago I noticed that my mother sent at least five of her guardsmen away. I don't know where they've gone, or why, but I do know they haven't returned yet. Have you heard anything of them?"

"No, my lord. Is this unusual?"

"Yes. At least it is unusual for my mother. She loves being surrounded by her servants and guardsmen more than she loves her own family—it makes her feel powerful. I wonder what she's planning."

"I'll be listening; I'll speak to my brother too."

"Thank you, Kaleb." He mused aloud, "But I hope my Master-Uncle and his servants don't know more about my mother's household than I do. That would be disgraceful."

"Indeed it would, my lord." Perturbed by this whole conversation, Kaleb followed Adoniyram down the tower stairs.

In the Lady Sharah's sumptuously overdecorated residence, Adoniyram bent and kissed his mother's cheek. She looked bleary this morning, but not unhappy, which was odd. He eyed her suspiciously as she motioned for her serving women to finish combing her hair and fastening her ornaments. She wore a particularly elaborate necklace this morning, a cascade of red stones mounted in gold.

"That's new, isn't it, Mother?"

"Yes." Sharah preened and checked her reflection in an obsidian mirror, smiling. "I traded some gifts to have it made a few weeks ago; I felt like celebrating."

"Celebrating what?"

"Nothing that concerns you." She threw him a fierce look. "If you've come here to quarrel, then you can leave. I'll listen to my people and accept their petitions without your help."

"I haven't come to quarrel, Mother; don't worry. I didn't want you to think I was neglecting you." Politely, he asked, "Have you heard from those missing guardsmen of yours? It's not like them to just disappear."

"They are retrieving some things for me—which is also not your concern."

"Forgive me." He should have waited to question her while she was drinking and too tired to consider what she was saying. Now he would simply have to wait until the missing guardsmen returned. Perhaps Kaleb would have better luck talking with his brother when they visited Ra-Anan's household tonight.

His mother was smiling again. "There *is* something I will tell you. Ra-Anan has sent an appeal out to all the other tribes—in my name—for the return of our Great King's body. Isn't that devoted of him?"

"Perfectly." *And it makes me wonder why you didn't send out the same request years ago, after his death.*

She hadn't loved Nimr-Rada, of course, Adoniyram decided. *She's never loved anyone except herself. Not even me.*

Tiyrac stared at his brother in Ra-Anan's evening-shadowed courtyard, wondering why Kaleb thought he had any information on that Lady Sharah's missing guardsmen. "No, I haven't heard anything."

Almost inaudibly, Kal muttered, "Why would she send her guardsmen away so mysteriously? Her son claims that she loves to be surrounded by them; they make her feel powerful. What else could be so important . . . unless they've found out that I'ma-Keren and Zekaryah and the others are in the Tribe of Metiyl?"

The thought made Tiyrac catch his breath sharply. "Do you think they have?"

"We'll know when those guardsmen return. Until then, we pray." Still quiet, Kaleb asked, "How is she?"

It took Tiyrac an instant to shift his thoughts. "Shoshannah? She's well." He had almost mistakenly said the name of the young lady Demamah. He had to forget her, particularly if their enemies had found Zekaryah, I'ma-Keren, Father Shem, and I'ma-Annah. Considering what might happen if I'ma-Keren and Zekaryah were caught—if they were all caught—Tiyrac felt his stomach churn. Truly, he had to forget Demamah; it was useless to think of her anyway. Her father would never approve of his only daughter marrying such a plain man as himself.

Perek entered the darkening courtyard just then and gave the brothers a suspicious look. Kaleb straightened and stared at Perek coolly. Tiyrac detested the rude man and silently echoed his brother's attitude. Perek sneered at them but turned away.

Coward, Tiyrac thought, pleased.

After stretching and studying the dawn, Annah carried a limp heap of water skins down a green hillside to a tree-sheltered, noisily rushing stream. She would fill these skins while Shem and Zekaryah were tending their horses, and while Keren finished binding the tents for their journey today. By tonight they would be well into the mountains again, farther away from the Great City.

Are we doing Your will? she asked the Most High as she lifted the first plump and dripping water skin from the cold rushing stream. *Should my Shem and I be avoiding the Great City and our rebellious children to the south? Or should we ride down there and confront them all?* She had been asking herself and the Most High this question for months with no definite answer. They could be in the Great City within weeks. But they didn't want to risk Keren's and Zekaryah's lives. *What should we do?*

A muffled clatter on the other side of the stream alerted her to the presence of another human; no animal made such a noise—like sticks rattled together. *Who are you?*

Fleece-cloaked, leather-clad, and watchful, a man stepped from behind a coarse green bush on the other side of the stream. His bow and arrow were readied, but not aimed directly at her. A quiverful of arrows clattered against a knife handle at his side. He warbled a bird call, bringing two other men from their own hiding places, their weapons also readied. Two additional horsemen came riding down the opposite hillside, leading three horses. Annah stood, alarmed.

They've found us—they've come for Keren.

Twenty-Three

SCARED AND INFURIATED, Annah watched the three guardsmen splash across the icy stream. *Look at their horrible faces. How can they be children of my own children?* But all of them were probably descended from her in some way. She wished they were small enough to spank. *Oh, you would be punished!*

She almost screamed to warn Keren and the others but realized that if Shem and Zekaryah thought she was in danger, they would fight these men. And the two of them would probably be defeated, wounded, or even killed. These guardsmen would also catch her if she ran, which could provoke the violence she feared. Exhaling a silent prayer, Annah tied the filled water skin, her hands shaking.

The first guardsman to reach her was apparently the leader, an arrogant, brawny, nut-brown man. Shifting his weapons, he grabbed her arm.

She raised her eyebrows at him severely. "Son, whichever one of mine you are, *behave.*"

His black eyes flickered, and his grip loosened for the slightest breath of time, then he held her more firmly. "You are Ma'adannah then. I thought so—you were described to us perfectly. Forgive me, but you must obey us. We have no quarrel with you."

"Oh, but you do have a quarrel with me, child!" Annah glared at him, furious now. "You are . . ."

The guardsman actually gave her a silencing shake as the other two drew near; Annah gritted her teeth and calmed herself somewhat. But she flashed the first guardsman a warning look.

He put his oily, bewhiskered face down to hers, saying, "We are commanded to bring the Lady Keren and her companions to the Great City. I'm sorry you disapprove, Ma'adannah, but you are one of those companions. I will follow my orders." Turning, he snapped to the nearest guardsman, "Erek, as soon as the others get here, we haul her into their camp and claim their weapons. And you, Abdiy, keep your aim toward that Zehker. And watch their Father Shem."

"Don't trust the Lady Keren; she will also have weapons," Erek said. He was such a sly-looking man that Annah mistrusted him at once.

"By the way, Ma'adannah," the chief guardsman said, "I am of the sons of Khawm; you are not my First Mother."

Annah eyed him critically. "Perhaps not. But you look and act too much like my dead brother Yerakh for the resemblance to be a coincidence. I'm sure you didn't listen to your elders enough. One of my own daughters probably married into your family."

His eyes flickered again, and she could almost hear

him silently recounting his lineage to himself, considering possibilities. He looked away. "Even so, Ma'adannah, you will go quietly with us to your encampment."

"Are you carrying any weapons?" the sly-faced Erek demanded.

"Will you search me, child?" Annah asked him gently, aware of her knife and tools secured beneath her robes.

His face turned crimson brown, and he hushed.

The other two horsemen joined them now, their five horses immediately lowering their heads to graze. Abdiy, the hitherto silent guardsman, warned the two horsemen, "This is the First Mother Ma'adannah."

Annah was gratified to see the two latecomers falter, embarrassed. Now she spoke to the guardsman who had her by the arm. "Child, what is your name?"

He looked offended. "You will call me Becay."

"Thank you, Becay-child."

They all shuffled around now, obviously uncertain how to manage her.

Let them be ashamed of themselves, Annah decided as they guiltily nudged her up the slope. *They should be ashamed.*

"How did you find us?" she asked, walking slowly up the grassy hill, wanting information. "We haven't been using cooking fires for days, so you had to know where to begin looking for tracks. Did someone tell you where we were?"

"We were told that you'd be somewhere along the river between the Tribe of Metiyl and the mountains," the guardsman Abdiy said, barely polite.

Becay scowled at him. "Tend your weapons and don't let her distract you; they might already know we're here."

"You should walk her into the camp first, Becay," Erek suggested, his dark eyes suddenly scheming. "If you use her as a shield, they won't shoot you. In fact, I'm sure the Lady Keren would give up her weapons immediately."

Becay sneered, "You'd know *that,* wouldn't you? Actually, Erek, if I didn't think you'd run like a whining coward, I'd have you do it." He shoved Annah slightly. "Let's hurry, Ma'adannah."

"Don't hurt *anyone,*" Annah commanded, feeling panicked now.

"That depends on how everyone else behaves."

The violent terrors of Annah's childhood arose, no longer memories but real again, full of cruel, bloody possibilities. *I beg You,* she cried to the Most High without words, *don't let anyone die. I don't want to see it!*

Keren glanced toward the tree and shrub-swathed hillside that led down to the stream. *Where is I'ma-Annah?* She called to Zekaryah, "I'll be right back; I'ma-Annah may need help with the water."

Shem lifted a genial hand, shaking his head. "Stay with your husband, Keren-child. I'll go find her."

You'll snatch any excuse to pursue your wife, Keren thought, smiling. She went to lift the last bundle of tent leather.

Zekaryah hurried to help her and to kiss her, snatching time alone with her as eagerly as Shem did with I'ma-Annah. "I've missed our children," he said, smiling. "But it's been good to have time to ourselves."

Pleased as always by the sight of his dimples, she hugged him. "I agree. If only we'd hear Shoshannah is safe . . ."

Zekaryah held her and kissed her hair, silent as always whenever she spoke of Shoshannah. He feared that his daughter and Kaleb and Tiyrac were dead, for there had been no messages from the two young men since they departed all those months ago.

Burying her face in his shoulder, Keren tried to convince herself that everything would be well. *They must be alive . . .*

Without warning, Zekaryah roughly yanked Keren behind him as he faced the direction Shem had gone. Keren caught her breath and peered around him, bewildered. Her confusion became terror.

Soldier-guardsmen. Five of them, all brandishing arrows or spears. One man was leading I'ma-Annah, who looked small and defenseless beside him. Two other guardsmen were confronting Shem.

This is Your answer, Shem thought, raising his arms as a thin, devious-looking guardsman searched him and took his knife and a small copper axe from his belt. *Now, because we have no weapons of our own, O Most High, I ask You to be our weapon.*

Accepting captivity for now, Shem looked at his beloved Annah. Her dark, beautiful eyes were huge, anguished, begging him without words to be careful. He winked at her in reassurance. And he smiled at the thin guardsman who was stashing Shem's weapons in his own belt, then backing away as if he feared Shem would attack him.

"Don't worry," Shem promised, "we'll go with you peaceably; there's no need to threaten us further."

"We'll threaten you as much as you deserve," the sly guardsman taunted, apparently feeling courageous now that Shem was unarmed. "Kneel and put your hands behind your back. And call to those others to kneel and wait. Do it!"

~~~

Shem's voice echoed to Keren and Zekaryah. "Kneel and wait; they won't harm you."

"We should obey," Keren told Zekaryah softly, hugging his waist, feeling his tension, his readiness to fight for her. "Perhaps later we'll have a chance to escape. Until then, we can hear about Shoshannah."

Zekaryah's voice lowered dangerously as they knelt together in the chill damp grass. "I knew we shouldn't have allowed Echuwd to speak to his relatives during their last visit."

It was the most logical explanation, Keren realized. When his relatives made their last visit to the Tribe of Metiyl, Yelahlah's husband, Echuwd, must have persuaded them to betray Keren and Zekaryah. *Yelahlah,* she groaned silently to her niece, *what made you love such a man as Echuwd?*

Obviously blaming himself, Zekaryah said, "We should have left immediately after they did."

We would have been in the mountains by now. Farther away from Shoshannah. Thinking of her firstborn, Keren tried to be hopeful. "Perhaps now that they have us, Shoshannah will be freed."

Zekaryah remained stonily silent, watching the guardsman bind Shem's hands. All at once, Keren heard her husband growl. "Ferret!"

Ferret Erek? Surprised, she scanned the guardsmen who were now approaching, leading their horses and Father Shem and I'ma-Annah with them. One of the guardsmen
~~~

was indeed the ferretlike Erek, who had spied on her household during her years in the Great City. She also recognized two others: the arrogant Becay and Abdiy, who had always detested Zekaryah.

She held her husband fervently and kissed his neck, whispering, "I love you! Don't let them provoke you to fight—we need you alive."

"Move away from him!" Becay snarled at Keren, still gripping I'ma-Annah's arm. To Zekaryah, he said, "Lift your hands and don't move; it's nothing to us if you die."

Protected by the threatening Abdiy, Erek gleefully searched Zekaryah and tossed his weapons a safe distance away, then bound Zekaryah's hands behind his back. Keren noticed that Erek didn't dare to speak to Zekaryah directly.

After all these years, you're still a sneaking little scoundrel, Erek, she thought, repulsed.

He noticed her and said, "The 'death order' no longer applies to you, *Lady,* so don't you threaten me now."

Everything and everyone threatens you, she reminded him in her thoughts. *You were never a true guardsman but always a spy.*

Swaggering up to her, he sneered. "Do you have any weapons?"

Keren swiftly unlaced the knife pouch from her belt and tossed it at his feet. "I have that, but nothing else. My bow and arrows are on my horse."

"As you say. Put your hands behind your back." Erek tied Keren's wrists together with cordage, then made her sit as he unlaced her boots and checked them. Keren submitted to his search quietly, aware of Zekaryah, who was smoldering, watching Erek's every move, no doubt longing to kill him.

"Will you tie my hands too, children?" I'ma-Annah demanded, frowning at the way Erek was treating Keren.

Becay shook his head. "As I said, Ma'adannah, we have no quarrel with *you*."

"And as I said, Becay-child, you do have a quarrel with me."

"Still, you are to be treated as our honored guest, unless you give us some reason to change our minds."

"Beloved," Shem urged I'ma-Annah tenderly, "don't give them a reason, please. I'm sure I speak for everyone when I say that we'd rather not see you bound."

Clearly frustrated, Annah gave her husband a reluctant nod. To Becay, she said, "Please, it's obvious my Keren-child has no more weapons. May I help tie her boots?"

Becay released Annah, seeming satisfied now that Keren, Zekaryah, and Shem were all bound.

Annah gave Erek a vicious look and shoved the filled water skin into his hands. "Now, *you*, back away and don't touch her again." He obeyed.

Keren almost laughed at Annah's boldness. "I'ma-Annah, now I see where my Shoshannah gets her willful nature—I've always blamed myself."

"I'll gladly take the blame for her. And for you." Annah relaced Keren's boots. "Come, child. Let me help you to your feet. This is going to be a dreadful journey." Still fierce, she whispered to Keren, "I have my knife and my sewing blades; don't give up hope yet!"

"You amaze me."

That night, Shem stared at Annah, incredulous. "What? You still have your knife?"

"And my sewing blades," Annah murmured into his ear. She rubbed his neck, back, and bound arms, which were aching. "Those overgrown children were afraid to search me. Do I dare cut you free?"

"Let's wait and watch for a few days. We have to be sure we can also free Zekaryah and Keren; they are in more danger than we are."

They looked across the searing, hissing flames of the hearth toward Zekaryah, who was also bound, and Keren, who was temporarily freed. Keren was coaxing her husband to drink some water; Zekaryah was grim, staring hard into the fire.

Shem continued, whispering, "Let's consider the plans of the Most High."

Less than a month before their High Day of Shemesh, Shoshannah thought, sickened. Kneeling beside Demamah, she watched as Ra-Anan, Lord Kuwsh, and the priests sat nearby in the sunlight on the tower's terrace, discussing their final plans for the celebrations. Adoniyram sat with them, unattended by Kaleb—to Shoshannah's regret. She would have loved to see Kaleb instead of just listening as these proud men discussed water supplies, foods, the new cylindrical merchant seals, and the buildings and open spaces that were being cleared for the city's expected guests.

"My four youngest sons have agreed to visit," Lord Kuwsh was saying, as if he had granted a favor to the Great City. "As will the sons of my brothers."

"All of the tribes will be represented," Ra-Anan said pointedly. "Sons of Khawm, sons of Yepheth, *and* sons of Shem."

All the rebellious ones who want to honor the death of that mighty hunter Nimr-Rada, Shoshannah thought.

"Which sons of Shem?" Lord Kuwsh demanded, looking as if he smelled something rotten.

"Elam and Aram. Perhaps Lud and even Arpakshad."

Kuwsh sneered. "Yes, let them come and bow to the memory of my son, who was butchered by their father!"

"Not all of them agreed with their Father Shem's decision," Ra-Anan said. "They will bring gifts."

"Gifts for the temple will be appreciated," the priest Rab-Mawg interposed smoothly, smiling. Shoshannah couldn't remember the last time he had looked so clear-eyed and well rested this early in the morning. But his Master Ra-Anan and Lord Kuwsh didn't seem to notice or appreciate the difference. They stared at him, offended.

But Adoniyram stared at Shoshannah, his gaze so concentrated, so compelling that she longed to hide.

Lord Kuwsh stood without acknowledging Rab-Mawg. "Now that we've discussed everything of importance, Ra-Anan, I must go; I'll speak with you later."

He inclined his head proudly to Ra-Anan. And he gave Shoshannah such a mistrustful glance that she bowed her head politely and didn't look up again until he had departed with his servants.

The instant Kuwsh was gone, Ra-Anan berated Rab-Mawg. "Your foolishness and lack of discretion is becoming indefensible! One more such lapse, Rab-Mawg, and I will strip you of that leopard-skin mantle and give your place to someone else! Be content with the ordinary offerings of the people."

Rab-Mawg lowered his head and didn't reply, but he was tensed, livid.

Turning sharply, Ra-Anan snapped, "Demamah!

Shoshannah! We're leaving. Rab-Mawg—and all of you—remember what I've said." His pristine linen robes flaring, his fine sandals slapping hard on the bricks, Ra-Anan stomped toward the tower steps, followed by his guardsmen.

Shoshannah stood with Demamah and bowed to Adoniyram and to the offended priests, frightened, not daring to look at them. As she fled with her cousin, she heard Rab-Mawg snarl to Adoniyram, "So he gets the gold, and we get dirty peas and barley!"

My next few lessons are going to be horrible, Shoshannah thought, despairing. *Rab-Mawg and the others will be furious for weeks.*

By the time she reached the tower courtyard, Ra-Anan was already mounted on the restless, perfectly groomed Khiysh—with Kaleb standing nearby, obviously pained, watching his cherished horse. Ra-Anan treated Khiysh with such flaunting arrogance and contempt that Shoshannah feared Kaleb would soon protest and be punished.

Kaleb saw Shoshannah now. A flicker of hurt and helplessness crossed his face, and he deliberately turned away as if he couldn't bear to watch her leave.

Shoshannah wept quietly as they rode away from the tower and over the bridge above the sparkling canal.

"Why are you upset?" Demamah begged in a whisper. "Was it that awful Rab-Mawg?"

"I don't want to face him anymore," Shoshannah said, snatching at Rab-Mawg's behavior as an excuse for her tears—he *was* partly to blame. She dabbed at her eyes, trying to compose herself before Ra-Anan or Perek noticed. "I don't want to face anyone—I'm tired of it all! I just want my family."

She was aware of someone riding close behind them now, a dark horse, tossing its head, full of high spirits. Tiyrac was there, riding his brazen Nashak. Unable to help herself, she stole a look at him, trying to comfort herself with the sight of a familiar face. He studied her, big, worried, and dear. If Kaleb couldn't be here, then at least she had a dependable ally in his brother.

Shoshannah straightened, reassuring Demamah, "I'm fine; just homesick."

"I'm sorry. I wish I could know what it's like to be homesick."

"You don't wish to be me."

"I wouldn't be as *rude* as you, but—"

Before Shoshannah could take refuge in a heartening quarrel with her cousin, a woman's voice called out, "Lady!"

Shoshannah glanced to her right and saw a matron swathed in a flowing blue gown and red beads; she offered her infant to Shoshannah with a pleading smile. Remembering Ra-Anan's lectures, Shoshannah halted her horse, flashed the eager mother a warm grin, and quickly turned to Tiyrac, saying, "Please, we need you to bring this child to Demamah—I'm not supposed to hold it myself."

Tiyrac obligingly asked another guardsman to hold Nashak, then dismounted and hurried over to the woman, bowing to her politely before carrying the infant to Demamah. Shoshannah had to nudge her cousin hard; Demamah seemed overcome. Whether it was from the thought of holding a baby or the prospect of facing Tiyrac, Shoshannah couldn't decide. But it was clear that Demamah had never held a baby before; she was wringing her hands, seeming afraid to touch the infant.

Having been raised in the rambunctious, child-fond

Tribe of Ashkenaz, Tiyrac looked as surprised as Shoshannah felt. "One hand beneath its rump, the other beneath its head, Lady," he instructed Demamah firmly, not releasing the infant until Demamah obeyed.

"Oh!" Demamah breathed, clearly thrilled. "Are all babies so light?"

Shoshannah laughed at her, and they admired the black-haired, adorably plump baby. But Tiyrac looked uncomfortable until he was allowed to return the infant safely to its mother.

As Tiyrac turned toward Shoshannah again, she lowered her head. Using her unruly hair to shield her face from Demamah, she murmured, "Listen: I have less than a year to escape—it's serious."

Tiyrac nodded politely, as if she had thanked him. Shoshannah wondered if he had truly heard.

I should not *continue to think of a city girl who doesn't even know how to hold a baby, not to mention that she's the daughter of Ra-Anan,* Tiyrac decided, still recovering from his shock at Demamah's ignorance. He was also aggravated at the way Ra-Anan was persistently goading the unhappy horse, Khiysh, with a flail. He hoped both Khiysh and his master would recover from this ordeal. Now, however, he had to warn Kal that Shoshannah needed to escape within the next year. Though his sister-in-law was often fond of pranks, Tiyrac believed her now.

I am more than ready to leave this place; Kal is too.

He wondered if he should tell Shoshannah that she and Kaleb were married. Tiyrac recoiled inwardly, afraid of shocking or offending her; best to leave *that* to Kaleb.

~ ~

"Kaleb."

Kal turned, watching as Adoniyram left the tower steps, his boots crunching across the gritty, unswept paving bricks in the tower's courtyard. *I'm in no mood to deal with you, Little Lord,* Kaleb thought, almost growling. He was too upset over being separated from Shoshannah and Khiysh. But he managed to bow and wait for orders.

To Kal's surprise, Adoniyram removed a corded gold pendant from beneath his tunic. "Here. Please take this up to those priests for me. Be courteous and tell them that I'm offering it as a gift. It's all I can think of to appease them for now—but don't tell them I said *that.*"

Kaleb bowed and hurried up the tower steps. He hadn't known that Adoniyram possessed any gold at all—he didn't live as richly as Sharah, Kuwsh, and Ra-Anan. Did the Young Lord have more gold hidden somewhere else? *Not that I covet it,* Kal thought emphatically. *I only want what's mine—my wife and my horse. Then I'll leave this place and never return.*

Halfway up the endless stairs, he realized he was about to speak to those disgusting priests. He would rather beat them for frightening Shoshannah. But he had to control himself, for Shoshannah's sake.

He strode briskly into the temple, bowed to the startled priests in polite greeting, then handed Adoniyram's gold pendant to the leopard-skin- and linen-draped head priest. "Forgive me for intruding, but my master, Adoniyram, offers this as a gift."

The thin bald priest stared at him intently. "You're that new guardsman."

"Yes." Kaleb bowed and made himself smile. He had

no intention of talking to these strange, scrawny men—they'd learn that he despised their false Shemesh, and *that* would be dangerous. "Again, forgive me; my master is waiting."

He couldn't leave the temple fast enough. The place was cold, lifeless, and eerie; he hated it. And they had Shoshannah visiting here constantly. He had to get her away.

Twenty-Four

KEREN TRUDGED ALONG beside her husband, exhausted, hungry, aching, and nauseated. She wished she could sit down, or at least ride her horse, but Becay and the others had decided that she and Zekaryah were less of a threat if they traveled on foot. Shem and Annah were also walking, but ahead of them for now.

Like Zekaryah's, Shem's arms were bound for most of their days and for all of their nights. Only the men's leather wrist guards prevented their bonds from chafing bloody sores into their skin.

Keren hated to see them subjugated this way. Blaming herself, she swiped tears from her cheeks.

Abruptly, Zekaryah said, "Look at me."

She looked up at him miserably, knowing he would guess what else was upsetting her. She'd been trying to count the days . . . the weeks . . .

"You're with child."

"I hope not."

"You have those shadows beneath your eyes."

She couldn't speak. Particularly not to argue. If she had those unusually dark shadows beneath her eyes, which had marked all her pregnancies, along with her other achingly familiar and usually welcomed symptoms, then he was probably right.

"Let us live to see this one." His prayer was almost inaudible.

Keren echoed her husband silently, grieving for this infant, which could be lost. She longed desperately to see this child, to embrace it—to hold all her cherished babies . . . Shoshannah, Adah, Qetuwrah, Ahyit, Sithry, Rinnah. She forced herself to continue walking.

Overcome with a severe bout of sickness, Keren knelt shakily in the damp grass. She had to rest. *I was never this sick with the others. Is fear making me weak?*

She *was* afraid—death seemed so near. She would be killed when she reached the Great City. And if she died, then this child would die with her. She hadn't told anyone else of her pregnancy yet. She and Zekaryah had been quietly agonizing over the prospect for days, wondering if it would be wise to tell their captors or not. But I'ma-Annah would certainly guess soon, if she hadn't already. Keren tried to calm herself and to will the nausea away.

Still bound, Zekaryah knelt beside her, his deep brown eyes worried; he looked as if he longed to hold her. Keren clasped his shoulder weakly, praying the nausea would pass.

But Erek rushed over to them, furious, prodding them with the butt of a spear. "Get up! What do you think you're doing?"

Clinging to her husband for support, while trying to defend him, Keren protested, "I'm sick." The effort of speaking was too much. She heaved in front of the startled guardsman, barely missing his boots.

Erek jumped back, revolted. The others laughed at him, while shaking their heads at her. I'ma-Annah hurried over to Keren, though Becay grabbed Shem.

"You're delaying us!" Becay cried to Keren. "We were ordered to return quickly."

You can blame me when we get there, Keren thought, too overcome and too embarrassed to talk. *My sister and the others will believe anything dreadful you might say about me.*

"Keren-child." I'ma-Annah was untying a water skin, pouring some of the warm liquid into a scrap of fleece, then mopping Keren's face as if she were a child. She peered at Keren, a delicate crease in her forehead. "Do you think you'll recover soon, or will this . . . be a while?"

Keren drooped, relieved. I'ma-Annah also seemed reluctant to share this information with their captor-guardsmen. "This will be a while." *I hope I have a while.*

They looked at each other for a long instant. I'ma-Annah nodded and held Keren comfortingly.

The unsociable guardsman Abdiy approached, staring down at them. "She has to get up; we don't have time for this."

"Abdiy-child," I'ma-Annah said gently, disapproving, "she's ill. If you are commanded to bring her alive to your Great City, then shouldn't you allow her to rest along the way?"

Abdiy stalked off to consult with the others. After a

long, muted debate, full of irritated hand waving and head shaking, they reluctantly allowed Keren to rest. She dropped into the grass beside her husband and shut her eyes gratefully, exhausted.

Whoever wanted her brought to the Great City, be it Sharah, Kuwsh, or Ra-Anan, they evidently wanted her alive. But they would have to wait.

Shoshannah swiftly raked a flint blade across the gleaming sides of a fish, sending shimmering, light-catching scales flying into a heap at her knees in Demamah's courtyard. She sliced the fish's belly lengthwise, scraped the slippery innards onto a swatch of leather, rinsed the fish in a tub of cold water, and tossed it into a nearby basket. Then she quickly snatched up another.

Plucking birds nearby, Demamah sighed, shaking her head at the mess. "Look at all the cleaning we'll have to do. At least we're not trapped inside with Tabbakhaw."

"Are you finished with those yet?" Ormah scurried into the courtyard, flushed and harassed. "Tabbakhaw wants the birds first, then the fish as soon as possible. We've got the lamb roasting and the wine cooling in the jars. Why did those people arrive so early? As if we don't have enough to do."

Those people. Shoshannah frowned to herself, scraping the fish hard with her blade. Shem's eldest son, Father Elam, was here a week earlier than they'd expected. And he had brought his wife and his youngest brother, Father Aram, who was Shoshannah's own great-grandfather. A boisterous, food-loving man, Aram had ignored everyone, talking instead with Ra-Anan of trade in the Great City.

I'ma-Annah didn't teach you to be so rude, Father Aram, Shoshannah thought. *You've become that way yourself. You've also betrayed the Ancient Ones and the Most High by attending this ceremony honoring that Nimr-Rada and his Shemesh. Your dear parents would be so hurt to see you . . .*

"Here." Demamah offered Ormah a basket of plucked birds. "That ought to be enough for the evening meal. Does Tabbakhaw really want more?"

"Will you argue with her?" the maidservant demanded huffily. "I won't. When you've finished the rest of those birds and the fish, you'll have to bring them to the kitchen. Hurry." Even as she spoke, Ormah rushed back into the house.

Demamah stared after her, perturbed. "She's being very bossy. If Mother hears her talking in such a way . . ."

"I agree—though I'm not one who should talk about manners." Shoshannah sighed, gutting and rinsing another fish. "At least I don't have lessons today; soon Rab-Mawg will try to teach me prayers to honor their Shemesh; then he'll try to kill me."

"Please, don't talk that way." Demamah shoved a fistful of dark feathers into a nearby basket. "Just obey him, Shoshannah, I beg you."

Shoshannah tossed the cleaned fish into her basket and reached for the next one. "How do I pray to a heartless object, Demamah? I can't. Also, he expects me to wear 'ceremonial' apparel and ornaments from some of the tradesmen."

"Just wear the garments and gold," Demamah advised. "And act forgetful. That should gain you some time."

"He probably won't believe me if I pretend to forget. What could I do then?"

"I don't know." Demamah didn't look at her. "Is your

Most High worth all this, Shoshannah? Is He worth your life?"

"Without Him I wouldn't be alive anyway," Shoshannah said, trying to draw comfort from this thought. "None of us would, Demamah." She sent rainbow flecks of scales flying off the fish with her blade. "I wish you could feel the presence of the Most High as I sense Him sometimes. He's there, *waiting* . . ."

Demamah shuddered, straightening as if she'd been dashed with cold water. "Oh, I wish you weren't so stubborn! And complicated."

Shoshannah shook her head, slicing open the fish. "I'm not complicated. It's all become very simple for me here in your Great City: Do I love the Most High, yes or no? And my answer has to be yes. I can't live with no."

"You won't live with yes either!" Demamah argued, flashing her an angry look. Then her expression softened into a plea. "Can't you just do what they want and keep your devotions to yourself?"

Cleaning and rinsing the fish, Shoshannah pondered her answer. "That would be like someone telling my mother, or any other loving wife, 'Be unfaithful to your beloved husband and keep your love for him a secret.' She couldn't do such a thing, and I wouldn't either. Could you?"

Demamah thrust another fistful of feathers into the basket, her sweet face troubled. They continued their work in silence.

"We cannot escape unless we abandon our Keren," Shem murmured to Annah as they settled down together for the night—beneath an open sky so the guardsmen could watch them. "And they're guarding us too closely; even if Keren weren't ill, we could easily be caught."

Annah listened, knowing her husband was correct. She tucked a woolen coverlet around Shem carefully—he was tied again for the night. Then she settled beside him, kissing his lips, whispering, "You're right. But we should still watch for some way to hide. Surely someone will shelter us—unless we are completely without friends in that Great City."

"Perhaps." Shem sounded doubtful. "The Most High alone knows what will happen. I pray His plans include mercy for our rebellious children."

Looking up at the far-flung, glistening stars, Annah half pretended a defiance of her own. "You pray for those rebellious ones! I'm praying for Zekaryah and Keren and their new infant. And for Shoshannah, Kaleb, and Tiyrac."

Shem chuckled, his breath warm in her hair. "You do that, beloved, as I will. I think I'm praying for you too—you're becoming so fierce. You sound like my mother—and that's not terrible; you just sound like her."

"I miss her." Wistfully, Annah added, "I miss your father too. I wonder what he would think, if he were here."

"He would be praying."

Annah hushed now, completely exhausted, staring up at the skies, praying and pondering the intentions of the Most High.

Shivering in the morning light, Keren emerged from the river. Her leather tunic dripped heavily, and bits of grass clung to her feet as she followed I'ma-Annah up the riverbank toward the small leather tent where they would change their garments.

Shem and Zekaryah sat nearby, both of them clean but bound, and watched their captor-guardsmen, who waited impatiently. Flinging I'ma-Annah a teasing look, Shem called, "Hurry, or we will leave without you."

"No doubt you would!" I'ma-Annah called back.

Keren managed a smile, which faded swiftly. She didn't feel like joking; they would be in the Great City tonight. Perhaps she would be dead before dawn. At least she would be relatively clean when she died. *My baby,* she thought to her unborn child, *I wish I could see you and hold you first.*

On the mats inside the tent, Keren wiped her feet, then changed into clean undergarments and a fresh leather tunic. As she sat down to work a comb through her tangled hair, I'ma-Annah gave her an appraising glance.

"Child, are you better or worse today?"

"Somewhat better. Not that it matters."

"Don't lose hope." I'ma-Annah knelt beside her, combing her own hair. "Perhaps someone will speak for us or offer us a place to hide."

Not while we're prisoners. But Keren remained silent, fighting a stubborn tangle.

I'ma-Annah continued, "I'm grateful they've allowed us to bathe."

"Sharah or Ra-Anan would insist that we must be clean. Kuwsh wouldn't; he'd prefer to kill me outright."

"And what of my Shem?" Annah asked quietly. "Would Kuwsh prefer to kill him 'outright' as you say?"

"I pray not. But if he is seeking revenge for Nimr-Rada's death and thinks of our Father Shem with such contempt, then yes . . . he might have him killed."

"How can this be the same Kuwsh-child I cared for as my own?" I'ma-Annah wondered aloud, sounding inconsolable. "And Shem played with Kuwsh and protected him as he did our own sons. I don't understand why he turned against us."

"Kuwsh wants his children to rule your children," Keren explained, yanking at her hair now—though she decided it was hopeless. "He wants to control us all."

"But does everyone else want him to control them? I think not." Annah slipped the comb through her dark wet hair so easily that Keren would have envied her if she weren't so dispirited. Annah paused now, seeming to remember something bitter. "I think Kuwsh's rebellion is because of his father Khawm's rebellion. Years ago, Khawm insulted and offended our Noakh horribly. Oh, but that was a terrible time. He—"

"You two hurry!" Erek's voice cried from outside, interrupting them. "Before we come in and drag you out!"

His threat angered Keren. And if she was angered, then Zekaryah must be furious. They hurried outside and began to dismantle the tent. As she worked, Keren heard the guardsmen talking.

"We can't let her be seen by anyone," Abdiy grumbled.

Becay sounded irritated. "We'll just throw something over her head."

They're talking about me, Keren realized, as she helped I'ma-Annah roll the deerskin covering away from the wooden tent ribs.

I'ma-Annah patted Keren's hand, giving her a questioning look while tipping her head toward the guardsmen. "They want to hide you from others, Keren-child?"

"It seems so," Keren agreed, upset. "I'm sure my presence will create chaos in the Great City if I'm seen."

Shaking her head, I'ma-Annah boldly approached the guardsmen, who all straightened as she spoke. "My sons, I have something she can use to remain hidden; you can't just throw a piece of leather or wool over—"

Becay swiftly nodded and raised a hand toward her—a silencing motion of agreement. The others retreated, unwilling to argue.

Annah smiled at them kindly, went to one of the packhorses, and unfastened a leather bundle. Returning to Keren, she said, "I knew you would be determined to find Shoshannah, so I thought it would be wise to bring this. I know you'll take care of it. I've mended it over the years."

Opening the bundle, Annah produced a light, fragile length of netting, scattered with tiny, intricate, naturally decorative knots. Keren didn't dare touch it.

"Your veil . . . the one you wore as a girl in the times before these . . ."

"I know you'll take care of it," I'ma-Annah repeated. "Let's finish packing our gear, then you can put it on."

"But I can't." Keren stared at the veil, scared, humbled. She could just imagine herself shredding the precious, delicate threads that were such a part of her heritage.

"Obey her, child," Shem commanded, very much the First Father.

Unnerved, Keren bowed her head in mute agreement. Then she glanced at her husband. Zekaryah returned her look, troubled.

"How did you survive beneath this veil for so many years?" Keren asked, peering through the fragile mesh toward I'ma-Annah, who was guiding her by the elbow. "I feel as if I'm walking through an endless mist."

"You'll become used to it," I'ma-Annah promised, "if you have to wear it for very long." She almost halted, staring ahead. "Keren-child, is that their tower?"

Focusing through the veil, Keren saw what she had prayed never to see again: a mountain created by man, that formidable brick heap they called a tower. "Yes. Though it's much higher now."

"O Living Word," Shem prayed aloud behind them, almost groaning, "be merciful. How it must offend You."

Zekaryah made a quiet sound of agreement. Keren longed to look back at him, to take refuge in his arms. To hide from the sight of the Great City. *Most High, please, I don't want to go there again!*

But Shoshannah was there. Keren willed herself to continue.

The path toward the Great City was widening now, and more travelers merged with them, carrying heavy packs of gear, or guiding horses, donkeys, and oxen. All of these travelers were laughing, chattering, and joking loudly, delighted to see the Great City.

Keren felt others staring at her curiously as they walked. Now she was glad for I'ma-Annah's veil; she didn't want to be recognized by any of these people. Neither did Shem or Annah; despite the summer warmth, they had both pulled light hoods over their heads, hiding their faces.

"Stay close!" Abdiy prodded Shem and Zekaryah sharply with a bow stave as they turned into the crowded city streets. Keren was almost limping. When had they paved the streets? Her feet already ached with so much walking, and now the brick pavings worsened her misery.

And being jostled by the arrogant citizens didn't help.

"Every faithless person on the face of the earth must be here," I'ma-Annah muttered to Keren, stepping around a small dung pile.

"It's so much more crowded than I remember," Keren whispered, overwhelmed.

"What's wrong with her?" An impudent young man called out to Erek, while pointing to the veiled Keren.

"It's not your business!" Erek retorted snidely. "Run back to your I'ma, boy, before we bind you too."

Keren felt as if she would stifle beneath the veil, amid the bustle and the warmth of the late-afternoon sun. Even the southern end of the city, which she remembered as being comparatively quiet, was teeming with noise and confusion. She was recognizing some of the houses, including the pale, wall-enclosed one she had used for more than six years. Its trees were amazingly tall now, their branches drooping over the high walls, lush and overgrown. This had been a place of despair for her, yet it was also here that she and Zekaryah had first acknowledged and nurtured their love.

Unable to help herself, she peeked over her shoulder, through the mists of the veil, at Zekaryah. He glanced from their former residence to her, his quiet expression mingling love and regret. *I'm sure he also believes we will die here . . . soon.* Keren had to force herself to keep moving and not to give in to her despair.

"There is Ra-Anan's home," she told I'ma-Annah later, as they passed the sprawling, wall-enclosed residence.

"It's too much of a home." Annah studied the residence from beneath her head covering, then looked away. Her tender voice infinitely saddened, she said, "How terrible that he has become so important and proud."

"I wonder where they've hidden Shoshannah."

"I have been praying for her. And for us."

I pray He listens. Keren had to fight her sense of betrayal against the Most High; it was affecting her badly, worse than the despair. Now they were walking toward the Great-King Nimr-Rada's massive wall- and guard-protected home.

Sharah. You sent these men for us, Keren realized. The thought brought up a nausea unrelated to her pregnancy. She didn't want to face her sister again. But would she rather face the vindictive Kuwsh? Or Ra-Anan, whose ambition was never restrained by compassion?

"Becay!" A thickset, rough-skinned guard, wearing an unshorn fleece-hide cloak, called out cheerfully. "You've finally returned. You were expected days ago! I'm glad I'm not *you*."

"Close your mouth and open the gate," Becay snarled, narrowing his dark eyes at the guard.

The coarse guardsman opened the wooden gate and bowed as they all passed through. Noticing Zekaryah's and Shem's bound wrists, he smirked. "An honor, my lords! A delight. Welcome."

Keren gritted her teeth at his sarcasm, and Annah exhaled, obviously indignant. "I hope his mother wasn't one of my own daughters!"

They were led inside Nimr-Rada's former home—which was certainly Sharah's now. All of Nimr-Rada's gruesome hunting trophies were gone, replaced by lavish linen draperies, sprawling black-outlined murals, thick furs, mats, piles of baskets, ornate red-painted vases, huge arrangements of garish iridescent plumed feathers, and low, wide wooden chairs strewn with heaps of fleeces. Keren stared through the veil, amazed at the transformation from a deathly stark room to a lush, overwhelmingly feminine retreat. It was too showy to be restful.

"Sit!" Abdiy commanded harshly, earning a frown from Becay. The two guardsmen were wearing on each other by now, enmeshed in a power struggle.

Soon a delicate metallic musical noise made them all look at the far side of the room, toward sheer linen draperies shielding a passageway. Sharah—overpainted, overdressed, overindulged, and wearing countless gold and jeweled bracelets—flung the draperies aside and swept into the room. The instant she saw Shem, I'ma-Annah, and Zekaryah, she laughed triumphantly.

"Oh, but welcome," she cooed, sounding like a falsely sweet variation of her guard at the gates. "Though you're so late, I should punish your guardsmen." Glancing at the five wary guards who had followed Keren and the others inside, she waved Erek off. "Go tell my son that he won't be eating dinner here tonight after all. Go!"

Erek bowed and departed, looking relieved.

Sharah smiled again, clasping her pale hands together beneath her chin—an exaggerated, condescending gesture. "Now, what will we do with you all? Keren, my own dear shadow sister, is that you?"

Reaching toward Keren, Sharah snatched the veil away, eyeing it. "A lovely old thing—what a pretty gift; thank you, my sister." She draped the veil over her shoulders like a shawl, then settled decorously into one of the fleece-draped chairs, saying to Keren, "You look horrible."

"I've been ill," Keren said quietly, watching Sharah pick at the fragile meshwork. "That is I'ma-Annah's veil; you must give it to her now. And where is my daughter?"

"You always *were* ready to quarrel." Sharah sniffed. "And never mind your daughter—she's nothing. Look: I can do whatever I want now, including ripping this sad old fishnet to bits. Not to mention that I'll decide *your* fate, so don't provoke me."

"What is there for you to decide?" Shem asked, his dark eyes very wide, intense, his voice dangerous. "Keren is your own sister."

"Are you saying I should forgive her for being a traitor to my people?" Sharah tossed her head. "That's not your problem. This is my kingdom. Anyway, didn't the Most High spare that Kayin in the Garden of Adan for killing his brother Hevel?"

If she weren't feeling so ill, Keren would have laughed at her sister's warped version of the earth's first murder.

Shem said, "At least you remembered their names. Return the veil to my wife, please. And answer us: where is Shoshannah?"

Her pale eyes glistening wrathfully, Sharah wadded up the veil and flung it hard at I'ma-Annah without looking at her. She focused on Shem instead. "That troublesome girl is not your concern. I'm remembering now why I've always disliked you—you're so haughty and sure of yourself. I won't put up with you!"

As Keren watched, infuriated by Sharah's rudeness, I'ma-Annah folded her veil neatly, then asked, "What will you do, Sharah-child?"

"Whatever I please, Ma'adannah. And don't call me 'child.' You don't rule here."

"It seems you've said that quite often," Shem observed. "But repeating something over and over doesn't make it true, child."

"Oh, but it is true, as you'll learn." Sharah settled herself into her padded chair again, hostile. "*You* can't endure it when someone has more authority than you!"

"You're being unjust," Keren said quietly. "All these things you've accused our First Father of . . . they aren't true." *They apply to you, not him.*

"Always the loyal follower, aren't you?" Sharah mocked Keren viciously. "But really, you're the worst liar of all—deceiving our elders with your 'sweetness,' trying to steal my place here, plotting to kill our Great King, and seducing this fool to help you!" She nodded toward Zekaryah, who smoldered at her, outraged.

"You've imagined all those things," Keren argued, not raising her voice. "And you don't need to insult my husband and I'ma-Annah and—"

A young man swept into the room now, handsome, as tall as Zekaryah, with smooth brown skin, an inviting smile, and such long-lashed, fascinating eyes that Keren was shocked beyond speech. His eyes were very much like those of a guardsman from years ago, Qaydawr. Bowing to the indignant Sharah, he kissed her cheek. "Mother, I've come to see if you're well—you called off our evening meal so suddenly that I was worried. But I see you have company, so I'll . . ."

He halted, seeming astonished, staring at Keren. She returned his stare in disbelief. His voice was the same, low and deliberately appealing. *There's no mistake; he is Qaydawr's son.*

"I am pleased to meet your son," Keren told her sister carefully.

Sharah glared at Keren and dismissed her son with a furious wave of her hand. "I will speak to you tomorrow morning, Adoniyram!"

"As you command. I look forward to seeing you." Adoniyram bowed politely, but he threw a searching look toward Keren just before he departed.

She watched him leave, then turned to Sharah again, wondering about Qaydawr. *Where is he?* She dared not ask. But she would ask about Shoshannah again.

Speaking coldly to the guards, Sharah pointed to Father Shem. "Put him out in the streets after dark, with his wife. Tomorrow their enemies will hunt them down and kill them like animals." Jerking her chin at Keren, she continued, "Put her—and her stupid husband—into one of my storage rooms and bar the door; then guard it. If they escape, I give you my word you'll be punished."

Frantic, Keren hugged Annah, whispering, "Find Yabal the potter, and his Meherah. I love you both! Tell our children I love them too. And my parents . . ."

By now, Erek had returned and was dragging Keren to her feet, while Abdiy took hold of Zekaryah. Keren's throat burned with the effort to control her tears. In despair, she prayed, wishing she'd been able to learn something hopeful about Shoshannah.

She knows who my father is, Adoniyram thought, going into his quiet sleeping room and dropping onto his wide, linen-curtained bed. There was no doubt in his mind that she was Shoshannah's mother, tired and thin but still lovely, with those amazingly pale eyes and the forthright nature he knew so well. And there was no doubt that she had recognized his face. He had noticed her surprise.

I have to speak to her. But how? My mother will certainly keep her hidden . . . but where?

Twenty-Five

"OUT!" SHARAH'S hefty, fleece-cloaked gateman thrust Shem and Annah into the dark street.

Unbound now, Shem looked back at the man, appalled by his behavior.

The gateman glared at him, pitiless. "Don't stand there staring at me! Whoever you are, you're not wanted here. Move on." The obnoxious guard shut the gate, settling the bar from inside with a resounding clunk.

"Beloved," Annah pleaded, her hand light upon Shem's arm, "let's leave this place for now."

They walked toward the dark market street. Shem looked around, detesting this Great City. He could hear voices, laughter, the muffled rasping of a grindstone, and two men arguing from one of the houses nearby. Most of the people of the earth seemed to be here. But he and his dear wife, who shared a small, vital part in the lives of these rebels, were alone in the murky streets with no food, shelter, or anything to barter for their safety. No doubt Sharah was thrilled by their plight, considering it revenge. The notion set Shem's teeth on edge.

Breaking into his thoughts, Annah murmured, "Our Keren said that the potter Yabal and his Meherah might help us."

Shem recalled the names from Keren and Zekaryah's stories: Yabal and Meherah, who had lost their firstborn son, Lawkham, to Nimr-Rada's violence. "Working with clay, they must live near the river." Choosing a house at random, he thumped on the door to track down the potter Yabal.

"Beloved, untie these," Zekaryah whispered as soon as he and Keren were alone in the dark, windowless storeroom. But even as he spoke, he felt Keren's soft fingertips moving along the cords at his wrists, picking at the leather knots that had frustrated him during these past few weeks.

Zekaryah waited in tense silence, exhaling his relief as the last knot finally opened. As Keren rubbed his hands and arms, Zekaryah turned and embraced his wife. He had been so afraid for her—was still afraid for her. Feeling her thinness beneath her garments, he muttered angrily, "You've lost too much weight."

"It doesn't matter."

"It does." He knelt now, peering at the slash of light streaming in beneath the doorway. Four big leather-booted heels were there. Two guards. And he'd been bound for so many days that his arms felt weak. He couldn't attack the guards outright. He had to think. What was in this storeroom? As his eyes adjusted to the dimness, he moved around noiselessly, inspecting the contents of the room. Jars. Baskets. Leather bags of grain. Relieved, he took Keren's hand, gently pulling her toward the bags of grain, making her sit on them. If need be, they could even recline upon these for the night. "Rest."

Reaching down into one of the jars, he moistened his fingertips, then sniffed and tasted the liquid warily. Water. Cool, scentless, tasteless. Reasonably fresh and clean. He sighed his gratitude. "Here," he beckoned. "Drink as much as you can."

They could chew on some of the grain too. He had to rest and gather his strength; he had to save his wife, their unborn child, and Shoshannah. *If anyone has hurt Shoshannah, I will be merciless.* Was he right to be so angry? Enough to almost kill? *Yes.*

Zekaryah made plans. As soon as that door opened, he would act.

Furious, Sharah poured some wine from a gold flask. Her hands were shaking, and she sloshed some of the dark red liquid onto her bedchamber floor, spattering her newest pair of sandals. Adoniyram had upset her badly.

"Why do you never listen to me?" she muttered.

She hadn't wanted Adoniyram to see Keren and the others. If he dared to feel sympathy for the worthless Keren and tried to argue in her defense, Sharah was going to have him beaten. Son or not, he must learn his place, and he had to stop treating her enemies like friends. *He knows Keren is here . . .*

Worse, Keren had obviously recognized Qaydawr's

beautiful features in Adoniyram's face. Beloved Qaydawr. Sharah had adored him more than any other man. How terrible it was that he had needed to die. Now, years later, she could see Ra-Anan's wisdom in having him killed. On occasion, she was sure that Adoniyram—and perhaps Kuwsh and others—suspected that the supposedly great Nimr-Rada was not Adoniyram's father. Fortunately her people still trusted and loved her more than they had ever loved Nimr-Rada, though they exalted *him* to the heavens. She didn't regret his death at all.

Nor will I regret your deaths, Sharah thought of Keren and the others. *How can you ragged idiot farmers be my own family?* They were an embarrassment.

She poured herself another drink. And another.

"Come in, come in! Quickly!" Meherah, the diminutive wife of the potter Yabal, pulled Annah and Shem into her modest clay-brick home, her dark eyes shining with delight. She embraced Annah and kissed her cheek. "Are you truly the First Mother Ma'adannah? And Father Shem? Oh, but you *are* just as the Lady Keren described you; we're honored! Have you come to take our Shoshannah-child from Ra-Anan's household? May the Most High bless you!"

Annah loved Meherah instantly. And Meherah's thin, work-toughened husband, Yabal, was also kind, though more reserved, as were their three unmarried children—a son and two daughters. Their family seemed prosperous though unpretentious, wearing simple woolen tunics and sturdy sandals.

"Sit and rest," Yabal urged. "Let us bring you a bit of food."

He hustled off, waving to his son and daughters for help. They followed him eagerly, almost dancing with excitement at having unexpected company.

Meherah, chattering happily, presented Annah and Shem with water and coarse cloths to scrub their faces, hands, and feet. "We'd invite you to sit on the roof where it's cooler, but a passerby might wonder who our guests are. People gossip so much in this Great City. And our home would be suspected as the first place you might take refuge in—we'll hide you elsewhere tonight with those who love you as we do. We've prayed you would come here if you *had* to come. Our son will guard you as you sleep. Oh, but first you must rest and eat."

Satisfied that they were comfortable, Meherah took away the used water and cloths, then presented them with tart, refreshing fruit juice, sweet sticky dates, and bread softened with oil.

Annah could smell meat searing, mingling with garlic and spices. Soon she realized that a bit of food to Yabal was apparently everything in their storeroom: rich olives, more dates, fresh white curds, beans, and choice, tender pieces of lamb.

As they ate, Annah and Shem told their story. Hearing that Keren and their adopted son, Zekaryah, had been captured by Sharah, Meherah burst into tears, praying softly, "Most High, save them!"

Yabal nodded, consoling his wife, trying to reason through the situation aloud. "Surely they aren't in immediate danger . . . Our friends will listen for talk tomorrow in the marketplace. If there's a way to save them, we will find it."

There was no need for Shem and Annah to ask for information about Shoshannah. Yabal, Meherah, and their children told them everything they knew of her troubles. From the beating Shoshannah received on the day of her arrival, and her tragically disrupted escape attempt, to the danger she had been in on the night of the women's festival, and her enforced visits to the Temple of Shemesh atop the tower.

Yabal's lean bearded face hardened when he spoke of that. He loathed the temple.

Meherah shivered dramatically. "How we've been praying for our Shoshannah-child! As has the wife of our Lord Kuwsh, his Achlai, who loves the Most High. She protected Shoshannah's clothes and sewed weapons into the child's garments after her arrival, hoping Shoshannah could use them to escape. But you know how sadly that ended. Oh, but we mourned for her."

Full of good food and lulled by the sultry night, Annah felt her tired limbs relaxing. She tried to stay alert, but Meherah noticed her fatigue. Patting Yabal's hand to get his attention, she nodded toward Annah and Shem. "Beloved, they are so tired; we'd be rude to keep them awake. Let our son take them away to rest."

"Ezriy." Yabal beckoned his son, fond but firm. "Guard our guests with your life, more than if they were your parents."

The young man nodded solemnly, looking at Annah and Shem with big brown eyes. His parents kissed him, and he gathered his weapons: a knife and a leather sling with a small bag of stones.

Meherah wept as she hugged Annah. "Be safe, be well! Let us see you again."

Annah hugged her hostess and thanked her fervently,

realizing that Meherah and her husband had sacrificed much for them tonight. Now they were offering their cherished youngest son, endangering his life as well as their own.

As they walked through a night-shadowed field, their feet rustling through the coarse straw, the young Ezriy confessed worriedly, "Every day I regret my panic in the marketplace when Shoshannah was taken. But I was so sure she was the Lady Keren—their resemblance is so close I was shocked. I beg your forgiveness, and hers."

"You have no need," Shem answered, his quiet voice reassuring in the darkness. "Shoshannah does look like her mother."

Sounding more at ease now, Ezriy confided, "I will always remember the Lady Keren bringing my brother Lawkham's body to us the day he died. She was as overwhelmed with grief as any of my sisters. My parents never once blamed her for his death; they turned to the Most High instead. They hate what my brother's death has become to the people of this city."

His young voice rising in exasperation, he continued, "Those women who place offerings in the river, then feast and dance in the streets, they don't remember our Lawkham as he was in life. I grow angry thinking about it. My parents tell me to forgive those who have forgotten Lawkham. The Most High knows the truth."

"Your parents are wise, Ezriy-child," Annah said gently, trying to keep up her pace.

"They *are* wise," Ezriy agreed, wonderfully matter-of-fact. Calmer now, he said, "I'm taking you to the merchant Tso'bebaw's home. He and his wife, Peletah, will be glad to see you. And perhaps they can plan a way to save our Zekaryah and Keren."

Annah followed Shem and the young man to a walled clay-brick house with a high roof. A lamp glowed from inside through a leather-shaded window.

"They're still awake," Ezriy said, pleased. Marching through the gate, he rapped on the door, calling, "Father Tso'bebaw? I'ma-Peletah . . . are you there?"

"Ezriy?" A man answered the door, blinking, his shoulders set in a deep slouch. "Is something wrong? What are you doing out so late, my son? You'll be tired and good for nothing tomorrow."

"I'll work as always tomorrow," the young man promised readily. "But look, I've brought guests to you. This is the First Father Shem and his Ma'adannah."

Annah feared the merchant would choke with shock. After sputtering and stammering incoherently, he motioned Shem, Annah, and Ezriy inside. There, on a low table, an oil lamp flickered beside a collection of carving tools and a flat disk of ivory. Nearby, a sturdy woman bounded to her feet, dropping a tunic she was mending—her mouth sagging open. "Is it true?"

"I'ma-Peletah," Ezriy begged, before Peletah released the shriek Annah was sure would emerge from her lips, "this must be secret. Our guests are in danger. I'll tell you everything. But my parents humbly ask a place for them to sleep tonight. Your roof is higher than ours, and I'll guard them."

"Yes, yes, certainly! Show them up the ladder at once!" Peletah rushed here and there, thrusting mats and fleeces into her husband's arms so he could carry them up to the roof. "I'll bring you some water and food and drinks—you must be exhausted after your journey. It shouldn't rain tonight, and our roof is high enough that you won't be seen easily."

Despite herself Annah drooped throughout the obligatory visit that followed—she was still full from her meal with Yabal and Meherah. But she ate again: bread, fruit, cold spiced meat, honey cakes, barley water, and fish charred over a brazier set on the roof. The young man, Ezriy, knew the merchant and his wife so well that he was soon able to maneuver them down the ladder again without offense, cheerfully begging them—as they loved the Most High—to guard the door below. As the merchant Tso'bebaw prepared to descend the ladder, he reassured Shem and Annah firmly. "Tomorrow we will try to find some way to help your loved ones. You can hide yourselves in my booth, if you wish."

"Thank you," Annah sighed. The stooped merchant beamed at her, then descended into his house again. Ezriy settled down in the farthest corner of the roof to keep watch, and Annah and Shem crawled onto the soft, freshly made pallets to rest. Annah barely had time to look up at the stars and thank the Most High for providing this place of refuge. One breath later, she was asleep.

Shoshannah stepped out into the courtyard, dreading this dawn. She prayed Rab-Mawg wouldn't insist that she learn prayers to recite to their nonexistent god Shemesh. *I can't "pretend" to forget them as Demamah suggested; Rab-Mawg won't believe me.*

He would probably throw her down the temple steps.

Uneasily she watched her Uncle Ra-Anan, wondering if she dared to plead with him to end these lessons. Ra-Anan was belligerent, speaking to some overseers who worked in the fields around the tower.

"You *will* clear all the canals surrounding the city. If you have to use your own bare hands, then do it! After our celebrations of Shemesh, I will inspect every canal. And I assure you that I know who is in charge of each one. When the rains return next year, we must be prepared." Eyeing the sullen men grimly, Ra-Anan said, "You know full well that if we have any trouble with flooding in our city, it will be because of *your* negligence!"

Some of the overseers lowered their eyes, but most of the men looked as if they wanted to argue. Ra-Anan sent them off with a wave of his hand, disturbingly reminiscent of their Queen-of-the-Heavens Sharah.

I won't ask for mercy today, Shoshannah decided. *There will be none. Most High, please be with me. And with Kaleb and Tiyrac.*

She didn't see Tiyrac anywhere in the courtyard, but his absence wasn't surprising; Demamah was staying home today to help Tabbakhaw cook for their guests. Therefore, Tiyrac was probably shoveling manure this morning. She envied him.

Followed by Kaleb, Adoniyram entered his mother's residence, looking around. Perhaps she was still asleep; it was early yet. "Wander around," he muttered to Kaleb. "If you see any rooms closed up and guarded, come tell me at once. I'm going to speak with my mother."

"Yes, my lord." Kaleb bowed obediently. But he gave Adoniyram a curious, searching look.

Adoniyram thought about telling his guardsman exactly what he was spying for but decided to not waste words. Kal would know the truth soon enough. Bracing himself for a tirade, Adoniyram strode down the dim corridor to his mother's private rooms and rapped on the wooden door.

"Come in," his mother's voice beckoned, stiff, preoccupied.

"It's only me." He stepped inside and bowed, surprised to find her awake. Her private rooms were even more overdone and cluttered than the feather- and linen-decked main room. He detested the stifling fussiness of it all. "I thought I should spare you the trouble of sending for me."

"Yes, you were right," his mother agreed coolly. She was seated, fully robed, adorned, and painted, with a maidservant combing her hair. But her eyes were tired, and she grimaced as if her head ached. "The next time I give you a command, Adoniyram, don't decide that you know better than I do. You were not welcome last night."

Although her command last night hadn't actually forbidden him to visit her, which meant that he hadn't acted inappropriately, Adoniyram knelt, pretending the utter misery she usually expected. "Please forgive me, but—"

"Don't question me about *anything* you saw last night; do you understand?"

"I won't," he agreed, infuriated.

"What are you doing today?" she asked—not as an interested mother, Adoniyram realized, but as one who would change his plans for him.

He shrugged. "I'll probably go hunting with my Master-Uncle, when he's finished receiving gifts at the tower—and when *she* is finished with her lessons."

"Lessons," Sharah scoffed. "Surely those priests know they've failed to teach her manners by now."

Pretending surprise, Adoniyram said, "But they aren't teaching her manners. They are teaching her to take her mother's place; she will receive gifts from the people for Shemesh."

High pink color flooded Sharah's face. "I forbade them to give her any power!"

"Rab-Mawg insists that she is bound by her mother's oaths," Adoniyram said, using his most apologetic tone. As he expected, it didn't help.

His mother stood, furious, shoving her maidservant out of the way. "Where are my sandals? Send for my horse! I am going to deal with this now!"

"Mother, it may be too—"

"Get my horse! Now, before I disown you!"

He bowed and left, sweating. Kaleb was waiting for him in the doorway of the main room, looking as serious as Adoniyram had ever seen him. The tall guardsman bowed and whispered, "You were right, my lord. There is a doorway, closed and guarded, near the kitchen."

"Did the guardsmen notice you?"

"No, my lord, they were both leaning against the wall, dozing as if they've been standing there all night."

Elated, Adoniyram looked around furtively before hissing, "Listen! Go to those guards and tell them you're there to take their places. Big as you are, they'll believe you. Tell them to eat and get some sleep immediately. As soon as my mother and I are gone—but not before—you bind any prisoners in that guarded room and take them to my residence. Bar them in one of *my* storerooms. If anyone stops you, resist them. Say that you were commanded to do this. Don't lose them for me! Hurry."

As Kaleb marched off to do his bidding, Adoniyram darted outside to call for someone to bring mother's horse. He had to get her out of here quickly.

Exhausted after his journey but determined to profit by his knowledge, the guardsman-spy Erek bowed to Lord Kuwsh within the quiet main room of Kuwsh's huge brick-and-timber home. Kneeling beside Kuwsh, the Lady Achlai watched Erek steadily; the guardsman felt her mistrust.

Lord Kuwsh had just finished his early meal and impatiently motioned for Erek to speak. The guardsman knew better than to waste words.

"We captured the First Father Shem and his Ma'adannah, as well as the Lady Keren and her husband. The First Father Shem and his wife are somewhere in the Great City— the Lady Sharah sent them away with nothing last night. But the Lady Keren and her husband are being guarded inside our Queen of the Heaven's own residence."

Kuwsh stood, snatching up a linen mantle, his dark eyes bright and hard as he waved off his wife's anguished protests. "We will find that Shem. And I'll go to the Lady Sharah and demand her traitor-sister's life! You've earned a new horse for this, Erek."

Erek bowed, pleased. It was more than he had dared to hope for.

When Kaleb knew that Adoniyram and the Lady Sharah were gone, thankfully with half of her household in attendance, Kaleb tapped lightly on the door, lifted the bar, and called inside, "Come this way; stand where I can see you."

There was a shifting, rustling sound inside the dark

room, then a slow, careful rasping sound, like a heavy clay jar being lifted from a stone. A shadowy human form moved into the thin ray of light shed by the open door. From behind the person, a second form whispered, "Kal!"

I'ma-Keren! And Zekaryah! Kaleb wanted to shout and hug them and whoop like a boy freed from chores. He restrained himself. But he couldn't help grinning like an idiot. "Forgive me; I have to tie you both—I'll be sure you're safe." He noticed Zekaryah setting down a large clay jar. "What were you doing with that?"

"I was planning to knock you senseless," Zekaryah muttered, turning around and putting his wrists behind his back. "Keep the knots loose."

Kaleb obeyed swiftly, eager to get them away from this place. He would take them through the back gates of both residences, which led to the stables, away from the streets. There would be few, if any, people there. Most of the guards would be gone with Adoniyram and the Lady Sharah. Those who remained were either eating or not fully awake yet, for it was still early in the morning—a blessing. *Guard us, Most High!*

In the secluded room behind the temple, Shoshannah shuddered, looking down at the gold ceremonial ornaments. Kneeling beside Shoshannah, Ormah whispered, "Just behave and put them on! It won't kill you!"

It just might. Slowly Shoshannah donned the two symbol-incised gold rings, the matching gold cuffs, flat gold throat collar, and the narrow gold band for her head.

Studying Shoshannah, Rab-Mawg frowned as if she were an unacceptable decoration. He was in a foul mood this morning—rough shaven, his dark eyes fiery, glittering. The other three priests moved forward now, staring.

"She looks like her mother," Ebed said quietly, as Ghez-ar nodded.

"But without the weapons," Awkawn sniffed.

Rab-Mawg whirled around, facing them. "You have other duties. Go get water, all of you. Be sure our robes are clean and start scrubbing the temple for the ceremonies. Awkawn, be sure the wine is set where it will remain cool. Ghez-ar, check the plants on the terrace; run some water from the cisterns down to the trees and shrubs before the day becomes too hot."

The attendant-priests scattered like wrongdoers who'd been caught. Rab-Mawg frowned at Shoshannah again. "You will wear these ornaments whenever you come to the temple. We'll have sandals made for you later, depending upon our Master Ra-Anan's generosity." He sounded bitter while speaking of Ra-Anan.

Ormah straightened, restless beside Shoshannah. The young magician-priest gave her a forbidding look, causing the maidservant to swallow nervously. Rab-Mawg eyed Shoshannah.

"For your lessons today, you'll draw the signs in the stars that you studied most recently. Then I will show you the proper way to approach the altar of our Shemesh during a ceremony; you've been disrespectful coming and going through the temple."

Shoshannah nodded, relieved. He hadn't mentioned that she must learn any words or praises to his god. Perhaps she would escape that terrible duty for today. Feeling awkward in the gold cuffs and rings, she pressed out a soft tablet of clay, flattening it carefully. Now, holding a slender reed marker, Shoshannah closed her eyes, trying to remember the last wretched nighttime lesson. *What were those patterns in the stars?*

"Move, Perek!" Sharah's voice echoed through the temple into the secluded area. "Go find your Master Ra-Anan and stay there!"

She sounds so angry . . . Hearing Sharah's swift footsteps, Shoshannah frantically tried to remove her rings, but she wasn't quick enough. The Queen of the Heavens flung the full linen curtains apart and stormed into the secluded area, her pale eyes immediately flashing to her niece.

"What's this?" Sharah demanded, slapping a hand toward Shoshannah's head, snatching the gold band and thrusting it beneath the hostile Rab-Mawg's nose. "I warned everyone that *she* is not to be honored in any way here! Particularly not with her mother's status in this temple!"

"She's bound to this temple by the same oath that binds you, Lady," Rab-Mawg said angrily, leaning toward Sharah, clearly eager to quarrel with her. "If she doesn't fulfill her mother's oaths, then you must."

"Who are you to tell me what I should do? You're no one! You're a miserable priest—and you won't be that for much longer!" Sharah screeched, her hands flailing in uncontrolled fury.

Ormah was scuttling away, apparently bent on escape. Shoshannah was bent on the same thought, but the Queen of the Heavens pointed at her, screaming, "She's leaving this place now—with me—and she won't return!"

"That's not for you to say!" Rab-Mawg snarled, putting his face directly in front of Sharah's. She struck at him with the gold circlet she had snatched from Shoshannah's head. The irate priest dashed the circlet away; it fell ringing against the stone floor, provoking Sharah further. She clawed toward him. He grabbed her wrists and shoved her viciously, their confrontation becoming a violent struggle.

Alarmed, Shoshannah jumped up and retreated as the priest and the proud would-be Queen of the Heavens went sprawling into the linen curtains, shredding them down. The Lady Sharah was wild with rage, clawing, kicking, biting, becoming entangled in the curtains like a fish in a net. Rab-Mawg flung more fabric over her thrashing limbs, then dragged her away from his beloved temple area, toward the carved stone brazier. Sharah was screeching unintelligible threats against the priest. Equally maddened, he seized the stone brazier and bludgeoned her, ashes and dead coals falling like dark spattering rain. Sharah screamed horribly, desperately.

He's killing her! Panicked, Shoshannah turned to call for help. Adoniyram was behind her, watching, unmoving as a carving. "We must help her!" Shoshannah gasped. She glanced toward the Lady Sharah and Rab-Mawg again. Sharah was struggling feebly within the linen curtains now, her cries fading beneath the magician-priest's frenzied blows. Shoshannah averted her gaze, horrified—the linen was deeply stained with blood.

Now Adoniyram moved, grabbing Shoshannah's elbow and pulling her toward the temple door. "Hurry, or you might be next!"

She went with him, stumbling down the stairs, pleading, "We have to help her! Adoniyram . . ."

He seemed to not hear.

Twenty-Six

"YOU HAVE TO HELP HER—she's your mother!" Shoshannah pleaded, breathless and frantic as Adoniyram rushed her down the steps.

"There was nothing I could do; you saw what happened." Adoniyram looked upset, but he sounded unexpectedly reasonable. "It was stupid of her to quarrel with Rab-Mawg. I tried to warn her, but she never listens to anyone."

But you could have saved her, Shoshannah argued silently. Horrible as Sharah was, still she *was* his mother. "Perek and the others might have gone to help her."

Adoniyram didn't answer.

Shoshannah glanced up at him, trying to comprehend his feelings. He was frowning at the servants and guards in the temple yard below. Didn't he care that his mother was probably dead? There had been so much blood on the curtains . . . and Sharah's awful cries . . . The memory made Shoshannah waver and stumble.

Adoniyram gripped her arm, dragging her from the steps. Loudly, he called to Sharah's and Ra-Anan's servants, "Get up there! Help my mother!"

The servants all stared, then bowed and ran up to the temple. Ormah had apparently gone to find Ra-Anan; Shoshannah didn't see either of them. Adoniyram pulled her toward her horse. "Hurry. We have to get you out of here. If my mother is alive, she'll insist upon killing Rab-Mawg and you."

Knowing he was probably right—about this at least—Shoshannah dashed to her horse. Adoniyram helped her up, then swiftly bounded onto his own restless creature. Anxious, Shoshannah looked around for Kaleb. He always accompanied Adoniyram. Why wasn't he here now?

Kal, what's happened to you? As Shoshannah envisioned the dreadful things that might have happened to Kaleb, Lord Kuwsh rode into the temple yard, accompanied by a number of guardsmen. He flung himself off his horse, glaring at Adoniyram.

"Where's your mother?"

Adoniyram nodded toward the tower. "She and Rab-Mawg have quarreled."

Followed by his guardsmen, Lord Kuwsh rushed up the stairs.

Adoniyram quickly leaned over and grabbed Shoshannah's horse by its bridle. "Let's go."

Shoshannah stared at Adoniyram, dazed, wondering how he could be so calm. Her own terror was eating at her like some merciless predator shredding a living victim. *O Most High* . . . She pleaded for His help over and over in wordless, jumbled anguish.

Rab-Mawg set down the stone brazier, leaning upon it heavily, his head pounding, his rage fading as he gazed at the unmoving, linen-wrapped body before him. Had he killed their Queen of the Heavens? Agitated, he sought a life pulse in her wrist but found none. *I only wanted to subdue her . . . I was defending myself . . . She was insane . . .* Excuses filled his mind, balancing his fears. Adoniyram, the maid-servant, and that girl, Shoshannah, had all witnessed the confrontation—they knew the truth. But they had all fled, leaving him to deal with the aftermath. *Traitor,* he thought of Adoniyram. *You don't deserve my loyalty; you've deserted me for protecting myself and my temple.*

He was right. He would tell his accusers so. Even now, he heard rough footsteps scuffling inside his temple. Sharah's and Ra-Anan's servants surrounded him, their faces all alike, shocked and disbelieving. Standing, he lifted his chin defiantly. *Cowards, all of you!*

"That was Kuwsh riding past us with his guards," Shem told Annah as they sat in the merchant Tso'bebaw's booth, their faces shielded with borrowed lengths of linen. "I have no doubt!"

"Should we go after him?" Annah asked reluctantly, distressed by her husband's anger at Kuwsh's gold-decked, power-flaunting pride.

His eyes very wide, dark, and kindling, Shem stood and offered Annah one long, work-hardened hand. Breathing a silent prayer heavenward, Annah drew the linen across her face, covering all but her eyes. Then she accepted her husband's hand.

Ezriy, son of the faithful Yabal and Meherah, started to his feet, but Shem refused the young man's protection firmly, gratefully, clasping his shoulder. "Thank you, Ezriy, but you must stay here."

The gentle merchant Tso'bebaw almost wept as they parted, whispering aloud, "Living Word, protect them! Spare all their lives . . ."

Throughout the morning, Meherah had been praying while she worked, as her dear Yabal had been praying. Surely Zekaryah and Keren would survive. There had been too much death. *O You who sees us, let it be enough.*

In her stately home, the Lady Achlai, wife of Lord Kuwsh, left her four youngest sons and daughters-in-law to finish their late, lingering morning meal. They were happy and laughing. She didn't want to worry them with her tears. In her own room, she huddled down on a mat, weeping, longing for a compassionate and final end to her husband's rage, his craving for vengeance. And, yes, for his ambition. *Forgive him! Forgive us.*

Let Us, then, go down . . .

Sick with dread, Annah walked north with her beloved husband through the crowded, brick-paved market street. She hated this loud, bustling, rude city, all that it meant, and all that it might yet become. How offensive it must be to the Most High! Worst of all, however, was that wretched tower—the symbol of Nimr-Rada's flagrant rebellion. The symbol so adored and uplifted by all these people. And there were so many people. It frightened Annah to think that these were her own descendants. Grief fell upon her, pitiless, heaped with regrets. *Have I somehow turned them against You?*

At the end of the market street, Shem stopped, and Annah paused with him, staring across the rippling, glittering waters of the canal that separated them from the tower. They had only to cross the hewn wooden bridge to find Kuwsh, Annah was sure. But she didn't want to move. And apparently, neither did Shem. Curious, Annah looked at her husband. His hand tightened around hers, but he wasn't looking at her. He was watching a traveler, robed and covered much as they were covered. *Do we know this man?* Annah wondered.

As if to answer her question, the traveler turned and looked at them. He could have been anyone's son: brown skin, dark hair, brown eyes. An ordinary man. But his expression . . . His eyes were passionately, vividly alive and full of . . . *everything*. Strange yet wonderfully familiar. *He trusts the Most High . . . His Presence is here.*

Nodding politely, the traveler turned away from the tower and walked past Shem and Annah into the city, vanishing among the crowd. Annah stared after the man, wishing they had spoken to him. He didn't seem to belong here any more than she and her husband did.

A breeze fluttered lightly past Annah's head covering,

easing the midmorning warmth. Shem started to say something to her; but they were both distracted by the thudding clatter of horses charging off the wooden bridge. Two horses passed, ridden by Sharah's son, Adoniyram, and a richly clad young woman with flowing dark brown curls. It took Annah an instant to recognize her. *Shoshannah.*

Raising her voice, she cried, "Shoshannah!"

But it was already too late. Adoniyram had turned their horses into the market street, barely slowing their pace. Shoshannah looked around almost wildly, without seeing Annah and Shem. The crowds in the street parted for the two young riders, then surged together again.

"She's more important to us than Kuwsh," Shem decided aloud. They turned and followed Shoshannah.

Shoshannah heard a woman calling her name—someone who sounded amazingly like I'ma-Annah. She looked around desperately but recognized no one in the crowd. Adoniyram was riding too fast; he was frightening her.

"Please, Adoniyram, slow down. There's no need for us to hurry so."

"There is," he insisted, his usually charming features cold. "We have to hide you away until I'm sure you'll be safe."

"I'll be safe. Ra-Anan won't kill me because of what's happened. Slow down, Adoniyram, please. If you're so worried, you should have brought your guardsman."

"There wasn't time."

"He might have saved your mother from—"

"Don't speak of her again."

Now his tone, his whole attitude, frightened her more

than his riding. Had he wanted his mother to die? *You did!* she thought, horrified, convinced she was right. *You wanted your mother dead.* The realization choked down all her arguments. If he could be so cruel that he would seek his own mother's death, then he would certainly turn against her if she pushed him too far. *I don't understand you! Nor do I want to.*

She was relieved to finally see Ra-Anan's walled home. As soon as she was inside, she would run to Demamah's room and stay there. She would never again speak to Adoniyram willingly. Never. To her shock, Adoniyram urged her horse past Ra-Anan's gate. She couldn't help calling out, "Stop! Adoniyram, where are you going?"

"Where you'll be safe." Obstinate—definitely lord-like—he said, "Shoshannah, if you start a scene, I give you my word I'll finish it. Now, listen to me; *trust* me; I'll be sure you're protected. You'll have no need . . ."

She felt a breathlike breeze, stirring both fear and wonder. Adoniyram was still speaking to her, but she couldn't understand him. She stared at his face, trying to comprehend his words. He was serious . . . and she didn't understand the chopped, garbled syllables emerging from his lips. *I don't understand . . . He's speaking to me . . . and I don't understand. It's all been too much; I'm going mad.*

Other voices lifted around her throughout the street, garbled like Adoniyram's but different. *I am going mad.*

Adoniyram looked away from her now, turning them toward a wall-enclosed residence, whistling sharply to the guardsmen. They seemed bewildered as they opened the wooden gate and bowed.

This must be his residence, Shoshannah told herself, looking around inside the unadorned garden courtyard. Her panic heightened. *He's taking me into his household!*

Frantically, she scrambled off her horse and ran, but

Adoniyram caught her arm before she even reached the gate, which the guardsmen had already closed. At once, Shoshannah dropped to her knees on the hard brick pavings. She would *not* go inside with him.

To her surprise, Adoniyram knelt with her, gripping her gold-cuffed wrists painfully but talking quietly, his appearance rational, his voice garbled and mangled unintelligibly. Overcome by her failing senses, by everything, Shoshannah felt herself breaking down into tears. "I don't understand what you're saying! Adoniyram, please, I don't understand."

What is she babbling? Adoniyram stared at Shoshannah, incredulous. She couldn't be joking at a time like this. Watching her hard, he realized she was serious. She was crying, her gray eyes were huge, bright with tears, almost wild as she pleaded with him in low, clipped phrases he couldn't comprehend. The only word Adoniyram could even half understand from her lips was his own name, and she was drawing it out all wrong. Was she that frightened of him? Wrapping his arms around her, trying to soothe her, he said, "Shoshannah, beloved, why are you so afraid? Calm yourself."

His words had the opposite effect. She cried despairingly, covering her ears, obviously pleading with him again but using words he couldn't decipher.

Kaleb paused near the kitchen in Adoniyram's home, baffled, listening. He was almost certain he could hear Shoshannah outside. Was she crying? Looking left and right, he leaned inside the hushed storeroom where he had hidden Zekaryah and I'ma-Keren. "Something's happening outside. Wait here, I beg you. I'll be right back."

"Be safe," I'ma-Keren whispered to him. Kaleb loved her for being concerned. She was in far more danger than he. Closing the door softly, he crept out to the courtyard and stared, appalled.

Two horses were nosing around the courtyard gardens for stray bits of greenery. And beyond them, near the gate, Adoniyram was kneeling on the bricked ground, holding Shoshannah in his arms. She was clutching her hands to her ears, crying, "I don't understand! You're not making sense! Adoniyram, stop this, please."

Adoniyram's other servants were backing away, looking thoroughly bewildered. Kaleb hoped they remained bewildered, because if Adoniyram didn't take his hands off Shoshannah very soon, then Young Lord or not, he was going to be flattened like a lump of stomped clay.

Controlling himself strictly, Kaleb knelt near Adoniyram, gaining the young man's attention. When Adoniyram threw him a secretive questioning look, Kal nodded tightly, knowing that he was wondering about their prisoners.

Yes, my lord, they are safe and in your household, but they won't remain here, and neither will my wife.

Adoniyram spoke to Kal in skewered, warped bits of sound. A command, Kaleb realized, startled. *Wonderful! This man has the power to kill me, and I don't understand a single word of what he just said.*

Shouts were arising in the streets outside the gate, women shrieking horribly, men snarling. Two guardsmen suddenly tumbled inside the gate, kneeling, burbling words at Adoniyram, making him stare at them, obviously confounded.

I didn't understand them either, Kaleb thought, swallowing hard. *Most High, has everyone forgotten how to talk?*

Turning again, Adoniyram said something unintelligible to Kaleb. To Kal's relief, however, Adoniyram followed the mumbled command with an unmistakable nonverbal look and a tilt of his head. He wanted Kaleb to take Shoshannah inside his residence. Kal nodded and bowed, then spoke to the now-hushed, tearful Shoshannah. "Come, Lady; I'll be sure you are safe."

"No." Shoshannah shook her head. "I'm not going in there. Don't you understand what he's doing? He wants to make me his wife!"

"Understand me, please," Kaleb said distinctly, fearing Adoniyram might suddenly recover his senses and comprehend what they were saying. "You'll be safe; I'll be sure of it."

"Truly?"

"You have my word."

Adoniyram felt Shoshannah trembling, but she seemed to recover as Kaleb spoke to her. She wiped her eyes, sucked in a shaky breath, and stood. Standing with her, Adoniyram kissed her wet cheek, then her hand, murmuring, "You'll be safe; go inside, beloved. I'll return to you as soon as I can."

Shoshannah studied him again, clearly not understanding what he had said. But she followed Kaleb obediently. She had understood the big guardsman. *How? Why didn't I understand him?* Mystified, Adoniyram watched

Shoshannah until she was safely inside his house. Then he caught his horse and followed his scared, incoherent gatemen out into the streets. Whatever was happening, Adoniyram was determined to confront it. He could not allow chaos to take hold in his city. *This is my kingdom now.*

He hoped Rab-Mawg and Kuwsh were fighting in the temple, and that Ra-Anan would join them; they could struggle for supremacy among themselves until they killed one another.

"You've ruined yourself," Kuwsh told Rab-Mawg coldly, pleased by the sight of the body and by the young magician-priest's disgrace. A breeze wafted through the temple, and Kuwsh inhaled it, feeling refreshed. Victorious. Now he had only to be rid of that useless, scheming Adoniyram. Not to mention Ra-Anan.

My own sons will help me deal with them, Kuwsh decided. *We will take control of this kingdom, as we should have done after Nimr-Rada's death. And I will deal with the Lady Keren. As soon as I find her.*

He would have to search for Keren himself, since Sharah was no longer able to reveal her sister's whereabouts. He would order his guardsmen to tear apart Sharah's residence as soon as he dealt with this fool Rab-Mawg.

The magician-priest glared at him, looking like a trapped wild animal. And he growled out words—deformed, hacked bits of noise that made no sense.

Kuwsh laughed at the thin, shaven priest contemptuously. "You've lost your mind, haven't you? And no wonder—after all the brewed herbs and poisons you've experimented with. Did you think I wouldn't hear of your doings? You are a fool." Glancing at his guards, Kuwsh said, "Kill him."

His guards blinked and stared. Impatient, Kuwsh repeated, "Kill him!"

One of his guards spoke now, his tone and manner respectful, his words guttural and strange. Two of Ra-Anan's servants gabbled at Kuwsh, agitated, shaking their heads.

They've all gone mad, Kuwsh thought, stunned.

Ra-Anan charged into the temple now, looking around, arrogant as ever. He eyed Kuwsh and snapped out words that sounded like rattling, whispering nonsense.

Kuwsh frowned at him. "What is wrong with you?"

Instantly, Ra-Anan's dark eyebrows went up quizzically. One of his servants muttered something, Rab-Mawg growled out more gibberish, then everyone began to jabber and yell, gesturing broadly. Ra-Anan stared at them all and fled from the tower as if chased by wild beasts.

Cold fear chilled and raised the hairs on Kuwsh's head and down his neck. *What have You done to us?* he wondered to the heavens—to the Most High, whom he had not deigned to address in years. Horrified, he scurried after Ra-Anan. *I have to get home.*

The priest Rab-Mawg stood within his glittering, golden temple, triumphant, watching his enemies flee like the cowards they were. Shemesh had saved him by confounding Kuwsh, Ra-Anan, and their servants. *I will live; I've escaped punishment.*

But now he had to get rid of this woman's corpse; it

was defiling his temple. Calmer, his heart settling into a more normal rhythm—though his head still ached and pounded thickly—Rab-Mawg looked around for his attendant-priests. Ebed, Ghez-ar, and Awkawn were clustered together uncertainly in the side doorway, watching him.

Irritated, Rab-Mawg motioned for them to help him remove the body. As they wrapped their defeated Queen of the Heavens in linen and carried her outside to bury her amid the plants, Rab-Mawg said, "She will be more useful to us now that she is dead; she will rule unseen, and we will speak for her!"

When he realized that his fellow priests were staring at him as if he were insane, or a babbling toddler, Rab-Mawg knew he had not escaped punishment after all. Who could accept his commands if they didn't understand him? How could he possibly rule this kingdom? *This cannot be true. I am ruined. I am mad . . .*

Trailed by Perek and the weeping Ormah, Ra-Anan rode with Kuwsh through the streets, feeling more vulnerable than he had after that would-be assassin, Dayag, had slashed at him in the darkness.

The citizens were yowling at each other or weeping and tearing their hair. Others were hastily packing up their belongings to flee. Many screamed at Ra-Anan and Kuwsh, as if condemning them for this chaos.

A man spat toward him, and a woman gestured expansively, her voice rising in hysterical accusation. Refusing to take the blame for this horror, Ra-Anan lifted his hands toward the sky, pointing emphatically. *There. Blame the heavens! Blame Him!*

He found the motion effective and profound enough to stop many people where they stood, reducing them to hopeless misery and tears. But numerous rough laborers and merchants were not so easily subdued; they glared threateningly and joined others who were running south, toward his and Kuwsh's residences.

Kuwsh frantically prodded his horse ahead, toward his home.

Unnerved, Ra-Anan followed Kuwsh's example.

Shoshannah frowned, doubtful, as Kaleb opened a door and urged her inside, murmuring, "Whatever you do, beloved, keep quiet. Give these to the others." He handed her a sheathed knife and a spear. "I'll get more weapons; then we'll reclaim our horses."

Others? Was Kaleb teasing her? Shoshannah stepped into the dim storeroom and hesitated, whispering as loudly as she dared, "Who's in here?"

A woman's voice answered softly. "Shoshannah?"

Shoshannah thought her heart would fail from shock. "I'ma!"

They found each other in the darkness. Shoshannah hastily set aside the spear and held her mother with all her might, crying—particularly when she heard Keren's stifled sobs and felt her tremble. A hand passed over Shoshannah's hair, and her father's voice, profoundly grateful, whispered, "Thank You."

Overwhelmed, Shoshannah hugged him and her mother, rejoicing until her father said, "Shhh. What's Kaleb doing? When he returns, we'll find the others and leave."

Averting their faces, Shem and Annah listened and watched amid the chaos outside the walled gate. "Shoshannah must be inside," Annah murmured to her husband. "That young man, Adoniyram, rode away from this gate."

"And Zekaryah and Keren are probably inside Sharah's home," Shem agreed. "I pray we can rejoin them soon." Around them, people were calling to each other, packing gear, departing . . . scattering just as their ancient patriarch, Noakh, had predicted.

As You planned, Annah thought to the Most High, amazed. *This is Your will.* "Shem, the stranger, the traveler we saw by the river . . . When we met him, did you feel the Presence of the Most High?"

"You sensed Him there too?"

Kuwsh dismounted in his courtyard, stunned. His household was teeming with people he didn't recognize. Everything was in turmoil. His four youngest sons, their wives, and Achlai were standing in the courtyard. Achlai hugged herself fearfully as their sons and daughters-in-law jabbered to each other, trying to communicate. Sabtekaw, his usually glib youngest son, spied Kuwsh first and rushed toward him, talking frenziedly. His three brothers joined him, anxious, letting citizens and servants loot his household while they tried to argue.

Achlai approached now, her face grave as always, her dark eyes tear dampened, grieving. "My husband, we have nothing left here now. Perhaps our eldest son will understand what we say . . ."

She wept and began to embrace her children as if bidding them farewell.

Sebaw, Kuwsh thought, dismayed. His second-born son—now the eldest—had always politely detested Nimr-Rada and avoided the Great City, and Kuwsh. *How can I possibly turn to Sebaw?*

Ra-Anan heard his wife screaming before he entered the house. Zeva'ah was in the main room, pummeling Demamah, who cowered and wept in a corner, heedless of their dumbfounded guests: Father Elam, Father Aram, and their elegantly robed, raven-braided wives and all the servants. And heedless of the intruders pouring into his house.

Desperate to bring his wife to reason, Ra-Anan grabbed Zeva'ah, shaking her. "Stop! Our household is being overrun by thieves! What's wrong with you?"

"Tell your father what's wrong!" Zeva'ah screamed, pushing the ashen, sobbing Demamah toward Ra-Anan. "Talk to him."

To Ra-Anan's horror, Demamah fell to her knees, pleading with him in low, tortuously fractured syllables. Ra-Anan shook his head at her, stupefied, "I don't know what you're saying. I don't know . . ." He had awakened at dawn, full of confidence in his life and his power. Now, at midmorning, he realized he had nothing at all.

Twenty-Seven

"HERE!" KALEB LEANED into the small storeroom and handed Keren, Zekaryah, and Shoshannah bows, quivers of arrows, and knives. "Hurry, before we're caught."

Elated at being with her parents and Kaleb again, Shoshannah slung the quiver over her back and tested her bow. It was her own bow, confiscated by Adoniyram; Kaleb had reclaimed it for her. She longed to hug him for his thoughtfulness. Quickly, she snatched an arrow and held it against her bow, ready to use.

"Go," her father urged quietly, pulling open the door.

Shoshannah darted from the storeroom, following Kaleb. *Let us be successful,* she prayed. *Not like last time.*

Her parents followed her, their arrows clattering softly against their bow staves, their boots scuffling as they rushed through another brick-and-bitumen room, obviously a kitchen. A matron-cook in a smudged tunic and two fleece-cloaked guardsmen were chattering at each other, flustered amid piles of vegetables, bread dough, and baskets of eggs and fruit. The cook gaped at Shoshannah and Keren and retreated, fearfully. The guardsmen eyed Kaleb, Zekaryah, and all their weapons, then backed into a wall trying to avoid them.

Encouraged, her pulse racing, Shoshannah dashed outside after Kaleb, her mother and father at her heels. Warm straw-horse-manure scents greeted them from a sprawling, wide-doored set of buildings, the stables shared by Adoniyram and Sharah's households.

"Let's find our horses and gear," Zekaryah muttered, looking around inside. To Keren and Shoshannah, he said, "We're lacking one horse; you'll have to share."

"I'm taking Khiysh when we go after Tiyrac," Kal said, resolute.

As Kaleb guarded them, they swiftly readied the horses and gathered what they could find of their travel packs and tents. Then Zekaryah helped Keren onto a light brown horse, handing her the reins and her weapons.

"Tiyrac will be in the stables behind Ra-Anan's home; he could bring our other horses," Shoshannah informed her father as he boosted her onto the horse behind Keren. With a pang of distress, she added, "I wish I could see Demamah before we leave."

"My little Demamah . . ." Shoshannah felt her mother sigh. "Kal told us that you've lived with her in Ra-Anan's household. But we have to find Tiyrac."

"Someone's coming!" Kal backed inside the shadowed doorway. "One of Sharah's guardsmen. He's got a horse we can borrow—then we'll have two for Father Shem and I'ma-Annah."

Zekaryah crept up behind Kal and waited. Keren kept the horse still, and Shoshannah lifted her bow, cautious. The instant the guardsman rode into the stable, Kal grabbed the unsuspecting rider's arm and tunic belt and threw him to the stable floor while Zekaryah caught the horse. As Kal dragged the squawking guardsman to his feet, Shoshannah begged, "Don't hurt him, Kal."

"I won't." Kaleb released the scrawny, terrified man.

Keren stiffened, recognizing him. "Erek."

Zekaryah growled. To Shoshannah's shock, he walloped the frightened guardsman in the stomach, then shoved him face-first into a manure heap and kicked him ferociously in the rump. "You're blessed I don't kill you!" Still glowering, Zekaryah leaped onto Erek's horse as Kaleb mounted another and snatched the spare animal's bridle.

The guardsman Erek was retching in the straw as they rode out of the stables.

"What did that Erek do to make Father so angry?" Shoshannah begged in a whisper.

"He was a coward and a spy—always," her mother explained, clearly convinced that Zekaryah was justified in attacking him. As they guided their horses into the crowded, disordered streets, Keren said, "Watch for I'ma-Annah and Father Shem."

"I knew I'd heard I'ma-Annah calling me this morning!"

Even as she spoke, Shoshannah heard Shem yell, "Zekaryah, wait! Here we are."

Shoshannah desperately wanted to jump down from the horse and hug I'ma-Annah and Father Shem, but she didn't dare. People were gathering now, gawking at Keren, yelling gibberish as Shem and I'ma-Annah mounted their own horses. Thankfully, the people seemed unable to talk among themselves coherently enough to plan an attack.

"What's happened to them?" Keren wondered aloud, incredulous.

"This is how Adoniyram sounded to me this morning," Shoshannah murmured, her earlier distress returning. "I couldn't understand anything he said—it's the same with everyone here." She felt ill, scared.

"Shoshannah-child," I'ma-Annah called to her above the din, "are you well?"

"Yes, but let's leave, please!" Shoshannah begged, her courage failing.

"As soon as we find Tiyrac," her mother promised.

They rode to Ra-Anan's residence, with Zekaryah and Keren brandishing their weapons at anyone who blocked their path. As they turned toward the stables, Zekaryah called out, "Keep your weapons ready and stay together. Tiyrac! Where are you? Tiyrac, answer us!"

They all began to shout themselves hoarse.

Demamah stood with her family and their guests in the main courtyard, weeping as gangs of furious men invaded her father's house, destroying whatever they didn't claim for themselves. If only they could be reasoned with . . . if only they could be placated. *But Father has no way to speak to them, and neither do I.*

The confusion of everyone's speech was the worst thing of all. Tabbakhaw had chased her from the kitchen, shrieking horribly; then their guests had backed away from her as if she was some bizarre, terrifying creature, and her mother had struck her face, her back, her arms.

Until her father had returned . . . angry and babbling as senselessly as everyone else.

And he had returned without Shoshannah.

Demamah feared the priests had killed Shoshannah after all. She tried to ask about her cousin, but no one could speak properly and tell her. She didn't know how she would survive without Shoshannah's companionship, her humor.

Have I deserved this? she cried silently, glaring up at the heavens through her tears. *Just kill me.*

"Tiyrac!" A man's voice resounded harshly beyond the walls. "Where are you? Tiyrac, answer us!"

Other voices joined the man's, causing Demamah to turn. *Shoshannah.* She heard Shoshannah's voice, calling Tiyrac, of all people. And she had understood Shoshannah's words.

Demamah bolted from the courtyard, passing her distressed relatives and her angry parents, determined to find her cousin.

Tiyrac appeared from behind the stables, carrying a bale of hay, looking baffled, then flabbergasted to see them all waiting for him. Shoshannah would have laughed at his expression if the situation weren't so serious.

Zekaryah rode forward, calling out, "Are you alone there? Hurry! Get your horse."

"And mine!" Kal bellowed as Tiyrac flung down the hay and raced into the stables.

And mine, Shoshannah thought. *Ma'khole.* "I'ma, please, I have to get Ma'khole."

"We may not have time," her mother began quietly.

"Shoshannah!" Demamah's voice echoed from the corner of the wall nearest the street. Shoshannah turned, surprised. Demamah halted, staring at her, at Keren, at all of them, her gentle face crumpling in despair like a lost child silently begging for help.

Shifting her bow and arrow in her hands, Shoshannah dismounted hastily, barely hearing her parents' cries of warning. *I have to* . . . The words lingered unfinished; the realization that she had to leave Demamah was too painful to crush into a simple thought. She ran to her cousin and hugged her.

Demamah clutched her and sobbed, "You're going? You can't!"

"If only . . ." Shoshannah faltered as Ra-Anan dashed around the corner of the wall, with Zeva'ah, Father Elam, Father Aram, and their two wives following him tentatively. They all stopped, gaping at Shoshannah, Keren, Father Shem, I'ma-Annah, and the others.

While Ra-Anan smoldered, Zeva'ah cried out hissing, rustling words that were unmistakably accusations. But Father Elam, Father Aram, and their dignified black-haired wives all retreated, watching Father Shem and I'ma-Annah dismount.

"Why do I find you in this evil city?" Shem asked his sons and their wives, sounding deeply wounded, stung almost to rage.

"My firstborn . . . and my youngest," I'ma-Annah murmured achingly, her big dark eyes betrayed, pleading. "Tell me you haven't forgotten our Most High."

Father Elam protested in a mangled babble. And Father Aram gave his parents an imploring look—his eyes wide and dark as I'ma-Annah's, while liquid, indecipherable noises poured from his lips.

"I don't understand my mother or our guests," Demamah whispered to Shoshannah. "Do you understand them?"

"Not at all. I think we've lost our minds."

Father Shem and I'ma-Annah were equally upset. They were trying, again, to talk to their sons, who couldn't communicate with them or with each other.

Shem turned to Annah, despairing. "Beloved, we are being separated from our children . . . scattered as my father has said."

"Separated?" Demamah asked, her voice rising shakily. "What do you mean? I'll never understand my father and mother again?"

As she began to sob, Ra-Anan spoke dry, whispery syllables, raging at Keren.

"You've won, haven't you, my sister!" Ra-Anan cried, clenching his hands into fists to keep from lunging at Keren and yanking her off her horse. He was unarmed, while she, her husband, Shoshannah, and that false guardsman, Kaleb, were all holding their bows and arrows ready. "You and your Ancient Ones and the Most High! You've brought this disaster upon us—you've stolen everything from me!"

While Ra-Anan was speaking, he saw Shoshannah adjust her own bow, then whisper to Demamah, who nodded tearfully, evidently understanding what Shoshannah had said. Focusing on his daughter now, Ra-Anan asked, "Do you understand me at all, Demamah? Have I lost you too?"

"What do you mean?" Zeva'ah demanded, the color ebbing from her face. "She's our daughter!"

Ra-Anan looked down at his wife. He had to compose

himself, to give his bitter realization words. "I think she's lost to us. By the will of their Most High."

"No." Zeva'ah shook her head vehemently. "You're wrong!"

"Speak to your daughter, beloved," Ra-Anan said, knowing it was hopeless. "If she understands you, then she is still yours. If she understands them . . . she is theirs."

"You're wrong," Zeva'ah insisted. Turning, she called out, "Demamah, come here! Leave that girl and her family; you don't belong with them. *Demamah!*"

Keren fought down her nausea, unable to believe what was happening. And while the others were trying once again to speak to each other, the horses were stirring, agitated by the delay and by Zeva'ah's rising hysteria.

Zeva'ah was grabbing Demamah now, pulling her away from Shoshannah, denying what was happening.

Reluctantly, Keren called out, "Demamah-child!"

When Demamah looked over at her with those somber, long-lashed eyes Keren remembered and loved so well, Keren said, "Don't be afraid, little one. Kiss your mother and give her a hug; she will understand you then. Kiss your father too, child—this is not your fault. They must know it's true."

Demamah nodded miserably. "Thank you, I'ma-Keren."

The young woman's gentle verbal agreement with Keren caused Zeva'ah to waver, then to shriek in anguish.

Following Shem, Annah hugged and kissed her first-born son and her youngest, grieving, uncertain if she would ever see them again. Elam and Aram looked ashamed and mournful, though Annah wondered if they were truly repentant—or if they fully understood what was happening. But she would not allow them to remember her as angry or unforgiving.

Their wives, daughters of Yepheth and Ghinnah, and Khawm and Tirtsah, wouldn't look Annah in the eyes. Determined, she put her hands on their proud, lovely faces and made them look at her. "Be wise. Be careful," she told each one, realizing that they couldn't understand. With difficulty, she restrained her tears. "I love you."

Turn again to the Most High . . .

Seated on Ma'khole now, Shoshannah watched as Ra-Anan helped Demamah onto her horse and sternly coerced the weeping Zeva'ah to give their daughter a farewell kiss. But then Ra-Anan glared at Keren once more, seeming to blame her for his predicament. Behind him, his residence was billowing with smoke, flaring and crackling with flames. Shoshannah felt almost sorry for him, and for Zeva'ah, yet she was ready and eager to leave.

By now Tiyrac had retrieved his gear and was astride his horse, Nashak, who was hungrily nosing through the pile of abandoned hay.

Kaleb, meanwhile, was soothing the nervous Khiysh, while trying to communicate with two guardsmen who had approached him. After failing to understand each other despite repeated shrugs and hand motions, the two guardsmen nodded at Kal and hurried into the stables.

"Ghid'ohn and Ye'uwsh. They're good men," Kal told Shoshannah, regretful. "They brought me here."

"I'm grateful to them," Shoshannah murmured tenderly. She looked ahead at her father.

Zekaryah was watching Father Shem and I'ma-Annah, who were settling onto their own horses again. They motioned their last, sad farewells to Elam and Aram, then nodded at Zekaryah, who swiftly urged his horse onward.

As Zekaryah led them around the back of Ra-Anan's walled residence, then south—apparently to avoid the chaotic main streets—Shoshannah prayed this escape would succeed where her own had failed. How ironic that they were taking the same route. But this time, she didn't want to cross paths with Perek or Adoniyram.

Particularly not with Adoniyram.

I'ma, she thought, distressed, watching her mother ride ahead, her weapons ready, *how will I tell you that your only sister is dead, and that Adoniyram allowed her to die?*

A glob of mud spattered over Kuwsh's shoulder as he walked away from his smoking, ransacked home. Kuwsh seethed but didn't dare to look back at the offender. He would never find the guilty one among the crowd who had forced him and his family onto the streets with almost nothing but the clothes they wore. Everything he had owned was now stolen or burned, including his gold and his favorite leopard-skin mantle.

Defiantly Kuwsh shook out the linen mantle he had snatched this morning and swathed it over his head. He had been certain this would be one of the best, most triumphant days of his life. Now, before midday, he was utterly vanquished.

Beside him, Achlai walked in silence, accepting this disaster as quietly as she accepted everything else in her life, both good and evil. He resented her composure. "See what your Most High has brought upon us?"

"Because of our rebellion," she agreed gently, as they turned south and west, toward Sebaw's tribe.

Kuwsh repressed a superstitious chill and glared at the trampled dirt road. Puffs of dust lifted into the air, roused by the footsteps of those traveling ahead of them. His four youngest sons and their wives followed him, bewildered, occasionally speaking aloud in their garbled fashion, as if hoping this chaos would pass like a bad dream.

As they joined others who were fleeing the pandemonium within the Great City, Kuwsh glanced at eight riders passing them. He envied the riders their horses and their possessions, until he recognized them: the traitor-guardsman, Zehker; the Lady Keren; Shoshannah; Demamah; those two stinking horseman-brothers, Kaleb and Tiyrac; and I'ma-Annah. And, worst of all, Nimr-Rada's executioner, Shem.

Kuwsh raved inwardly. *I was so close to avenging my son!* Now he was powerless against their weapons. They didn't notice him amid the crowd, for they were riding toward the river, talking among themselves. Communicating.

Furious, Kuwsh looked away, hating them. But Achlai sighed, her head turning as she watched them depart. He saw longing in her expression. And grief. "Forget them!" he snapped, scowling at her.

"I cannot forget those I have loved, my lord," Achlai said, her gaze and her words including him.

She put him to shame.

Shoshannah watched anxiously as her father dismounted in front of a modest clay-brick home. An ample earthen oven smoldered in front, but no one was visible until her father gave a sharp whistle.

A thin, sun-darkened man peered around the side of the dwelling. When he saw Zekaryah and the others, he threw his muddied hands up high, laughing. Alerted by his laughter, I'ma-Meherah, the ivory merchant Tso'bebaw, I'ma-Peletah, and the young man Shoshannah remembered from her first day in the Great City all came running around to the front of the house. Exultant, I'ma-Meherah hugged Zekaryah. He kissed her cheek and picked her up briefly as if she were a child.

Meherah scolded Zekaryah tenderly. Hearing her voice, Shoshannah sagged in despair. I'ma-Meherah and her family and friends had been separated from them by the awful confusion of speech that had swept through the Great City. Silently Zekaryah hugged his adoptive mother again, then embraced his adoptive father, Yabal. When Shoshannah next saw her father's face, she realized there were tears in his eyes.

Father, I'm so sorry! Following her mother's lead, and Father Shem and I'ma-Annah's, she slowly dismounted to hug I'ma-Meherah and the others good-bye.

Meherah fought down tears, realizing she didn't have time to indulge her own emotions. Obviously Tso'bebaw and Peletah had been telling the truth: The Most High had separated the tribes and was scattering them. Mercifully, it was only their speech that He had chosen to impair. She couldn't tell her dear Zekaryah and his Keren how much she loved them, how much she would miss them.

But at least she could hug them before they made their escape. And she could smile at the cherished Ancient Ones and the lovely, wild-haired girl who had been in her prayers for so long. Shoshannah managed to smile in return. Moved, Meherah embraced the young woman and kissed her dimpled cheek. "You're a good, brave girl! Like one of my own—how glad I am that we met!"

To her distress, Shoshannah cried. They parted in sorrow.

Adoniyram rode along the market street, yelling, "Who hears me and understands? Who remains?" A number of people called out to him gladly. Some of Ra-Anan's own guardsmen, Ghid'ohn, Ye'uwsh, and the usually irritable Dibriy were riding with him now, protecting him because they could no longer understand Master Ra-Anan. Adoniyram was grateful for their presence. Not that he needed their protection—his people still loved him—but the guardsmen gave Adoniyram the appearance of normality and authority, which were necessary to calm his people.

Now, Ghid'ohn—a sensible, steady man—urged Adoniyram, "My lord, consider searching the temple; people are gathering there, trying to appeal to the priests and Shemesh to remove this disaster from us."

Adoniyram reluctantly agreed and rode toward the tower. He hoped that someone had discreetly removed his mother's body—and that Rab-Mawg had been effectively silenced. Otherwise, Rab-Mawg could accuse him of not intervening to save his mother.

Maintaining his poise, Adoniyram nodded pleasantly to those people who didn't understand his greetings. And he encouraged those who did understand him, "Stay! Don't flee." About one or two of every ten people comprehended his words and followed him. *My kingdom will be badly diminished.* He dismounted in the tower's courtyard and forced himself to march up the steps to the temple.

The air was permeated with sharp-sweet clouds of smoking incense. And someone had rearranged the remaining linen curtains to hide the priests' unfinished living area. Rab-Mawg was still there, but silent, huddled in a corner, his head in his hands, rocking back and forth. Ebed stood quietly before the altar, garbed in linen robes and a leopard-skin mantle that declared his status, comforting worshipers.

Summoning his courage, Adoniyram approached the priest. The worshipers around them backed away. Hushed, the young man asked, "Where's my mother?"

Ebed seemed to wilt. "Haven't you heard, my lord?"

"I have heard—I saw the attack," Adoniyram agreed sadly, allowing the priest to see his regrets, which were few. "Has Rab-Mawg explained what happened?"

"No one can understand him, my lord. I fear he's gone mad; he's been sitting there for quite some time. Show him compassion, I beg you."

"I will. He's not entirely to blame; my mother provoked him." Adoniyram sighed loudly now and drooped from relief, not sorrow, though the priest didn't have to know that. "Where are the others? Ghez-ar and Awkawn?"

"I think they've fled to their families—I couldn't understand them."

"Will you flee also?" Adoniyram asked softly, hoping that this priest—the most easily manipulated one—would stay to serve him.

"I feel I'm needed here, my lord."

"Thank you, Ebed. I hope you'll stay." *And I hope you'll be satisfied with the temple as it is; we won't be able to finish it.* "Where is . . . my mother's body?"

Barely audible, the priest whispered, "We buried her among the plants and trees on the terrace. Later we can build a small tomb . . ."

Adoniyram nodded and left Ebed to comfort those who had rushed to the temple for solace. The Young Lord understood his people's desire for heavenly reassurance.

However, those who cannot understand and obey me, as their king, will have to leave. Except Shoshannah, of course. She would be safer now; one of her enemies was half mad, and two others were the objects of devastating retribution. Adoniyram had seen smoke rising from Kuwsh's and Ra'Anan's homes, and he knew their servants and guards had abandoned them. As for Shoshannah's fourth enemy . . .

The Young Lord searched the gardens until he discovered a newly disturbed mound of earth: his mother's burial place. Ebed was right; they should make a small tomb for her, but discreet and unmarked. The circumstances of her death would be kept secret if possible.

You will be exalted, Adoniyram told his mother, deciding to make restitution to her in the most practical yet glorious way he could imagine. *You will be finer than you ever were in life . . . adored and revered as Nimr-Rada is now. Perhaps more.*

When all this chaos was settled, his priest, Ebed, would declare that Sharah had rejoined her "husband" Nimr-Rada. And Ebed would proclaim a sign in the stars for her . . . a crown for their Queen of the Heavens. Then, if she had a spirit, it might be satisfied.

At dusk Adoniyram returned to his house, exhausted. Their footsteps echoing, Ghid'ohn walked with him throughout his residence, checking for looters. But his house seemed untouched; no one else was here. No servants to tend him, no guards to protect him, no Lady Keren and her companions to tell him of his past . . . and no Shoshannah to take as his wife.

Unable to believe the truth, Adoniyram tore through his home, calling, "Kaleb? Kaleb! Where did you hide them?"

Ghid'ohn said, "Kaleb is gone, my lord. With the young lady and her family. I saw them ride away together—they understood each other."

They took her. He took her. And I can't leave my people, my kingdom, to go after them. Adoniyram stumbled into his sleeping room and dropped onto his bed, shocked. *I am alone.*

For the first time in years, he wept.

Twenty-Eight

THROUGHOUT THE LONG DAY, as they rode in fear for their lives, Demamah alternately wept, then composed herself sternly. By sunset she was exhausted, starving, and aching. She was unused to riding for such a long time—they had paused only twice today to rest their horses and themselves. And this was only the beginning of their journey.

"We aren't being chased," the guardsman Kaleb announced, as he and Tiyrac rode up to join them; they had stayed behind the others all day, watching for pursuers.

"I don't see anyone," Tiyrac agreed, looking from the river to their right and across the vast, rippling, grass-filled plain that separated them from the Great City.

"Will we be safe to rest and camp for the night?" I'ma-Annah wondered aloud. She peered at I'ma-Keren worriedly.

For the first time today, Demamah forgot her own troubles; I'ma-Keren looked ill and ready to fall off her horse. Zekaryah halted and rushed to help his wife down.

"I'm just hungry and tired," Keren protested, leaning against her husband, sighing comfortably, easing everyone's concerns.

Now Kaleb dismounted and—to Demamah's horror—hauled Shoshannah off her horse possessively, hugging her, kissing her, and growling. "I have you now!"

Even more appalling, Shoshannah wrapped her arms around the guardsman's neck and kissed him, laughing, seeming . . . delighted.

Kaleb noticed Demamah's shock and grinned. "Don't worry; we're married."

"We are not," Shoshannah argued.

"We are. Ask Tiyrac. Ask your parents." Kaleb set Shoshannah on her feet.

Speechless, Shoshannah looked over at her parents. Zekaryah nodded, and Keren smiled in weary affirmation. Shoshannah eyed Tiyrac indignantly. "You knew this and didn't tell me!"

"It wasn't my place to say so," Tiyrac objected, looking flustered despite his gruffness. "You're Kal's problem."

"I'm sure I'll manage," Kal said, earning a mock-stern look from Shoshannah.

They've known each other for years, Demamah realized. She felt like a fool. How could she have been so blind? As she sat there on her horse, limp, stupefied, Tiyrac came to assist her, as he'd done for months.

"Don't touch her!" Zekaryah warned. Apparently satisfied that I'ma-Keren was comfortable, Zekaryah approached Demamah. She remembered being frightened of him as a child, when he was I'ma-Keren's guardsman.

But he nodded to her now, his brown eyes keen and not unkind. "Child, come get some food and water." He helped Demamah from her horse protectively, as if she were one of his own daughters. And he frowned at Tiyrac as if he considered the young man to be overly bold.

Demamah looked away, flushing, but grateful for Zekaryah's fatherly protectiveness. She didn't want to think of Tiyrac or of anything else; Zekaryah was welcome to take charge of the situation for now. Aching and unsteady, she went to sit with I'ma-Keren, who soothed her with a loving, tired hug.

"Demamah-child . . . how I've missed you . . ."

Though she returned Keren's hug thankfully, Demamah thought, *Why couldn't my mother have been like you?* It was a grief to her, a terrible wound.

Zekaryah's firm voice snapped her to reality. "Let's set up the tents."

Shoshannah offered her mother some warm broth made from simmered herbs, salt, and dried meat. "I'ma, you look more than just tired. What's wrong?"

Her eyes shining despite her fatigue, Keren looked from Demamah to Shoshannah. "Nothing's wrong. I am with child."

"Finally!" Exultant, Shoshannah hugged her mother and laughed. "Our Rinnah will be glad not to be the baby anymore. I can't wait to see her and the others!"

"Neither can I," Keren sighed, as Demamah gave her a sweet-sad kiss. "But right now, I'm just glad to be alive. This has been such a terrible day for us all."

Sobering, Shoshannah knelt worriedly. "I'ma . . . can

you endure some dreadful news . . . about your sister?"

"Sharah? What about her?"

Though she was still upset by what she'd seen, Shoshannah told her mother, I'ma-Annah, and Demamah of the violent confrontation between Rab-Mawg and Sharah in the temple this morning. Could it really have been just this morning? Too much had happened today. Scared again, Shoshannah finished softly, "I'm sure he killed her; she wasn't moving when Adoniyram took me away. And there was so much blood."

"How could he?" Demamah asked in a thin little voice.

"His own mother." I'ma-Annah was horrified.

Keren shook her head in disbelief and whispered, "Sharah always did as she pleased; nothing ever made her happy. I shouldn't be shocked . . . but I am."

They sat together, all of them grieving and miserable, staring into the popping, hissing fire they had built from dry twigs, grass, and small branches off the trees lining the river. The men finished tending the horses and came to sit with them.

Kal boldly pulled Shoshannah into his arms and held her, kissing her hair, then whispering in her ear, tickling her delightfully. "I'll be so sad when you can't wear your hair loose anymore."

"That won't be for months yet, beloved." Married or not, it didn't matter how she wore her hair; they had only two tents for this journey, one for the men and one for the women. Besides, she wouldn't feel truly married until their Ancient One, Noakh, could bless their union. Until then Kaleb, and hair braids, had to wait.

"You're so cruel." Kal didn't sound terribly hurt. Grinning, he whispered, "Look at Tiyrac watching Demamah. Do you think they'll marry?"

"That's for them to decide." Shoshannah hugged her husband, tired and grateful, kissing his warm, whiskered neck, loving him. "Thank you for coming to find me. I've been so afraid for you. The risk you took . . ."

He nuzzled her, scraping her cheek, whispering fervently, "The sight of you in those scandalous clothes was worth any risk!"

Chafing under the burden of an old, barely salvaged traveling pack, Ra-Anan trudged eastward across the plains. Zeva'ah walked beside him in resentful silence. Behind them, their fellow travelers were grumbling, quarreling, whining. Ra-Anan cast a dark look at them, embittered.

Of all the people who could have understood him and joined with him to create a new realm, he'd inherited too many malcontents. One was Awkawn, the former priest, and his sarcastic family who had coerced Awkawn to marry a tall, austere reed of a woman named Romaw. Another was the irritable Tabbakhaw, not to mention her short, thickset, always-pessimistic husband, Chuwriy, who was a linen worker.

Equally troublesome was the guardsman Erek, who was desperately courting Tabbakhaw's reluctant mirror-image daughter, Salkah, because the only other unwed girl who understood him now was the maidservant Ormah—and *she* wanted nothing to do with him. However, Ormah also wanted nothing to do with the sullen guardsman Perek, though he was the only other unmarried man in their new tribe.

The best of the lot, for now, was Nekhosheth, a metalworker—who was so closemouthed that Zeva'ah remarked he had no language to change. *At least he and his family don't complain,* Ra-Anan thought, eyeing Nekhosheth's timid wife, Shavsha, and their five sons and three young daughters, who were taking turns riding a pair of small dirt-brown horses.

"When will we get to where we are going?" Ormah demanded in a very unmaidservantly tone. She was walking at Ra-Anan's heels. "I'm sick of these people!"

"These people are all you have, until we find others who understand us," Ra-Anan snapped. He devoutly hoped they could live with his eldest son's tribe, just beyond the eastern river. "Until then, keep ten paces behind me; if you step on my sandals and break them, I'll beat you and leave you where you drop."

Zeva'ah walked beside Ra-Anan, carrying the few garments and ornaments she'd been able to keep from the looters. She began to lag now, looking exhausted, making a complaining sound in her throat. Ra-Anan narrowed his eyes at her. "Don't you *dare* begin to sound like these others!"

They trudged on in angry silence.

"Eriy!" Ra-Anan strode through the midday heat toward his eldest son's home in a modestly prosperous settlement of tidy, round, clay-bricked houses, edged with canals, orchards, and fields. Here and there, people looked out of doorways and small windows, frowning, chattering softly, shaking their dark heads at each other. A growing dread ate at Ra-Anan's hopes. "Eriy!"

"Why is he not answering?" Zeva'ah demanded in a furious whisper. "That boy!"

"Eriy!" Ra-Anan pounded on the hewn-wood door, his unease mounting.

The door creaked open, and Eriy stepped outside, his hard-angled face and fine black eyes mistrustful. He stared at his father. And he spoke politely, in an unintelligible jargon.

The people of Eriy's settlement were gathering now, chattering at Eriy, shaking their heads, motioning to all of Ra-Anan's companions. Zeva'ah put a hand to her mouth, stifling a sob. Ra-Anan wearily rubbed one hand over his face, not wanting to comprehend the obvious: They could not stay here among Eriy's tribe. Three and a half days of miserable walking with these malcontents, listening to their gripes, and giving Zeva'ah's ornaments to boatmen to take them across the eastern river . . . for nothing.

No, Ra-Anan told himself. *Not for nothing.* Sternly, he motioned to his worried eldest son, as if eating and drinking. He would at least get some food. As much food as Eriy's people could spare. They would also rest for a day or so.

Then they would move on. They had no choice.

Slowly, reluctantly, Kuwsh rapped on the gate of his eldest son's wall-enclosed home. "Sebaw? Sebaw!"

A thin, coppery-dark boy wearing a simple fleece wrap opened the gate, blinked at Kuwsh, then darted toward the house without a word.

Discomfited at the boy's reaction, Kuwsh stepped inside, followed by his wife and their four sons and daughters-in-law, who were dragging wearily. *What will we do if Sebaw doesn't understand us?* Kuwsh wondered. The thought was too appalling to consider.

Sebaw appeared now, tall and dark with a wide-boned face eerily similar to Nimr-Rada's, but without Nimr-Rada's fire or charisma. He gave his father a formal embrace of greeting, then kissed Achlai affectionately. "I'ma, it's good to see you again." He nodded to Kuwsh and his brothers and sisters-in-law quietly. "Father, come sit in the shade and rest; my wife is preparing food."

Kuwsh followed Sebaw, amazed that he could understand him. Sebaw offered his father the place of honor, then said, "Forgive me, Father, but after all these years of silence, why have you come to visit me?"

Unable to even think where to begin, or how to explain, Kuwsh stared at his son. After an uncomfortable pause, Achlai leaned forward and said gently, "We've come to ask your help, my son. To begin again. By your love for the Most High, we ask you to help us begin again."

Kuwsh covered his face, humiliated beyond words. *To begin again.* And everything he might gain from this time onward would come from whatever he was given by this son, who loved the Most High.

Shoshannah and the others rode into the Tribe of Metiyl. They were greeted with an enthusiastic, unintelligible outpouring of joy—though Shoshannah's cousin Yelahlah and her husband, Echuwd, fearfully retreated into their circular mud-brick home.

Shoshannah watched them hide, and she listened sadly as the others talked. Half of what the boisterous Metiyl and his Tebuwnaw said was garbled, but many of their words made strangely intoned sense. Communication was possible. Barely.

Though Metiyl, Tebuwnaw, their son Khawrawsh, and his beloved Tsinnah were all grieved by this complication, they didn't seem entirely surprised. They finally settled inside Metiyl's restfully cool mud-brick home—with a host of Metiyl's cousins, children, and grandchildren—for an afternoon feast.

As they visited, Shoshannah enjoyed Tsinnah's dimpled, busy toddler, Tavah, and half listened as Metiyl repeated the words "Akhood" and "Yawlulaw" over and over. *Echuwd and Yelahlah.* Surprised, Shoshannah turned, listening hard.

With emphatic hand motions, and much nodding and shaking of heads, Metiyl, Tebuwnaw, and the others described Echuwd and Yelahlah's loss of plain, understandable speech. "Upsat . . . tarrible . . . bad," Metiyl explained, motioning that Echuwd had seemed about to lose his mind in despair.

Shoshannah understood completely; Echuwd's trading skills would be severely hindered without his gift of speech. Echuwd was probably devastated.

Nodding his wild-curled head at Shoshannah, obviously pleased to see her safely returned to her family, Metiyl grinned at Kaleb. "Akhood . . . Yawlulaw . . . fray, ah?"

He had to repeat himself before Kaleb understood, laughing, nodding. "Yes. Echuwd and Yelahlah are freed."

But when they went to see Echuwd and Yelahlah, the pair babbled frantically, pleadingly, waking their young son, Rakal, howling from his nap. At last, Shoshannah handed Yelahlah one of her gold rings—given to her by that murderous Rab-Mawg in the temple. Yelahlah wept and hugged Shoshannah, accepting her peace offering. That same day, Echuwd and Yelahlah packed their belongings and departed, obviously knowing they were safe from pursuit and retribution.

"How like the two of you to create such a commotion," Noakh teased Shoshannah and Kaleb as they walked ahead, leading his horse and I'ma-Naomi's into their home settlement, the Tribe of Ashkenaz. Kaleb grinned. "The commotion is for you and our I'ma-Naomi, O Ancient One. They love you! If it were just Shoshannah and me, they'd chase us away with spears."

Shoshannah swatted him, and he laughed.

The entire Tribe of Ashkenaz had been forewarned that Father Shem, I'ma-Annah, and the Ancient Ones would be visiting to celebrate Kal and Shoshannah's wedding. Now everyone in the tribe rushed from their homes, fields, and stables, whooping, laughing, clapping, and uttering raucous, tongue-rattling cries of welcome.

"Huh!" Naomi feigned irritation. "Such a fuss! Didn't I teach these children to behave? You are too noisy, son of my sons," she scolded Ashkenaz, who had come to lift Naomi off her horse.

Ashkenaz beamed at her, undeceived, his eyes crinkling warmly above his long, rough, dark beard. "If you'd come to visit us more often, I'ma-Naomi, we wouldn't carry on this way! Father of my Fathers"—he bowed his head to Noakh fondly—"we have all your favorite foods prepared, and you'll have my lodge for tonight! Come and rest!"

"See," Kaleb pretended to grumble to Shoshannah, "we don't matter at all."

But even as he complained, their families charged at them—Shoshannah's siblings, Adah, Qetuwrah, Ahyit, Sithriy, Rinnah—all shrieking and laughing, joined by their grandparents, Meshek and Chaciydah, who had been summoned for the celebrations. And Kaleb's parents, Regem and Pakhdaw, also came to hug them, jubilant.

Just behind them were Kal's eldest brother, Ozniy, and Mithqah, who was radiant, holding a baby in her arms—a solemn, husky miniature of Ozniy, with Mithqah's lovely, bristly dark eyelashes.

"I want one like this," Kaleb told Shoshannah. "Actually quite a few more than one." To his brother Ozniy, he said, "A boy? Well, he can't be yours—he's too good-looking!"

"He is, isn't he?" Ozniy agreed, admiring his small son.

Shoshannah hugged her dear friend, then glided a fingertip over the baby's tender nose, making him blink and stare. "Mithqah, he's beautiful! And you look wonderful! I'm so glad for you—didn't I say you'd marry Ozniy?"

Mithqah seemed about to laugh and cry. "You're really here! I've been praying for you since the day you were taken, and we've been tending your lodge—though we've built our own . . . We hoped you'd return months ago." She looked over Shoshannah's shoulder at Demamah, who approached shyly. "Now, who's this?"

"Mithqah, this is Demamah, another cousin. She's much too serious, but you'll love her anyway. Demamah, come meet my dear friend Mithqah, and her little one." As she spoke, Shoshannah lifted the hefty baby from Mithqah's arms, jostling him playfully until he smiled a toothless grin.

"Kaleb! Shoshannah!" Father Ashkenaz yelled at them. "Get over here. Let's have the marriage blessing, so we can feed our guests!" Loudly he asked the ancient Noakh, "Do you think it'll improve those two wild ones at all—blessing them?"

"They aren't completely hopeless," Noakh answered warmly. "Come here, my children. Let us pray the Most High continues to protect you from your recklessness."

"Such a marriage blessing!" Kal protested to Shoshannah beneath his breath.

She laughed and hushed him softly, taking his hand.

"Wait," I'ma-Annah said. "She's had no time to make wedding apparel. Child, if you wish, you may borrow this." She offered Shoshannah her ancient, carefully protected veil.

Shoshannah felt her throat constrict with unshed tears as I'ma-Annah draped her lightly with the soft, fragile mesh, then hugged her in silent affection. A marriage blessing . . . more than she could have ever desired. And for once, her beloved rascal Kaleb had nothing to add. Together, surrounded by their grateful families, they stood before the ancient Noakh. *We are truly blessed . . . Thank You, Most High.*

After an evening of feasting and stories, the entire Tribe of Ashkenaz danced to the thunderous rhythm of drums and flutes, laughing, singing, shouting in celebration before the Most High. Stars glistened in the darkness above a massive, almost frightfully huge bonfire that sparked and crackled loudly, seeming to exude a life of its own.

Jubilant, Shoshannah danced with her sisters and Demamah and Mithqah, following each other's steps in tempo. And for the first time in months—since they'd departed from the Great City—Shoshannah heard Demamah laughing.

She's enjoying herself, Shoshannah thought, pleased, turning to look over her shoulder. But before she could glimpse her cousin and sisters, someone snatched her, scaring her. Kaleb.

He grinned roguishly and swooped an arm beneath her knees, lifting her off the ground, making her laugh.

"Kal!"

"We see you, Kaleb!" Mithqah's father, Uzziel, bellowed. "Don't think we don't!"

"I'm taking my wife home," Kaleb yelled in reply. "Perhaps you'll see us again in a few days!"

"You're very bad," Shoshannah scolded him beneath her breath as he carried her away from the bonfire, though she was delighted.

He tossed her slightly, making her gasp and cling to him. Grinning, he argued, "Bad? I've waited for you longer than any other man has ever waited for his wife beneath these heavens; I'd say I've been amazingly patient. And, if I were truly misbehaving, your father would give me a thrashing—but I don't see him following us. Do you?"

"No." Shoshannah peeked over his shoulder; the dancing had continued despite their departure.

Kal shifted her now, nudging the door open with his foot, carrying her inside their small lodge. Mithqah and her sisters had cleaned everything and decorated the walls with garlands of leaves and vines. Ozniy, in gratitude for Kaleb's loan of this place during the past year, had made them a storage chest, a low bed, and a weaponry rack, which was pegged into the wall by the door.

Still holding Shoshannah, Kaleb pushed the door shut, saying, "There's a leather loop hanging up there on the door frame; pull it down over the first plank in the door—there's a slot to hold it."

Shoshannah obeyed, fastening the door by touch—she couldn't see in the darkness. Finished, she said, "You can set me down now."

"I'll set us both down now." Kaleb edged his way through the darkness, colliding with the bed unexpectedly, dropping her into the fur coverlets. "I didn't mean to do that."

She laughed at him. In return, he kissed her, apologizing, almost smothering her in an embrace that made her forget everything.

Two months of hiking through the eastern mountains had honed Ra-Anan's temper to an edge. They were now descending from forests into grasslands, and the quarreling amid his small tribe hadn't stopped. Tabbakhaw's attempts to control Ormah had failed. Ormah refused to be treated as a maidservant now, because they were all walking the same miserable paths, eating the same dull food, and carrying the same tiring loads. Her rebellion made Tabbakhaw furious.

"Give me that look again and I'll beat you, child! How dare you. I've treated you like my own daughter, and this is how you behave." Fuming, she called to Ra-Anan, "See how she is? Do you see this? Kicking at my shoes when she walks behind me, and deliberately slowing down when she walks ahead!"

His patience gone, Ra-Anan hushed Tabbakhaw with

a killing look and snatched the startled Ormah by the arm, dragging her away.

Offended, Ormah argued, "Why do you always believe her? I wasn't doing anything wrong! If she thinks I am—"

Ra-Anan shoved the young woman at Perek and said, "Here. She's your wife now; make her behave before I kill her."

Ormah's mouth opened and closed soundlessly. When she could finally speak, she sputtered, "You c-can't just give me to him—you're not my father!"

"Where is your father? Go complain to him!" Ra-Anan snapped.

Ormah had been separated from her parents and siblings by the confusion in the Great City, a loss that hadn't affected her too badly.

"Go back through those mountains alone—you'll starve to death if the animals don't kill you first." To Perek, Ra-Anan said, "She's yours. You both need to marry anyway."

"But not to Perek!" Ormah wailed, her mouth so wide open that the youngest children of their new tribe—sons and daughters of the metalworker, Nekhosheth, whimpered in sympathy.

Remorseless, Ra-Anan glared at Ormah. Perek smugly took her by the arm.

Adoniyram awoke with the dawn, immediately plotting mental lists of tasks he needed to accomplish for the day: Finish inspecting the canals, encourage the workers, and check on the priest Ebed—who was proving to be as quiet, orderly, and wise as Rab-Mawg had been ambitious, unpredictable, and self-destructive.

I'm glad you're gone, Adoniyram thought to the now-departed Rab-Mawg, whose family had retrieved him from the tower three days after the chaos had descended from the skies. *And I'm grateful you're here,* he thought, turning, hearing his young wife sigh and stretch herself awake.

She was Ghid'ohn's sister, a pretty girl with gentle dark eyes and an unresisting personality. They had been married for seven weeks, and she had yet to argue with him about anything. She had even let him rename her, Atarah, without a murmur. He hadn't liked her name—Telathah—which unimaginatively designated her as the third child in her family after Ghid'ohn and another sister. Shoshannah, he knew, would have argued to keep her first name—if he had been able to understand her.

One day, Shoshannah, I'll go looking for you, he thought, determined. *I'll find you, and that brother, Gibbawr, you insisted was mine. And I'll see the Ancient Ones with my own eyes . . .*

Musing, he drew Atarah into his arms and kissed her, gratified by her softness and her obvious adoration of him. She would never be as amusing as Shoshannah had been, but for now, she was a comfort, and that was enough.

For now.

Twenty-Nine

STEPPING OUT of his new reed hut, binding his straight black hair into a severe horseman's plait, Ra-Anan studied the sun-gilded morning contentedly. Five years of slow, difficult travel had brought him and his tribe to this eastern coastline—a deep, curving bay teeming with fish, crabs, and shellfish, pleasingly enhanced by a fertile marsh to the north populated by flocks of raucous—and edible—birds. Best of all, his quarrelsome tribe had finally agreed this past month that they would stay here permanently.

Nekhosheth and Perek were already awake and busy, hollowing out a fallen tree, carefully burning and chipping its interior to create a boat.

Ra-Anan approved. "Do you think you'll finish it today?"

"Maybe," Perek grunted, as Nekhosheth nodded.

The low nickering of a horse stopped them cold. As one, the men turned and saw a tribe of horsemen approaching from the south—followed by their families, who were also on horses. They had apparently been drawn to Ra-Anan's settlement by the plumes of smoke rising from their work and from the morning fires. Jolted, Ra-Anan stared at the horsemen, recognizing some of them as former merchants from the Great City. *They must have taken half the horses in the city—some of those are mine!*

Worse, these horse thieves had weapons aimed at Ra-Anan, Perek, and Nekhosheth. Apparently recognizing one of the men, Nekhosheth called out, "Peh-ayr! You've become a horseman?"

Peh-ayr, a dark, sparse-bearded, sneering man, called to Nekhosheth in ringing, rhythmic accents, nodding at Ra-Anan and Perek as if to ask, "Why are you with them?"

Another horseman, bony and surly, unmistakably motioned for Ra-Anan and all the others—who had emerged from their reed huts—to leave.

Seeing this, Ra-Anan's former priest Awkawn cried, "They're chasing us from our own homes that we've built? No!"

The surly horseman responded by shooting an arrow at Awkawn's feet. Awkawn retreated as his wife and everyone in the tribe yelled in protest. Ra-Anan called to his wife and the other women, "Zeva'ah, gather everything you can! All the gear you can carry! Quickly before they decide they should have that too!"

Peh-ayr followed Ra-Anan's every move with a readied arrow. Seeing this, Nekhosheth muttered, "He still hates you—always has."

Ra-Anan felt all the hair on his head prickle with apprehension. "We'll go," he told Perek, who looked ready to fight. "We'll start again. We don't have much to lose yet, except our lives—and the children's."

Apparently remembering his young son, whose birth had settled him—and Ormah—tremendously, Perek nodded. But he scowled at the former merchant-thieves.

"Boats," Nekhosheth said abruptly, as soon as they were safely away from the invading tribe.

Peering ahead at the northern coastline, Ra-Anan said, "What about boats?"

"Easier than walking. We *can* swim if there's an accident—but we'll be careful."

Nekhosheth was obviously thinking of the tribe's children. The invaders had taken his children's horses, which meant that the littlest ones would have to be carried. The journey—wherever it took them—would be dismally slowed.

Ra-Anan agreed reluctantly. "Boats it will be then."

That night, as Ra-Anan sat down at the evening fire, Zeva'ah rolled her dark-shadowed eyes at him—the expression of a woman who has had enough. He expected her to berate him for not defending their settlement. Beneath his breath, he snapped, "Say it!"

"I think I'm with child." She lowered her face into her hands, rocking, weeping.

After all these years? Shocked, he pulled her into his arms as she cried for this new infant, and for everything she had lost: their home, luxuries, their sons, and their

Demamah. Ra-Anan soothed her, aware of the others staring curiously. "Things will be better in a few years, you'll see. As our tribe grows, we will have a city again." Frowning, he asked, "Can you swim?"

Weeks piled upon months, then became years, which Ra-Anan had always tracked by systematic knots in cordage: small knots for days, large knots for weeks, thread-marked knots for months, each cord ending with a year. The cords fringed to six . . . eight . . . nine years after the scattering of the tribes. Nine years of travel.

Using laboriously crafted wooden boats, carefully balanced with adjoining planks, Ra-Anan's growing tribe cautiously worked their way up the northern coast. Eventually the land curved east, then south. Vistas of lush, misty grasslands filled with wildlife tempted them to linger, while pouring, chilling rains compelled them to flee, turning south with the coastline. Often they took refuge in caves to escape the weather. And they fought over where to settle. They had not yet found a place as wonderful as the deep, sparkling bay so rudely stolen from them by the merchant-thieves—a crime they all mourned.

Ra-Anan began to doubt that his young daughter, Tereyn, an unexpectedly happy child, and her constantly hungry infant brother, Nebat, would ever know a true home.

"That looks like a fine cave!" Tabbakhaw announced,

to Ra-Anan's irritation, pointing toward a dark-hollowed outcropping of limestone along the shore.

Waving an oar from their boat adjoining Ra-Anan's, Erek called to Tabbakhaw, "As you say." Being their son-in-law, he was now almost subservient to Tabbakhaw and her husband, Chuwriy.

Behind Erek, his wife, the pregnant Salkah, sniffed loudly. "Let's hope it's a fine cave; the last one was so damp I felt as if I were living in a puddle."

"I didn't pick that one," Tabbakhaw reminded her in a huff.

"You agreed to it, though," Awkawn's wife, the lanky Romaw, called to her from another boat. "I said we should move on, but no one ever listens to me. I think this one's probably worse than the other."

"Let's try it," Awkawn said, always ready to argue with his wife.

In her place behind Ra-Anan, Zeva'ah shifted the nursing Nebat. "I am tired."

Ra-Anan had intended to push them farther down the coast today, but the women seemed determined to camp early. He subdued his frustration while his tribe carefully maneuvered their boats into the tides that would carry them to shore.

As the women bickered and unloaded the boats, the men took their weapons and climbed up the sandy beach to explore the cave. Putrid, musty, dripping darkness greeted them, with a seething, rustling sound unlike anything Ra-Anan had ever heard.

Erek sounded as if he were gagging on the stench. "Something's in here."

"Out," Ra-Anan muttered, backing away from the sound, a spear ready in his hand. The seething sound formed into a mass that arose, unfurling like a dark, lifted, shaken cloth. Ra-Anan's fear expanded with the form. "Out!"

To his horror, the creature followed them. In the light of day, it was not as tall as a man but a hitherto unimagined nightmare—lightly fuzzed, deep shadowed colors, a narrow sharp-toothed snout on a long, thin, bony head with piercing eyes and leathery claw-fingered wings that opened to an astonishing width before it charged them menacingly on clawed feet. *Like a carrion eater from one of I'ma-Annah's old stories . . .*

They retreated, facing it, fending it off with their weapons while the women and children screamed from behind them on the beach. Piling everything and everyone back into the boats, Ra-Anan and his tribe fled. The creature glided into the sky, circling above, diving at them until they were well away from its portion of the coast.

In the eighteenth year after the division of the tribes, Adoniyram felt confident enough to leave his beloved Great City in the care of his guardsman Ghid'ohn and his priest, Ebed. He intended to search for his brother, Gibbawr. In addition, he had heard muddled rumors of a celebration to honor the Ancient Ones this year; he was determined to visit them, hoping to somehow communicate with them.

For the first time in their married lives, however, Atarah tried to argue. She was bearing their tenth child and feared he wouldn't return to see this little one.

"I have to find my family," he told her firmly, not

mentioning Gibbawr. "Even now, it may be too late—the tribes are all so scattered and confused." *And I want to find Shoshannah. I want to meet the Ancient Ones in the mountains—to decide for myself if they will outlive me. You in the heavens, whoever You are . . . let me find them.*

Accompanied by his guardsmen Ye'uwsh and Dibriy, Adoniyram rode north for weeks—using some of the few horses that had not been stolen from his Great City.

Searching for telltale smoke from hearths, he led his companions into the foothills and the mountains to find the Tribe of Bezeq. He repeated the names over and over to various tribal leaders. *Bezeq. Gibbawr.* Most shook their heads at his words, but some nodded. And, thankfully, Adoniyram told himself, a nod was still yes in any language. He was heading in the right direction.

"Is this the place?" Dibriy demanded, tired, glaring around as they rode into a comfortable, well-established village of rustic stone-and-timber lodges.

"Smile, Dibriy," Adoniyram encouraged him. "If they think you're angry, we'll be chased off like scoundrels. Yes, I think this is the place."

Women and children bounded from various homes, chattering, whistling, hurrying. Adoniyram dismounted, smiling, and led his weary horse to the largest lodge. A big, sinewy, bold-looking man emerged from this lodge, lifting his chin at Adoniyram, Ye'uwsh, and Dibriy in wary welcome.

Carefully Adoniyram repeated the names. "Bezeq? Gibbawr?"

Relaxing, the bold-faced man tapped himself, drawing

out the name sharply. "Bezeq." Turning, he called out an order, of which Adoniyram understood one distinct, lingering word: Gibbawr. Seeming satisfied with verbal responses from others in his village, the big man motioned Adoniyram inside the lodge.

"Stay with the horses," Adoniyram muttered to Ye'uwsh and Dibriy. He didn't want them hearing what he would say.

A dignified, sharp-faced woman served drinks, berries, grain cakes, and honey, which Adoniyram accepted gratefully. The sharp-faced woman then knelt beside a sour, rugged man, who was most likely her husband—and the tribe's patriarch.

Others were filing into the lodge now, studying Adoniyram eagerly, the girls whispering behind their hands, giggling. A sturdy, friendly seeming matron appeared, followed by a tall, handsome leather-clad man and a younger matron, who was quite pretty and heavily pregnant. She reminded Adoniyram painfully of Atarah; he missed her more acutely than he'd realized. Three gangly adolescent boys and a small girl moved after the young matron in a line, like half-grown brown ducklings.

As if trained, the three boys sat near Bezeq and the dour man. The little girl, however, climbed into the sharp-faced woman's lap and relaxed, playing with some cordage and beads. The tall, leather-clad man sat with Bezeq, while nodding to Adoniyram sociably.

Adoniyram returned the man's nod, wondering if he was imagining a resemblance, hints of his own features reflected in this young man's face. "Gibbawr?"

Exchanging glances with Bezeq, the leather-clad man nodded in polite agreement. "Gibbawr."

"I am Adoniyram." He had to say this twice before Gibbawr attempted it.

"Adyon-ee-raaawm."

Good enough. Adoniyram nodded, wary now. "Sharah's son." Receiving blank stares, he repeated her name again. "Sharah."

The sturdy, friendly looking matron gasped in apparent realization. "Shaw-raw!" Turning, she chattered at the entire tribe, then swept a questioning look from Adoniyram to Gibbawr. Instantly, Bezeq smoldered, the dour, rugged man sneered, and everyone in the tribe seemed to stiffen and stare, indignant.

No doubt they are remembering my mother, Adoniyram thought, grimly amused. To put their minds at ease, he repeated her name, then briefly, mournfully hung his head. If necessary, he would tell of her death with dust, ashes, and a grief he didn't feel.

Bezeq leaned forward now, still smoldering. His powerful face hard, he grabbed a chunk of clay from beside the cold hearth, crumbled it, and let it fall to the floor near his mat. "Shaw-raw?"

When Adoniyram nodded, Bezeq spat vigorously, insultingly, onto the crumbled clay beside him. Unoffended, Adoniyram removed a dark leather bag from his belt and offered it to the perplexed Gibbawr. *To you, my own brother, mere gold from the brother you should never have had.*

He longed to tell them everything. He desperately wished he could gain their acceptance and trust. Their steadfast kinship. But their mangled words stopped them. And Gibbawr's expression was suddenly too polite. While Bezeq was and would always be—Adoniyram thought—too full of hatred for Sharah to welcome her ill-gotten son.

~ ~

Bezeq's mother, Nihyah, sighed regretfully, snuggling her cherished great-granddaughter in her lap. "I wish we could actually speak to our guest."

"So my own mother is dead?" Gibbawr asked, staring down at the gold rings and red-stoned gold cuffs in his hands.

"It would seem so," his adoptive mother, Khuldah, sighed. "Though this Adyoneerawm doesn't seem much grieved; she must have died years ago."

"Someone must have killed her," Bezeq said, openly pleased.

His father, Ramah, snorted, "Good riddance. Her and her sister, that Keren."

Nihyah stiffened, dignified and cool. "Keren was never the terrible woman you thought her to be. It was that Nimr-Rada king who was the evil one . . ."

"Do not start that argument again!" Ramah warned his wife, his dark eyes ferocious in his bearded, raw-boned face. "Let's feed this young man and his companions and encourage them to leave in the morning."

Gibbawr's wife, Meleah, straightened now, pressing her hands to her heavily pregnant sides—for the unborn child was kicking visibly. "Gibbawr, beloved," she said, her brown, rounded face warm and worried, "I do think you should at least share one meal with your brother. He *has* brought you gifts. You may never see him again. Let there be no regrets."

"We should part in peace," Gibbawr agreed, clearly unwilling to offend his father.

Bezeq remained silent. Ramah nudged him. "Now that

she's dead, you should marry again. A true wife this time. Perhaps a girl from your brother Yithran's tribe."

"Perhaps." Grudgingly, Bezeq turned to his son, Gibbawr. "Your Meleah is right. Go share some food with your brother before he leaves. If he had Sharah as his mother, he deserves some compassion."

Clubs in hand, Mithqah, Demamah, and Shoshannah knelt in the sunshine before the lodge of the Ancient Ones, pummeling a long, leather-wrapped mat of damp wool, felting it to be used for winter boots and caps.

As they pounded in rhythm, they laughed at the antics of their younger children. Demamah's toddler daughter, Ghiylath—a busy, prattling mite with Demamah's brown eyes and Tiyrac's thick, dark, red-tinged hair—was trying to escape to play in the stream, which she loved. The other children encircled her to keep her penned. Ghiylath howled. Shoshannah's only daughter, Meherah —twelve, stick thin and earnest, with her mother's tousled brown curls—finally grabbed the unhappy toddler and swung her in circles until Ghiylath was too dizzy to stand.

"Why did Tiyrac and I get such a little wild woman?" Demamah complained fondly. "She should be one of yours, Shoshannah, really."

"Oh, thank you," Shoshannah said, watching dear, naughty Ghiylath wobble to her feet. Timing her rhythm with the others, Shoshannah called to the frustrated Meherah, "Make her dance! Wear her out. Ghiylath-child, dance!"

Catching on, Ghiylath's eyes brightened as she began

to stamp her feet and flap her hands in delightful disorder.

Mithqah laughed, calling to the other children, "Dance! Hands high to Him! Step, step, step! We'll practice for the celebration."

Celebration. Shoshannah sobered as she pounded on the felt. They were here to prepare for their First Father Shem's third kentum—his three hundredth year. Language barriers notwithstanding, all the neighboring tribes, and many from beyond—including Shem's brothers—would be arriving within days, bearing gifts and full of joy, which Shem seemed reluctant to acknowledge.

It's because he knows he will outlive most of us here.

"Shoshannah!"

Eliy'ezer—Shoshannah's lanky pale-eyed youngest brother, born the winter after the confusion in the Great City—came charging up the slope toward the lodge. Shoshannah stood, alarmed by Eliy'ezer's breathless shock; he was usually rock calm.

"Kaleb said to warn you! Adoniyram of the Great City is coming with two guardsmen. Our Noakh and Shem and Father and the uncles are going out to meet them."

"What?" Shoshannah abandoned her work and herded the little ones together. Her second thought—after gathering the children—was to fetch her bow. But Meherah was almost underfoot, agitated by Eliy'ezer's panic. And Eliy'ezer had gone inside to warn I'ma-Naomi and I'ma-Annah and all the aunts. They would insist upon welcoming Adoniyram, though cautiously. Shoshannah willed her fears down hard, telling herself that Adoniyram and his men were too heavily outnumbered to create trouble.

I'ma-Naomi and I'ma-Annah were already hurrying to create a resting place for the travelers just outside the lodge. Shoshannah soothed her daughter and coaxed her to help with the food. "We're fussing over nothing, Meherah-child, I'm sure."

She watched as the men climbed the slope, surrounding Adoniyram and his men, "leading" them and their horses. Adoniyram was as smoothly handsome as ever, yet to Shoshannah, he lacked her Kaleb's warmth and strength.

Kaleb strode over to Shoshannah, kissed her, then possessively wrapped an arm around her shoulders as a silent warning. Three of Shoshannah's tawny, wild-haired young sons, Khaziy'el, Eythan, and Zebul, joined them now, mistrustful of Adoniyram. Nine-year-old Eythan, in particular, glowered.

Shoshannah nudged him. "Behave!"

"*Your* son," Kal muttered.

Shoshannah gave him a look to match Eythan's.

Adoniyram noticed this interplay, eyebrows lifted. Shoshannah realized that he didn't seem surprised to find her with Kaleb, or Demamah with Tiyrac.

Smiling politely, he addressed them in the same dreadful chopped, garbled syllables that had frightened her so badly years ago. Even now, her stomach churned to hear him. It was hopeless; she still couldn't understand him.

Adoniyram felt a sinking despair. They couldn't understand him. And he would never understand them—his own family. No uncles, no grandparents, no close cousins would ever perceive his words, much less behave as true kindred toward him. *I'm alone.*

He subdued the longing to weep. He could never tell

Shoshannah and Kaleb that he forgave their deception. That Shoshannah was still lovely and precious to him—though she was Kaleb's. He couldn't tell Demamah that he was glad to see her safe and obviously loved by her husband, Tiryac, who was guarding her against him as warily as Kaleb was guarding Shoshannah. He also couldn't discuss their children and trade a father's stories with them.

Worse, he could not question the Ancient Ones, which he wanted to do more than anything else in the world. *Tell me I will live to be as old as you . . .*

Noakh—*the* Noakh, and his Naomi—approached Adoniyram now. The young man stared, amazed that anyone could be so ancient, silver haired, yet dark eyed. They were living legends, warm, agreeable, and surely the most significant people he'd ever seen. Yet he could ask them nothing. He felt so frustrated and helpless. Thoughts stabbed him cold and hard: *You are not the Promised One. And compared to these Ancient Ones, you are nothing but a man who will die with nothing.* A mere man.

The Ancient Ones embraced him, welcoming him with words beyond his comprehension. His journey, and his hopes, were futile. Already, he longed to leave.

After visiting for only a day and a half—unable to communicate with anyone—Adoniyram rode off with his men. Shoshannah watched him leave. He didn't seem like a great lord now. Only a bereaved man. She pitied him. Until she remembered the morning he had deliberately allowed his mother to die in the temple. He still wasn't sorry, Shoshannah was certain.

Demamah approached Shoshannah now, thoughtful. "I think he wanted to see all this for himself. He remembers your stories. And your warning of our foreshortened lives."

Shoshannah looked at her cousin, her dear friend. "And now what do you think? Did I lie to you or to him?"

"No," Demamah said slowly. "I knew you were telling the truth. And I'm sure Adoniyram knows it too—he looked so unhappy." Sighing, she added, "After all this time, I can say that I'm glad to be with you now. And with my Tiyrac. Sometimes I miss my parents, but there was no mercy with those in the Great City. Or their Shemesh."

Pondering these things, Shoshannah approached her parents, Kaleb, Shem, I'ma-Annah, and the Ancient Ones, who were also watching Adoniyram leave. "Demamah and I think Adoniyram wanted to speak with you, our Ancient Ones," she told them quietly. "He wanted you to tell him that he would live to be as old as you."

The Ancient Ones looked at her, then away, as if unwilling to discuss this hurtful subject. Her father was staring hard into the distance, beyond Adoniyram. Her mother put a hand to her mouth, clearly on the verge of tears. But Kal nodded in firm agreement.

Summoning her courage, Shoshannah continued, "I want to tell you . . . before the Most High . . . however long I live, or don't live . . . whatever comes, *I've been happy.*"

"And so have I." Kaleb wrapped his arms around her, but the others didn't respond. Couldn't respond. Shoshannah prayed they would remember.

Remind them, O Most High.

"Were you able to understand the Ancient Ones at all, my lord?" asked the priest, Ebed, as he walked down the tower steps with Adoniyram in the late autumn sunlight.

"Oh, I understood them perfectly," Adoniyram answered, sarcastic. "They told me that I'll be immortal and loved forever."

"Forgive me. Obviously your journey wasn't what you hoped it would be." Pausing now, the priest said gently, "But you've been missed. Your people and your lady-wife have come here almost daily to offer prayers and gifts to Shemesh for your safe return. It would have pleased you to see it."

"You're telling me to be satisfied with what I have?"

"Others long to be you," Ebed murmured. "You have everything they desire. And now you've had this adventure . . . visiting the Ancient Ones." Kindly, the priest said, "Perhaps you and your men shouldn't discourage the people with your own disappointments. Let them believe that you had a journey they can only imagine—it should be your duty as a king to give them such dreams."

Dispirited, Adoniyram smiled at him. "I'll leave the dreams and storytelling to you; I'd rather forget this whole 'adventure.' Now, forgive me, but I'm going to go see my wife and children."

"And practice contentment?"

"If I find it." Adoniyram doubted he would.

You are not the Promised One. You are nothing but a man who will die with nothing. A mere man. Bitter knowledge for a king.

In the eighteenth year after the chaotic division of the earth, Ra-Anan led his tribe from a warm coastal beach up into a sultry, lush forest, teeming with colors, with water. With life.

"This is the place," Awkawn announced firmly, daring the others to disagree. "We can make a clearing and build a new temple nearby—a tower to the sun."

Everyone began to argue eagerly over campsites and food.

Slowly, followed by his intrepid, dusky nine-year-old son, Nebat, Ra-Anan lifted a spear and moved into the lush, sultry foliage, staring, amazed . . . disturbed.

"Father," Nebat asked, hushed and respectful as Ra-Anan required, "are we going hunting? Is something wrong?"

What is wrong? Ra-Anan asked himself, frowning. A brilliantly colored bird flew before them fearlessly from one rich-flowered tree to another, its elegant feathers tempting Ra-Anan to catch it for Zeva'ah. The bird was as dazzling as the flowers, the landscape, the river. It dawned on Ra-Anan then what was wrong. I'ma-Annah's voice whispered to him in fragments, unseen.

The earth was not always as you see it today, Ra-Anan-child. Before the Great Destruction, the trees were enormous—beautiful and fruitful. And the flowers—they were so sweet that we sometimes ate them! But even more wonderful, little one, were the animals in the world of that time. They did not fear people as predators and prey . . .

He was seeing these exquisite things with his own eyes . . . glimpses of the creatures and the earth she had known. He was going to hear her voice forever in this lush place. He could see the hand of her unacknowledged Most High.

He stared about in silence, haunted.

Epilogue

THEY WALKED TOGETHER, mother and daughter, through a cold, autumn-misted field near their homes. The daughter had the silver hair of old age, while the mother—still youthful in her middle years—supported her child.

At last, Shoshannah set a frail hand on Keren's arm. "I'ma . . . please, I am tired."

Keren paused, knowing her daughter wasn't talking about this walk through the misty field. She was talking about life itself. She was tired. She was asking Keren's acceptance. More than that, she was asking Keren to be strong and at peace with herself and the Most High.

"I miss my Kaleb," Shoshannah sighed. Smiling wistfully, she said, "I've had a good life. A *good* life. I've been happy. But now I'm tired . . ."

Aching, Keren held her daughter, kissed her, then walked her home.

Inside their hushed, lamplit lodge, Annah studied her dear in-laws, who were sleeping, exhausted. Noakh's spirits had begun to fail in the years after Kaleb's and Shoshannah's deaths. Naomi, too, lacked the vitality that had been so much a part of her being for as long as Annah had known her. Grief had struck them hard. But it was more than that; like Shoshannah, they were tired of this life.

But I'm not ready to lose you, Annah thought, dismayed. *It was terrible enough to lose Shoshannah.*

As she sat there, neglected sewing in her lap, struggling with this new torment, Annah's beloved Shem sat down with her, taking her in his arms, kissing her cheek, despondent, whispering, "Beloved, I must send for my brothers."

His brothers and their wives were visiting nearby tribes, drawn together by their mutual languages. It wouldn't be long before they arrived. For the first time ever, Annah dreaded seeing them.

Weeping, Annah watched as her tearful sister-in-law Ghinnah knelt and placed a small, ancient, elaborately painted box in the grave beside their Noakh. Within the box were the mysterious sun stones that Ghinnah had given Noakh while they were living in the ancient ship during the Great Flood. It was best, they had all agreed, that the sun stones be buried with the ancient man, in a place known only to them.

The stones were an enigma, a wonder that might be

used in worship against the Most High. The Ancient Noakh's grave, too, might become a place of unholy worship. It was best kept a secret.

Shem, Annah, Yepheth, Ghinnah, Khawm, and Tirtsah covered the grave together, mute in their grief. And in their memories.

I would have died as a young woman if you had not lived and loved the Most High, Annah told the ancient patriarch silently. *And He was merciful for the sake of your love . . .*

Finished, they hurried back to the lodge to console their I'ma-Naomi, who was fading, overwhelmed by grief at being separated from her beloved Noakh.

In the flickering lamplight, Shem gathered and perused the writings, the histories of all. The passing of ages—of precious lives—were griefs that seared like endless burns. Nimr-Rada's story, for example, was too painful to record beyond the minimal facts. And even if he wrote the truth, Shem knew that other tribes, enemy tribes, would sneer and deride his words. He meant nothing to them now; only a few still followed the Most High. Mere handfuls among many. *How merciful of You, O Most High, to allow these faithless rebels to live.*

"What will we do with these?" Annah asked, sitting beside him now, touching one of the leather rolls with a small, work-worn hand. How he loved that hand. Soothed, he kissed her fingertips and looked into her dark eyes, seeing the girl he had first loved in a marvelous world long since vanished.

"We take them to someone who will listen to Him."

❧ ☙

"Look at *that*," Keren muttered to Annah, almost stopping her horse. Her pale eyes glittered with rage as she gazed upon their destination, a walled river city in the fertile northern plains.

Annah was already looking at the object of Keren's wrath, a huge brick mountain—a replica of the tower in the former Great City, now called Babel, the place of confusion. This city was merely an echo of the first. Nothing had changed for the children of her children here—sons of Arpakshad and Aram. "This makes me want to tear out my hair," Annah said darkly. "The Most High must truly love us—being so patient with *that*."

Keren sighed heavily, aggrieved. Annah and Shem had invited her and Zekaryah to accompany them here for a needed respite from the mountains, from mourning their children. Instead, Annah feared this place would sharpen their sorrow.

Even so, they covered their heads, dismounted, and entered the gates, then the marketplace, which offered gold, fabrics, honey, wine, and luxuries. Many of the residents wore delicate crescents and stars of gold—tributes to their god of the moon and other "rulers of the heavens." Obviously Nimr-Rada and Sharah, in all their vile deified forms, ruled this place. Annah looked away from these disgusting ornaments as Shem and Zekaryah inquired directions, repeating the names of Arpakshad and all his descendants whom they knew of, ending with, "Terakh?"

Some of the merchants looked at them strangely, but one gabbled at a rough-robed companion, who grudgingly led them through the dusty streets to a remarkably large house. Pounding on the wooden gate, he marched off, shaking his dark head.

A servant opened the door, flashed them a well-trained smile, and bowed them into a brick-paved courtyard, motioning at two other servants to guard the horses.

This can't be the place, Annah thought, looking upward, amazed by the two-storied skylit courtyard and the wooden stairs and railing that led to—and around—beautifully timbered and arcaded upper rooms.

A man appeared at the central upper railing now, middle-aged, neither tall nor short but with fine dark eyes and handsomely clad in light woolen robes. Seeing his visitors, he hurried down, his sandals clattering on the wooden stairs as he smiled and greeted them kindly. "Abram," he said, in cordial, half-familiar accents.

Shem questioned, "Of Terakh?"

Abram nodded his head gently, sadly, indicating that Terakh was no more.

Annah drooped with disappointment. But Shem persisted, tapping himself. "Shem. Shem, son of Noakh."

"No-akh? Shem?" Abram stared, shocked, retaliating with, "Arpakshad? Arawm? Elawm?" He was gripping Shem's arm now, his warm brown eyes growing wider and wider as Shem nodded agreement with each name of his own sons.

Annah thought the man, Abram, might faint. But then he laughed and embraced Shem, delighted, raising his voice, calling to the rooms above. "Sarai!"

A very beautiful woman appeared at the railings above, clad in flowing linen robes; her luminous skin, dark hair, and eyes were as perfect as Annah could imagine. She seemed somewhat irritated, until Abram beckoned her and called to the servants authoritatively, sending them in all directions to welcome his guests.

As the jubilant Abram rushed to make them comfortable, Shem glanced at Annah, Zekaryah, and Keren, his eyes shining with joy, lifting Annah's spirits. He had no need to speak; they had found the man they sought. Beside Annah, Keren wept.

That night, while his wife and guests slept, Abram gripped the wooden railing of the courtyard balcony, exultant, staring up at the stars. He felt a need to see them. A need to be quiet and to wait for the Presence he had felt in the past. All his possessions, his wealth—they were nothing to the treasure he had been granted today: an answer.

He finally had an answer. There was a plan. He could leave this idolatrous place. Abram smiled, contented. A breath of wind touched his face, and he felt as if he had been granted more blessings than there were stars in the skies.

And he felt the Presence with him, whispering, *I am the Lord . . .*

Glossary

Abdiy (Ab-dee) Servicable.
Abram (Ab-rawm) High father. Contraction of Abiyram (ab-ee-rawm), father of height.
Achlai (Akh-lah-ee) Wishful.
Adah (Aw-daw) Ornament.
Adoniyram (Ad-o-nee-rawm) Lord of height.
Ahyit (Ah-yit) A hawk.
Annah (Awn-naw) A plea: "I beseech thee" or "Oh now!"
Aram (Arawm) Highland.
Ashkenaz (Ash-ken-az) Meaning unknown.
Atarah (At-aw-raw) Crown.
Awkawn (Aw-kawn) To twist; tortuous.
Bariyach (Baw-ree-akh) A fugitive; i.e. the serpent (as fleeing).
Becay (Bes-ah-ee) Domineering.
Bezeq (Beh-zek) Lightning.
Chaciydah (Khas-ee-daw) Kind (maternal) bird; i.e. a stork.
Chayeh (Khaw-yeh) Vigorous; lively.
Chuwriy (Khoo-ree) Linen worker.
Dawkar (Daw-kar) To stab; [by analogy] to starve.
Dayag (Dah-yawg) Fisherman.

Demamah (Dem-aw-maw) Quiet.
Dibriy (Dib-ree) Wordy.
Ebed (Eh-bed) Servant.
Echuwd (Ay-khood) United.
Elam (Ay-lawm) Hidden.
Eliy'ezer (El-ee-eh'zer) God of help.
Erek (Eh-rek) Length.
Eriy (Ay-ree) Watchful.
Eythan (Ay-thawn) Permanent; specifically, a chieftain, hard, mighty, rough.
Ezriy (Ez-ree) Helpful.
Ghez-ar (Ghez-ar) Soothsayer.
Ghid'ohn (Ghid-ohn) Feller; i.e. warrior.
Ghinnah (Ghin-naw) Garden.
Ghiylath (Ghee-lath) Joy; rejoicing.
Gibbawr (Gib-bawr) Valiant.
Hadarah (Had-aw-raw) Decoration: beauty, honor.
I'ma (Ame-aw) Derived from "Im" or "Em" and the syllable "Ma." Mother; bond of the family.
Kaleb (Kaw-labe) Forcible.
Keren (Keh-ren) A ray of light.
Khawrawsh (Khaw-rawsh) Craftsman.
Khawm (Khawm) Heat; i.e. a tropical climate.
Khaziy'el (Khaz-ee-ale) Seen of God.
Khiysh (Kheesh) Make haste.
Khuldah (Khool-daw) A weasel (from its gliding motion).
Kuwsh (Koosh) Possible meanings: to scatter; confusion; chaos.
Laheh'beth (Lah-eh-beth) To gleam; a flame, or the point of a weapon.
Lawkham (Law-kham) To feed on or (figuratively) consume.
Ma'adannah (Mah-ad-an-aw) Pleasure; dainty; delight. Also, a bond or influence.
Ma'khole (Ma'khole) Dancing.
Meherah (Me-hay-raw) Hurry.
Meleah (Mel-ay-aw) Fulfilled; i.e. abundance (of produce or fruit).
Meshek (Meh-shek) Sowing; also a possession; precious.
Metiyl (Met-eel) Bar; in the sense of "hammering out" or "as forged."
Mithqah (Mith-kaw) Sweetness.
Naomi (No-om-ee) Pleasant.
Nashak (Naw-shak) To strike with a sting (as a serpent); to bite.
Nebat (Neb-awt) Regard; to regard with pleasure.
Nekhosheth (Nekh-o-sheth) Copper.
Nihyah (Nih-yaw) Doleful.

Nimr-Rada (Nem-ar-raw-daw) From *Nimar*—leopard and *Radah*—to tread down; subjugate.
Noakh (No-akh) Rest.
Ormah (Or-maw) Trickery.
Ozniy (Oz-nee) Having quick ears.
Pakhdaw (Pakh-daw) Fear.
Peh-ayr (Peh-ayr) Embellishment.
Peletah (Pel-ay-taw) Deliverance.
Perek (Peh-rek) To break apart; severity; cruelty.
Qasheh (Kaw-sheh) Severe; churlish; stubborn; in trouble.
Qaydawr (Kay-dawr) Dusky.
Qetuwrah (Ket-oo-raw) Perfumed.
Ra-Anan (Ra-an-awn) Prosperous: green; flourishing.
Rab-Mawg (Rab-mawg) Chief magician.
Rakal (Raw-kal) To travel for trading; (spice) merchant.
Ramah (Raw-maw) To delude or betray.
Regem (Reh-gem) A stone heap.
Revakhaw (Rev-aw-khaw) Relief; breathing; respite.
Rinnah (Rin-naw) A shrill sound; shout of joy.
Ritspah (Rits-paw) Hot stone.
Romaw (Ro-maw) Haughty; proudly.
Sabtekaw (Sab-tek-aw) Unknown meaning. Compare to *Sebaw.*
Salkah (Sal-kaw) To walk.
Sarai (Saw-rah-ee) Dominative.
Sebaw (Seb-aw) Unknown meaning. Similar to *Saw-baw:* to become tipsy.
Sharah (Shaw-raw) A fortification; wall.
Shavsha (Shav-shaw) Joyful.
Shem (Shame) Denotes honor; literally name. Also, appointed one; to desolate.
Shemesh (Sheh-mesh) The sun.
Shoshannah (Sho-shan-naw) Lily.
Sithriy (Sith-ree) Protective.
Tabbakhaw (Ta-baw-khaw) A female cook.
Tavah (Taw-vaw) To grieve.
Tebuwnaw (Teb-oo-naw) Intelligence.
Telathah (Tel-aw-thaw) Third.
Terakh (Teh-rakh) Of uncertain derivation.
Tereyn (Ter-ane) Two; second.
Tirtsah (Teer-tsaw) Delightsomeness.
Tiyrac (Tee-rawce) Unknown meaning. Probably of foreign origin.
Tsinnah (Tsin-naw) A hook; a large shield.
Tso'bebaw (Tso-bay-baw) Canopier.

Uzziel (Ooz-zee-ale) Strength of God.
Yabal (Yaw-bawl) A stream.
Ye'uwsh (Yeh-oosh) Hasty.
Yelahlah (Yel-aw-law) Howling.
Yepheth (Yeh-feth) Expansion.
Yithran (Yith-rawn) Excellence.
Zebul (Zeb-ool) Dwelling; a residence.
Zeh-abe (Zeh-abe) To be yellow; a wolf.
Zehker (Zeh-ker) A memento.
Zekaryah (Zek-ar-yaw) God has remembered.
Zeva'ah (Zev-aw-aw) Agitation; fear.

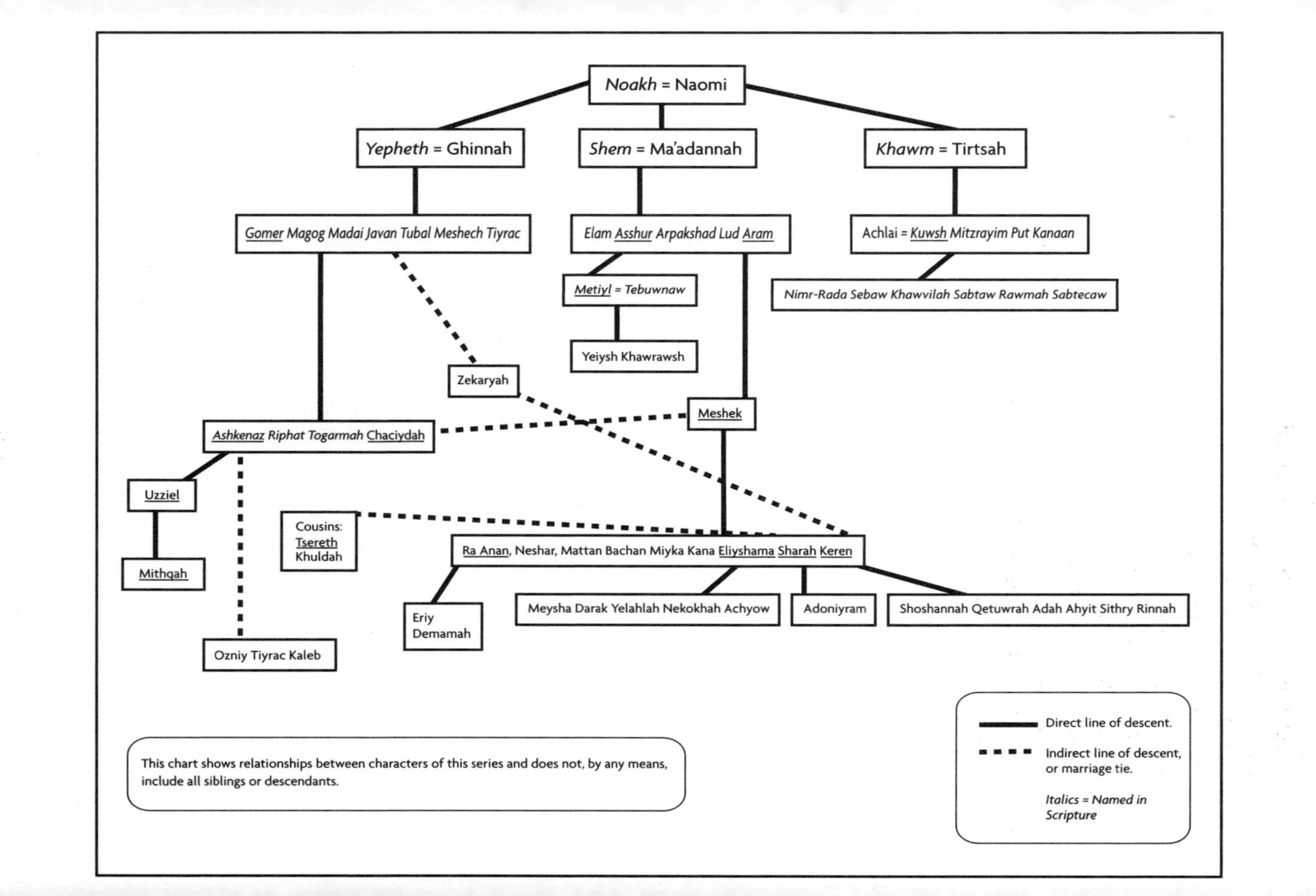

Noakh = Naomi
Yepheth = Ghinnah
Shem = Ma'adannah
Khawm = Tirtsah
Gomer Magog Madai Javan Tubal Meshech Tiyrac
Elam Asshur Arpakshad Lud Aram
Achlai = Kuwsh Mitzrayim Put Kanaan
Metiyl = Tebuwnaw
Nimr-Rada Sebaw Khawvilah Sabtaw Rawmah Sabtecaw
Yeiysh Khawrawsh
Zekaryah
Meshek
Ashkenaz Riphat Togarmah Chaciydah
Uzziel
Cousins: Tsereth Khuldah
Ra Anan, Neshar, Mattan Bachan Miyka Kana Eliyshama Sharah Keren
Mithqah
Eriy Demamah
Meysha Darak Yelahlah Nekokhah Achyow
Adoniyram
Shoshannah Qetuwrah Adah Ahyit Sithry Rinnah
Ozniy Tiyrac Kaleb
Direct line of descent.
Indirect line of descent, or marriage tie.
Italics = Named in Scripture
This chart shows relationships between characters of this series and does not, by any means, include all siblings or descendants.

More from Kacy Barnett-Gramckow & Moody Publishers!

The Genesis Trilogy

The Heavens Before retells the enthralling biblical account of the Great Flood—as seen through the eyes of a courageous woman. In a world of astonishing beauty and appalling violence, Annah dares to believe in the Most High, the God who is nothing more than foolish legend to the people of her settlement.

The Heavens Before
ISBN: 0-8024-1363-3
ISBN-13: 978-0-8024-1363-5

He Who Lifts the Skies retells the biblical account of the building of the tower of babel. The Mighty Hunter, Great-King Nimr-Rada, offers mankind freedom from the judgment of God. But Nimr-Rada's promises of freedom will only bring his people enslavement to a false god, and to Nimr-Rada himself. Keren must risk death to defy the Great King and end his tyranny.

He Who Lifts the Skies
ISBN: 0-8024-1368-4
ISBN-13: 978-0-8024-1368-0

SINCE 1894, Moody Publishers has been dedicated to equip and motivate people to advance the cause of Christ by publishing evangelical Christian literature and other media for all ages around the world. Because we are a ministry of the Moody Bible Institute of Chicago, a portion of the proceeds from the sale of this book go to train the next generation of Christian leaders.

If we may serve you in any way in your spiritual journey toward understanding Christ and the Christian life, please contact us at www.moodypublishers.com.

"All Scripture is God-breathed and is useful for teaching, rebuking, correcting and training in righteousness, so that the man of God may be thoroughly equipped for every good work."

—2 TIMOTHY 3:16, 17

THE NAME YOU CAN TRUST®

A Crown in the Stars Team

Acquiring Editor
Andy McGuire

Copy Editor
LB Norton

Back Cover Copy
Michele Straubel

Cover Design
Barb Fisher, LeVan Fisher Design

Cover Photo
Steve Gardner, pixelworksstudio.net,
Daryl Benson/Masterfile

Interior Design
Ragont Design

Printing and Binding
Bethany Press International

The typeface for the text of this book is
Weiss